SHADOW OF A LADY

'Vintage Aiken Hodge' *Sunday Times*

'Miss Hodge knows her period and provides the right measure of thrills and romance'
Good Housekeeping

'A colourful romance and an interesting sidelight on Nelson' *Women's Journal with Flair*

'The plot moves along at a spanking pace'
Catholic Herald

Born in Massachusetts, Jane Aiken Hodge is the daughter of Conrad Aiken, the poet, and sister of novelist Joan Aiken. Educated at Oxford and Harvard, she has worked as a journalist in New York and London, and now lives in Lewes with her husband, Alan Hodge, editor of *History Today*, and her two daughters. Her previous books available in the Coronet list include *Runaway Bride*, *Strangers in Company*, *Here Comes a Candle*, *Savannah Purchase* and *Greek Wedding*.

Shadow of a Lady

Jane Aiken Hodge

CORONET BOOKS
Hodder and Stoughton

Copyright © 1974 by Jane Aiken Hodge

First published in Great Britain 1974 by
Hodder and Stoughton Limited

Coronet edition 1976
Second impression 1977

Printed and bound in Great Britain for
Hodder and Stoughton Paperbacks, a
division of Hodder and Stoughton Ltd.,
Mill Road, Dunton Green, Sevenoaks, Kent
(Editorial Office: 47 Bedford Square,
London, WC1 3DP) by
Hunt Barnard Printing Ltd., Aylesbury, Bucks.

ISBN 0 340 20757 4

SHADOW OF A LADY

Chapter 1

DRAWN by the sound of music, Helen wriggled through the familiar gap in the park palings. It was child-size only, so pursuit, if it came, must come by the gate, with explanations to old Ben who kept the lodge. The thoughts slid unformulated through Helen's eight-year-old mind, the joy of escape predominant. Grandfather had reduced Mother to tears again at breakfast and Mrs. Telfair had retreated to her room with one of her headaches. Helen, consigned to the random care of cook and maids, had soon made her escape and taken the now familiar path to Uppark. She had found it the first time she ran away, when the primroses were out.

Today there was a good smell of grass. The men must have been out with their scythes in the park. She pushed her way cautiously through the evergreens that masked the inside of the park fence, the music calling her, nearer now, loud and joyful. There were voices, too, and laughter. She moved more slowly. No one had found out, yet, where she came when she managed to get away, and every instinct urged caution. But she must see what they were doing in the park. The laurels gave way to rhododendrons, heavy with strange-scented blossoms, and she found that she could climb through their branches, her own height above ground, safely masked by green leaves and purple flowers. Ahead, the music danced to a halt and there was a spattering of hand-clapping and a great deal of laughter. Lying along two branches, Helen pushed aside a head of bloom, and saw.

Sir Harry was having a party in his garden. Canvas had been laid across the new-scythed grass to make a dancing floor. There was a long table beside it, and men in the Featherstonehaugh livery were clearing away the remains of a meal. Helen saw one of the fiddlers reach out and snatch a leg of chicken. They were the ones from the village; she remembered their faces from May Day; but they were playing different music today. They were tuning up now, ready to start again, and she saw Sir Harry emerge from the group of young men who were drinking and talking beside the long table.

"What's it to be then?" Speaking, he seemed to be looking directly at Helen, and she cowered in her hiding-place. She did not like Sir Harry, though he was kind enough on the rare occasions when she met him with Grandfather or Mother.

"Who cares?" This was a young man rather more formally dressed than the others, whose shirts and breeches had struck even eight-year-old Helen as odd at a party. But then, it was a very hot day. "Who cares, so long as the divine Emmy dances for us. Mr. Haydn's new air perhaps? They have it pretty well now, I think."

"Thanks to you, Greville." Sir Harry turned and spoke to the fiddlers, who nodded rather dubiously and scraped away harder than ever at their tuning.

"Look!" This was a young man Helen knew, one of the neighbours she saw from time to time in church. Today his face was very red. "Here's your stage, Emmy." The table was almost clear now. He seized a corner of the damask cloth that covered it, gave a good pull, and brought the last dishes clattering to the ground. "Up with you!"

"But I'm in a mook sweat already." The woman's voice, from the centre of the group of young men, surprised Helen. She had thought this a men's party, and besides, the accent was very strange, neither like Sir Harry's nor the villagers'. She peered eagerly through the screen of flowers to see this woman who was at a party with such a great many men.

Sir Harry was looking cross, and no wonder, with his silver all over the grass. He spoke again to the musicians, who bobbed nervously in assent, then strode over to the group of his guests. "I'll put her up."

The group parted before him, and Helen saw an angel. She had been talking to the grave young man called Greville, but now turned to Sir Harry, all sweet compliance. Dark auburn curls tumbled on bare shoulders. Her face was far more beautiful than that of the lady in the picture Grandfather was so proud of, and her dress infinitely brighter than any of Mother's. She was laughing, and holding out her hands to Sir Harry, "All right then." The "A" was flat. "If I moost, I moost."

Sir Harry picked her up, with a tumble of dishevelled petticoats, a flash of red shoes and neat ankles that brought a whistle from the young men. On the table, she dropped a deep curtsy, then struck an attitude. "So, what's it to be?" Her voice was lovely, when you got used to the accent.

"Greville's Haydn," said Sir Harry. "If you can do it?"

"I can do anything." This time the curtsy was stately, like the ones Helen remembered her mother practising once. The word "court" flashed uncomprehended through her mind. It had been a long time ago . . .

The fiddlers struck up, uncertainly at first, then coming out strongly with the most beautiful tune she had ever heard, and, lovelier still, the girl began to dance, dipping and swaying, her nimble feet always just on the table, her face grave, serene, an angel's still. It was too beautiful to be borne, and Helen, lost in wonder, lost, also, her grip on the rhododendron branches, and tumbled helplessly out onto the grass.

The music stopped, with a scream of discordant notes, and Helen, picking herself up unhurt, heard Sir Harry saying one of Grandfather's words as he moved towards her. She cowered for a moment, then straightened. Her hands, black from the rhododendrons, were clasped tight across her dirty pinafore. It was the end, of course.

"Who the hell are you?" asked Sir Harry.

He did not know her. Why should he? There was hope yet. But she would not lie. "Helen," she said.

It caused, for some reason, a roar of laughter. The grave young man, Greville, came over to stand beside Sir Harry and look down at her. " 'Was this the face that launched a thousand ships?' " he asked, puzzling Helen.

"Please let me go." She did not like him any better than Sir Harry, to whom she instinctively addressed her plea. "I meant no harm, truly, sir."

"A young lady," said Sir Harry, surprised.

"A very young lady," said the other man. "Can you find your way home, young lady?"

"Of course I can." Indignantly. "Please, sir," again she spoke to Sir Harry. "Let me go. I was only watching the angel."

This brought another roar of laughter, frightening, horrid. But it also brought help. "What, me?" said the angel, appearing behind Sir Harry. "Coom on, Harry, luv, let her go. She's only a tiddler. And whipping'll be the least of it, if her folks find out she's been here, whoever she is. You sure you can find your way home?" Her smile, bent full on Helen, was exquisite, if a trifle gap-toothed.

"Oh, yes, please!" Helen smiled back.

"Then, scoot," said the angel, and turned to throw an affectionate arm round Sir Harry's neck. "Much simpler that-a-way, luv." And, as Helen obediently scooted, "That'll be a smasher one of these days, and no mistake."

Safe back among the rhododendrons, Helen hesitated for a moment. The temptation to stay was strong. The heavenly music was striking up again. Even if she dared not look, she might listen. But suppose Sir Harry changed his mind? It was too great a risk. She crawled back through the fence and headed for home. It was sheer bad luck that she met her grandfather face to face in the back hall.

"Filthy!" Look and tone were crushing. "That any son of mine . . ." Helen had learned not to listen when he talked like this, but she got her whipping just the same.

It was raining. Dead leaves lay sadly by the roadside and the carriage was damp and full of draughts. Helen was glad when they got to Petersfield, even if it did mean dragging through the rain with her mother as she did the errands. There were to be more of them than usual. They were celebrating, and Mother and Grandfather were on good terms for once. Helen did not entirely understand what it was all about, but Father had been very brave on his ship and there was going to be something called prize money.

It was hard to remember what Father looked like. Helen obediently jumped down out of the carriage in her mother's wake and found with relief that it had stopped raining. "Watch where you go, child." Mrs. Telfair picked up shabby skirts to avoid a huge puddle. "We must go to Miss Brown." She looked down at tired flounces with distaste. "If your father should get home, I can't greet him looking like this."

Helen's heart sank. A visit to the dressmaker meant endless waiting in a stuffy room while Mother and Miss Brown talked caps and sleeves, poplins and muslins. But Mother had stopped to talk to a neighbour. Helen made her curtsy and stood dutifully quiet, as she had been taught, half listening to their talk. Mother sounded really happy for once. "A Spanish convoy," she said. "Promoted on the spot. If the Admiralty only confirm it . . ."

"Commander . . . hmm," said old Mr. Masters. "It's when he's made post captain, Mrs. Telfair, that you should really rejoice. Mind you, this—ahem—war looks like going on forever. What with the Frogs and the Spanish, and those—ahem—American rebels, the navy's got its hands full. Your husband will likely be an admiral before you see him home."

"Oh, don't say that." But Mother sounded half pleased at the idea, and suddenly Helen had a picture of her father's face, very like Grandfather's.

Mother was beginning to shiver. She was so thin, it was no wonder if she felt the cold. Helen pulled her hand very gently and looked up at her.

"Quite right, pet." It was Mother's kind voice. "We ought to be getting on with our errands." Characteristically, she made no move. "You really think this war will go on so long?"

"I see no end to it," said Mr. Masters. "We'll be lucky if it's over by 1790. You'll be a young lady by then, won't you, miss? With ringlets and beaux and billets doux. And that reminds me, there was something my son said. Now, what was it?"

Helen remembered, suddenly, the young man with the red face that day last summer when she had seen the angel. Mr. Masters's son. She was shivering now, as badly as her mother. Mr. Masters was ruminating, winding himself slowly up to say something, when Mother intervened. "Look! There's the Uppark carriage."

It was drawing up outside the Red Lion where the London coaches stopped, and Helen, expecting Sir Harry's tall figure, and dreading possible recognition, was relieved to see a footman out of livery let down the steps and give a rather careless hand to a heavily cloaked girl.

"Hmm," said Mr. Masters. "Turned off. I rather fancied it would end like that." And then, "I cry your pardon, ma'am. Talking to myself. Bad habit of mine. May I conduct you to your next station? If you understand me. Naval man myself once." He talked almost at random as he guided them along the street, the carriage now between them and the cloaked girl. "Dressmaker's, ha!" He answered her mother. "Quite right, my dear. Must put out all our flags in case the commander gets home." He left them at Miss Brown's door with a gallant bow, and it was only as he walked away that he remembered what he had thought of saying to Mrs. Telfair. But probably best left alone. The boy had no doubt been in his cups and mistaken some village child for little Miss Telfair. A sweet-looking child; pity about that grandfather. Pity about the father, come to that. A grandfather himself, he sighed gustily and turned into his favourite tavern.

The session with Miss Brown was just as lengthy as Helen had feared, but the conversation was more lively than usual, since here, too, there were the subjects of promotion and prize money to be discussed. Helen, settled on the window seat with a handful of Miss Brown's stale sugar-candy, half listened, half watched as shoppers splashed through the puddles below. It was market day and the little town was full, despite the rain, which was beginning again and in earnest. She saw the Uppark groom emerge from the inn, wiping his mouth, followed by the footman, and wondered idly what was the matter with the coachman, who usually drove Sir Harry's bays. The two men were laughing—jeering almost, their eyes fixed on someone concealed by the coach. They swung themselves up into their places, the boy who was holding the horses' heads stood away, a touch of the whip, and the carriage swung forward at the speed Sir Harry liked. It revealed the figure in the cloak, standing in the rain beside a very small box. She had pulled her hood more closely round her face, perhaps in defence against the men's jibes, but, now they were gone, it fell back as she looked up to study the time on the church clock.

Helen gasped. It was her angel, but pitiful somehow, and diminished, bowed down by the heavy cloak, bright skirts spattered already with mud.

"What's the matter, child?" Her mother had heard the gasp, and looked up impatiently from the copy of the *Belle Assemblée* that she and Miss Brown were studying.

"I feel a little sick," said Helen, lying for the first conscious time in her life. "May I just run down to the front door? I wouldn't like——" She left the sentence delicately unfinished.

"Sugar-candy," said her mother, and, "Perhaps it might be best," said Miss Brown.

"Very well, pet." Today, nothing could damp Mrs. Telfair's unusual spirits. "But not outside the door, mind, and don't, for anything, speak to strangers."

"Of course not, Mamma." Helen got demurely down from the window seat, wrapped her cloak quickly round her, and left the room.

"You're sure about the sleeve?" Her mother had already forgotten her.

Miss Brown's tiny apartment was, appropriately, above a draper's shop, but it had its own separate entrance, and Helen stood there for a moment, the door ajar, peering out. It was raining harder than ever and the street had emptied. A boy hurried by with a baker's tray; a farmer urged two reluctant, new-bought cows towards the London road; the angel was still there, huddled under the overhang of the inn, her eyes fixed on the church clock. Two men, hurrying past Helen to cross the road, explained this. "Coach is almost due," said one of them.

The London coach. "Turned off," Mr. Masters had said. Helen knew about that. Cook before last had been turned off for making free with Grandfather's port. But how could you turn off an angel? She took a deep breath, a quick, frightened look up at the window above, and plunged across the street, almost under the hooves of a tinker's horse. As she ran, her hands were busy under her cloak, loosening the gold chain her godmother had given her. The tinker screamed frightened abuse at her, but she had the little gold crucifix safe in the palm of her right hand.

The man's shouting had brought the angel's eyes down from the clock to gaze for a moment vaguely at Helen. If she was an angel still, she was a sad one. Dark circles smudged eyes that seemed deep-set in the pale face; auburn ringlets hung limp under the hood . . . Helen was a child, but she had known despair, and could feel it. "Please?" Smiling timidly up at her lost angel, she remembered the voice that had said, "I can do anything."

"Please," she said again. "Do you remember me?"

The angel's eyes focussed on her with difficulty. Then, miraculously, the grey face smiled that heavenly, gap-toothed smile. "Sure, it's me peeping Tom," she said. "Did you get home safe, luv?"

"Oh, yes, thank you." Helen glanced nervously back over her shoulder. "Please, I haven't much time. Are you all right?"

"Am I—?" Horribly, the angel burst into Mother's kind of laughter. But she was young and strong. She saw the recoil in Helen's eyes, and steadied herself. "No, luv," she said. "I'm not all right. I'm"—she laughed again, more quietly—"in trouble. But all the better for seeing you."

"You'll always be my angel." Helen held out the golden cross and chain. "Please, will you take this? From me? It's mine, truly. My godmother gave it to me. She's dead."

For a moment she thought it would be refused. Then, the angel took it and, surprisingly, bit the cross with strong, irregular white teeth. "Dear God," she said. "It's gold." She swooped down to envelop Helen in a damp embrace, and, oddly, in that moment of crisis, Helen noticed that she smelled quite different from the maids or cook, sweet and spicy, for all the mud that draggled her

14

skirts. "If I'm your angel," she said, in her lovely, strange voice, "then you're mine, luv. I'll pay you back, one day, truly I will." For a moment, her voice had resembled Helen's own. "But here's the coach. God bless you, child." The crucifix was in the breast of her gown. "I needed this. Now scoot, luv."

And once again, Helen scooted.

Mrs. Telfair's new poplin had to wait a year before her husband came home, and when he did, it was in a very bad temper, on half pay, on the outbreak, as he would have put it, of peace in 1783. It was not a good moment for a middle-aged, short-tempered naval man to have achieved his long-desired post-captaincy, though at least, as he pointed out with monotonous regularity, his name was now safely on its way up the naval lists. He had only to keep alive while others died, and wait, hopefully, for a new war, a new ship and, he was sure, in the end, an admiralship.

In the meantime there was nothing for it but to live at home with his father, who did not want him. His half pay came to less than fifty pounds a year, and the expectations on which he had married his wife had failed to materialise. Her aristocratic relatives refused to help a girl who had married, in their view, to spite them. Though respectable country gentry, the Telfairs were not at all in the same class as the Glendales, who had wide influence and a handful of rotten boroughs in their control, but saw no reason to advance the interests of a man who had neither intelligence nor manner to recommend him.

"They might at least do something for the child." Captain Telfair returned again and again to this, and Helen was increasingly aware that he looked on it as somehow her fault. The only one of her great-aunts she had ever met was Aunt Helen, her godmother, who had visited them once, had given her the gold crucifix and chain, quarrelled violently with her father, changed her will, and died. Mention of Helen Stott brought Captain Telfair close to apoplexy, so she was never mentioned. Helen sometimes thought that even her own name irritated her father.

Her childhood, from the age of nine, when he came home, apparently for good, was even less happy than it had been when alone with her frail mother and irascible grandfather. But she was older now, and had learned a new way of escape. Her father, who thought education wasted on a girl, had dismissed the idea of a governess, and Helen might well have grown up in a state of ignorance worthy of a Rousseau heroine, if the vicar's sister had not intervened. Meeting Helen and her mother in the street one day, this lady had paused to ask when Helen was to start her schooling, had learned the dismal state of the case, and had dismissed Mrs. Telfair's explanation that she herself intended to undertake her daughter's education with the scorn it deserved.

"Nonsense, my dear," said Miss Tillingdon. "Daughters never learn from their mothers. And, besides, what, pray, have you to teach her? Oh—accomplishments, I grant you them. You shall teach her satin-stitch and sketching, so she may waste silk and spoil paper, but send her to me, I beg you, in the mornings, and I will teach her to read. It will be an entertainment for me. I worked for a while with my friend Miss Wollstonecraft at her school in Newington Green. It was the happiest time of my life."

And, as she grew up, Helen's mornings, at least, were happy. Miss Tillingdon was not a methodical teacher, but she was an instinctive one. They studied what she chose and studied it from the heart. Her brother, the bachelor vicar of Up Harting, gave them the run of the very considerable library he no longer used, retiring, himself, to the "den" where he kept the collection of other people's sermons from which he took his Sunday pick.

So Helen learned to read in quite a new sense, and was soon carrying off volumes from the vicarage library for afternoon consumption. She also learned a useful lesson when her father caught her with *Tom Jones* and, predictably, exploded. She was too old by then to whip, but he made both her and her mother's lives a misery to them for several weeks. What girl reared on such improper stuff would ever make a good marriage? And marry, of course, Helen must, preferably as soon as possible, and someone with parliamentary or naval influence, or both.

"Though how he expects me to," said sixteen-year-old Helen to her friend Miss Tillingdon, "when he knows I meet no one, I cannot begin to imagine."

"Marriage," said Miss Tillingdon, "is a very doubtful blessing. At least for a woman."

Helen could not help laughing. "There would be few marriages, dear Miss Tillingdon, if all the women refused."

"Just so. My friend Miss Wollstonecraft writes me that she is engaged in composing a *Vindication of the Rights of Woman,* in answer to Mr. Burke. She believes that marriage is an outmoded superstition, and has even persuaded her sister to abandon her brute of a husband."

"I shall never marry," said Helen.

"Then we had best work hard at your education, my dear. Miss Wollstonecraft is most fortunately able to support herself by her pen, but hers is a most unusual case. I, as you see, have found myself compelled to keep house—for a brother."

"Yes." Helen had a practical turn of mind. "But I have no brothers."

"You have something better," said Miss Tillingdon. "You have an income of your own."

"What?" said Helen.

"I thought you had not been told. From things your mother has said, I think it possible that even your parents do not know, surprising though it seems. So perhaps the less said about it, the better. But I do think you should know. Your great-aunt, Helen Stott—Helen Glendale that was—left you her fortune. I do not know the exact figure, but it should provide an income sufficient to keep you in comfort. It is in trust, I think, until you come of age. Naturally, if you marry, it will become your husband's."

"Yes," said Helen. "I shall certainly never marry. Dear Miss Tillingdon, thank you for telling me."

Chapter 2

WHILE Helen and Miss Tillingdon worked their way simultaneously through the works of Rousseau and those of Richardson, the political scene darkened and Captain Telfair's hopes rose. Revolution broke out in France and he made the valet he could not afford refurbish his uniforms. "You never can tell," he said, "when I may need them."

"Yes, my dear," said Mrs. Telfair. The years that had rested him had wasted her. There were no more quarrels now, because she agreed with everything he said. Domestic duties exhausted her, and after old Mr. Telfair had made a particularly disagreeable scene over the way his house was run—or not run—Helen had quietly taken over the housekeeping. It meant that she could no longer go to the vicarage in the mornings, but she went in the afternoons instead, and she and Miss Tillingdon continued their happy, random process of education, but as companions rather than pupil and teacher. They were studying Italian together, since Helen was rather more fluent than her preceptress in French. She thought, sometimes, how surprised her father would be to know how much she knew, but took every precaution against his finding out. Her first action, after that disastrous episode over *Tom Jones,* had been to embroider an elegant book-cover in her best satin stitch, and now everything she read looked like the Bible. Nor had she ever betrayed, by look or hint, that she knew herself an heiress, and no one had told her. In fact she was convinced by now that Miss Tillingdon had been right. Her parents quite certainly knew nothing of her expectations. It was very odd, and she only hoped Miss Tillingdon knew what she was talking about. Pressed as to the source of her information, she had subsided into tears and incoherence, and Helen, appalled at this sign of weakness in the only person in the world that she admired, abandoned the painful subject.

When she was seventeen, the year after the Bastille fell, and her grandfather died, the invitation Helen's father had stopped even grumbling about actually arrived. It was from the youngest of Mrs. Telfair's aunts, who had married late in life and was now bringing out her own youngest daughter. She wrote to suggest that Helen come and stay with them and "do" the London season with her Charlotte. Reading between the lines of the letter, Helen decided that Charlotte must be a problem of some kind, and that she herself was to be made use of. But it was a chance to get away from home, and as such, not to be resisted. Her only qualm, as she confided to Miss Tillingdon, was that she knew herself to be going on false pretences. "Nothing could induce me to marry," she said. "And here is poor Mamma spending all this money on rigging me out to catch a husband."

"Never mind," said Miss Tillingdon comfortably. "They can afford it now old Mr. Telfair's dead, and you need the clothes."

Arriving in St. James's Square, Helen was interested to find herself treated as a pauper. Apparently the facts of Great-Aunt Helen's will were not known even to her immediate family, and she wondered, with some respect for her dead relative, how she had contrived this. She was immensely grateful to her. As a pauper, the chances of attracting the kind of marriage offer for which her parents hoped were slight enough. She knew she was handsome, in a rather formidable, dark-haired way, but her wide reading of novels had taught her that when it came to marriage, good looks were seldom enough. Anyway, she did not mean to marry. If Miss Tillingdon's information about her inheritance proved false, she would have to teach, or even write for money, like her heroine, Mary Wollstonecraft.

Charlotte was away when Helen arrived, staying with one of her married sisters, and Mrs. Standish's few references to her youngest daughter confirmed Helen's suspicions that Charlotte was a problem. It was all too obvious that her mother disliked her, and Helen, working hard with her aunt's sewing woman to refurbish her wardrobe out of her married cousins' cast-offs, resisted the temptation to ask the mildest of leading questions about Miss Charlotte. Her father, too, was out of town, hunting with the Belvoir, so they were a quiet household for the first week of Helen's stay, but when he brought her back on a wet February Monday, everything changed. The house came alive; servants ran about; doors banged, invitations began to pour in. And in the middle of all the excitement was Charlotte, pretty as a picture, tiny, golden-haired, and unable to speak to her mother without a stammer so pronounced as to be agonising.

Aunt Standish had calculated well, Helen thought, when she invited her to join Charlotte for the season. She could only wonder what kind of enquiries had been made, and how. Her looks were the perfect foil for Charlotte's and she understood why her aunt had felt she could afford to be generous in outfitting her. And—had her aunt known this too?—conversation came easily to her. She could not remember when she had outgrown her dread of her father and grandfather, but outgrown it she had, and if she was not afraid of them, she feared nobody. At that first, dreadful family dinner, when Charlotte, asked by her mother for a report on her sister, who was breeding, had got as far as "She m . . . m . . ." and then stammered to an anguished, tear-laden halt, Helen had plunged in with a knowledgeable question to Mr. Standish about hunting conditions in the shires. He was not a sensible man, but he could talk about hunting, and did, for the rest of the meal.

It set the pattern for the whole extraordinary season. Charlotte looked ravishing, and stammered. Helen looked handsome, and talked. In fact, after two younger sons had asked for her hand and been ruthlessly refused without reference to either uncle or father, she talked a great deal. It had been Miss Tillingdon's advice. "Make them think you a bluestocking," she had said, "and you will be quite safe."

In the main, it worked admirably. Just occasionally, it worked rather better than she had intended, as when one of the younger sons was actually inspired to invite her and Charlotte to visit the winter exhibition of the Royal Academy at Somerset House with him. It was, Aunt Standish said, an unusual invitation, but she could see no harm in it, so long, resignedly, as she herself went too. Since Charlotte stammered much worse when her mother was present, this made the excursion to Somerset House less agreeable than it would otherwise have been to Helen, who had to act, all the time, as a protective screen between Charlotte and the others. Young Mr. Scroope had brought an equally young friend, Mr. Fysshe, to balance their numbers, and Helen hoped, for a while, that the party might separate, leaving Charlotte alone with Mr. Fysshe, who was so timid himself as to be almost beyond stammering at. But Mrs. Standish knew her duty and did it. They all drifted round the handsome galleries together, and Helen was between Mr. Scroope and Mr. Fysshe when she gave a gasp. "Who in the world is that?" It was years since she had thought about her angel, but there she was in a gold frame, unmistakable, even dressed as a bacchante.

Mr. Scroope went red, Mr. Fysshe went redder. "It's a picture by Mr. Romney," said Mr. Scroope, recovering.

"But of whom?" Helen was aware of her aunt in the background, apparently making faces at her, but refused to notice. "I'm sure I met her once."

"Impossible," said Charles Scroope.

"An imaginary subject?" suggested Mr. Fysshe hopefully.

"No." When she knew more, Helen was to respect Mr. Scroope for his answer. "I believe the young lady was a favourite model of Mr. Romney's."

"Was?" Still Helen would not notice her aunt's forbidding face.

"Oh, she's still alive," said Mr. Scroope. "Very much so." His colour was high. "She is in Naples now, staying with our ambassador there, Sir William Hamilton."

"It is time," said Mrs. Standish, awfully, "for us to go home."

She sat portentously silent in the carriage, and Helen thought the two young men had showed extreme good sense in abandoning the doomed expedition so promptly. Doomed, indeed, it seemed to be. One of the horses cast a shoe in the Strand, and the coachman, who feared his master even more than his mistress, refused to budge until it had been replaced at the nearest smithy. The three ladies, meanwhile, sat in painful silence, Helen busy wondering how she could find out more about the fate of her angel. She had not even, she realised with regret, learned her name, remembering her only as Emmy.

Her resolution was more easily fulfilled than she had expected. Reaching the Standish house, Mrs. Standish dismissed Charlotte to her room and led Helen into her own little downstairs parlour, used mainly for the castigation of servants.

"Now, miss." She did not sit down, but stood by the fireplace, drawing off her gloves. "You will be so good as to tell me what you meant by that disgraceful scene."

"Scene?" Helen, who found the house intolerably hot, dropped her pelisse onto a chair. "I do not seem quite to understand you, Aunt."

"No? You really expect me to believe that it was all sheer ignorance and innocence? From my Charlotte, poor creature, I might be prepared to credit it, but from you, with your learned airs and graces, I rather think not. 'I'm sure I met her once.'" She quoted Helen's own words furiously back at her. "The notorious Mrs. Hart. 'Mrs!' Well she has as much right, I imagine, to that as to the 'Hart.' And you must needs lay claim to knowing her. It will be all over town tomorrow. It's too good a story to waste. Mr. Fysshe has not sense enough to see it, but Mr. Scroope . . . and Charlotte there, too. Inevitably involved. I wish to God I had left you in the mud where you belong."

"Thank you." Now Helen was angry too. "I'll go home tomorrow."

"You'll do nothing of the kind. It would merely confirm the scandal."

"I wish . . ." Helen reached for patience. "I wish, Aunt, that you would explain to me just what this scandal

22

is." She saw Mrs. Standish nearing explosion point again, and threw up a hand. "But first, please let me tell you all I know about the matter. Once, years ago, when I was a little girl, I got into the garden of Uppark."

"Oh my God!" Mrs. Standish interrupted her. "It's too much, I shall swoon; I feel it coming."

"Here." Helen took her arm and guided her to the sofa. "Sal volatile, Aunt? Or would you prefer a drop of your cherry cordial?"

Limp on the sofa, Mrs. Standish fanned herself weakly. "The cordial, child. Not the small glass, the other one. You had best have some yourself." It was the smallest possible olive branch, but Helen accepted it as such, merely wishing, as she filled the two glasses, that her aunt kept brandy or port in her theoretically secret cupboard, as well as the oversweet cordial.

Sipping greedily, Mrs. Standish gazed over the glass at Helen with large, curious eyes. "Uppark. When you were a child. What did you see?"

"Nothing much." The older woman's eagerness was disgusting. "Sir Harry was having a party. The fiddlers were there from the village. That's when I saw this Mrs. Hart—if that's her name. They called her Emmy. She danced for them; on the table. It was beautiful." She would never admit to having thought Emmy Hart an angel.

"Danced on the table." Mrs. Standish leaned forward, spilling a little of the precious cordial. "Not . . . Helen . . . Not . . ." She stopped, for once at a loss for words.

"Not what, Aunt?"

"Was she dressed?" asked Mrs. Standish, simply.

"Of course she was." Helen was beginning to understand the kind of orgy Mrs. Standish was imagining. "I thought it the most beautiful dress I had ever seen. She was so lovely. And kind." But she would not tell Mrs. Standish how she had fallen out of the bushes and been discovered.

"Kind!" Mrs. Standish picked up the word. "Too kind by a half, poor girl." She emptied her glass and held it imperiously out for more. "That's why Sir Harry turned her off. Increasing, of course, and not by him."

"Oh." Helen remembered the day she had last seen her angel, waiting for the coach in Petersfield. "Turned off" had been the phrase old Mr. Masters had used, and Emmy herself had admitted to being "in trouble." The phrase had a meaning for Helen now that it had not had then, and she remembered Emmy's strange laughter, and the desperate way those strong teeth had bitten the crucifix, and was glad that she had given it. But this was something else not to tell Mrs. Standish. "What happened to her then?" she asked instead, handing back the filled glass and making a pretence at sipping from her own.

"That was the extraordinary thing." Mrs. Standish had forgotten that she was not talking to a woman of her own age. "She turned up a while later, demure as you please, pretty as a picture, in keeping with Mr. Greville at Paddington Green. That's when Romney painted her. You couldn't go to a gallery without her languishing at you from some canvas of his or other. As a muse, a Venus . . . oh, a whole range of most unsuitable subjects. But faithful to Mr. Greville." She conceded it grudgingly. "I even heard that Mr. Romney had to get in a professional model to do the . . ." she coughed. "The limbs."

"What happened about the baby?" Remembering that wan face, with the dark-circled eyes, Helen was sure this part, at least, of the extraordinary story must be true.

"Nobody knows. Well, Greville's a very sharp young man." Mrs. Standish laughed harshly. "So sharp he may cut himself yet, people say." She looked up sharply at Helen. "This is a most extraordinary conversation." The syllables blurred a little.

"Yes." Helen did not attempt to deny it. "But, don't you see, Aunt, I need to know just what has happened; how bad things really are." She managed to suppress a laugh. "I do see, now, that I put the cat among the pigeons, back there when I said I'd met Mr. Greville's Mrs. Hart. We must put our heads together, you and I, and see how we can best make a recovery, for Charlotte's sake. Mr. Scroope seemed to know a great deal about Mrs. Hart," she went on thoughtfully.

"He's a friend of Greville's," said Mrs. Standish. "Oh, it's hopeless . . . hopeless."

"But if Greville is in Naples?"

"Greville is not in Naples." Mrs. Standish sat up straight on the sofa. "That's the cream of it. He sent her out there. To his uncle, Sir William Hamilton. The great connoisseur." She pronounced the word oddly. "Our representative at the Court of Naples. He married money, years ago, when I was a girl. What was her name? Catherine something or other. Played the pianoforte like an angel." She did not see Helen wince at the last word. "And died childless. There was talk of his remarrying. Well, there always is. Lady Clarges nearly had him, I believe. Which would not have suited Charles Greville at all."

"Why not?" Helen was at sea.

"Why not? Because young Greville has always looked on himself as his uncle's heir, that's why. A second marriage is the last thing he would want, with the chance of children this time. Though, mind you, I've always thought Sir William . . ." She dwindled to a stop, then started again. "Anyway, last time Sir William was home on leave, he paid his *devoirs* to Mrs. Hart, as all Greville's men friends do." She put a heavy accent on the word "men." "And it ended with young Greville packing her up, for all the world like one of his uncle's precious antique vases, and sending her off to him at Naples. Oh, very respectable; she has a mother these days, who goes by the name of Mrs. Cadogan, with as much right, no doubt, as her daughter has to be Mrs. Hart. That was about four years ago, as I recall; and Greville was dangling after one of Lord Middleton's girls, but nothing came of it. And serve him right, say I!" Drink mellowed Mrs. Standish. "A man who will cast off a mistress so, hardly promises well as a husband. I thought Middleton showed good sense, myself. And, besides, Greville's expectations are all from Sir William, and it begins to look as if he may have been fair and far off in that business."

"What do you mean, Aunt?" Helen's heart was rent at the idea of the girl's fate . . . looking back, she realised how young her angel must have been that day in Uppark. And after all, to be passed on, like a bit of used goods, from nephew to uncle. Intolerable. "How old is Sir William?" she asked.

"Old enough to be the girl's grandfather. He must be sixty if he's a day. But that's the cream of it. She's a clever one, that Emmy Hart. By all reports she held the old man off for so long that he was almost a figure of fun, but now everything's going her way and the talk is he'll marry her in the end. And then where will Charles Greville be?"

"Serve him right," said Helen. "But would Sir William really? In his position?"

"You would hardly think so, but it seems that Queen Maria Carolina of Naples has taken a great fancy to Mrs. Hart. Of course they can't meet formally as things stand now, but there's nothing much formal, by all reports, about the Court of Naples."

"Good God." Helen was taking it all in. "Maria Carolina? The Queen of France's sister?"

"Yes, one of those stiff-necked daughters of the Empress of Austria. Well"—Mrs. Standish finished her drink and rose to her feet—"Maria Carolina may receive her, if she does catch Sir William and make herself Lady Hamilton, but I know our own Queen Charlotte will do nothing of the kind."

"No." It was certainly hard to imagine.

"And in the meanwhile"—the glow faded from Mrs. Standish's cheek—"what in the world are we to do about this hell broth of a scandal you've stirred up?"

"I've been thinking about that, Aunt, and, truly, I believe you are taking the business too hard. Oh, I grant you, it was an appalling gaffe of mine, but I think you do Mr. Scroope and Mr. Fysshe less than justice. Why should they repeat it?"

"Why should they not?" asked Mrs. Standish. "A couple of young rattles like that with nothing to do but talk and drink. You might just as well expect my macaw to keep silent. Yes, James?" She turned her basilisk stare on the footman.

"A note, ma'am. Most urgent. For Miss Telfair."

"Thank you." She held out an imperious hand, and he proffered his silver salver with the hint of an apologetic glance at Helen. "That will do." And, as the door closed on him, she rounded on Helen. "So now it's secret correspondence?" She tore open the folded letter without more ado and scanned its contents rapidly, while Helen fought down fury. "Oh, well." At last Mrs. Standish condescended to hand over the note. "It could be worse, I suppose. That young Scroope seems to have more sense than I gave him credit for."

He had a great deal, Helen thought, for he had quite evidently drafted his missive on the assumption that Mrs. Standish would read it. It was short and to the point. He was sorry their pleasure party had been spoiled by such an unlucky misunderstanding. He himself had only realised after they parted that Miss Telfair must have seen the subject of Mr. Romney's picture many years ago, when she was a child—an infant he might say—and presumably in the street at Petersfield. No wonder if she had been surprised at sight of Mr. Romney's excellent picture, but perhaps it was a subject best forgotten. And then, a significant afterthought: "Mr. Fysshe and I have been at Tattersall's, he has bought a bay mare and thinks of nothing else." He was hers to command, Charles Scroope.

"Well, thank God for that." Mrs. Standish summed it up, and then with a logical connection Helen found at once inevitable and distasteful, "A sensible young man. Pity he has no prospects."

Chapter 3

ONE of the last big parties of that season was given by Pitt's friend Henry Dundas at his house in Wimbledon, and for once Helen was eager to go. Pitt, she knew, often went home from Parliament with Dundas, and indeed had his own rooms in the house his friend had bought a few years before, and above all things Helen longed to meet the great statesman. But for a while it looked as if Mrs. Standish was going to jib at the effort involved, and Mr. Standish at the fatigue to the horses of the long drive out of town. "Besides," he said darkly, "you might meet with a highwayman on the way back."

"From a breakfast," Helen objected. "I know the name's an absurd one, but we would hardly be as late as that."

"All a waste of time," said Mr. Standish. "Spent money like water on you two girls, and not a proposal to show for it."

It was a fortunate interjection for Helen. Mrs. Standish made a point of disagreeing with her husband wherever this was at all possible, and now she came down firmly in favour of going. "Dundas is a coming man, I believe. There's talk of a cabinet post . . . And young Robert must be rising twenty. We'll go."

The day of the party was brilliantly fine, but Helen soon learned that her main hope was to be disappointed. Mr. Pitt was in the house, but suffering from one of his bouts of ill health, and would not appear. "I can't say that I blame him," Helen confided to Charlotte as they walked out into the sunken garden beside the house. "It's pretty much of a crush, isn't it?"

"And not a soul one knows." Charlotte was looking about her gloomily. "I don't know what M . . . M . . . M . . ."

"Will say at our walking about together," said Helen helpfully. "Never mind, love, here comes rescue. Will you have Mr. Fysshe and I Mr. Scroope, or vice versa?"

"Perhaps we should let them choose," said Charlotte.

"Nonsense." But curiously enough, Helen did, five minutes later, find herself, without intention of her own, walking down on Mr. Scroope's arm to look at the ornamental pond where, he said, Mr. Dundas was experimenting with various kinds of rare waterfowl.

"No need to look so anxious," he said, as she glanced quickly back to where Charlotte and Fysshe were standing, obviously at a loss. "Fysshe may not be rich, but he's well born and harmless. The old dragon can't possibly object."

"The old . . ." Helen could hardly believe her ears.

"We all call her that." Cheerfully. "Married off six daughters by *force majeure* and it won't be her fault if she don't succeed with this one."

"Poor Charlotte."

"What about poor Helen?" And then, frozen by a glance, "Oh, very well, poor Miss Telfair."

"She is wondering," said Helen frostily, as they came to a halt, again at his instigation, beside the pond, "what has become of Mr. Dundas's ornamental fowls."

"You may well ask." The small pond was ornamented only by water plants and a gracefully drooping willow. "But I had to get you away somehow."

"Oh?"

"Yes." He was looking, for him, remarkably grave. "I have something to say to you. I've no right to, and I know it, but, Helen, I love you. No, please hear me out. No need for you to tell me that we are both penniless, with not a prospect between us, but if you would only give me hope, I promise you I'd be a different man. I'm not stupid," he said it without either pride or false modesty. "Just lazy. So far. There's never seemed an inducement to do anything. Now . . . there is. I have an uncle with some influence. I'd thought of politics. You'd be worth a fortune as a politician's wife."

"Thank you." Dryly. "Had you, by any chance, decided which party you would favour with your patronage?"

He coloured angrily, then threw out a deprecatory hand. "I suppose I deserve that. The war party, of course. Mr. Pitt's. To tell truth, I had hoped to see him today. As well as you," he hurried on.

"Thank you again. And, I take it, your useful uncle is of Mr. Pitt's persuasion."

"Oh, very much so. He thinks me, I should tell you, a useless young scoundrel. He told me so last time we met."

"And on that basis you expect him to advance your career?"

"Well, he told me that too. It was he, in fact, who said

29

I was not stupid. I have been thinking it over since, and do you know, I find myself inclined to agree with him. Only give me the faintest shadow of encouragement. Let me hope that I shall be working for you as well as for myself, and, seriously, I believe I might find myself moving mountains. And, Helen"—she had given up trying to protest at his use of her name—"before you demolish me with a word, think a little. We are two solitaries, you and I. You must know what a pleasure your company has been to me, what a refreshment in the vapidities of the season. And, sometimes, I have flattered myself that you, too, found a certain ease in talking to me. And . . . forgive me if I speak plainly, but it would be idle to pretend that your prospects are bright. God knows you're lovely enough to turn a man's heart over, but what is that in the marriage market as it exists today? Besides, you frighten people."

"I know," said Helen. She did not mean to tell him, any more than she had her aunt, of the surprising proposals she had rejected, or, better still, managed to cut off unmade. "But"—after going through rage to unwilling sympathy and back to rage again, she had decided that his frankness deserved to be reciprocated—"you see, I do not intend to marry."

"Not marry?" He was appalled. "But how will you live? Have you considered, Helen, what life is like for a single lady?"

"Yes. I don't care." No need to tell him of the legacy that she hoped would make her life tolerable. But odd to think what a difference it would make if she should be tempted to accept his surprising offer. Suppose she were to let him find his political niche and then surprise him with the news that she was not the penniless bride he had worked for. It was curiously tempting. He looked, in his earnest eagerness, handsomer than she had ever seen him, but also younger. If there had been a moment of doubt, of actual wavering, this settled it. "Madness." Was she saying it to herself as well as to him? "It would be sheer lunacy, and, Mr. Scroope, you must know it as well as I do. An engagement so long, so doubtful . . . It is not to be thought of, even if . . ." She stopped. Where was this taking her?

"Even if you cared for me? Helen, only tell me there is a shadow of hope and I shall be bound, and you free." They had been moving, as they talked, up a slight hill into one of the shrubberies with which Mr. Dundas had ornamented his garden, and now found themselves alone for a moment, deep among flowering bushes. He took her hand and turned her to face him. "Look me in the eye, Helen, and tell me you care nothing for me, and I will go to the devil any way you please."

"No! Don't do that." Was the surprising magic of his touch to destroy all the plans she and Miss Tillingdon had laid between them? Was this how all the disastrous marriages she had seen came about? She pulled her hand away. "Of course I care for you—as a friend. No more." It was hard to say it, but she managed, and with conviction. "And as your friend," she went on before he had time to intervene, "let me beg you to go ahead with your plans for a career. I have minded seeing the idle life you lead, now, when the world needs good men."

He looked suddenly much older, the bones of his face showing the shape of things to come. Still facing her, "I wonder, Helen, what would happen if I were to kiss you. Forcibly."

"I suppose I should scream," she said.

"Mrs. Standish would not be pleased." But his tone was light again, the crisis past. "Nor will she like our spending so much time together. I had better return you to her tender care." He took her arm to guide her up the path, where a little spring had roughened the ground, and once again she felt herself succumbing to the extraordinary magic of his touch. She must say something, anything, and quickly. "I shall come and listen to your first speech in the House."

"You won't," he said. "Politics would have done for Benedict, the married man, but without you, I've nothing to lose. I shall join the navy—we'll be at war within the year. Perhaps by then I shall be fit for service. My uncle is an admiral. His dearest wish has always been that I

31

should go to sea. How surprised he will be to find it grati-
fied."

"Oh—" Intolerable to have driven him to what might
so easily mean his death. But before she could muster her
wits, they had emerged on to the open lawn, where, as
Charles Scroope had predicted, her aunt was waiting with
a brow of thunder.

"My apologies, ma'am." As always, he was quick to
deal with the situation. "I have been boring your niece
with talk of my plans to join the navy. My uncle the admiral has been urging it this long time past, and Miss
Telfair, as a member of a naval family herself, has been
so good as to encourage me."

It was all over. He was bowing over her hand as if this
was indeed all they had been talking about. He would join
the navy; presently she would read of his death, and know
that she had killed him.

"The heat is insufferable," said Mrs. Standish. "Charlotte is tired already, and you looked fagged to death,
Helen. Perhaps, Mr. Scroope, you would be so good as to
have our carriage called." If Helen half hoped her aunt
might invite him to join them in the drive back to London, she was to be disappointed. Helping her into the
carriage, he held her hand for one almost unbearable moment. "This must be good-bye," he said. "My uncle lives
in Norwich. I shall ride there tomorrow."

"Quite right too," said Mrs. Standish. "Come, Helen,
the men are waiting."

"Good-bye." What else could she say? "Good"—she
swallowed something that felt like a sob—"good luck."

"Thank you." He stood back, the horses sprang forward. It was over.

Helen did not sleep that night, and was angry with herself for it. But in the long, wretched hours she at least
made up her mind to a course of action that she had often
considered but never so far undertaken. Before the season
ended, and she went home to face her parents' re-
proaches, she must find out more about her own expectations, those financial hopes that were to make life with
Miss Tillingdon a possibility. It had been easy enough to

learn the name and address of the lawyers who handled the Glendale family affairs. Mrs. Standish wrote to them once a week about what she considered the grave mismanagement of her own.

But to know that the answer to her question must lie with one of the partners of the law firm of Presse, Presse, Bartlett, and Furnival was one thing. To get in touch with them at their office in Chancery Lane was quite another. Mrs. Standish did not always open her niece's letters, as she did her daughter's, but she often did. Helen did not dare risk writing to ask for an appointment. Inspiration came with a short notice in the morning paper, to which she had acquired a kind of right after her uncle had finished muttering over it. Mr. Flood, M.P., was to introduce a bill for the reform of Parliament. To appear, suitably escorted, in the Stranger's Gallery of the House of Commons was as respectable, she knew, as to attend the endless trial of Warren Hastings, which was providing a Roman holiday for society. Lying ruthlessly, she invented a female cousin for Mr. Fysshe and convinced her aunt that he had arranged the outing when they had met at the opera a few nights before.

Luck was on her side. Her aunt was suffering from the exhaustion of the long, unsuccessful season. Lying prone on her sofa, she merely muttered that Helen had the oddest tastes of any girl she had ever encountered, and closed her eyes again. Charlotte was visiting a school friend. The only problem now was to get out of the house. Helen waited until the butler would have retired to his parlour, went downstairs to the hall where only James was in attendance, and asked him to call her a sedan chair.

"A sedan? But, miss!"

"*Please,* James." She had considered trying to bribe him, but decided against it. She thought him her friend, in a quiet way, and was justified. "It's nothing out of the way, I promise you," she said. "Just an errand I must do before I go home."

"You'll be careful, miss? It's not at all the thing." But he had yielded.

It was delightful to be jogging through the streets of

London alone, and fascinating to find herself in the narrow lanes of the city, far farther east than she had ever been before. And the lawyers' offices, when the men stopped in front of them, looked reassuringly respectable. She debated asking the men to wait, but decided against it. She had no idea how long she might have to wait herself.

She had dressed, on purpose, as quietly as possible, in a rather unfashionable blue cloak she had brought from home, but just the same her appearance caused a stir in the outer office, where a group of very young men stopped their careful engrossing to look at her open-mouthed.

"Miss Telfair." She had rehearsed what she would say, but her hands were damp on her reticule just the same. "To see Mr. Presse."

"By appointment?" asked the antique clerk who had risen to greet her.

"No." She was sure he knew she had none.

He rubbed dry, white hands dubiously. "Which Mr. Presse?"

This was a facer, but not entirely unexpected. "The one who handled Mrs. Helen Stott's affairs."

"Ah." The clerk's eyes were bright with intelligence in his withered face. "That would be Mr. Horace Presse."

"Thank you. If I might see him? With apologies, of course, for my failure to make an appointment?"

There was a kind of rustle among the young men, who had apparently resumed their writing. A pen fell to the floor. "That would be difficult," said the clerk. "Mr. Presse has been dead fifteen years."

"Has he?" Was the clerk merely old and obstructive, or actively hostile? Helen drew up to her rather considerable height and looked at him with, she hoped, the expression she had seen old Lady Spencer use with withering effect on Mr. Fysshe. "In that case," she said, "I think perhaps by now that someone might have taken over his business. I will see *him,* if you please, and the sooner the better."

"Mr. Furnival, that would be." The clerk's tone, and a sympathetic rustle from the young scribes, told her that she had scored a moral victory. "I'll just step up and find out if by any fortunate chance he is free. If you will take a seat, miss?" Grudgingly, he opened the door of a small, dark waiting room and left her to the thought that aristocratic clients presumably were never kept waiting. This was a place for humble petitioners to cool their heels.

She did not, however, have to wait long. A clatter of footsteps on the uncarpeted stairs could hardly herald the aged clerk. The door swung open and a surprisingly young, fair-faced man bounced into the room. "Miss Telfair!" He held out a warm hand. "I am delighted to see you. I have been meaning to . . . But it's all quite remarkably difficult. If you will have the goodness to step up to my office . . . It's not very elegant, I'm afraid."

"Neither am I," said Helen, liking him.

"Very sensible." He was ushering her upstairs, past the visibly interested scribes. "Your maid is outside, I take it, in the carriage."

She did not answer until he had led the way down a long corridor and into a very small room at the back of the building. Then, "I came by myself," she said.

"Enterprising, if unusual." He dusted a chair with his handkerchief and pulled it forward to face his antique desk. "As the most junior of partners," he apologised, "I am seldom so fortunate as to have visitors like yourself. But let me say again how delighted I am to see you. I have beaten my brains for means of getting in touch with you, since I read that you were in town with Mrs. Standish, and I confess, I've been gravelled."

"But surely," said Helen, "it would have been simple enough."

"It's in the will, you see." He had sat down facing her, but now jumped up again to fetch a file from a cabinet even more antique than his desk. "Of all the devilish documents. . . . I beg your pardon, Miss Telfair, but how old Presse came to draw it up is beyond me. He must have been in his second childhood. Here we are." He produced a faded parchment. "I doubt if you could either read or understand it. . . . Besides, if you'll just forgive me while I refresh my memory. . . . Yes, quite as bad as I thought. Do you know anything about the background, Miss Telfair?"

"Not much. And, by the way, you have not asked me to prove that I am indeed Miss Telfair."

"I don't need to." His tone held respect for her point. "When I read that you were in town I made a point of looking out for you. Naturally, as a miserable scrivener I do not attend the *ton* parties, but I have friends who do. It was easy enough to learn when Mrs. Standish was taking a party to the opera, and easier still to decide which was Miss Charlotte and which Miss Telfair."

"I see." In her turn, she was impressed with him. "Thank you."

"No trouble," he said. "I enjoy the opera. And now, this wretched will." He tapped it with an irritated finger. "In her later years, as you may or may not know, Mrs. Stott—Miss Helen Glendale that was—quarrelled with her entire family. She had inherited a rather pleasant competence from her husband, Mr. Stott. An unfortunate surname that was, I understand, a matter of jest with the other Glendales. Also, he was in trade, in quite a thriving way of business, but not precisely an elegant one."

"I see," said Helen. "So the family twitted her with the source of her money."

"Just so." Again he was pleased with her. "And at the same time let it be known that they expected to inherit. She was the eldest by some years, and childless. A lady of considerable character, I suspect." He laughed. "She must have been, to make Horace Presse draw up this will."

"Do explain."

"She wanted no one to know what she had done with her money. Well, of course, on the face of it, that was impossible. Wills are publicly read, and on file for anyone to inspect."

"Yes. So what did she do?"

"She made a double will. The public one was simple enough. It left everything of which she could die possessed to a clerical friend of hers, to be used"—he ran a finger quickly down the faded document, and quoted—"for the charitable relief of deserving females."

"Females!" Helen was delighted with this sidelight on her great-aunt.

"Just so. Mr. Presse told me that there was a quite appalling scene when the will was read. The family tried all they could to shake it, but they failed, and failed also to discover the existence of what I might call the secondary or secret testament. Its terms are entirely different. The clerical gentleman was to administer the estate as trustee . . . for you. Until you reach the age of twenty-one, half the income is, in fact, to be used for the relief of deserving females. You will, I am sure, understand the purpose of that. Mrs. Stott had suffered for most of her life from the burden of her money; she did not wish you to be so burdened, and she knew her family. So money must be seen to be disbursed on—"

"Deserving females," supplied Helen helpfully.

"Precisely. When you come of age, you inherit the whole, absolutely; or rather"—for the first time he showed signs of nervousness—"on two conditions."

"And they are?"

"The first, that the secret has been kept." He looked, for a moment, unhappy. "I do hope, Miss Telfair, that you have kept it. Our instructions were that either we or the trustee should inform you at such time as we thought fit. I take it that Mr. Tillingdon has, in fact, done so."

"No. It was his sister." A great many odd little things were falling into place. "Mr. Tillingdon moved to Up Harting to keep an eye on me?" And, a logical deduction: "It must be quite a pleasant competence."

"He gets his expenses. They have been"—he paused for a moment—"quite considerable. But within the terms of the trust," he hastened to reassure her.

"I see." She could not help laughing. "I always thought Mr. Tillingdon such a wonderfully generous man. His benefactions to the distressed ladies of his parish have been a byword for as long as I can remember. But," anxiously, "will Miss Tillingdon's knowledge invalidate the trust?"

"No, I'm glad to say. Horace Presse had the wits to insert a special clause about her. He obviously thought it inevitable that, living as she always has with her brother, she would learn at least something of the facts of the case. But what else did she tell you?"

It came out sharply, a crucial question. Luckily, it was also easy to answer. "Nothing. I am quite sure that is all she knew."

"Simply that you are your great-aunt's heir?"

"Yes."

"She did not even advise you to say nothing about it?"

"No, it's lucky for me, is it not, that there was no need."

"It most certainly is. She is your friend, I take it?" And, as Helen nodded, "Then we can assume that she told you all she knew."

"I'm sure we can. What happens, by the way, to the money if I don't get it?"

"It is to be used to found a home for aged or infirm governesses."

"And a very good idea too. But just the same I shall make every effort to keep my secret. And what, pray, is the other condition?"

Now Mr. Furnival looked very unhappy indeed. "That, I fear, I am not at liberty to tell you."

"Oh dear," said Helen.

"Just so. I told you it was a deplorable will." He looked it over again with disfavour. "On the other hand," more cheerfully, "I think I can honestly tell you that it is not a condition that is likely to affect you."

"Ah," said Helen, "so it's not something about my possible marriage, for instance." She read his agreement in his face. "Not that I intend to," she added.

"I'm sorry to hear that." And then, aware of her glance of quick enquiry, "No, no . . . pray don't misunderstand me . . . nothing of that kind." He rose to his feet. "Miss Telfair, I hope you will forgive me if I say that it is time we ended this conversation. I shall look forward to a long and happy association in the future. In the present, I think I have said all that can safely be said. May I say again what a pleasure it has been to meet you? You are returning shortly to Up Harting?" She nodded. "Perhaps you would be so good as to let me know of any future changes of address?"

"I shall indeed." She held out her hand. "Thank you,

Mr. Furnival. Of course, I long to stay here and play guessing games with you, but I can see it might be a dangerous indulgence. Perhaps you would be so good as to have your clerk call me a chair?"

Left alone, Mr. Furnival mopped his forehead. "And only seventeen," he reminded himself. "Phew." He carefully returned the will to its file. At least he thought, her inheritance should be safe enough.

The King's birthday had come and gone, and people were leaving town daily. The Standishes were planning a visit to Weymouth, a seaside resort made popular by the King's patronage, and there was a half suggestion that they should make a detour and take Helen home to Up Harting on their way.

She escaped this with relief, and reached home as she had left it, chaperoned by her aunt's second maid on the stagecoach. There had been a fond, unusually lucid farewell from Charlotte, and a chilly one from Mrs. Standish. "Give my apologies to your mother," were that lady's last words.

It was disconcerting to find that these were hardly needed. Helen's absence had taught her parents how useful she was as unpaid housekeeper, and though her father inevitably jibed at her for her failure to catch a husband he was glad enough to have her firm hand in control of his household once more. As for Mrs. Telfair, she burst into tears at sight of her daughter and took to her bed.

The household was indeed in a bad way. The great spring wash had not been done, and neither had the spring cleaning. The decanters were filthy, and the cook was having a tempestuous affair with the coachman. One of the housemaids was pregnant and would not say by whom, and Captain Telfair's valet had taken to helping himself liberally to his master's port. As soon as she could get away, Helen hurried to the vicarage, to scandalise Miss Tillingdon by describing her visit to the lawyers, and ask eagerly whether her friend had known about Mrs. Stott's extraordinary will.

"Good gracious, no," said Miss Tillingdon. "I only knew you were the heiress because my brother said something once, when he was not feeling quite the thing." It was the nearest she ever came to mentioning her brother's drinking habits.

It was also what Helen had expected, but a blow just the same. "That's a pity. I had hoped you might have some clue about that secret condition of my great aunt's. It would be sad to lose it all just for not knowing. I must say, I do find myself in agreement with Mr. Furnival about that will."

"Yes," wailed Miss Tillingdon, "but what are we to *do?*"

"Wait," said Helen. "Hope for the best, and, in your case, listen with all your ears to everything your brother says, in the hope he may unwittingly give us another clue. It's only four years after all," bracingly, "and then, if all goes well, we'll have our cottage in the country, you and I."

"Only four years!" It was less a wail than a hiccough. "I don't know how I shall bear it."

"You will have to," said Helen.

Chapter 4

TROUBLE with Spain threatened war that summer, and Captain Telfair had his uniforms out and ready once more, but to his disappointment, and Helen's, nothing came of it. She thought that if she could have her mother to herself for a while, she might do something for her shattered nerves and consequent ill health, but Captain Telfair would not even consider the trip to Bath she suggested, throwing it in her teeth that he could not afford it after the wasted expense of her season.

The London visit soon had the unreality of a dream, its

only tangible result a rather erratic correspondence with Charlotte Standish. It was from her that Helen learned, next year, that her angel had achieved respectability at last. On a visit to London, Sir William Hamilton had quietly married the young lady who had been his "guest" in Naples for the last five years. Helen was at once amazed and delighted. She never crossed Uppark to visit the vicarage without thinking of the angel with the warm heart and the strong accent. It was good to think that Emma Hart had actually achieved a recovery from that disastrous beginning of hers. "Of course," wrote Charlotte, "our Queen will not receive her, but it may be otherwise in Naples."

Sir William and the new Lady Hamilton, Charlotte reported, were returning to Naples by way of Paris, still a mecca for English tourists, despite the revolutionary changes that had begun with the fall of the Bastille two years before.

"Just think," Helen told Miss Tillingdon, "Queen Marie Antoinette actually received Lady Hamilton."

"Good gracious!" Miss Tillingdon was always a little shocked by Helen's interest in the one-time Emmy Hart. She believed that women should be liberated, but not, perhaps, quite so liberated as Lady Hamilton. "I expect," she said now, after thinking it over, "that the Queen of France wished to send messages to her sister, the Queen of Naples."

"Very likely," Helen agreed. "In which case, no doubt, the Queen of Naples, too, will receive Lady Hamilton."

"Our Queen never will," said Miss Tillingdon.

"It's monstrous," said Helen. "And there's Sir Harry goes wherever he pleases. No one holds it against him."

"My dear Helen!" As she got older, Miss Tillingdon's views were growing noticeably less liberal. Now she looked anxiously at her young friend. "I worry about you sometimes," she said. "Since you were in London, you behave as if you were thirty, not eighteen."

"I sometimes feel a hundred." Helen could not help remembering Charlotte's last letter, with its casual reference to a farewell visit from Charles Scroope, on his way to join his ship. With an effort, she made her tone more cheerful. "Never mind. I promise to get younger, year by year, once we are settled in our cottage." And yet, did she entirely believe in that cottage? Nothing she saw at home had altered her determination never to marry, but she did, guiltily, sometimes wonder what it would be like to spend the rest of her life tête à tête with Mary Tillingdon.

Seventeen-ninety-two brought terror and massacre to France. Charlotte wrote that Lord Gower had been recalled as ambassador at the French Court, and, in a scribbled postscript, that Helen's old friend Charles Scroope, who had made rapid progress in the navy, had distinguished himself under Lord Cornwallis on the East Indian Station, and been promoted lieutenant. This was not a piece of news with which to regale Captain Telfair, who had himself applied unsuccessfully to serve under Lord Cornwallis. But it pleased Helen, who could not help a curious feeling of responsibility about Charles Scroope's career. How glad he must be, she told herself, that she had refused that rash offer of his, and left him free to make his own way in the world.

But the news made her curiously restless. The trouble was that she envied him. He could carve out his own career, while she must stay at home, acting nurse to her mother, and housekeeper to her father, and waiting for a dead woman's money. Which, in the end, she might not get. She had tried in vain to inspire Miss Tillingdon with the courage to embark on a tactful cross-examination of her brother about Helen Stott's will. Mary Tillingdon was not cut out for a conspirator, and her one attempt at a leading question had secured her so resounding a setdown from her brother that she tearfully refused to try again. It was no use Helen's telling her that their whole future together might be at stake. She simply could not do it.

Mary Tillingdon had been shocked and shaken by the news that their idol Mary Wollstonecraft was in Paris, watching the bloody activities of the revolutionaries. Here, as in the case of Emma Hamilton, she found that there were limits to the amount of female liberation she could admire. At first, Helen was inclined to disagree with her, but as the news from France went from bad to worse, she too stopped calling the French insurgents revolutionaries, and called them murderers instead. Their King and Queen were in prison now, and that monstrous invention, the guillotine, at its dreadful work. But still Helen could not approve of the manifesto of the Duke of Brunswick, who was leading an army of the European powers against France. "To threaten to burn every house in Paris if they hurt the King is merely to harden them against him," she told Miss Tillingdon. "No good will come of it, I am sure."

"But how can the French possibly resist the Duke?" asked Miss Tillingdon. "A rabble like that! His army will cut through France like a knife through butter."

"I wonder," said Helen. "I would have agreed with you, I think, if it had not been for this foolish manifesto. What would you do if someone talked of burning every house in London? I know I would be out in the lanes with my father's pistols, peppering them as they went by."

"Oh dear," sighed Miss Tillingdon. "I really believe you would."

Events were to prove Helen right. The Duke of Brunswick swaggered into France in July. By October came the news of his crushing defeat by Dumouriez and the French "rabble" at Valmy. The allied armies were in full retreat, and the French had taken the offensive.

"Will Fox and his Whig friends never see the danger we are in?" Captain Telfair was furiously reading the *Times* one dark December morning. "If there had been a few regiments of good English redcoats at Valmy it would have been another story. And if our navy were to go into action against them, they'd soon be crying for peace. *And* on their knees for pardon to King Louis."

"Poor man," said Helen. "I doubt if he'll leave the Temple now, except for the guillotine."

"Oh, pray, don't speak of such things." Mrs. Telfair poured tea with a shaking hand. "It is more than my poor nerves can stand."

"Your poor nerves!" Captain Telfair's voice was even rougher than usual. "What right have you to be indulging in nerves, here in England, with every comfort around you? Think of the Queen of France, in prison, with no women about her, and even forced to empty her own slops!"

"Oh, I can't bear it!" Mrs. Telfair put down the teapot, tears streaming down her face, rose from the table and tottered from the room.

Helen encouraged her mother to take to her bed for a few days, but was disconcerted when the days drew into weeks. Christmas came and went, with the barest minimum of necessary celebration, and still Mrs. Telfair lay in bed, dissolving into tears at any suggestion that she even consider getting up. In the end, Helen made her father send for the doctor, who spent a long time with his patient and emerged from her room looking grave.

His interview with Captain Telfair reduced that short-tempered gentleman to almost speechless rage, the best of which he saved for his daughter. "A warm climate," he fulminated. "He wants me to take her to a warm climate! On half pay! Bankrupt by her extravagance and yours! Of all the nonsensical——"

"A more practical point"—Helen interrupted a fruitless outburst of oaths—"is that we could hardly get her to a warmer climate if we could afford to. The way lies through France, and no one but a madman would go there now."

"How like you," he sneered, "to forget that the easiest way to the Mediterranean is by sea."

She was to remember this a few weeks later, when the news of the execution of the King of France was closely followed by the amazing announcement that France had declared war on England.

"That'll teach Fox and company what the Frogs think of them and their friendship!" Captain Telfair was busy packing for a journey to London. This time he would leave nothing to chance. He would get a ship, he said, if he had to swing his hammock across the Admiralty doors.

"I'll stay with your Aunt Standish," he told Helen. "You can direct to me there, if your mother should show any sign of improvement. Or the other thing." Helen knew that he longed now for his wife's death, and rather wondered what he would like to have happen to his daughter. He was desperate, she knew, to get to sea and be free from both of them.

But that being the case, he had made, it turned out, a bad mistake when he went to stay with Mrs. Standish. He returned, a few weeks later, proud with the news of a command, but it was one with strings attached. Mrs. Standish had used her influence to some effect, and he owed his command of the *Trojan* very largely to her good offices. According to him, it was only when he returned from the Admiralty with this news that Mrs. Standish had put in for her reward. The *Trojan* was ordered to Mediterranean waters. His wife, she knew, had been ordered there by her doctor. And it so happened that Charlotte, too, worn out by three unsuccessful seasons, was in need of balmier airs. What more logical than that Captain Telfair should take his wife and the two girls with him when he sailed?

This was the way Captain Telfair described the course of events. Helen, knowing both him and her aunt, was certain that a hard bargain had been drawn between them before Mrs. Standish used that influence of hers. It was obvious that the last thing Captain Telfair wanted was the company of his wife, daughter, and niece, and Helen herself was dismayed at the prospect of life in the cramped conditions of a man-of-war. If it had not been for the state of her mother's health, she would have argued strongly against it, but the doctor, sensing her reaction, took her aside and warned her that, for her mother, it was literally a choice between a warmer climate and death.

A letter from Charlotte was encouraging. Captain Telfair's new command, it seemed, was a large, old-fashioned seventy-four-gun ship with unusually roomy living quarters for her captain, and a stern deck opening off his main saloon, where, Charlotte said, her Aunt Telfair would be able to sun herself back to health in peace and privacy. It seemed an odd enough prospect on a battleship in time of war, but then, no one expected much active opposition from the French navy, depleted of its aristocratic officers. Charlotte wrote eagerly, as if they were going on a pleasure cruise, and Helen could only hope she knew what she was talking about.

The *Trojan* had been laid up at Portsmouth, and with the whole navy struggling to get back on to a wartime basis, her refitting was inevitably slow. On Captain Telfair's rare visits home, he talked angrily about shortage of stores, of men, of ammunition, of everything that he needed. But he seemed, to Helen, a different man. In action he was in his element. On the beach, he had been grinding himself to pieces; now all his energy was thrown into getting his ship ready to sail, and Helen had her first glimpse of the man who had distinguished himself first as lieutenant and then as commander. Perhaps life on the *Trojan* would be better than she had feared.

Charlotte arrived to stay with them early in June, stammering hard, but improved remarkably when she found Mrs. Telfair too ill and Helen too busy to notice whether she finished her sentences or not. She was as pretty as ever, and not much more sensible, but Helen was genuinely pleased to see her and grateful for her company on what seemed to be a wild enough venture. Saying good-bye to Miss Tillingdon, she said something of this, and Miss Tillingdon replied bracingly that she had sense enough for the three of them, "So long as you don't give too much way to your wild notions."

It seemed a sad change of front on the part of the friend who had first introduced Helen to these "wild notions" about the rights of women. But it was no more than Helen had expected. Whatever plans she might have now for her future, they did not include that cottage with Miss Tillingdon.

"Poor M . . . M . . . M . . ." Charlotte was on her knees folding a muslin ball gown into the smallest possible compass. And then, when Helen went placidly on with her own packing, "I hope she won't be too disappointed."

"Why should she be?" Helen straightened her weary back for a moment.

"Because I shan't m . . . m . . . m . . . Because no one will propose to m . . . m . . . m . . ." Charlotte gave up and shoved the gown ruthlessly into place at the top of the already overflowing box.

So that was it. Charlotte was being sent to sea as other girls were sent to India, to make the best marriage she could. Well, Helen thought, her own parents very likely had the same plans for her. She was doubtless supposed to snap up some fine young aristocratic naval officer. This revolting prospect was confirmed when they finally went on board the *Trojan* and found that other passengers had already arrived. Lord Merritt was a friend of Lady Standish's, and like Mrs. Telfair, had been ordered south for his health. He, his secretary, a Mr. Trenche, and his valet, Price, were to have the quarters below the captain's that were usually allocated to the first and second lieutenants. It was just as well, Helen thought, that the *Trojan* was such a roomy ship, but she was still sorry for the two lieutenants, whose faces she liked, though she had not yet managed to remember their names.

Charlotte and Lord Merritt, it seemed, were old friends. If that was the word, which Helen rather doubted after witnessing Lord Merritt's unenthusiastic surprise, and Charlotte's extraordinary outburst of stammering, when they met. Mrs. Standish would be lucky, she thought, if the voyage resulted in an engagement in that quarter. But then, Mrs. Standish had never been in the least aware of other people's feelings. Of course, it might be young Trenche she intended for her daughter, but it seemed unlikely as he was a younger son, earning his living in attendance on Lord Merritt who was, it soon became apparent, a very rich man indeed.

He liked being rich, and made no secret of it. He had spent his first afternoon on board in a minute scrutiny of the captain's stores and had then sent so comprehensive an order ashore that Captain Telfair, when the results were swayed on deck, had had to reorganise his entire between-decks cargo.

"Necessities of life," said Lord Merritt with satisfaction when it was all over.

Helen had come on board at the same time as the last of his cargo. "You look on champagne as a necessity?" The sight of the crates being loaded at the same time as the men's salt beef and biscuit had shocked her profoundly and she had been more shocked still at her father's meek acquiescence in this disruption of plans for his ship.

"Part of civilisation. Even if it does come from France." This was a joke, and Mr. Trenche laughed dutifully, giving the lead to all the others save Helen.

"And how, exactly, do you define civilisation?" Helen had taken a dislike to this plump, middle-aged man in his overfashionable clothes, but thought she was giving him one more chance.

"Interesting question." He turned to Mr. Trenche. "Philip. Civilisation?"

"The *douceur de vivre,* sir? And, perhaps," with a comprehensive bow, "the company of charming ladies?"

"Excellent, excellent. Thoughts in a nutshell." Merritt flourished his own bow, his eyes on Helen. "Charming ladies," he repeated Trenche's phrase. "And ladies . . . most unusual . . . who think."

This made the compliment pointedly for Helen, but she would have none of it. "I think it is time we went below and saw to our unpacking." She turned and led the way.

The convoy of merchant ships that the *Trojan* was to escort to Gibraltar was already assembled; the wind was fair; they sailed that night. By next morning, all the passengers but Helen were very ill indeed, and even she only kept going by resolutely making herself eat small quantities of bread, and spending as much time as possible on the stern deck, away from the multifarious smells of ship. Necessity joined with fresh air to keep her on her feet. Rose, Charlotte's maid, whom Captain Telfair had grudgingly allowed to accompany the three ladies, was as sick as anyone else. Leaving her to her fate, Helen was kept occupied ministering to her mother and Charlotte, providing basins, rags soaked in vinegar, sal volatile, and encouragement. Price, Lord Merritt's man, was busy about the same dismal office. She wished she could like him. He made himself invaluable, but all the time she felt that his shifty grey eyes were looking this way and that for advantage to himself. She thought him jealous of Trenche and thought herself absurd to think so.

Too busy to give way, Helen soon began to feel better, and ventured up on deck next afternoon to see the ships of the convoy ploughing along ahead, their sails brilliant white in the sun. Her father was not in sight, but the officer of the watch was coming along the deck to greet her, with a friendly "Good-day," and then, aware of her difficulty: "First Lieutenant Forbes, ma'am. I had the honour of being presented to you before we sailed."

She smiled at him gratefully. "Thank you, Mr. Forbes. I'm afraid the last two days have got a trifle confused in my mind."

"As well they might." His smile was friendly. "I gather you're the only survivor so far." He turned away, with an apology, to shout an order to the helmsman. "It's difficult to keep our speed down to those tubs." A scornful gesture indicated the ships of the convoy. "The *Trojan* could sail rings around them if she wanted to."

"She's fast?"

"Said to be. Faster than you'd expect from her build. And Captain Telfair will get every ounce out of her, you can rely on that. You'll see some action, ma'am, I hope, once we've cleared Gibraltar, left this lot behind, and joined the Mediterranean Fleet."

He seemed to think this so delightful a prospect for her that she had not the heart to tell him that action was the last thing she wished to see. It was extraordinary, and horrible, to think of these shining white decks stained with blood, the sails that sang above her ragged with gunfire, men all around groaning and dying.

"I beg your pardon." Once again, disconcertingly, he had read her thoughts. "I quite forgot myself. Naturally, I very much hope that we get you and your mother safe on shore before we are lucky enough to go into action."

She smiled at him gratefully. "Frankly, Mr. Forbes, so do I. If one only knew what that shore was going to be."

"Yes." She saw the mask of professional discretion close over his face. Then it lightened again into his rather engaging smile. "Frankly, Miss Telfair, I have no more idea than you do. I doubt if even Captain Telfair knows what will happen to us after Gibraltar."

"Then it's not much use worrying, is it?"

But she did worry. It was impossible not to, when Charlotte recovered and appeared on deck, gay as a bird, and still her mother lay in the exiguous cabin they shared, tossing helplessly, eating nothing, endlessly sick. Their plan had been that Captain Telfair would land them at the first Italian port they reached, and Lord Merritt, who planned to make a slow progress southwards to Naples, would escort them to some suitable, inexpensive spot where Mrs. Telfair could be nursed, in sunshine, back to strength.

It had all seemed practical enough at home in Up Harting. Now it struck Helen as little short of madness. The more she talked to the pleasant young officers of the ship, the more she realised how ruthless was naval discipline. If Lord Hood, commanding the Mediterranean Fleet, were to decide that the *Trojan* must be detached on some dangerous duty, Captain Telfair neither could nor would suggest that first he must put his passengers safe on shore.

Lord Merritt, who claimed to owe his recovery entirely to the extensive consumption of champagne, caught her alone in the main salon and confessed to the same doubts.

"Seemed a good enough plan when Mrs. Standish suggested it. Not so sure now. Perhaps"—here was the point of his remarks—"Speak to your father?"

"It would be no use." She wished to settle this once and for all. "With my mother as ill as she is, he would consult her convenience if he could." It was not true but how was he to know that? "I think, Lord Merritt, that we can do nothing but pray for a fair wind, and the right order at Gibraltar."

"I wish you would call me Henry."

Here was an unpleasant surprise. He had achieved a whole sentence; his tone was actually languishing, and he was, to the best of his ability, making eyes at her. It was a deplorably comic performance, and she ignored it as best she might. "My father has such rigid ideas of propriety," she kept it light. "I am sure you will understand, my lord."

"Hard world." He was fretful now. "Buy you—God dammit—buy you Corsica if you wanted. Won't even call me by my name."

Worse and worse. And—a comic underthought—what in the world would Aunt Standish think if she learned that

her careful plans had come to this? "Dear Lord Merritt"
—at all costs she must not quarrel with her father's afflu-
ent passenger—"you are kindness itself, but, do you
know, I do not particularly want Corsica."

"Sensible." Even this remark, intended to be quelling,
met with his approval. "What do we think of Corsica,
Trenche?"

"We think it a barbarous island, my lord." Philip
Trenche had just entered the cabin, and Helen was surprised how relieved she was to see him.

Chapter 5

⌇ IF the Bay of Biscay had been rough, the
passage round Cape St. Vincent was tempestuous. While
the rest of the party ate their way ravenously through the
more perishable of the cabin dainties, Mrs. Telfair lay
helpless in her cot, supporting existence on thin soup and
Lord Merritt's champagne, for which Helen now found
herself blessing him. She seemed weaker every day, and
Helen even wondered whether she should suggest that
they go ashore at Gibraltar. But when she managed to
catch her father alone and tentatively raised the idea, she
got a short answer. "If the wind's fair for the gut, we're
not stopping at the Rock," he told her. "Besides, Merritt
intends to go in to Italy, and I can't leave you three
women alone here. Spain's not much more to be trusted
than France. You and your invalid might find yourselves
standing siege on the Rock."

"Oh!" She had not thought of that unpleasant possibility. "You mean, we leave the convoy at Gibraltar and go
on alone?"

"Just so. To rendezvous with Hood and the fleet off Toulon. And then the sooner I can get you passage on a ship bound for Italy, the happier I shall be."

There was no more to be said, and in the end they passed the Rock of Gibraltar at night after a flurry of farewell signals from the convoy, whose captains seemed to Helen almost excessively grateful for the protection they had received, considering that they had not sighted a single enemy ship.

"Well, there aren't many of them," said Lieutenant Forbes, to whom she had remarked on this. They were in the Mediterranean now, sailing up the east coast of Spain to their rendezvous at Toulon, and Helen was on deck, enjoying the balmy air and steady motion of the ship, and straining her eyes to make out the details of the wooded, unhospitable-looking shore.

"Heavenly air," she said, breathing it in.

"Yes. It will be hot later. Miss Telfair, I've been thinking about your mother. It cannot be good for her to lie in that dismal cabin all day. If Captain Telfair would give permission, I could easily have a cot rigged for her on the stern deck. We could have her carried out, in the daytime, to get the benefit of the sea breeze. The doctor would not agree with me, I know," he went on bravely, "but I have never thought it could be good for an invalid to lie and breathe the same air over and over again."

"I'm sure you're right!" She turned to him eagerly. "We found this at home—a friend of mine and I. In the summer, we used to try and get the sick out of doors. It often helped. Pray let us try it with my mother."

"You will have to get the captain's permission." He did not sound hopeful.

But Captain Telfair did not use the stern gallery, much preferring the peace and quietness of his own portion of the main deck. He listened to Helen's request calmly enough, and merely suggested dryly that she should consult the other passengers before she made her arrangements, which must not, of course, interfere with the management of the ship. "I won't have a moment added to the time we take to clear for action."

It was a chilling thought, but one for which Lieutenant

Forbes had prepared Helen. If the ship should encounter a French warship, the place of passengers was far below decks, in the cable tier. He had offered to show it to her, "Just in case," but she had thanked him and refused, knowing herself a coward. If she must face the foul, dark air below, she would, but she took her duty as chief nurse to her mother too seriously to take any unnecessary risks. Or was she making excuses for herself? Probably. As for the actual clearing for action, Forbes had assured her that it would make no difference whether her mother was in her cabin or out on the stern deck. That point gained, Helen nerved herself most unwillingly to approach Lord Merritt. He proved, as she had feared, quite overwhelmingly cooperative. Her wish was his command. More obligingly still, he offered the services of Trenche and Price to help move Mrs. Telfair to and fro between cabin and stern deck.

Mrs. Telfair was horrified at the idea of being moved out on deck in the daytime, and it took all Helen's blandishments, and the loan of an excessively becoming swansdown-trimmed daygown by Charlotte, to persuade her, but once she had been carried out, still feebly protesting, by Price and Trench, the improvement in her health, though slow, was steady and obvious.

They had run into contrary winds, much to Captain Telfair's fury, but when they got to Toulon at last, it was to stirring news. A royalist revolution had broken out in the south of France, and the city fathers of Toulon had actually handed their town, harbour, and the ships it contained over to the protective custody of the British navy. "It's the beginning of the end, if you ask me." Captain Telfair hardly tried to pretend that this was not bad news to him. "We'll consolidate our position, make a landing here, march on Paris, and it's all over."

"If the government at home send the troops," said Helen. "Aren't we pretty heavily committed up in the Netherlands?"

"Pah!" said her father. "Setting up as a strategist now, are you? If we can raise a navy, we can surely raise an army." His tone showed how little he thought of the land forces.

"Might that not be the strength of our position, sir?" Trenche spoke, with his usual deference, to Captain Telfair. "A pincers movement, with the Duke of York marching inland from Dunkirk, and another body of troops moving north from here? I am sure that when Sir Gilbert Elliott arrives to take over as civil commissioner here at Toulon we shall see some action."

"In that case, he can't get here too soon for me," said Captain Telfair. "I'm sick to death of all this cursed merry-making. Bowing and scraping and giving full honours to a lot of Frogs one can't even talk to. It's not at all what I expected when I came to sea."

Helen actually felt sorry for him. He had strained every nerve to get his ship to sea, in the eager expectation of action, and now found himself compelled to act host to some of the very "Frogs" he had expected to fight. The royalists of Toulon must be treated with every possible courtesy, and indeed even Helen felt that, granted their hazardous situation, their rigid insistence on all the forms of precedence, the jots and tittles of etiquette, bordered on the ridiculous. A few weeks before, most of these elegant ladies and gentlemen had been hunted fugitives, afraid for their lives; now they were very much Monsieur this and Madame that, and a captain who made a mistake in precedence might actually imperil the precarious alliance between ships and shore.

"I must say I had hoped that Sir Gilbert's arrival would make more difference," Helen told Philip Trenche as they made ready for yet another of the parties her father was so ill-equipped to give. The two of them were the only fluent French-speakers on board, and a good deal of the burden fell on them, Helen acting as interpreter, where possible, for her father, and Trenche for Lord Merritt. Helen's main anxiety, as she added the necessary Gallic grace-notes to her father's curt speeches, was lest some of their French guests might understand more English than they admitted.

But today's occasion should be easier. At Forbes's suggestion, discreetly passed on to her father by Helen, the guests were to be entertained under an awning on the main deck. The October day was fine and calm, so that they came on board without difficulty, and the al fresco entertainment was universally voted a great success. Helen, dancing a quadrille with Mr. Forbes, congratulated him on the idea and then laughed at his look of quick anxiety. "Don't fret," she smiled. "I won't give you the credit for it." But she had lost his attention. "What is it?"

He had been looking beyond her, out to the open sea, with those clear blue eyes of his. "A ship of the line," he said. "You'll excuse me?"

"Of course." She had learned soon what Charlotte never would, that always the call of duty came first. Now she moved over to the rail, straining her eyes in vain to see what Forbes had.

"All alone?" Lord Merritt was the last person she would have wished to find her thus. "Call of duty?" He had clearly seen Forbes leave her, but managed to make his reason seem more than dubious.

"No doubt," she responded dryly. If there really was a new ship joining the fleet, perhaps with news from England, they would know soon enough. She saw her father hurry across the deck to where Admiral Lord Hood was holding a small court, his flag captain in attendance.

By now, everyone who owned a spyglass had it out and fixed on the strange ship and the signals at her masthead. "It's the *Agamemnon*." Jones, the second lieutenant, paused by Helen and Lord Merritt. "Captain Nelson, back from Naples. Now we should see some action. He's a regular fire-eater; a death or glory man."

"Fire-eating at Naples?" Merritt's tone with the officers was always just wrong. "The volcano?"

"Hardly." Jones coloured. "It's an open secret, sir—my lord—that the Admiral sent Nelson to ask for naval as well as military aid from the Court of Naples. The first contingent of troops have arrived already. Let us hope that Captain Nelson brings news of more. Ah!" A new set of signals had gone up from the *Trojan*. "They're signalling for him to come aboard. If you will excuse me . . ."

"Sideboys and bosun's pipes!" Merritt made it a sneer. "Sick of them both. Go down and see how your mother is?"

Helen had wanted to do just this, but not with Lord

Merritt. Still, there seemed no help for it, and she let him hand her over-gallantly down to the stern deck, where, to her dismay, they found Mrs. Telfair fast asleep on her cot.

"Shh . . ." Merritt's elaborate pantomime was both unnecessary and irritating. But worse was to follow. He closed the door from the stern deck quietly behind him, then moved quickly across the large cabin to make sure that the other door into the companionway was closed. "At last," he said.

"I beg your pardon?" Helen would not understand him.

"Modest *and* beautiful. Really don't know? Schemed, prayed (almost), conspired (quite) to get you here."

"Conspired?" Helen did not like the sound of it.

"Price. Useful man. Out in the companionway. Gives me a chance. Ask you to marry me. Devoted slave; adored you from a distance; all of that."

"A lot of nonsense."

"Nothing of the kind." He had got hold of her hand and was kissing it without conviction. "Surprised. Does you credit." Another kiss, rather damp. "My heart and hand at your feet." She released her hand and started to speak but a peremptory gesture silenced her, and, after all, best hear him out and get it over with. "Miss Telfair!" Now his hand was on his heart, or where his heart might be presumed to lurk under layers of well-fed flesh. "My respect for you, so great; my admiration, so profound. Nothing for it but to tell you all."

"All?"

"Find myself," he said. "Found myself, while ago; most absurd case. Frankly, no plan to marry. Oh, marriage a blessing, of course, but——" He paused.

"No need to say more." For the first time, Helen found herself feeling quite kindly towards him. "I have always thought marriage a very mixed blessing myself."

"Knew it. The very girl." He laughed, not pleasantly. "Poor Mrs. Standish."

"I beg your pardon?"

"No need to play the innocent. Know you." A pause, a gesture. "Love you too well. No fool. Course you've seen through the old bitch's plans. Knows everything. Bound

to know I must marry. Pricked me down for that s . . . s
. . . stammering chit. Well; true enough. Good breeders,
those Glendale girls. But girl's the word. What's that to
the purpose?"

"Lord Merritt." She must not quarrel with him. "I do
not understand a word you are saying."

"Never a one for gossip. Not you." Nothing she could
say would puncture his self-assurance. "Virtue in a wife.
It's like this." Suddenly, and unpleasantly, they were conspirators. "Lot of damned nonsense. Fuss and bother.
Scandal. Had to come away. Must marry. Get an heir."

"Why?"

"Damned—excuse me—most unfair. Ought to be a law
against old people; ridiculous wills. My uncle," he explained, unaware that at last he had caught both her attention and her sympathy. "Heard the gossip. Damn fool
will. All to me if I have an heir male when he kicks it.
Thinks I'm a fribble. Well, perhaps I am. What's wrong
with it? No harm to anyone. Good for trade. Worst of all;
old codger never told me till he took ill the other day.
Suppose he had died! Never have forgiven myself. Or
him."

"I take it he recovered?" Helen could not help but be
fascinated by his story, so oddly like her own.

"Fit as a fiddle; lots of time; comfortable wedding here
on board; no hurry . . ." He coloured and looked unhappy. "No hurry about anything. Besides." More cheerfully.
"My uncle; odd fish; crazy ideas. Meet you. Like you.
Change his will."

"Oh. Why?"

"Thinks nothing of me. Never did. Doesn't like the
idea of me for an heir. No one else; lucky for me. But if I
married you. Well, different kettle of fish. A man, after
all."

"I see." She did indeed see, and felt herself profoundly
sorry for him in his absurd predicament. He still had her
hand but seemed not to know quite what to do with it.
"You'd be good to me," he said. "Only wife I can imagine. I'd be good to you. Everything . . . anything. Your
mother . . . Only to ask . . ."

She believed him. How could she make him see it as

impossible? "But, Lord Merritt, you have so much money already. Surely you can afford to snap your fingers at this ridiculous uncle of yours?"

"At all that money? Well—" his weak eyes met hers. "Thought of it. But—all that fuss in England. Go back with a wife. Settle it. Be rich—very rich—" He loved the thought. "No need to be together all the time. If you wanted to run a salon, a school even . . . try out some of these ideas of yours . . . Anything, anything you say." He had gone white with the effort of what he was trying to tell her. "Helen: strange conversation . . . strange proposal, but, believe me: I love you."

There was a qualification lurking in that speech, and she recognised it. What he was saying was that, insofar as he could love a woman, he loved her. It was at once oddly touching, and, if it had been needed, decisive. Gently, firmly, she released her hand. "Lord Merritt, I am more flattered than I can say by your proposal, but I must tell you, I mean never to marry."

"Never?" She had taken the wind quite out of his sails. And, mercifully, as if on cue, came a tapping on the cabin door, and Price's voice. "My lord, they're coming!"

When Captain Telfair ushered in an extremely distinguished party of senior officers, Helen was out on the stern deck bending over her mother's cot, and Lord Merritt, rather red in the face, was looking at one of the books Helen had insisted on bringing on board. Lord Hood's keen glance took in the situation instantly. This was no place for the full report he wanted from his newly joined captain. "We'll take a glass of wine with you, Telfair, and then Nelson and I must adjourn to the *Victory* and lay our heads together. We'll not disturb your invalid, but I'm sure Miss Telfair would like to join us and hear what Captain Nelson has to tell of that extraordinary court at Naples."

Helen, who had been hovering in the open doorway of the stern gallery, took her cue gratefully and joined the party. The strange captain had just been presented to Lord Merritt and now crossed the cabin to bow over her hand. He was a small man, undistinguished-looking at first, with thinning hair of an indeterminate colour, and a pair of eyes of such brilliance that she forgot everything else about him. "Captain Telfair is fortunate," he said with instinctive tact. "I have a wife at home in Norfolk. It would be almost worth having her an invalid to have her here with me."

In the background, Helen was aware of her father's simmering rage at being found thus encumbered, and, smiling at Captain Nelson, thought he too had felt it. "And a daughter!" he went on. "I have a stepson of whom I'm more than a little proud, but to have a daughter . . . You're a fortunate man, Telfair."

"Thank you." Luckily, Price, passing round Lord Merritt's excellent madeira, caused an inevitable redistribution of the party. The other officers were gathered eagerly round Nelson, plying him with questions. His had been altogether a most encouraging visit to Naples. The King had received him cordially. "For what that's worth," said Nelson. "Everyone knows the Queen and her first minister, Acton, rule the country, while the King hunts and fishes like the overgrown schoolboy he is."

"You met the Queen?" asked a captain whose name Helen did not know.

"No. Breeding, poor woman, as usual. A fine family of young princes and princesses." Helen thought there was something faintly wistful in his tone. "But there's no doubt of her sympathies," he went on. "She's Marie Antoinette's sister, after all. I've heard it said that she'd fight the French single-handed if she only got the chance. A regular amazon of a woman."

"And our ambassador?" asked another captain. "You found Sir William agreeable?"

"Kindness itself. And a man it's a pleasure to do business with. Why, he and Lady Hamilton actually insisted I stay with them in that palace of theirs."

"Lady Hamilton!" There was a ripple of interest in the crowd of men, and Helen was quite forgotten as her father spoke. "The new Lady Hamilton!" A wealth of innuendo in his tone. "Don't tell me that trollop is received at Court."

Captain Nelson stiffened and seemed to grow taller. "Lady Hamilton is on the best of terms with Queen Maria

Carolina." His tone was icy. "She is a young woman of amiable manners, and who does honour to the station to which she is raised."

Chapter 6

◁ THE whole fleet soon knew that Captain Nelson had done brilliantly well at the Court of Naples. More troops and even some Neapolitan ships were coming to join the blockade of Toulon. It was just as well they were. Hopes of a march on Paris had long since dwindled into anxious discussion of how long Toulon would be able to stand the siege that was being mounted by the revolutionary French army. The news from Dunkirk was bad, too, and a rhyme was beginning to circulate, behind hands, in private:

> The noble Duke of York
> He had ten thousand men;
> He marched them up to the top of the hill,
> And he marched them down again.

They lived daily in the expectation of news of the evacuation of Dunkirk, which would, inevitably, mean an increase of pressure on Toulon. And, already, the pressure was getting hard to bear. They were not to know that out in the barren countryside to the north, a young artillery officer called Bonaparte was distinguishing himself, for the first time, by his handling of guns and men.

The weather was getting colder and the sea rougher. There were fewer parties now on the blockading ships, and much less coming and going between them, since this

60

tended to mean a good wetting at one end or the other. Helen was growing increasingly anxious for the passage to an Italian port of which her father had spoken before they left England. Ships were frequently detached from the blockading fleet and sent to Leghorn, but each time she raised the question, her father produced one difficulty or another. The ship was not equipped to take females on board. . . . The notice had been too short. . . . The weather was too bad.

It baffled her. Since that uncomfortable moment when Hood and Nelson had had to postpone their conference because of the presence of passengers in the cabin of the *Trojan*, Helen had been more acutely aware than ever of how her father hated to be cumbered with four females, one of them an invalid. So, why did he not get rid of them at the first opportunity? Lord Merritt provided her with the answer one evening when she had gone up on deck for a breath of air at sunset. She had half hoped to find Forbes on watch, but it was Jones who saluted her, and then irritated her by vanishing to the farthest part of the deck when Lord Merritt appeared.

He had brought her a shawl. "Night breezes treacherous." He put it round her shoulders with those damp hands of his. "Weather worsening. Time your mother was safe ashore."

"It is indeed." She turned to him gratefully. "If you would but speak to my father. I cannot understand why he has not arranged our passage to Leghorn long since."

"Cannot?" He was laughing at her, and she did not like it. "Charming simpleton! Hard to tell: more irresistible wise or foolish?"

"What in the world do you mean?"

"Father's no fool. Nod's better than a wink to him. Wedding bells first. Then Leghorn. Shipboard marriage. Just the thing. No trouble. No fuss. No need for you to fret either. We'll make it all right and tight in Leghorn. Must be that for my uncle."

"Oh, my God." She had listened to him with growing horror, wondering what form of bribery he had used on her father. It must have been powerful indeed to have outweighed Captain Telfair's dislike of having them on board. "I don't know what to do." She was ashamed of herself as she said it.

"All your troubles on my shoulders. Surprised how different they'll look. Mother in the sun at Naples by Christmas. Not a minute too soon. Losing strength daily."

"I know. I must talk to my father." It was a forlorn hope, but seemed her only one.

"Good. Knew I could rely on your sense."

"Nothing of the kind." She rounded on him. "I mean to appeal to his feelings as a husband."

He actually looked sorry for her. "Wasting your time. Ours. No use; must know it. Suit your father too well. Rich son-in-law. Just the ticket. Up to you. Refuse me. Your mother stays here. Accept. Naples. After all, if you really meant not to marry . . . could do worse than marry me. Rich, too."

She could have laughed if she had not been so close to angry tears. Turning from him, she stumbled down to the tiny cabin where bad weather now kept her mother almost permanently immured. Charlotte was sitting with her, and put her finger on her lips. Mrs. Telfair was lightly asleep. "Helen! I'm afraid she's worse. Her mind is wandering. I think we should send for the doctor. Or even Lord Hood's?"

"I'll just take another look at her." Helen returned to the tiny cabin, followed by Charlotte. Mrs. Telfair's eyes were open now but fixed on a remote point somewhere beyond Helen's shoulder. "Help me, Aunt Helen," she said. "Help . . ." The words were lost in a fit of coughing. Charlotte and Helen gazed at each other, speechless, as red blood flowed on the sheets.

The Admiral's doctor could do no more than the *Trojan*'s. All he did was insist that it was too late now for anything; a move ashore was impossible; a move from the cabin might mean death. And either way, whatever they did, death was there, waiting, inevitable. It was unspeakably horrible to Helen to find herself thinking that this disaster freed her from Lord Merritt. They would never journey south together now, for that sunny Christmas in Naples that was to cure her mother.

And all the time, the ring of batteries was closing round Toulon, with that active young gunner, Napoleon Bonaparte, busy setting and resetting his guns, to do the maximum damage to the beleaguered city.

"Those poor souls in Toulon," said Helen, "when we go, what will become of them?" Her "when" told the whole disastrous story from the summer's hope to the winter's despair. Everyone knew that the day was not far off when the revolutionary batteries would make it impossible for the British fleet to go on protecting Toulon. The question was not if, but when they would evacuate the town.

Mrs. Telfair died, quietly, on a bleak day of early December, and Helen, crying in the empty cabin, could not banish the thought that if she had accepted Lord Merritt, it might have saved her life. But at least it was a relief to be alone for once. Lord Merritt had taken Charlotte to a party at Lord Hood's quarters on shore, and, if Helen thought this heartless so soon after the funeral, she was still grateful for the solitude.

It was not to last. Her father joined her in one of his worst moods. "I hope you're proud of what you've done."

"Done?" Worn out with nursing, she raised great, listless eyes to his.

"Don't pretend to be more of a fool than you are. If you'd taken Merritt, she'd be alive now."

"Or if you'd let us go." But what was the use of arguing? It was actually a relief when Philip Trenche appeared with a white face and news of increased activity from the French inshore batteries.

Captain Telfair got to his feet. "This may be the end," he said. "If it comes to it, Trenche, I count on you to see Miss Telfair down to the cable tier."

Night fell, and still Charlotte and Lord Merritt had not returned. Helen stayed on deck well into twilight, watching the unusual activity between ships and shore, wishing that their station was not at the extreme outer verge of the protective ring of ships, longing for news that did not come. Lieutenant Forbes paused beside her for a moment in the gathering dusk. "I don't like the look of things," he said. "Look! There—and there!"

Helen knew the flash of gunfire well enough by now. "But—" She was puzzling out the position in the deceptive evening light. "That's on the Faron heights."

"Yes. Our last tenable defence. And pointed against us."

"You mean—"

"The French must have taken them. There have been rumours all day of panic in the town. The Spanish troops have been doubtful from the first. I've heard that the Neapolitans are not much better. Miss Telfair, I think you should go below and get the best night's sleep you can. Tomorrow may be a bad day."

"But Miss Standish—"

"I doubt if they'll be back tonight. I've seen the Admiral's barge to and fro, to and fro all afternoon. As busy as that, there'll be no time for guests."

"Oh, poor Charlotte, she'll be so worried." It was only when she got below that it occurred to Helen to worry about herself as well as about Charlotte. Her father had eaten a few hasty bites of food, told her briskly not to fret, and gone back on deck. Philip Trenche sat across the cabin from her, visibly sweating with fright, and asking, from time to time, if she did not think the sound of gunfire nearer. She did, but would not admit it, and retired to bed as early as she decently could. Now, she would even have been glad of Rose's cheerful chatter, but Rose had gone with her mistress.

Next morning, the gunfire sounded very close indeed, and Price, bringing breakfast for her and Philip Trenche, brought a message that was an order. "Captain says you're to stay below."

"What's happening?" Trenche looked sallow this morning, and Helen did not find it comforting to realise how frightened he was.

"We're quitting." Price seemed to be enjoying himself. "And not before time, if you ask me. The Frogs have got the batteries overlooking the town. We'll be lucky if we get off without bloodshed. The soldiers are beginning to board already."

"And what about the poor French royalists?" asked Helen.

"God knows," and then, "Poor devils, even if they are Frogs." He poured coffee. "Might as well enjoy your breakfast, miss. Anything may happen between this and dinner. But one good thing, the wind's fair out of the harbour."

The result of this, of course, was that nothing could be seen from the stern gallery. Trenche was biting his nails. "Our draught's too great for us to go in for them," he said. "They'll have to be ferried out to us. I hope to God we get Englishmen."

"Or those poor French," said Helen, abandoning the pretence at breakfast. "Yes, Price, you may clear."

It was an endless, horrible, newsless day. In the harbour, the grim process of evacuation went on, but Helen and Trenche were dependent on Price for such fragments of news as he was able to glean on his way to and from the ship's galley. Lord Hood and Sir Gilbert Elliott, the commissioner for Toulon, were safe aboard the *Victory,* he told them, and so, presumably, were Charlotte and Lord Merritt. Both Spanish and Neapolitan troops had panicked, and the Neapolitan admiral, Forteguerri, had actually sailed for Naples without consulting his allies.

"It sounds like a question of *sauve qui peut,"* said Trenche. "I hope to God Captain Telfair has the sense to save us while there is time."

"My father will do his duty," said Helen. It was, in fact, a small comfort to be sure of this. "I wish there was something one could *do.*"

"Talk to me," said Trenche.

She recognised the frantic appeal in his tone and did her best to keep him entertained with the kind of London gossip he enjoyed. It seemed an extraordinary way to be spending the day of the evacuation of Toulon. With dusk came movement at last, but from Trenche's point of view, movement in the wrong direction. He had been over-optimistic in his conviction that the evacuees would be ferried out to the *Trojan.* Time was running out; panic-stricken soldiers were firing into the boats that would not take them on board. Lord Hood had ordered the *Trojan* into the harbour to control the situation with her guns.

Price brought the news, and an order. "Captain Telfair

says I'm to take you and Mr. Trenche down to the cable tier," he said. And, aware of Helen's instinctive recoil, "Captain's orders." Once again she had the strange feeling that he was enjoying himself.

And she was the captain's daughter. Already, they could hear the scurry of bare feet across the deck, the gigantic creaking as the anchor was got up. "Very well." She picked up her embroidery. "Let's go."

"It's dark in the cable tier," said Price.

"Oh." She dropped the embroidery and they followed him in silence.

Dimly illuminated by the lamp Price carried, the cable tier was so horrible a place that Helen thought perhaps she would be grateful for darkness. Well below the water line, it was a compound of all the worst of the shipboard odours she hated. Trenche was begging, with a hint of tears in his voice, for Price to leave them the lamp.

"Sorry, sir." Price, who had been apparently courteous to Helen, was short with Trenche. "Captain's orders. And I'm on duty in the cockpit."

"Then we mustn't keep you," said Helen. She had looked quickly round the horrible place, selected what seemed to be a dry coil of huge cable, and sat down on it with a deliberate arrangement of her skirts. "At least"—she managed to keep her voice light as Price and his lamp went flickering away from them—"we seem to have been spared the anchor cable, which, presumably, would be soaking wet." They had heard the anchor come in as they were on their way down, and now a new movement of the ship indicated that she was under sail, doubtless beating her way into harbour, and the danger of death. But at least the wind that made entry into the harbour difficult would make escape easy. She thought of saying this to Trenche, but decided against it. The word "escape" might be a dangerous one to use to anyone in his state of obvious terror. Now, in the stinking darkness, she could hear a rustle that she thought must be rats, and a strange, clicking noise that she finally identified as the chattering of Philip Trenche's teeth.

She must talk about something. "I do hope Charlotte and Lord Merritt are safe aboard the *Victory*."

"I'm sure they are. Doubtless sitting down to a fine dinner in the Admiral's quarters, with young Charlotte stut . . . stut . . . stuttering to beat the band."

The change from his normal tone was so extraordinary that for a moment she could not believe her ears. Then, "Charlotte is my dear friend," she said.

"More fool you. She's rich; you're poor. There can be no real friendship between you. You might as well expect me to be devoted to Lord Plutocrat."

"And you are not?" She decided to overlook the slighting nickname. "You always seemed so."

"Seemed! Of course I seemed so. I'm the youngest of eight sons, Miss Telfair, and you wonder that I 'seem' devoted to my patron. I'm lucky to be alive, am I not?"

"I suppose so." Horribly, giving unexpected point to her words, something thudded against the planking above them. It took Helen a moment to understand. "We're under fire," she said, and wished she had not.

"Oh, my God! Under water too. If we're sunk, we haven't a chance, down here below the water line. And suppose she catches fire, who'll think of us? Not that father of yours, who thinks of nothing but his 'duty.'"

"And quite right too." Helen managed a briskness she was very far from feeling. More and more she wished that her father's idea of duty had not sent her down here, to this black, stinking hole, with a coward for company. "Sit down, Mr. Trenche," she said, she hoped bracingly, "you will feel better so." A moment later, and a lifetime too late, she was wishing the words unsaid. He had not so much sat down beside her as fallen across her.

"Miss Telfair—Helen—I'm so frightened." His arms were round her, pushing her back against the hard, unyielding rope, so that it hurt through the thin stuff of her dress.

"Nonsense!" She pulled her face away from his questing lips to say it, and felt his hold on her slacken as reason, please God, began to return. And at that moment, a nearer hit somewhere close above them in the blackness sent a shudder through the ship and rats scurrying past them away into the dark far side of the hold. She felt his mind crack. The hands that held her were strong now with the madness of terror. They pushed her back, down against the rough cable that hurt so much less than what he was doing to her. Most horrible of all, somehow, was his mouth, so hard on hers that she could not speak, could hardly breathe through the whole shameful, fumbling business. His hands were cold where Lord Merritt's had been damp. The whole weight of him held her down as he struggled horribly in the darkness with buttons, skirts, petticoats . . . something tore; general pain became specific, intolerable, but must be borne. And then, too late, she felt him loosen, relax; pulled her mouth away from his, herself from him, shaking, violated, and thinking with a strange, horrible clarity. Later, there would be time for tears. Now: "I could have you killed for this," she said.

Disgustingly, he was crying, his head among the skirts he had torn. It was the last straw. "If you were worth it," she said, "which you are not. But get away from me, if you want to live. And don't speak." She had anticipated him by half a second. What use were apologies now? Another cannonball hit the ship's side above them somewhere. Her mind was still working with that strange, cool lucidity. "I don't know how we will look when we get out of here," she said, "but we will say the gunfire knocked us about a bit. And we will stick to that. Otherwise, remember, my father is captain of this ship. If you ever speak of what you have done today, you're ruined."

"And so would you be." But he moved away from her, fumbling in the darkness that made everything at once horrible and, somehow, just endurable because they could not see each other's faces.

New noises above were a violent distraction. Helen had heard the guns run out and fired often enough in practice, but never in earnest before, nor had she been prepared for the hideous din and vibration when the firing came, as now, from above. The whole ship seemed about to rack itself to pieces; the smell of powder seeped down to join all the other smells of that unspeakable place; above them, feet moved in ordered confusion as the guns were reloaded. But there was no second broadside. Presumably, the first one had temporarily silenced the shore batteries and cleared the way for the refugee boats that could now be heard coming alongside. Above them, the ship became a Babel. Impossible down here to distinguish words or language; it was merely clear that an immense number of people were pouring on board.

"My God, we'll sink!" Trenche forgot shame in terror. "Captain Telfair's mad to let so many on board."

"My father knows his business." She could not remind him too often that her father was the captain, with power, at sea, of life and death. Presently, there would be time to think of what had happened to her; for the moment she could not afford to, simply did not dare. One shot echoed from forward somewhere. "He's warning them off," she said. It was extraordinary to be talking like this to the man who had just ravished her, but at all costs when Price came, he must notice nothing.

The ship was moving again, faster now, presumably with the wind, and therefore out of harbour, and here, thank God, came the flickering light of Price's lantern. She had done her best in the darkness to hide all signs of that brief, horrible, unavailing struggle, and was reasonably certain that it was only a petticoat that had torn.

"Are you all right, miss?" Price hailed her before he could possibly see them. "We took a shot not far forward of here."

"We heard it," said Helen, dryly. "Yes, we're all right." Only Trenche would recognise the bitterness of her tone. "We got a bit of a shaking, that's all." The light was nearer now, and a quick, horrible, anxious glance showed her that Trenche too had had the wits to fumble his clothes together in the darkness. "It threw us down," she went on to explain. "My God, I'll be glad to get out of here. Lead the way, Price, and we'll follow you." She moved in front of the dishevelled Trenche without so much as a glance.

They had to pass the cockpit on their way up. "Don't look in there, miss." Was it by accident that the warning came too late? Helen had seen the surgeon and his assistants busy at their grisly work, the scrubbed table running blood. Behind her, Trenche gasped like a fish.

"How many?" She made her voice calm.

"I don't rightly know, miss. One whole gun's crew, I think. The one just forward from where you were. You were lucky."

"Was I not."

There was blood on the companionway, and Helen thought dryly that she need not worry about any possible stains on her clothes. Incredible to have her mind moving in this clear, cold, detached way. She had remembered something else too. "Are you not on duty in the cockpit, Price?" She wanted to be free of those too-observant eyes.

"Should be. Lieutenant Forbes sent me down for you. We're well out of range now."

"You'd best get back there," said Helen. "Mr. Trenche will see me safe to my cabin."

"You'll find it crowded."

"Never mind that." She was the captain's daughter.

"Very good, miss. You won't need the lantern now." He turned reluctantly, she thought, and vanished back towards the hell below.

"My God, look at that." They had emerged on the gun deck, close to where a direct hit had been scored on one of the guns, but it was not the bloodstained deck that had caught Trenche's attention, but the crowds of people who were pouring down from above. "We'll never get through," he said.

"Yes, we will. Try to remember that you are a man." She moved aside to let him lead the way, certain that in this crowd of desperate refugees there was no need to worry about anything strange in her own appearance. They had troubles enough of their own. It was hard work pushing their way through the frantic crowds who seemed to speak every language but English, but at last they reached the captain's quarters and Helen breathed a sigh of relief at sight of a marine on duty at the door. He saluted at sight of her, stepped back smartly to let her pass, then moved forward again. "Ladies only," he said.

"Oh," Trenche hesitated pitifully. "But where do I go?"

"That's your affair, sir." It was the first time Helen had

realised to what extent Trenche had contrived to make himself disliked by the crew.

She forgot him when she entered the main cabin and saw Charlotte. "Charlotte!" When had she started crying? "Oh, Charlotte!"

Charlotte had her arms round her; Charlotte was soothing her, as she used to do her mother. Charlotte was urging her towards the tiny cabin they shared, was explaining something in her fluent French to a group of ladies who seemed to fade and reappeared through the veil of tears. Charlotte was now calling sharply for Rose.

"No, Charlotte!" Helen managed to speak through waves of dizziness. "Not Rose. Just you."

Chapter 7

◢◢◣ HELEN slept for what felt like hours and woke to find Charlotte sitting beside her, busy with her embroidery.

"Well." Charlotte smiled at her. "You're better!" Her tone as well as her expression told Helen that as she had hoped, her innocent eyes had not noticed what Rose's sharp ones might have. "I never thought to see you faint," Charlotte went on. "A lioness like you. Was it very dreadful down there?" And then, "Forgive m . . . m . . ."

The stammer was wonderfully bracing. "Nothing to forgive, love." She had never called Charlotte that before. "And much to thank you for. You got me to bed?"

"Yes, poor lamb. Your skirt's all bloody from that terrible cockpit. But we won't talk about that." Charlotte paused, then changed the subject. "I've been so grateful to you for the excuse to keep away from those good ladies out there."

"Who are they?" Helen remembered them now, vaguely.

"Royalist refugees, poor things. Lord Hood sent me over with your father's share. All of the best family, of course, and so busy about precedence, even in these cramped quarters, you wouldn't believe."

"What's going to happen to them?"

"God knows. We're on our way to a rendezvous in the Bay of Hyères. Perhaps Admiral Hood will have some orders about them when we get there. I certainly hope he has. The ship's bedlam as it is. You should just see it. Price tells me it's terrible below decks." She smiled wickedly. "And your poor Lord M . . . M . . ."

"Not *my* Lord Merritt," said Helen, more sharply than she meant. "But what's happened to him?"

"Sharing with the lieutenants," said Charlotte with simple pleasure. "And Trenche is in with the m . . . m . . ."

"The midshipmen?" Helen almost found herself joining in Charlotte's laughter. But it could not last. She began to think about Trenche, and all that had happened down in that stinking darkness. She bit her lip, not to cry. What in the world was the use of crying? Besides, was it so very important after all? Something had happened to her, not of her own volition. Why should she feel herself changed by that? Only . . . "What day is it?" she asked.

"Sunday, dear. You've slept the clock round. You must be famished. I'll ask Price to see what he can find for you."

Left alone, Helen's calculations were brief and bleak. "Sunday." December the twentieth. Five days till Christmas, and ten until she would begin to know whether Trenche's assault had had its possible disastrous effect.

The time passed quickly enough in the intolerably crowded captain's quarters where everyone had some private terror of her own. In the last panic of the evacuation of Toulon, wives had lost their husbands, mothers their children. When the fleet made its rendezvous in the Bay of Hyères, there was good news for some, but not for many. Helen's own anxiety seemed merely childish compared with that of these women, worn out with years of terror, who now faced exile, many of them alone. Helen's heart bled for them. But she had something else to think of. Reluctantly, desperately, she was beginning to face her own situation. Of course, after such an experience, three or four days might mean nothing, but they might also mean that her whole life was changed. Characteristically, she was beginning to try and persuade herself that it might even be a change for the better. There had always been one major drawback for her about those plans she had shared with Miss Tillingdon for a placid bluestocking life in a cottage. She liked children. It was one thing not to marry; nothing would induce her to do that; but where Miss Tillingdon had recoiled with horror when she had suggested that they might, in the fulness of time, find some suitable subject for adoption, she had privately stuck to this plan. It was one of the vital points on which her plans for their future and Miss Tillingdon's had begun to diverge. Now, perhaps, the problem of adoption was to be solved for her. It began, as the month drew on, to seem increasingly probable that she was to have a child of her own.

By the end of January, she was in no more doubt about the fact of the child, and was beginning to face the most acute of her problems. There were scandal and shame ahead, to be lived through, but she found she did not much care about them. The one thing that she found she passionately wanted to avoid was Trenche's knowledge of his responsibility. And that was a facer, if ever there was one. For herself, she would have been prepared to brazen it out, to have the child and refuse to name the father. But, inevitably, if she did this, Trenche would know. And she knew she did not trust him. Well, how could she?

There was only one year to go now until her twenty-first birthday when she would come into her inheritance and be able to support both herself and her child. But for just this vital year, she was penniless, dependent on her father. Presently, she would have to tell him, but not until the last possible moment; not, simply, until she had decided what to do.

In the meantime, they were back on station, blockading Toulon. It was tedious work, but she was grateful for the bad weather and rough seas that provided an admirable excuse for her own bouts of sickness. She was even grateful now for the pressure Lord Merritt must be continuing to put on her father not to send her and Charlotte ashore. He had a good reason for his own continued presence on board. "Not a brave man," he would say cheerfully. "Don't half like the look of things in Italy. Greedy lot at best; treacherous at worst. Mean to get to Naples safe and sound. King's ship's the best way. I'll bide my time if you'll have me, sir."

Captain Telfair was only too happy to keep a passenger who paid his way so lavishly, who had contrived to replenish his cabin stores on a brief trip to Leghorn, and who would end, he devoutly hoped, by taking his formidable daughter off his hands. He had said no more about this aspect of the situation to Helen, on what amounted to orders from Lord Merritt. "Take it easy and slow," Merritt had said, and Telfair, who disliked scenes, except those he made himself, was happy to do so.

It suited Helen too, specially as Trenche was obviously quite as eager to avoid her as she him. She even managed to endure Lord Merritt's second proposal with a good grace, if a firm answer. This was not, in fact, couched at all in the same language as her first refusal, but only Lord Merritt was aware of this. He thought, with some justice, that she felt more kindly towards him, and began to believe that it was only a question of time. But how much time had he? An immense batch of mail reached the fleet in January and brought him the news that his uncle's health was failing again. He wrote off at once, with sympathies and an over-optimistic description of his hopes. Helen, he was able truthfully to say, was just the kind of strong-minded woman of whom his uncle would approve. Trenche, as usual, helped him draft his letter, and gave him a strange look when they reached this point, but Lord Merritt was much too full of his own affairs to notice.

Helen had had a letter too. Recognising Mary Tillingdon's neat hand, she had opened it expecting the usual dullish catalogue of Up Harting affairs, and had not at first been disappointed. Mr. Tillingdon had had trouble with the choir. . . . Sir Harry had come down from London with another set of scandalous friends. . . . Miss Tillingdon's joints pained her worse than ever, and she had had to give up all attempts at gardening. "You'll find me but an ineffective companion in our cottage, my love," wrote Mary Tillingdon. And then, quite casually: "By the by: I can now set your mind at rest about the secret proviso in Mrs. Stott's will. It need not concern you at all. My brother had a fit of the dismals when the bad weather started"—this was a familiar euphemism for one of Mr. Tillingdon's drinking bouts. "He told me one night," went on the neat scratch, "that we would lose half our income next year. 'Whichever way,' he said. So I remembered you, my love, and was brave as a lion and asked him what he meant. And, 'Why,' said he, and I will spare you his language, which was not at all the thing, 'if she behaves herself, it all goes to that bluestocking friend of yours. And if she don't, why the governesses get it. Either way, unless the Bishop comes up trumps, you and I will starve on my stipend.' It was on the tip of my tongue," went on Miss Tillingdon, "to tell him that at least he would starve alone, since I would be happily settled with you, dearest Helen, but you will be glad to hear that I restrained myself. You will be glad, too, to know that the mysterious condition turns out to be so unimportant."

"Unimportant." Helen folded the letter with hands that shook. "If she behaves herself." Doubtless the casual phrase covered a whole paragraph of lawyers' jargon, but there was no blinking at what it meant. The mother of an illegitimate child, however unfortunate, would never be considered to have behaved herself. She actually ground her teeth, and remembered, horribly, how Philip Trenche's had chattered the day this all began.

There was no doubt in her mind now. She remembered too well the symptoms of the errant cook back at Up Harting. Her child would be born in September. She had until then to provide for its future. No, that was wrong. She had no time at all. If she could count forward, so could other people, backwards. She had heard it done often enough, sometimes in friendly, sometimes in malicious spirit. "Married in March, and the child born in September." And a wealth of meaning behind the words. For herself, she thought she would not have cared. But the child was different. It was her responsibility, and she must think for it, more than for herself. All very well to face her father's rage, the probability of being set ashore at the first Italian port he touched. By herself she could have done it. Night after night, lying awake with Charlotte breathing easily on the other side of the cabin, she thought this. By herself she would have turned her hand to something, have found employment of one kind or other at one of the small courts of Italy. Her Italian, after all, was nearly as good as her French, and knowledge of languages, in a world in chaos, was at a premium.

By herself she could have managed. But, heavily, obviously pregnant? Impossible. She had seen it happen too often to other women, unfortunates she and Miss Tillingdon had contrived to assist out of those generous funds provided by her great-aunt's will. A pity, she thought now wryly, that she had not had the wits to embezzle some of her own money to safeguard her future. Miss Tillingdon would never have noticed. Too late now for thoughts like these. She faced the decision that had made itself, almost without her being aware, some time during that wet, wretched January. After all those plans for a free and independent life, she must mortgage her own future to protect her child. She must marry, and since there was no one else, marry Lord Merritt.

But what would she tell him? And how? Bad weather made tête-à-têtes on deck an impossibility, and there was no chance of an uninterrupted conversation in the main saloon they all shared. Time was her enemy now, and her child's. At all costs, she must do something, and do it fast. Her one comfort was the businesslike nature of Lord Merritt's own proposal. It made it possible for her to re-open the question. And, though she thought little of his intelligence, she had a considerable respect for his capacity to arrange things to suit himself. In the end, after another sleepless night, she wrote him one line, "I need to speak to you," and handed it to Price when he came to take away her bitter cup of breakfast coffee. Inevitably, Charlotte was in the cabin too, and looked a question, but, receiving no answer, Charlotte could be relied on not to pry.

That was both unfair and absurd. The sooner she started crossing her bridges, the better. She looked up at Charlotte and made herself smile. "I have decided to marry Lord Merritt," she said.

"Helen!" They had never discussed this, but Charlotte could be in no doubt about her feelings.

"I know." Helen managed a convincing shrug. "It's not ideal, but he's a reasonable man, and rich. I find I am beginning to value the comfort wealth entails." She looked round the tiny cabin. "And, besides, I'm sick of this life. He's persuaded my father, you know, to keep us all on board until I accept him."

"What?"

"Yes. You could say I was responsible for my mother's death."

"I'd never say anything of the kind, and you mustn't think it."

"Thank you." Helen found she was crying, and realised with a twinge of surprise that it was the first time since the day it happened. Well, what use were tears? She dried them angrily, and held out a hand to Charlotte. "You'll come with us, won't you?"

"If you want me."

"More than anything. And, Charlotte, I've simply asked for a word alone with Lord Merritt. Help me, won't you?"

"Of course. But, Helen, are you sure? I thought you didn't even like him."

"I shall learn to."

"Oh . . ." and then, with an effort, "I wish I understood you, Helen."

Since this was the last thing Helen wanted, it was a profound relief to her when Rose knocked on the cabin door to announce that Lord Merritt would be grateful for a word, alone, with Miss Telfair. Helen's eyes met Charlotte's. "You have to admit," she said, "that he's capable. I wonder what he's done with Father. Sent him up on deck?"

"Very likely," said Charlotte. "M . . . m . . ." it was only the second time she had stammered in the whole extraordinary conversation. She took a deep breath.

"Money is power," she said. "Is that what you want, Helen?"

"Perhaps. Security, certainly." For the child. She gave herself a quick look in the cabin's tiny glass. "Tell Lord Merritt I will be with him directly, Rose." She gave Charlotte a quick, hard kiss. "Wish me luck." Only she knew how badly she needed it. Sending her note, it had not occurred to her that Lord Merritt would act on it so fast. What was she going to say to him? She should have decided before she wrote. Was everything she did always going to be either too late or too early? But she was keeping Lord Merritt waiting. She opened the cabin door with a firm hand and joined him in the salon.

He was, as she expected, alone, and, she saw, as nervous as herself. He had been staring out the stern window at vacancy, but turned at once as she entered and came forward to greet her. "Had your note. Price is at the door."

"And Miss Standish stays in our cabin." Where did one go from there? "I am grateful to you for acting so promptly." It was true, in a way. Surely this conversation was best got over with.

"And I for the message. Hope it means . . ." he paused. "What I hope it means."

"Yes." Was it so easy to sign away a lifetime's freedom?

Apparently it was. He had her hand and was kissing it lightly. "More grateful than I can say. You have made me . . ." another pause . . . "happiest of men."

If it was not true, it was gallant. Curiously, it decided her. "There is something," she said, "that I must tell you first. On your promise of secrecy." It was odd, and a relief, to find that though she had often thought him negligible, she had never thought him untrustworthy.

"Secrecy?" Surprised. "Well—a wife's secrets—her husband's."

It was a frightening thought. But she made herself go on. "When you know, you may change your mind. I beg you will feel free to do so."

"Impossible." For once, his expression was unfathomable.

"Thank you." She bolted into it. "When you were away, on the *Victory,* in the confusion of the retreat . . ." She stopped. This was incredibly harder than she had expected.

"Yes?"

"I was raped."

"God." And the inevitable question. "By whom?"

"That I will never tell you." Would he find out for himself? "And I beg you not to ask, not to think, not to wonder. . . . It is bad enough as it is. If you still wish to marry me, it must be at once. The child will be born in September."

He had dropped her hand and now stood for a long moment staring at her with the slightly pop-eyed look she always found irritating. At last, "No need to tell me. Brave woman."

"To tell truth, I did not mean to. But I found I must."

"Thank you." He was thinking it over, slowly. "Call it my child? Your idea? September, you say?"

"Yes." Now she was into it, she would spare neither of them anything. "Nine months to the day from the evacuation of Toulon. It's the child, you understand, that I am thinking of."

"Not my *beaux yeux.*" But his tone was encouraging. "Swear it was rape?"

"Yes."

"End of January now. Seven and a half months to go. Could be done. Letters take ages. A little mystification. . . . Yes; could be done. A fright, perhaps?"

Interesting, in a horrible way, to watch him grasping and coping with the facts of their case. If it was their case, which his next question put back into doubt. "But the father. Child's to be my heir. Must know something of the father."

It was a fair question. "He's a gentleman, though he did not behave like one. More than that, I will not say. There is no reason why he, or anyone else, should ever know. You remember what that night was like." Thank God he had not been on board.

"Yes." He turned, as Price put his head round the door.

"Captain Telfair on the way down, sir."

"Thank you." When Captain Telfair entered the salon, Merritt had Helen's hand in his. "The very man," he said. "Captain Telfair, glad to tell you, your daughter's made me the happiest of men."

"And about time too," said Captain Telfair.

Chapter 8

⟨⟨ THERE was no time for second thoughts. Lord Merritt saw to that. He had himself rowed over next day to the Admiral's flagship and returned with Lord Hood's chaplain and what he described as excellent news. "All arranged," he told Helen. "Lord Hood kindness itself. All sorts of polite messages; quite understands; happier on shore. There's a young captain—what's his name? Can't for the life of me remember; can't say it matters much. Just joined the fleet. . . . Distinguished himself on detached service . . . Wasn't really listening, sounds like a good enough sort of fellow. And the *Gannet*'s quite done up with all the action she's been in—has to go and refit at Naples. Suit us down to the ground. Not luxurious quarters. Very small ship—frigate, I believe; cabin for you and Miss Standish and Rose . . . Hope you won't mind. Odd kind of honeymoon. Don't like it?" He had noticed her blanched face.

"Did you say the *Gannet?*"

"Yes. What of it?"

"Oh, nothing." She swallowed what felt like a lump of hot ice. "I believe she's commanded by an old London acquaintance of mine—Captain Scroope. I read about his actions in the *Gazette*. A very successful man, by the sound of it. We should be safe enough with him." The prospect was almost beyond bearing, but must be borne.

"Old acquaintance!" said Lord Merritt. "Admirable. Persuade him not to get up to any of his gallant tricks while we're on board. Need to get to Naples as fast as we can," he added, fending off the hint of cowardice.

"Yes." She had recognised the implication of his remark about the cabin she was to share with Charlotte and Rose, and also the fact that this was as much of a relief to him as it was to her. . . . Just so long as the voyage did not take too long. How horrible it would be to make this disastrous marriage for her child's sake and then have it branded as a bastard after all. But Charlotte had joined them. Charlotte was explaining something with a mixture of tact and stammering. She and Rose had it all arranged. This one night, after the wedding and before they transferred to the *Gannet*, Charlotte would share Rose's cabin, as she had before Mrs. Telfair died, so that the bride and groom might be together. Lord Merritt's eyes met Helen's. "Too kind," he said.

Trenche and Price had been busy covering the guns in the main salon with flags and improvising an altar out of the table on which they dined. The clergyman, whose name Helen would never remember, had retired to don his robes. Captain Telfair, resplendent in full dress uniform, could hardly conceal his impatience to give away the bride, and the clergyman, returning in full pomp, shared his sense of urgency. He had had an uncomfortable enough trip over from the *Victory* and longed to be safe back on board before the weather worsened.

Incredible that something so final should take so little time. Her father was kissing her with what seemed almost like affection. Charlotte was crying. Mr. Trenche was coming forward to take her cold hand in his colder one, and offer congratulations. He looked drawn with anxiety, as well he might. She longed to ask Lord Merritt—good God, her husband—to get rid of him, but she knew she must not. It would inevitably give a direction to his suspicions. Trenche was simply another of the burdens she would have to bear.

Price was producing a wedding breakfast to which the officers who were not on watch had been invited. Helen was glad to see Forbes, who seemed today like an old friend. He was talking bracingly to Charlotte, who had dried her tears and seemed to be managing to answer him without stammering. Price was pouring out champagne and, horribly, for a moment Helen remembered her mother and wondered whether, if she had yielded thus earlier, she might have saved her life.

Useless speculation. And no time for it now, or to wonder how Charles Scroope would receive her, while Forbes toasted the bride and groom and Lord Merritt looked increasingly uneasy as he recognised the need to reply. And, of all things, this was the moment when Helen began to feel sick. The rest of the party had gathered in a kind of loose half-circle round the two of them; Lord Merritt was nervously fingering his neck cloth. He cleared his throat, once, twice, then plunged into it. "Not a public speaker," he said. "No trick for it. Grateful, just the same. Happiest of men. Thank you all. Most grateful, but no trick for it. . . ."

Was he going to go round and round like this for ever? Bile rose in Helen's throat. With an effort, she swallowed it, laid a hand lightly on—her husband's, and spoke: "My dear. All this excitement. I find myself a little faint. I am sure our guests will understand." Her eyes, sweeping the little group, met Trenche's, and she wondered for a sickening instant whether he might not understand all too well.

But her intervention had had the desired effect. The clergyman was delighted at the excuse to take his leave, after congratulating "the happy couple" once more, and urging, as he had done already, that they solemnise the marriage again "on terra firma" when they reached Naples. "If Lady Merritt understands me," he added waggishly.

Lady Merritt, surprised at the title, did understand, but was aware that her husband did not. Suddenly, surprisingly, she felt responsible for him, and forgot her sickness in coming to his rescue. "Yes, indeed," she said, "we will most certainly ask Sir William Hamilton to arrange it for us."

"Or Lady Hamilton," said Trenche. "She is adept, I believe, at arranging marriages."

This time there was no Captain Nelson to come to Lady Hamilton's defence, and Helen listened, helpless with anger, to the subdued masculine titter that greeted this sally. Lord Merritt, she noticed with pleasure, did not join in. She felt him beside her, wrestling with an idea. At last he brought it out, "Our Ambassadress," he said.

"Not precisely," said the clergyman. "But the point is well taken, just the same. Caesar's wife, and all that."

The party was breaking up at last. The endless day stretched before the newly married couple, and beyond it, worse still, the night. Helen racked her brains. Impossible to pretend it was just a day like any other, and get on with the reading and note-taking which were her usual occupations. Her father and the other officers had escaped to their various duties. Only Trenche and Charlotte remained with them in the salon, from which Price was swiftly removing all traces of the party. And Trenche, she now saw, must have contrived to come by a good deal more champagne than the rest of them. It explained, if it did not excuse, his remarks about Lady Hamilton. Now, he withdrew to his own tiny cabin with a muttered apology, and Helen saw him go with relief.

But at least she had stopped feeling sick. She looked from Charlotte to Lord Merritt. "We should do something to celebrate," she said. "But it is hard to think just what."

"A game of cards?" suggested Charlotte.

"Capital notion." Lord Merritt welcomed the idea with enthusiasm, then turned to Helen. "Would you mind?"

Helen had tended to avoid the card games he liked, since she and Miss Tillingdon had always looked on every form of gambling, whether for money or not, with disapproval. But today was different. "If it could be whist," she said diffidently. "It is the only game I know." Her father had a passion for the game, and she had often made a reluctant fourth when Mr. Tillingdon came to call. But at least it was a game of skill rather than of chance.

"Need a fourth," said Merritt. "Rout out young Trenche, sore head and all?"

"Oh, no," said Helen. "I cannot help feeling that he would be useless as a player. Could we not play three-handed?"

Her father, returning from the deck at this moment, settled the question by greeting the idea of a game with enthusiasm, and they were soon cutting for partners on the green baize cloth Price had produced for the table that had so recently served as altar. Helen, finding herself partnering her husband, could not help an odd, superstitious qualm, but her father commented on it jovially, with an inevitable remark about "partners for life."

And, in fact, Lord Merritt played a surprisingly good game of a straightforward kind which Helen found easy enough to understand. Since Charlotte had no head for cards, they were soon winning consistently, and Helen was glad that there had been no suggestion of playing for money. She was becoming increasingly anxious about Charlotte's finances. Mrs. Standish had certainly paid lavishly enough in advance for her daughter's passage, but whether she had also thought to supply Charlotte herself with adequate funds was very much another question, and one that Helen intended to have answered, now that she found herself suddenly in a position of such extraordinary affluence. Her father and Lord Merritt, she knew, had had a man-to-man discussion about settlements and pin money, and doubtless, sooner or later, the results would find their way to her in the form of actual cash. In the meantime, the day was drawing on; Price had lit the salon lamps; it was time to clear the table once more for the last, light meal of the day. Once again, there was champagne, and Helen, sick with nerves, was glad of it. So, she saw, was Trenche, who emerged from his cabin looking haggard, but was making an obvious effort to be agreeable, particularly to her. He was, she knew, penniless, and to be turned away when they reached Naples would be a disaster for him. From now on, he would watch his step. But he would also, inevitably, watch her. It was almost a relief when the rather silent meal ended and she and

Charlotte rose, as their habit was, to say good night and leave the men to their wine.

Here habit ended. Charlotte kissed her impulsively, close to tears. Lord Merritt rose ceremoniously to usher her towards the cabin they were to share. "Follow you very soon."

Helen had always refused Rose's offers of help with her dress, and was particularly glad of it tonight. If she had believed in anything but the greatest good of the greatest number, she would have fallen on her knees by her narrow cot and prayed for help. As it was, she got herself as quickly as possible into the ruffled flannel nightgown that had been a farewell present from Miss Tillingdon, and crept, shivering, into the cot. She longed to blow out the light and wait in the dark, but it seemed somehow an unfriendly act. She turned her face to the wall and would not think. Not about her own plight. Not about her husband. And, above all, not about Charles Scroope, whom she must meet tomorrow. How could she help it? What must he be thinking about her? Or had he, as she must hope, forgotten her long ago? But she must not cry either. Their situation—her husband's and hers—was unpromising enough without his finding her in her bridal bed (cot, she reminded herself angrily) in tears.

She lay rigid on the hard, narrow bed, fighting sobs and sickness together. She had not thought her plight could be made worse. How little she had known. The idea of meeting Charles Scroope ate at her like slow poison. He had told her he loved her, and she had answered that she would never marry. The sun had shone in the garden, and he had told her that they were both solitaries. He had taken her hand and threatened to kiss her. If he had, would the spell have been broken? Would she have had the wits to forget her fear of marriage, and engage herself to him? How long was it since she had recognised that she loved him?

Too late now, a lifetime too late to be thinking like this. She lay still at last, the tears fought down, and waited for her husband. She could hear the rumble of voices in the salon, but she knew from long experience that it was impossible to distinguish words. The old *Trojan* had been solidly built.

At last, after what seemed at once no time at all and an eternity, a louder outburst of sound suggested that the party was breaking up. Her father would be going up for his last look around on deck, Trenche would doubtless be glad to return to his bed. And her husband . . .

The cabin door opened. It would be a coward's part to pretend to be asleep, but surely reasonable to turn over and act a sleepy welcome.

"Left the light for me." Lord Merritt closed the door behind him. "Obliging." He sounded as ill at ease as she felt. "No dressing room." He looked with disfavour round the tiny cell that imprisoned them. "Not my idea of a honeymoon. Not yours either, I expect." He stood there for a moment, looking at her as she lay rigid under the protecting bedclothes. "Long, hard day," he said at last. "Not at all the thing for you." He stopped for a moment. "Proud of you," he said. "Thought for a moment you didn't feel quite the thing, out there. Carried it off. Proud of you." He repeated it. "Must be tired out. Plenty of time, later, in Naples." Was he reassuring himself, or her? "For tonight, I'll just blow out the light and get myself to bed as best I may."

"No need," she managed. "I'm half asleep already; I'll just turn my back."

"I'm a lucky man." He sounded as if he meant it.

Luckily the high wind that had plagued them all through January abated a little in the night, and the transfer from the *Trojan* to the *Gannet* presented no serious problem. If Helen looked white and ill, it was reasonably to be attributed to the parting from her father, brief and formal though that had been. He was glad to be rid of the lot of them. She knew it and hardly cared. All her thoughts were thrown anxiously forward, to the inevitable confrontation with Charles Scroope. He must, of course, know who Lord Merritt's wife was. What would he think of her? At best, that she was a fortune-hunter. . . . At worst . . . But nothing could be worse than the real facts of her case.

She bit her lips and lost her temper with Rose, who was making a tremendous fuss about the hazards of being swayed down into the tossing little boat that was to take them over to the *Gannet*. It won her quick looks of surprise from Lord Merritt and Charlotte, but it astonished Rose into good behaviour. All too soon, they were being deposited, safe if a little damp, on the deck of the *Gannet*. She seemed tiny after the *Trojan,* but Helen could see nothing beyond Charles Scroope's set face as he waited to greet them.

He looked years older than the frivolous young man who had turned so suddenly serious that sunny, far-off day in Wimbledon. Fair hair, bleached almost white, set off the deep tan of a face that bore the marks of hard service, both in the fine wrinkles that criss-crossed cheeks and brow, and in one savage scar, livid from hairline to chin on the left side.

And yet she would have known him anywhere. Worse still, she found she still knew him well enough to be sure that this meeting was as painful to him as to her. He was saying everything proper, everything polite and agreeable to Lord Merritt, who had been swayed up first. At last, he turned, with the tact she remembered, to greet her and Charlotte when they had had time to shake out crumpled petticoats and settle themselves a little on this small, un-familiar deck.

His hand was cold in hers. "Lady Merritt, Miss Standish and I are old friends." He spoke across her to her husband, then turned with a noticeably warmer greeting for Charlotte, who was surprised into one of her increasingly rare stammering fits.

For once, Helen could not come to her help; she was swallowing something between tears and sickness.

"Lady Merritt not quite the thing." Her husband surprised her by recognising her plight. "Parted from her father. Best below. All of us. Got a wetting coming over. Don't want a pack of invalids on your hands. Feels the motion a bit, don't she, your *Gannet?*"

A swift look from husband to wife told Helen just what Charles Scroope thought of her choice, but his reply was courtesy itself. "More than the *Trojan,* I must admit. And you will find your quarters, I am afraid, sadly confined after life on board a seventy-four. But, such as they are, I will have you taken to them at once. I will hope to present my officers when you dine with me."

"Mighty stiff, that young man." Lord Merritt summed it up as they settled themselves resignedly in the two small adjoining cabins that had been made ready for them. "Must hope for a fast passage to Naples."

"Yes, indeed." Helen echoed his hope fervently. This was worse than anything she had imagined, and only pride prevented her from pleading illness and dining in her cabin. Or was it only pride? Dare she plead illness with Trenche's cold eye perpetually upon her? She rather thought not. Besides—was there no end to these painful thoughts—she could not leave her husband to expose his full gamut of absurdity to Charles Scroope and his officers.

Over dinner, she was ashamed of this thought. Lord Merritt might not be a sensible man, but he was used to the conversation of his equals, and, if only he had put the occasional verb into his sentences, might almost have passed at the mess table for a reasonable man, especially with her beside him to extricate him deftly from his more unmanageable attempts at thought. Inevitably, the talk turned to their destination, Naples, and Helen was relieved to hear that Charles Scroope was as anxious to get there as she could wish.

"Since our last action," he explained to Lord Merritt, "we are in need of everything, and the crew sickly, as is to be expected after so long at sea."

"Sickly?" Lord Merritt, Helen had noticed, was something of a valetudinarian. "Nothing catching, I hope?"

"Scurvy," said Scroope. "You're not likely to catch that, my lord."

"No . . . no, I suppose not." He sounded unhappy. "Deuced unpleasant if one did. Fingers fall off and all that."

"Toes too," said Captain Scroope. "I'm hoping for lemons at the least of it in Naples. They're ripe there all the year round, I understand."

"You've not been there?"

"Never. My service, so far, has been entirely on the Atlantic and Channel stations."

"You'll be looking forward to the Neapolitan luxury," suggested Philip Trenche from farther down the cramped table. "And a sight of our renowned Ambassadress." His tone, if not his words, was just faintly off key, and Helen, looking up with quick anger, caught Charles Scroope's eye. So he did remember. She felt hot colour flood to her cheeks and busied herself with the unappetising food on her plate as Scroope replied, in his curiously level voice: "Ambassadors are quite above my touch," he said. "I'll be lucky to meet Mr. Lock, our consul. And glad of any help he can get me towards a refit. This is no time to be idling in harbour, however luxurious. God knows what will follow on the fall of Toulon, but nothing good in the Mediterranean, I am sure."

Lord Merritt leaned forward anxiously across the narrow table. "No good—hey? No chance the French will attack Italy?"

"Nothing more likely," said Captain Scroope. "But you and your party should be safe enough in Naples. The Kingdom of the Two Sicilies has proved our best ally in the Mediterranean, and we're not likely to let them down."

"Two Sicilies?" asked Merritt. "What's that?"

"Naples and Sicily," explained Scroope patiently. "It's true they hardly covered themselves with glory at Toulon, but at least they came."

"Saw and didn't conquer," said Trenche, who seemed to be making a point of his position as a social equal at Captain Scroope's table.

But Lord Merritt had thought of a new source of anxiety. "The French," he said. "No chance of encountering one of their ships? Eh?"

"Not much, alas," said Scroope. "But you never know your luck." And then, at a gasp of dismay from his guest, "We may be in need of everything, and short-handed to boot, but that's not to say we can't deal with any Frenchman we may be happy enough to meet."

"Quite so. Naturally." Even Lord Merritt was aware of the atmosphere among the junior officers. "One Englishman worth ten Frogs. All that. Quite so." But, later, alone for a moment with Helen, he changed his tune. "Just my luck to get a fire-eater for a captain. Action in this tub! Not at all the thing for you." And then, a happy thought. "Old friend of his. Perhaps a hint from you? Anxious to get to Naples. Not quite so keen on action as he is. Pity we can't make an excuse of your—ahem—condition."

"If we could," said Helen, "we would not."

"No . . . no. Naturally not. Just a thought." He was beginning to find his new wife rather more formidable than he had expected, and it added a note of unusual conviction to the letter that he sat down that afternoon and wrote, under conditions of considerable inconvenience, to his uncle. He must have it ready for the first chance for England. Just occasionally, when Helen gave him one of those straight looks of hers, he thought with horror of the possibility that his uncle might die before he had heard of their marriage, or before the child was born. Suppose he had already changed his will? His last letter did not make this clear, no doubt intentionally, and it was a possibility to make a man sweat. To find himself saddled with a wife, and without the fortune she was intended to ensure . . . It would be almost past bearing. And, another irritant, Captain Telfair, sensing his impatience for the match, had been ruthless in the matter of settlements and pin money. Helen would be a considerable expense to him as well as a wife. His uncle had better turn up trumps.

No hostile sail loomed over the horizon, and the voyage to Naples was mercifully brief, though too long for Lord Merritt, compelled to share a cabin with Trenche, and, curiously, too short for Helen. More than anything, she longed to reach, well—what? Some kind of understanding with the formal young captain who had once been her good friend Charles Scroope, and who now addressed her so stiffly as Lady Merritt, and all his conversation, where politeness permitted, to Charlotte, who was blooming visibly, and whom Helen actually saw stammering and laughing all at once in the middle of a group of the *Gannet*'s officers.

It was a sight to make Helen realise just what she had

done to herself in that desperate marriage. Lady Merritt could not stand laughing and talking in the midst of a group of cheerful young officers, nor would they think of grouping themselves round her. Lady Merritt had to spend her time saving her husband from making more of a fool of himself than she could help. And combined with the misery about Charles Scroope's cold politeness was another anxiety. How would things be for them at the Court of Naples? She had heard a good deal about Sir William Hamilton, who was by all reports an extremely cultivated man, a connoisseur of antiquities, and, surprisingly, an expert student of the activities of the volcano that loomed over the city where he was Ambassador. It seemed unlikely that he would extend more than the most official of welcomes to a man, however titled, who could hardly complete an intelligent sentence.

And what of Lady Hamilton? Extraordinary to think that she was to meet her angel again in this remarkable guise. Would the girl who had been Emmy Hart and danced on Sir Harry Featherstonehaugh's table remember her? And if she did, would she admit to it? Probably not, Helen thought. But then, why should she remember a nameless child, encountered only twice, and so briefly? Much simpler, of course, if she did not, and Helen thought she would rather die than remind her. Having come, herself, however innocently, to the very verge of social ruin, she had a new awareness of Lady Hamilton's situation, and, with it, an immense new sympathy and respect for her. She too had retrieved her position by marrying an older man. Helen wondered if she knew how lucky she was to have found someone of such distinction. Perhaps, when they got to Naples, she would find out.

They arrived at last very early one fine February morning, and Helen, making her way rather slowly and carefully up to the deck, as she did these days, gave a gasp of pure pleasure at sight of the famous bay with its pastel-coloured houses scattered among evergreen trees up the hillside and, beyond them, Vesuvius with a small, warning plume of smoke above it.

"Vesuvius." Her husband had joined her at the rail. "Not so nice to live under a volcano."

"The Neapolitans don't seem to mind."

"No. Ignorant lot of barbarians. Sir William Hamilton knows all about volcanoes. Most unusual hobby for an Ambassador, but could be useful. Must ask him, safest place to settle."

"Yes." Helen was getting used to this cowardice of her husband's, but was gladder than ever that she had never dreamed of mentioning her brief previous acquaintance with Lady Hamilton. She knew him well enough by now to know that this was the kind of thing on which he would seize, and of which he would shamelessly make use. As it was, he obviously intended that Sir William should invite them to stay until they could find themselves a house, and he went ashore with Captain Scroope as soon as they had received pratique. Left behind, Helen and Charlotte stood at the rail, enjoying the new mildness of the air and steadiness of the ship, and gazing shorewards trying to identify the larger buildings of that romantic waterfront. The Castle dell'Ovo, jutting out darkly into the bay on their left, was easily recognisable from its name. But which of the two fortresses that loomed over the city was the Castle Nuovo and which the Sant' Elmo?

Charlotte shivered. "What a lot of fortresses."

"Yes. I suppose they must need them." They gave Helen an uncomfortable feeling too. "That must be the palace." She pointed to a large, undistinguished building set back from the quay. "It doesn't look so formidable."

"No." Neither of them was really thinking about the strange new town that awaited them. Charlotte suddenly turned to Helen. "What am I going to *do?*" she wailed.

"Stay with us, of course. Dear Charlotte, how can you imagine doing anything else. Besides, I need you." Impossible, yet, to explain just how badly she was going to need her. She had decided that this news must wait at least until March, but in the meantime there was surely reason enough for wanting Charlotte's company. Besides: "What else can you do?" she asked unanswerably.

"I know. Helen, you didn't do it for m . . . m . . ."

"For your sake? Good God, no. I did it for my own." She hoped Charlotte would never know what a curious half truth that was. "But I am glad it means I can help you—and, best of all, keep you with me." Out here, on deck, it was possible to speak more freely than in the cramped cabin. "You must see that I will be glad of some other company but my husband's."

Charlotte's easy tears were flowing again. "Oh, Helen, I can't bear it for you. After all your plans. What will Miss Tillingdon say? And m...m..."

"What your mother says, thank goodness, is something we are not likely to know for some time. And in the meanwhile I propose to enjoy being a rich woman, and you are to share everything with me. Time enough to worry about England when we see a chance of getting back there, but now he's here, I very much doubt if Lord Merritt will want to brave the Mediterranean again for quite some time." Not, certainly, until the child was safely born. How much easier it would be when she could explain this to Charlotte.

Lord Merritt returned all bustle and enthusiasm. Sir William had been everything that was kind, and Lady Hamilton had joined him in the most pressing invitation for the three of them to stay at the Palazzo Sessa until they could find a home of their own. "Charming!" Merritt called her, and then again, with emphasis, "Most charming! Speaks the lingo like a native." He looked a little anxiously at his wife. "Of course, her English . . ." He thought about it for a moment. "Not quite what you'd expect. But goes everywhere; sees everyone; nothing wrong with staying there."

"Of course not." Helen was delighted to be able to agree with him. "We're lucky to be asked."

"Oh, Sir William quite keeps open house for us British. Told me so himself. Prince Augustus there just the other day. Good enough for a prince of the blood, good enough for us. Lady Hamilton quite the thing. Says she'll see to our remarriage. Close friend of the Queen's. Extraordinary story."

"Yes." It was not one that Helen wished to discuss.

They went ashore that afternoon and found Naples a good deal less romantic at close quarters than it had looked from the ship. Once they had left the broad promenade by the harbour, it was to find themselves apparently lost in a network of narrow, stinking lanes. Half-naked beggars swarmed everywhere, running beside the carriage Sir William had sent for them, shouting unintelligibly for alms.

"Lazzaroni," Lord Merritt explained. "Sir William says give them nothing. Harmless, really. But a great many of them." He sounded unhappy.

"Yes." Helen had been straining her ears to see if she could understand what they were saying, but their accent was too strange. "Are they republicans?" She was ashamed to sound almost as nervous as her husband.

"Nothing of the kind. Devoted to the royal family, Sir William said. Mostly to the King. Well; odd kind of character. Likes the lazzaroni. Gets on well with them. Good thing." He looked nervously at the Italian coachman and grooms. "Can't be too careful, Sir William says." He lowered his voice. "They don't like the Queen. Can't quite understand it. Daughter of Maria Theresa; fine woman, large family; runs the country, with that minister, what's his name? General Acton."

"An Englishman?" asked Charlotte.

"Well, not exactly," Helen explained. "He comes from an English family, and indeed is now Sir John—an English baronet. But he's a Catholic and has spent all his life abroad."

"Yes," said Lord Merritt. "That captain—what was his name—? Came here from Toulon?"

"Nelson?"

"That's the fellow. Said Acton didn't speak English worth a damn. Beg pardon, Miss Standish. Look on you as family. What was I saying? Got it. What Sir William said. Careful who you make friends with. Italians. I said, don't want Italian friends. Don't speak the lingo. What's the use? And he said, it's the ones who speak English might be dangerous."

"Dangerous?" asked Helen.

"Jacobins." He leaned closer and whispered it. Then: "Excuse me, Miss Standish. Helen will explain." He leaned close to Helen again, and she was aware, as she had been before, of the curious mixed smell of him. Snuff, and man, and some kind of perfume that she did not much like. If she thought like this, she would be sick.

"Do explain," she said. "I can't, if I don't understand myself."

"Place full of plots and plotters." Again he had an anxious look for coachman and running footmen. "Freemasons; Jacobins; a couple of seditious clubs with odd names. Roma and Loma—something like that. Young people. Young aristocrats, Sir William says. Can't understand it myself, but there it is. So, can't be too careful, you and Miss Standish."

"But if they know all about them," said Helen, "why don't they do something?"

"Just what I asked." He turned to her with real pleasure. "Just the very thing I asked."

"And what did Sir William say?"

"Not Sir William. Lady Hamilton. Said the chief of police—Medici his name is—anyway, too soft-hearted by a half. If the Queen had her way, they'd all be in Sant' Elmo. As it is, meet them at the San Carlo—the opera," he explained, for the benefit of his female companions. "Meet them everywhere. Just have to be careful, that's all."

"It sounds quite delightful," said Helen wryly.

"Oh, yes." It was always disconcerting when he missed her irony. "Altogether delightful. Just in time for the Carnival, Sir William says. Must get ourselves masks. Lady Hamilton said she'd help. Can't wait for you to meet her." Once again a cloud of anxiety crossed his cheerful, open face. "Delightful lady. You'll understand."

"Of course I will," said Helen, with more truth than he could possibly have imagined.

Chapter 9

THE Hamiltons lived in considerable luxury on two spacious floors of the Palazzo Sessa, overlooking the great curve of the Bay of Naples. Arriving, the travellers were greeted only by Lady Hamilton, who apologised for her husband's absence. Sir William had been sent for urgently to the palace. "They always send for him when there's trouble." The Lancashire accent was still there, though less pronounced than Helen remembered it. The beauty was still there too, but Helen's angel had put on weight since Romney painted her as a nymph. Now, with her violet-blue eyes and dark, tawny hair, her superb complexion just beginning to show the signs of consistent overindulgence, she would have made, Helen thought, a more suitable model for Rubens.

But she was a splendid creature, just the same, and her welcome was heart-warming. "You poor girls must be worn out!" She had a hand of each. "That tiny ship!" A gesture led their eyes down to the *Gannet,* looking small indeed in the foreground of the famous view. "I'll send you to your apartments now, and you can tell me all your adventures when you have rested."

But, "Trouble?" asked Lord Merritt anxiously. "There's trouble?"

"There's always trouble." Lady Hamilton's expression was eloquent. "I don't know what they'd do without Sir William. But this is nothing to trouble *you,* Lord Merritt." She was quick, Helen thought, to recognise other people's feelings, and perhaps this, combined with the famous beauty, was the secret of her success. "It's just the news from Toulon," she now explained. "It's the first we'd heard of the evacuation. One of our ships—the Neapolitans' I mean—came into harbour just after yours. It's terrible. All those brave young men." In emotion, her accent broadened. "I can't bear to think what my poor darling Queen will be suffering. I must go to her this evening. You won't mind if I leave you alone? Tomorrow we must arrange for your remarriage; your presentation; everything; but today, if you will forgive me, all my duty is to my beloved Queen."

"Naturally." Lord Merritt was impressed. "Mustn't mind us in the slightest. Don't wish to be a nuisance. Glad to rest. Most grateful for your hospitality. Must find ourselves a house, of course. In the meantime, my wife and I, Miss Standish, all three of us, most grateful."

"Yes, indeed," Helen seconded this warmly and got a quick look from Lady Hamilton.

"We've not met before, have we?" she asked. "It's odd: your voice. I never forget a voice. You remind me of someone."

"I hope it's someone you liked," said Helen.

"Ooh . . ." again the accent broadened, "it was so long ago. But, yes, I loved her."

"Then I'm glad if I remind you of her. But we mustn't keep you from your duties. Miss Standish and I would really be grateful for a quiet day."

"I'm sure you would. You must meet my mother."

Mrs. Cadogan was as kind as her daughter, and as used to dealing with exhausted guests. They soon found themselves established in blessed peace and a handsome suite of rooms. "Not the ones Prince Augustus occupied." Lord Merritt showed signs of going into a miff over this, but Helen quickly pointed out that they were a much larger party. "What luxury to have so much space to ourselves."

Mrs. Cadogan had told them that it was not one of Lady Hamilton's nights to receive company and had promised them an early dinner. "A long night's sleep will do you all good, and God knows when they'll get back from the palace. The Queen really counts on my Emma in a crisis." Having made every possible arrangement for their comfort, she left them with final, faintly suggestive wishes for a good night's sleep.

Alone, Helen stood staring with dismay at the vast double bed. Lord Merritt was busy with Price in the dressing room next door, but now joined her to gaze, she thought with similar feelings, at the bed they must share. "Shan't be a trouble to you," he said now, unexpectedly. "Must consider the child, you know. Must consider the child."

"Yes. Thank you." It was more than she had hoped, but perhaps what she should have expected. If the first night of their marriage had been strange, this one was to be stranger still. It was easy enough to plead fatigue and get herself to bed early, but impossible to fall asleep until she saw the glimmer of her husband's light in the dressing room next door, heard him talking in an undertone to Price, heard the connecting door open, and decided that this time she would let herself play the coward's part and pretend sleep. Stretched out on the far side of the bed, she made herself breathe deep and easily, and felt her husband pause for a moment to listen, then, she thought, breathe a tiny sigh of relief before he climbed very quietly into the other side of the bed.

Outside, the city was still awake, with all the multifarious sounds of a southern climate, where so much living is done out of doors and in the cool of the evening. In the room it was strangely quiet as the two of them lay, each pretending sleep, until mercifully fatigue had its way with them, and the pretence became real. Helen had promised herself that she would wake early and make her escape to her own tiny dressing room, but the bed was blissfully comfortable after all those nights on ship's cots, and she was exhausted. When she woke at last to glints of morning sunlight round the curtains, it was to find herself alone. She lay, savouring it, the first real moment of solitude since she had left England, and refusing to let herself think beyond it.

It was a strange, quiet day. Lady Hamilton, calling on them soon after they had finished their breakfast, explained that the bad news from Toulon had caused the cancellation of the usual Carnival festivities, and even of most public and private engagements. "Well, the poor things; how can they feel like parties when there's hardly a family but has some relative to fret for? There'll not be much jollification here until all our ships are home."

Helen had already noticed that Lady Hamilton tended to use "we" and "our" almost interchangeably for British and Neapolitans. It made talking to her a little confusing, but then she talked so much herself that it was often not necessary to provide more than the briefest of answers. On the other hand, when one did speak, she listened with a passionate attention that could not help but be flattering. She had also exerted herself to some purpose on their account. Her secretary, Mr. Smith, had been making enquiries about houses for them, and there were a couple for them to look at.

"And your remarriage is all arranged," her ravishing smile was for Helen. "I had a word with my angel Queen about it. There'll be no difficulty. And we can have a small party for that, without treading on any toes." And, when Helen protested at the trouble involved, she smiled more deliciously than ever. "No trouble. I love giving parties, and Mother does all the work anyway. Would you like me to ask that Captain Scroope who brought you? He seemed a pleasant enough young man, if you like them young." Her tone reminded Helen that they both had husbands older than themsleves.

"Oh, yes, please." Helen's parting from Charles Scroope had somehow, in the general confusion, happened before she had realised. "I never thanked him properly."

"Quite right." Lord Merritt approved. "Must have young Scroope. Here for a while. Ship refitting. Pleasant company."

Thinking it all over that evening as she changed her dress for what Lady Hamilton had described as a quiet family dinner with Sir William, Helen admitted herself lucky. Or rather, that it could all have been infinitely worse. Her husband might not be possessed of even average intelligence, but at least he seemed willing to be guided by her. It was she, in fact, who had chosen the smaller of the two houses they had looked at, pointing out that its situation was much the quieter, and he had agreed, with a proviso about a country cottage presently, before the weather got too hot. "Must ask Sir William." This was a phrase that recurred frequently in his conversation, and Helen found herself looking forward to meeting the man who had made such an impression.

When she did so, she liked him at once. He was even older than she had expected, a surprising mate for her buxom angel, and looked exhausted tonight, as well he might after a day devoted to advising the King and Queen, or rather, as Emma soon revealed, of helping the Queen persuade the King that after the disastrous news from Toulon the Carnival festivities simply had to be cancelled. In the end, it was Sir William who had suggested, as a compromise, that they might stage naval manoeuvres or a naval pageant of some kind in the bay.

"The King jumped at that," said Emma. "He loves a party, and the rowdier the better. Don't be surprised if he comes to your wedding party, Lady Merritt, but incognito, of course." It was becoming increasingly obvious that the "little party" she was to give for the newly married couple was going to be little in name only. Helen turned a faintly anxious glance to Sir William, on whose right she was sitting, got a reassuring one in return, and realised that he was as quick as his wife to read one's feelings. It must be one of the things they had in common. He was also, she soon found, formidably intelligent, and glad to enlighten her on many points that had puzzled her about the situation in Naples. And all the time, behind his apparently free discussion of the problem of the young Neapolitan aristocrat who had been carried away by the dangerous tide of liberal enthusiasm, she was aware of a vast, gentle discretion. He was telling her a great deal that would be extremely useful to her, but only a tiny portion of what he actually knew.

After dinner, he paid her what she was to learn was a considerable compliment by carrying her off to see his collection of antique vases, and in this field, too, proved himself a knowledgable and entertaining instructor. They were interrupted by a rather impatient summons from Lady Hamilton in the next room. "I promised Lord Merritt a special view of my attitudes," she told him. "And you know I am nothing without you."

There was only one possible response to this adept mixture of command and flattery, and they joined the rest of the party to watch Lady Hamilton go through the famous performance that had won the surprised admiration of such different spectators as the poet Goethe and the Duchess of Devonshire. Helen was to see them many times, but always with amazement. Equipped with a bare minimum of accessories, Lady Hamilton struck pose after graceful pose, twisting a couple of shawls so that they were one moment the veils of a sweeping Niobe, the next a headdress for a triumphant Cleopatra. Sir William, standing by with the lamp, stage-managed the whole thing, and, Helen suspected, had somehow contrived to suggest to his wife the passions that informed her graceful figure and made the series of mimes so effective. How much Lady Hamilton herself understood of the despair of Niobe or the pride of Cleopatra, was another question. Helen had already noticed her quick perceptiveness about people. Somehow, she seemed able, without very much of her own, to draw on her husband's intelligence. Helen, sadly, found herself wondering whether she and her husband might not work out some such relationship, but in reverse.

Now, Lady Hamilton was balking. "Not that one," she protested, and then, on Sir William's insistence, "Very well then, just for a moment. I don't much like it," she confided in Helen, her accent broadening.

Sir William, lamp in hand, led the way to the far end of the room, where a tall black box stood against the wall. "The perfect frame," he said.

His wife stepped into the box and turned to face them, every inch a Madonna. "No, no," said Sir William impatiently. "The other one."

"Ouch," said Lady Hamilton, and for a moment, was still, was dead, was death. Then she was out among them, talking rather loudly.

"What a strange box." Helen turned to Sir William. "It looks almost like a coffin."

"It is a coffin," he said. "It was dug up, with its mistress inside it, at Pompeii."

Next day, trying to explain the attitudes to her husband, who had been baffled by them, Helen could not help a certain sympathy with his final comment. "Not quite the thing, hey? Any of those women! And as for that last one. Surprised at Sir William."

He would never understand Sir William's passion for antiquities of every kind. A pot was a pot to Henry Merritt, whether it had been made by Mr. Wedgwood last week, or dug up from among bones and lava at Pompeii, or raised, at risk of life and limb, by a diver from the depths of the bay. Helen longed to visit the famous sites of which Sir William told her, but for the moment her husband was unpersuadable and her life too busy. The house they had taken needed everything, and, most particularly, cleaning, and the cheerful, dirty Neapolitan women found for her by Mrs. Cadogan had to be supervised every inch of the way if they were not to leave things worse than they found them. "I wish we had a Mrs. Cadogan," Helen confided to Charlotte.

"I've been thinking about that," said Charlotte. "Couldn't I be your Mrs. Cadogan, Helen?" She coloured painfully. "You've been so good to m . . . m . . . m . . ."

"Nothing of the kind," said Helen briskly. "You know how I love to have you with me. And so does Henry; he said so, just the other day."

"I'm glad," said Charlotte. "But, Helen, I've got to tell you. I've no m . . ." She stopped. "If you hadn't taken over paying Rose, I'd not have been able to."

"Oh dear." It was exactly what Helen had feared.

"Mother said . . ." Was it a measure of Charlotte's desperation that she got the word out without a stumble? "That she'd give me enough for six m . . . m . . . months. After that, she said, I was on my own."

"You made it last longer," said Helen.

Charlotte laughed, a reassuring sound. "Well, no one could call life on board ship expensive. But if I'm not to disgrace you here in Naples, I must earn some m . . . m . . ." She took a deep breath. "Or marry. Helen, I'd so much rather be your housekeeper. Please?" If she realised, as she spoke, what an appalling, unspoken comment this was on Helen's own marriage, she managed, admirably, to conceal it.

"You really mean it?" Helen felt both sympathy and respect. Here was a new, a surprising Charlotte.

"I do indeed. God knows, I've done it for Mother long enough. And my Italian may not be as good as yours, but it's not bad. And, Helen, you won't, please, think I'm prying, but isn't there perhaps a reason why you shouldn't be doing too m . . . m . . ." She took a deep breath. "Mother always sent me to stay with my sisters when they were increasing," she explained. "And, forgive me, I couldn't help noticing."

But not, thank God, and judging by her tone, too soon. "You're an angel." Helen embraced her. "And, yes, you're quite right. I do so hope I won't be sick at my second wedding breakfast. But we're so pleased, my husband and I. Of all things, he wants an heir." It was all, beautifully, true.

"I am so glad." Charlotte kissed her back warmly. "It will make everything so much easier for you. And now I know, I'll see to it that you aren't sick at the party. You've no idea how expert I am in these matters. So, please, Helen, don't make me ask again?"

"But what would your mother say?"

Charlotte gave her a very straight look. "I don't care a farthing dip what my mother says. She sent me here to sink or swim. If it weren't for you, it looks to me as if I'd sink. If she don't like my acting housekeeper to you, she's only herself to thank."

It was true enough. And, even more interesting to Helen, was the way Charlotte's stammer seemed to be falling away from her with the idea of independence. She had managed her worst word of all—mother—twice in the last few sentences.

"Selfishly," she said, "I can't think of anything I'd like better. But, of course, I must ask my husband."

"Of course," said Charlotte, and they both knew the matter settled.

Lord Merritt, predictably, was at once delighted and alarmed at the idea. "Miss Standish! Our housekeeper?" He thought for a moment. "But: Mrs. Standish?"

"Charlotte says she doesn't care, and I am inclined to agree with her. She needs the money; I need the help. What could be more sensible?" And, seeing him still look alarmed at the thought of the old harridan back in London, "Think what a long way off London is. We'll keep it all very casual," she improvised now, as she went along. "Nothing said to anyone about paying her."

"Not even to Trenche?"

"Specially not to Trenche. I shall pay her out of my pin money." She longed to suggest he get rid of Trenche but knew she did not dare.

They moved into the Palazzo Trevi the day before Lady Hamilton's party, and Helen was delighted with it. Close to the Palazzo Sessa, but a little lower down, it commanded its own segment of the great bay, with Vesuvius lowering in the distance, and, best of all, had a small terraced garden, already sweet with early violets and heliotrope, growing in a great tangle after a year of neglect. Sitting there, resting in the warm sun, where Charlotte had firmly sent her, Helen leaned back to savour an extraordinary sensation. Could it possibly be happiness?

If it was, it did not last. Closing her eyes for a moment of complete repose, she opened them to the sight of Trenche, who must inevitably move back to join them now they were settled. He had just arrived from his lodgings and had come out, he said, to pay his respects. It was actually the first time they had been alone together since the day of her disaster, and she was amazed how much she disliked it. And him. How had she ever thought of him as negligible?

After the usual respectful greetings, which she found so hard to bear, he came quickly to his point, making her wonder whether he perhaps disliked her company as much as she did his. "Miss Standish appears to be managing everything in there," he said.

"Yes. I asked her to."

"She has given me a room that is practically in the cellar. I have a weak chest. That is why I wished to come to Italy. I must have light and air. I trust that you will explain to Miss Standish."

"I have seen the room." Helen sensed that this, in its quiet way, was a moment of crisis. If she gave in to him now, she was giving way to endless blackmail. "Miss Standish and I went over the house together and chose it for you. I am sorry if it does not please you, but, frankly, it is the best there is. I am sure, if you really find it bad for your health, that Lord Merritt would make some arrangement about lodgings for you." What an extraordinary relief it would be.

"Oh, dear me, no. I must be at hand when Lord Merritt needs me. If it is your decision, Lady Merritt, then naturally I must abide by it. After all, I shall be spending most of my time in Lord Merritt's study."

"Yes, of course." It was disappointing that he would not move out, but, on the other hand, a relief that he should have yielded so easily. "I know how indispensable my husband finds you." Absurd to think of Lord Merritt with a study, but one of the advantages of this house was the small, charming ground-floor room that could be dedicated entirely to him. He would not study there, being incapable of it, but he could sleep, or pretend to read the latest papers from England, or dictate long letters to his uncle to Trenche, who, Helen had noticed, was adept at improving their style.

But Trenche had another point to raise with her. "About the party tomorrow," he said. "Have I been invited, Lady Merritt?"

This, she knew at once, was what he really cared about. The question of the room had merely been a preliminary. She could see his point. He had not yet been to the Palazzo Sessa. If he did not appear at Lady Hamilton's party, he was relegated forever to the ranks of servants. "Miss Standish goes, I take it?" he said now, making it just faintly a question.

One had to admit it. He was no fool. She looked up at him lazily in the warm sunshine. "Naturally Miss Standish comes," she said. "As for you, to tell you the truth, I have no idea whether Lady Hamilton even knows that you exist, but of course you must come with us. Lord Merritt may need you."

He gave her a look that was not all gratitude, thanked

her, and left her in ruined peace. He had noticed that Charlotte had taken over the housekeeping. He noticed everything. But what conclusions did he draw? And what others would he, if her child was born nine months to the day from the evacuation of Toulon? If he was already making tentative moves towards blackmail, what in the world would happen to her then? If only she could consult Charlotte, so surprisingly knowledgeable about the problems of childbearing. Might she not know of some method of delaying a birth, or at least of making an early one seem explicable? But, so far, whatever Trenche might suspect, the secret was hers and her husband's, and she had not the right to speak of it to anyone else. Nor, unfortunately, could she possibly hope for help from her husband. She sat there, cold now in the sunshine, racking her brains for expedients, and finding none.

Chapter 10

◞◖◖ LADY Hamilton's party was a success, because her parties always were, but just the same, Helen was aware of strange cross-currents under the apparently gay chatter that filled the crowded rooms. Two more ships had limped home from Toulon that morning, with their quota of bad news, and families were exchanging gloomy reports in undertones. Looking round, Helen noticed a strange thing. There were hardly any people there as young or younger than herself and Charlotte.

She was puzzling over this when her heart gave an uncontrollable, maddening leap at the sight of Captain Scroope, immensely elegant in full dress uniform, making his controlled way through the chattering crowd towards where she and her husband stood together, receiving the congratulations of Lady Hamilton's friends. Would he repeat the stiff words of felicitation with which he had greeted them on the *Gannet?* And could she bear it if he did?

Fortunately, Lord Merritt was carried off at the last moment by Lady Hamilton, who wanted to present him to a particular friend of hers, and Helen found herself waiting, in more agitation than she liked, for Scroope to reach her through the crowded room. "I am so glad to see you." She kept her tone casual, but managed to anticipate his greeting. "We never had a chance to thank you properly for all your kindness on the *Gannet.*"

"It was nothing." Now that he was closer, she saw that he looked fine-drawn with fatigue, the scar standing out more livid than usual because the colour had ebbed from under his tan. "I only wish we had been able to give you better accommodation."

His eyes flickered past her to where Charlotte was standing, but she could not let him go yet. "You look worn out." Surely, as an old friend she had the right to say it.

"It's nothing." Almost the same phrase as before. "The refit. And of course the Neapolitan ships have first call on supplies."

"Yes." She remembered what had been puzzling her when she first saw him. Here, surely, was a safe, neutral topic of conversation. "Have you noticed," she asked, "that there are no young people here?"

He looked quickly round, as if to make sure that they were near enough to the musicians, who were in full fling with an air of Mr. Haydn's, so that they could not possibly be overheard. "You have not perhaps heard the rumours, Lady Merritt?"

"Rumours?" She hated having him use her title. "No."

"I thought not." His glance took in the splendidly furnished rooms. "I think you should know that there is talk of a Jacobin conspiracy among the young aristocrats here."

"Oh," she said. "That. Yes, Sir William did say something, but I did not think he meant it seriously."

"I have a great respect for Sir William," said Captain

Scroope. "But do you not find that it is sometimes hard to be sure whether he is serious or not?" At last he was talking to her almost like the friend he had once been.

Friend? She bit back tears, but kept her voice casual. "And you think this serious?"

"Serious enough so that the young Neapolitans do not come to Lady Hamilton's parties. They are doubtless at the French Ambassador's at this moment. You did not know?"

"Know?"

"That he is giving an impromptu party today."

"And very ill-attended it will be." A tall, strongly built man in a mask had come up behind Scroope as he spoke, and now interrupted him in rather broad Italian. "We're much better here, with the divine Emma and our new star." Here a curious bob of a bow for Helen. "As beautiful as I had heard," he said, eyes behind the mask making an obvious inventory of Helen's white dress and crimson sash. "You wear red?" The question had more overtones than Helen liked, and it was a relief when Charles Scroope took it up.

"Crimson, sire." His Italian was surprisingly good. "No intelligent person wears any other red these days."

"No," grunted the mask, "but then there are so many fools."

That was Helen's first encounter with King Ferdinand of Naples, the eccentric monarch whose subjects called him either *Il Re Nasone* because of his enormous Bourbon nose, or, affectionately, the King of the Lazzaroni, who adored him. It was far from being her last. King Ferdinand, who had succeeded to the throne at the ripe age of eight, had had about as little education as her own husband, and it proved an immediate bond between them. The fact that Ferdinand's English was as bad as Merritt's Italian merely seemed to constitute an additional tie, and, in fact, as Ferdinand had proved by his disconcerting interruption at the party, he could understand more English than he spoke. Most important of all, they shared a passion for hunting, in which Ferdinand spent the greater part of his time, leaving the conduct of his kingdom to his wife, and their first minister, General Acton. Even now, with Naples abuzz with rumours of Jacobin meetings, of Freemasons who swore strange oaths in secret, and of French agents who had been smuggled back with the evacuated royalists from Toulon, Ferdinand spent his time as he always had, at one or other of his country houses, slaughtering great battues of driven game, with Lord Merritt now as his constant companion.

"Odd kind of fellow," Merritt confided to his wife, after one of these excursions. "Cuts them up himself. Like a butcher."

Helen shuddered. "Horrible. No wonder Sir William is glad to have you take his place." For Sir William, who had achieved early and lasting popularity with the King by joining him in these bloody outings, had made it tactfully clear that he was more than pleased to surrender the doubtful privilege to Lord Merritt.

It suited Helen too. It was late in March, and the sun was warmer every day. She felt progressively better every day and was beginning to enjoy the social life of Naples, quieter than usual because of Lent and the general mourning, but still absorbing enough to a girl who had not been to a real party for four years. She had her own box now at the San Carlo Opera, and had learned that ladies entertained in their boxes, as in a salon, providing refreshments on certain nights for the gentlemen who wandered freely from box to box. The only thing that maddened her was that the audience, respectfully quiet during the ballet, always burst into vigorous conversation when the opera began. And the occasion, on Shrove Tuesday, when the King made one of his infrequent appearances and threw macaroni to the delighted mob in the pit, shocked her to the core. The Queen, she noticed, stayed well out of the way at the back of the royal box until the orgy was over.

Emma Hamilton's angelic queen was an impressive figure, if she could never have been a beautiful one, like her dead sister, Marie Antoinette. Presented to her, Helen had been aware of sharp, cold eyes in the high-complexioned face. "You're very young," Her Majesty had said. "I think I should warn you, Lady Merritt, that youth here in Naples is not always a guarantee of respectability."

Helen remembered these rather chilling words on Shrove Tuesday, aware of a subdued titter among the young people who seemed to gravitate naturally to her box. This was very pleasant for Charlotte, whose Italian was improving by leaps and bounds, but just the same, Helen found herself increasingly wondering whether it was wise to encourage them. Besides, she had noticed something else about them. They often arrived late, or left early, or even disappeared for a whole act of the opera, returning in the highest possible spirits, rather like schoolboys back from a successful bit of mischief. She began to wonder if she and Charlotte might be being used as cover for some sinister activity.

It was hard to believe it of these charming, intelligent young men, who were so invariably courteous and such a pleasure to entertain, but then, what did she know of the realities of life here in Naples? And where could she turn for advice? Her husband was a cipher, she distrusted Trenche from the bottom of her heart, and Lady Hamilton, who might have seemed the obvious choice, was so closely in touch with the Queen that Helen feared the consequences to her group of young friends if she were to breathe a word of her doubts about them in that quarter. They might so easily be entirely innocent, merely up to the kind of mischief young men do indulge in, and she had been in Naples long enough now to know that the threat of the secret police and the great prison fortresses that loomed even more menacing than Vesuvius over the city was a real one. She refused to listen to the rumours that the Queen actually interviewed secret agents herself in a secret room—the *sala oscura* at the palace, but on the other hand she found she could not entirely disbelieve them.

And could you blame the Queen? She had seen the fate of her sister and brother-in-law in France. There was no doubt that liberal, or even revolutionary feeling was strong in Naples. A few years before, when a detachment of the French fleet had sailed aggressively into the harbour, a group of rash young men had gone on board wearing the cap of liberty and drunk, Helen had heard, a series of foolhardy toasts. As the Court had had to yield to all the French commander, La Touche Treville's, demands, the occasion had inevitably rankled and had probably had a good deal to do with the treaty that Naples had finally signed with England. Queen Maria Carolina had realised, if her husband had not, that a country as exposed as theirs must have an ally with a fleet to protect it.

Helen was sitting in her sweet-scented garden, brooding anxiously about all this, when one of the servants appeared to announce Captain Scroope. Her heart leapt at the name. He had been away in Sicily, choosing timbers for the refit of the *Gannet*, since the supplies in Naples had been exhausted by the Toulon disaster, and, inevitably, the needs of the battered Neapolitan ships came first. Making herself greet him with formal casualness, she thought he looked brown and well and anxious.

"No, thank you." He refused her offer of refreshment. "May we stay out here? I had been hoping for a word alone with you."

"Oh?" What in the world could he have to say to her? She felt herself blushing uncontrollably, and turned away, inwardly raging, to hide it. "Yes, Lady Merritt"— he paused, momentarily at a loss—"you must forgive me, if you think me presuming on our old acquaintance-ship : . ."

"Friendship." She could not help saying it.

"Thank you. That makes it easier." Suddenly, delightfully, he laughed, the young man's laugh that she had thought lost in the captain's dignity. "Do you remember that time you recognised Lady Hamilton's picture, and what a dust your aunt kicked up?"

"Do I not! Nor how grateful I was to you for the way you helped me out of the scrape."

"Does she know?"

"Lady Hamilton? No; I thought it perhaps best forgotten."

"Like many things." And then, on the same grave note, he said, "But I hope you will bear with me, if I give you what you may think a foolish warning."

"A warning?" This was not at all what she had expected. But then, what on earth had she expected?

"Yes. I got back to town last night to find it alive with rumours. Much worse than when we last talked."

"I know," she said helpfully. "There's all kinds of gossip. One can't help hearing it. But you don't think there's any truth in it, do you?"

"I wish I was sure. It may all be just young men's nonsense." And then, aware of her quick smile: "No, of course, I'm not so old myself, but I hope I have more sense than to go round talking of France and liberty here in Naples. The trouble is, even if it is nonsense, it may not be taken as such. There are spies everywhere. I know de Medici, the chief of police, seems the mildest of men——"

"Yes," she interrupted. "And, besides, do you know two of the leading revolutionaries—which I honestly do not believe they are—actually live in his house."

"The Giordano brothers. But don't you see, you can look even at that more ways than one. They may be fooling him, or he may be fooling them, or there may really be nothing to it. But, Lady Merritt, what I came to say was that I have heard your box at the opera mentioned oftener than I like in connection with that group of young madcaps."

"Not the Giordano brothers."

"No, they are hardly of a class to appear there. But they are in constant association with men like Vincenzo Vitaliani and Emmanuele de Deo, and that poetess, what's her name? Pimentel."

"But she's charming! Charlotte and I like her best of all the Neapolitan ladies we have met. And surely she wrote an ode or something in honour of the Queen not long ago."

"Long enough to have changed her mind since. So it's true that there's a constant coming and going of these young lunatics between her box and yours?"

"Well, yes." Here, surely, was the adviser she had wanted. "To tell you the truth, I have been a little worried myself."

"A little worried! Helen, I beg you, don't forget you're not in England now. There's no presumption of innocence here."

"Well," she said reasonably, "there's not all that much there. Think of Wilkes."

"He survived," said Scroope grimly. "If there really is a plot afoot and the Queen were to think you implicated, you might just disappear, and neither nationality nor title would avail you much when no one knew where you were."

Helen shivered. "You think it as bad as that?"

"It's happened before," he said. "Two years ago, after the visit the French squadron paid here. Some of the young men who visited the French admiral on his flagship and toasted 'Liberty' in red caps just vanished afterwards and have not been heard of since."

"I didn't know." She was appalled.

"Of course not. Their families have more sense than to mention them. But I have no doubt that every time there is a royal fête, an occasion for clemency, one of those constant childbearings of the Queen's, there are families all over Naples saying secret prayers for the life of a beloved son. They don't even know whether they are alive or dead you see. Once you're in the cells below Sant' Elmo, you might as well be dead."

"It's horrible."

"You're beginning to understand. Lady Merritt"—had they either of them noticed that he had called her "Helen" before?—"I do seriously beg you to think of a pretext not to attend the opera tonight, and then to find some means of changing your company."

"But how?"

"I don't know." Impatiently. "But you'll think of something."

"If you really think it necessary."

He was, incredibly, on the verge of losing his temper with her. "It depends whether you value your life—and that of Miss Standish, who is inevitably involved. Lord Merritt, I know, is on such good terms with the King that he would probably get off scot-free, but whether he would be able to save you is another question." His dry tone suggested that he doubted her husband's capability in every sense of the word.

"You're right, of course." It was a relief to admit it. "Tonight, in fact, I have to go. It's Charlotte's birthday and we have invited several people."

"Plead illness."

It was the last thing she wanted to do, and almost a relief when the appearance of Trenche on the terrace put an end to the conversation. Scroope had never tried to conceal his dislike of Trenche, and now took his leave, pressing Helen's hand, hard, once, and urging her to think over what he had said.

"Secrets?" asked Trenche, with an attempt at roguishness that she found repellent.

"Just some good advice from an old friend." She made her tone as quelling as possible, and wished Charlotte would join them.

"What a coincidence. Good advice was precisely what I had come to give—and to ask."

"Oh?" She turned negligently half away from him, and bent to pick herself a fragrant cluster of violets.

She was standing, and was therefore surprised to see Trenche seat himself negligently on the arm of one of the terrace's marble benches. "Just so," he said, "advice from an old"—he had the grace to hesitate—"friend. Do you think it wise, circumstanced as you are, to give tête-à-tête interviews to single gentlemen?"

"What in the world do you mean?" But she was horribly afraid that she knew.

"Lady Merritt, I'm not quite a fool. I was puzzled, at first, as anyone might have been, over that sudden marriage of yours. I have thought you many things, but never mercenary."

"Thank you." Her mouth was dry. The less she said, the better.

"So, of course, I have watched you," he went on blandly. "Oh, my congratulations. You have been superb. No one without cause to suspect would have done so. But I—had cause. What do you plan? A fright of some kind?

114

A premature birth? Even Lord Merritt can count, you know."

The scorn in his voice when he spoke of her husband put angry heart into her. And, besides, here was a tiny scruple of hope. He might know of her condition, but he had not guessed that Lord Merritt did. "How dare you speak of your employer in that tone?" She asked it angrily, giving herself a breathing space to think, to try frantically to plan.

"Oh, Helen, between ourselves? With so much already between us? You must allow me the privilege of an old friend, at least." And, when she turned away from him, too angry for words: "Besides, I have come to offer my help. I don't want to stand in my child's way. Or in yours. I have too much to gain as things stand. Nearer the time, I am sure we can think of something, between us. But, in the meanwhile, there are a couple of small favours you can do me."

Here it came, the inevitable blackmail. "Yes?" She had swiftly decided that to deny his allegations would be worse than useless. Once he had suspected, the facts would speak all too clearly for themselves.

"You have been leaving me out of your parties, when Lord Merritt is away. I should like to be included. For instance, you and Miss Standish go to the San Carlo tonight. Surely I am as respectable a cicisbeo—I believe that is the correct term?" Again that intolerable note of mockery in his voice. "Surely a safer cicisbeo," he reiterated the insulting word with obvious pleasure, "than these young Neapolitan fire-eaters of yours. Besides," now he was coming to the heart of the matter, "I rely on your influence with the divine Charlotte."

"With Miss Standish?" Could she understand him correctly?

"Yes. I won't say I hadn't hoped for better things, but needs must, you know . . . I have the strangest feeling that now he has you to do his thinking for him, Lord Merritt may decide, after a while, to dispense with my invaluable services, and, in that case, what can I do but marry money? Oh, I know"—he raised a hand to silence her—

"Miss Standish has nothing much, and that mother of hers won't be best pleased, but, when you come to think of it, what could be more suitable? Secretary marries housekeeper. What I can't decide—the point upon which I need your advice, and, indeed, your help, is whether it would be best to play the honourable man, and face all the delay that involves, or to compromise the girl and let the old harridan make the best bargain she can."

"I find you absolutely intolerable." She spat it at him.

"Oh, that's of course." He would not be ruffled. "Forgive me; I have pushed you, perhaps, a little far for a first interview, but when you have thought a little, I am sure you will see the advantages of an alliance with me. I can help you immensely. Or I can ruin you. Suppose I were to write to Lord Merritt's uncle?"

"You would ruin yourself." But the threat went home.

"It might even be worth it." His tone told her how much he hated her. "But, in the meantime, Lady Merritt." He rose, his voice a mockery of respect: "I beg you will do me the honour of allowing me to escort you to the opera tonight."

"Oh, very well." She knew it for the beginning of the end, but what else could she say?

The King and Queen had just returned from their palace at Caserta, and the opera was unusually well attended. Since it was a favourite of hers, Gluck's *Orfeo,* Helen could have wished this otherwise, but on the other hand, after Charles Scroope's warning, she soothed herself with the thought that there must be some kind of safety in the crowds that thronged the great opera house. The Hamiltons and her own husband had returned with the royal party, and Lady Hamilton waved to her graciously from her box, close to the royal one. Even Lord Merritt, who detested music, had promised to look in later on. Trenche, on the other hand, had accompanied her and Charlotte in the carriage, and was now paying unmistakable attention to Charlotte, so that during Orfeo's first great lament for his lost Euridice Helen was moved to turn round and hush him angrily.

"Everyone else is talking." There was a new note in his

116

tone when he spoke to Helen, and she saw Charlotte's quick look of surprise.

This was a horrible evening. Trenche did, in fact, keep quiet after that, but Helen was aware of him edging his chair nearer and nearer to Charlotte's, and of the latter's instinctive recoil. It was positively a relief when the first interval brought the usual group of callers. Or it should have been. But, freed by their presence from the fear that Trenche would say or do something disastrous, she had time to be aware of a feeling of tension in the great auditorium. Or was she imagining things because of the turmoil of her own feelings? But surely more of the royal guard than usual were present tonight? Because the King and Queen were just back, no doubt. She had not been long enough in Naples to be sure about a point like this, but it certainly seemed logical.

And her feeling that her own guests were in a state of suppressed excitement was doubtless simply a transference of her own nervous state. Were they drinking rather more than usual of the excellent light wine she provided? Were their voices sometimes higher, sometimes a little lower than politeness indicated? She found herself actually glad when her husband and Sir William Hamilton entered the box and inevitably changed the course of what had seemed to her a curiously fragmentary conversation, with odd pauses and strangely exchanged glances. Lord Merritt could be relied on to lower the intellectual tone of any conversation, and, if Sir William looked momentarily taken aback at sight of the company she was entertaining, he was soon his usual urbane self, complimenting her on what he called a marked improvement in her looks since he had seen her last.

Thanking him, she thought bitterly how surprised he would be if she gave him a straight answer. Naturally, she looked better now that she had stopped being sick in the mornings. Instead, she enquired after the success of the latest royal hunting party, and the health of the royal children. The conversation found its usual safe if not very interesting channel for a few minutes, until it was suddenly interrupted by Charlotte pushing her way almost rudely across the crowded box from the corner where, Helen saw, she had left Trenche white with fury.

"Helen!" Charlotte curtsied almost automatically to Sir William. "I don't feel well. May we, please, go home?"

Sir William looked as nearly shocked as he would ever let himself. The bells were ringing for the end of the interval; the royal party were settling back in their sumptuous chairs; it was absolutely impossible to leave.

"Nonsense," said Lord Merritt, as their own guests began to take their leave. "Going to stay myself, though I'll hate every minute of it."

In fact, he rather enjoyed the ballet of the Elysian spirits, and as he had absentmindedly taken the chair by Charlotte that Trenche had previously occupied, Helen began to hope that they would get through the rest of the evening without actual disaster. In the final interval, their box was emptier than usual, and Helen, seeing her usual crowd of young men in Eleanora Pimentel's box on the other side of the house, felt a mixture of relief and disappointment. Did they find her husband's company as tedious as that?

But when the last curtain fell to a roar of well-earned applause, they all came back to see her and Charlotte to their carriage, and she was delighted to see Trenche relegated to the background where he belonged, when a young Neapolitan aristocrat took Charlotte's arm to help her through the crowd. Lord Merritt was doing the same for her, with the rest of the group following along behind, Trenche in their midst. They were outside now, in the mild southern darkness, and Helen was standing with her foot on the carriage step, wondering whether their cavaliers were hoping to be invited back to the Villa Trevi, when it happened.

The crowd around them, a moment before cheerfully talking and shouting for carriages, was suddenly silent, shrinking into itself. A small group of dark-clad men making their way purposefully through it seemed to have a basilisk effect as they passed. Helen saw one extraordinarily significant exchange of glances between Vitaliani and de Deo, and then the dark, silent men were upon them.

Lord Merritt, showing unexpected presence of mind, pushed her up into the carriage and jumped in after her. Charlotte screamed. There was a scuffle, out there in the curiously patchy darkness, illuminated here and there by light from the opera house, or a carriage lamp. Outside the scene of action, Helen was aware of the other members of the audience, forming, as it were, a circle of lookers-on, silent, doing nothing. "Charlotte's out there," she told her husband. "Do something!"

"What can I do?" He peered out anxiously into the darkness, his ineffective face illuminated by the carriage lamps.

Charlotte screamed again, and then, miraculously, appeared at the carriage step, her face showing white and her eyes huge in the uncertain light.

"Thank God!" Helen reached down a hand to help her up, and heard, as she did so, a voice from the middle of the silently, horribly struggling crowd below the carriage steps. "I'm English!" shouted Trenche. "Lord Merritt, Helen, tell them I'm English!"

"Lord Merritt!" One of the black-clad men appeared at the carriage door and spoke in surprisingly good English. "You will take the ladies home. At once. This is no place for strangers." He gave a quick order to the servants, who began to take up the carriage steps.

"But," as Helen began her protest, she looked out into the struggling crowd, saw a truncheon rise and come down, with a crunch, in the face of one of the young men who had been drinking her wine half an hour before. He fell silently under the blow. The world began to whirl around her. Once again, she heard Trenche's voice, agonised now with fear, "Tell them I'm English!"

"We must do something," but as she spoke, she swayed where she sat, and Charlotte was just in time to catch her as she fell. For the second time in her life, Helen had fainted.

Chapter 11

✑ "WELL," said Lord Merritt reasonably next morning, sitting on his wife's bed and sipping chocolate, "what could we do? You perhaps dying? Nothing for it. Brought you home fast as we could. As for Trenche; chose his company; must take the consequences. No one knows where any of them are," he went on with a certain relish. "The earth might have opened and swallowed them. And no one asks."

"But we must do something," said Helen.

"Foolish."

"It's not a question of being wise, or foolish, it's doing what one must. Ring for Rose, would you? If you will do nothing, I must go and see Lady Hamilton." She knew it for a mistake the moment she had said it. She should have gone, but without making a challenge of it like this. His face closed obstinately against her.

"Expect you'll do what you want, as usual." He left her to her dressing.

Lady Hamilton received her with a preoccupied air, but, as she had hoped, Helen found her alone, and lost no time in telling her story, fearing that at any moment they might be interrupted.

Lady Hamilton listened in uneasy silence, the beautiful face unusally grave, the deep violet eyes, with that strange, dark fleck in them, serious. At last, "Oh, the poor man," she said. "I feel it all my fault. I have been meaning for ever so long to warn you about the company you've been keeping. But my position with the dear Queen makes me extra careful what I say."

"I wish you had spoken," said Helen. "I have been

wanting advice. But, now that it's happened, what can we do?" She did not, granted Lady Hamilton's tone, say, "What will you do?"

"Nothing, I'm afraid," said Emma Hamilton. "I have never seen my adorable Queen so angry. It was a plot against their very lives. If de Medici had not acted last night, we might find ourselves living in the Neapolitan Republic this morning."

"I doubt that," said Helen. "The lazzaroni are devoted to the King."

"And the aristocrats hate the Queen. Just think of those young men you've been entertaining actually plotting her death. No, Lady Merritt, I am sorry to disappoint you, but this is no moment for me to go to her with a request that has anything to do with your household. I had it in mind, already—in fact, Sir William had suggested it to me that it might be wise for you to retire for a while to that house your husband took at Torre del Greco."

"Oh!" Helen had, in fact, been longing to get out of town to the country villa her husband had rented, but she could not leave it like this. "That poor Mr. Trenche," she tried again. "He was only with the conspirators by accident. Surely something could be done for him?"

"Not by me," said Emma Hamilton.

This was horrible. Helen had been so certain that she had only to tell her story to get help, and the worst of it was that just because it would be such an extraordinary relief to her to have Trenche safely out of the way, silenced, perhaps forever, in one of those horrible dungeons, she felt it all the more incumbent on her to do her utmost to get him released. "Lady Hamilton," this was an appeal she had hardly even considered making. "You have never remembered me."

"Remembered you?" Emma Hamilton looked discreetly at the gold-and-glass clock on the chimneypiece.

"From long ago," Helen plunged into it. "Do you remember, once, at Uppark, a child who fell out of the rhododendrons?"

"Me peeping Tom!" said Emma Hamilton, human for a moment. But the moment passed, and Helen knew that for the second time this unlucky morning she had made a mistake. How extraordinary that for the sake of Trenche, whom she loathed and feared, she should have alienated both her husband and Lady Hamilton.

Lady Hamilton was looking at her now with frank dislike. "I suppose it would make a good story," she said in a tone Helen had never heard before.

"Good God! You must know I'd never tell it." Horrible to be suspected of the very blackmail Trenche himself had used on her.

"No?" asked Emma Hamilton. "Then what are we talking about? Oh—" as if inspiration had suddenly dawned, "I owe you a gold crucifix. You shall have it, Lady Merritt. It was most useful to me at the time, and I am grateful." Her tone was still icy, and Helen spared a moment to think how extraordinarily well she could act the great lady when she chose.

"No," she said. "Please. You must know that's not what I meant at all. I just meant—" What had she meant? She plunged on doubtful whether she could save the situation, but desperately trying. "I meant," she started again, "that you felt—well, kindly towards me when I was a child, and I've never forgotten you." This was easier. "I always thought of you as my angel," she said. "Won't you be my angel now?"

"I can't," said Emma Hamilton. "There's my angelic Queen to be considered. The only way I could do anything would be through her, and, frankly, she wouldn't listen. Not today." At last her tone was kinder. "But give it time," she said, "and maybe I can manage something. When the first shock of it has worn off. You see, what you're forgetting is that coming as he does from your household, Trenche is automatically suspect."

"Dear God," said Helen.

"I said you'd be better at Torre del Greco. And take that stammering child with you. She makes the Queen nervous. As for Mr. Trenche, leave it to me. If I can do anything, for old times' sake I will." The beautiful eyes were kind at last. "That gold crucifix saw me through a bad time," she said. "You were a proper poppet, weren't you, love?"

"I thought you an angel," said Helen again. "You were

so lovely." Another mistake; she knew it the moment the words were out.

"I'm reckoned quite a beauty now," said Lady Hamilton.

Lord Merritt was delighted when Helen suggested that she and Charlotte go to the Villa Rosa at Torre del Greco for a while. "Sound notion," he said. "Funny thing. The King said something about it just the other day. Said he thought the country air would do you good. Kind man."

"I wish you'd speak to him about poor Mr. Trenche," said Helen.

"Not a bit of use," said her husband. "The King don't run affairs; you know it as well as I do. The Queen and Acton see to everything. No use talking to the King. How did you get on with Lady Hamilton?"

"Not well." Helen hoped that the admission would mollify him, for she had felt a disturbing change in his attitude to her since that scene about Trenche. He no longer asked her advice about things, turning instead to Price, who showed every sign of taking Trenche's place. Since she disliked and distrusted Price, she could only deplore his increasing influence over her husband. She had a pretty fair idea, by now, of the kind of scandal that had driven Lord Merritt into marriage, and intensely disliked the idea of leaving him alone with Price.

But it was too late now for such doubts. "Capital notion; Torre del Greco," said her husband. "Why not go today?"

Helen had not seen the Villa Rosa before, having been unwell the day her husband rode out to look at it, and she was taken aback to find the village nestling quite so close under Vesuvius. It seemed a poor enough place, with pigs, chickens, and peasants scratching a lazy living from the rich volcanic soil, and Helen was relieved when the carriage drove straight through the village. But it was disconcerting to reach the villa at last and find it isolated on its own small promontory, with no other human habitation in sight.

Charlotte jumped down from the carriage and stood for a moment thoughtfully surveying the charming miniature classical front of the villa. Then she turned back to hold up a hand for Helen to descend. "One thing's certain," she said. "We must be sure to be in Naples when the baby is due. But of course that won't be till well on in the winter. Plenty of time to think about the arrangements."

If only there were. But there was a good deal just the same, and Helen, who hated lying to Charlotte, even tacitly like this, turned the subject by suggesting that they explore the house. "I know what we'll find," said Charlotte. "Dirt."

In fact, Rose, who had come on ahead with a detachment of servants, had done wonders in getting the place aired and ready, and the two girls were soon sitting in the sun on their own little terrace overlooking a quiet inlet.

"This is restful," said Charlotte. "This is just what we both needed. Peace, quiet, and safety."

Helen felt a queer little pang of anxiety, but kept her voice light as she said, "Yes, it certainly seems quiet enough. But I confess I wish the village was nearer."

"And the volcano farther off." Charlotte looked up to where the usual plume of smoke rose from Vesuvius.

It looked larger from here, Helen thought. Or was it larger? This was no way to be thinking. Anxiety, she knew, was bad for the child she was carrying, the child that had changed her life. For a moment, Helen felt a fierce pang, almost of hatred, for the unborn infant. Inevitably, her thoughts turned to Trenche. "I wonder if there is anything else I can do for him," she said.

"Him? Oh, Trenche. Helen, I really think you'd best not try. Sir William undoubtedly knows all about it by now. He will do what he can. After all, it's his job." Charlotte spoke with the comfortable certainty of someone who has grown up in circles where the right people only had to be approached for the right results to follow.

"I suppose so," Helen sighed. "I actually find myself hoping that Lord Merritt will miss him, now we are away, and be moved to speak to the King." But she had a horrid feeling that Price would prevent this.

"Personally," said Charlotte roundly, "I think prison's the best place for Trenche, and I don't care how long he stays."

"Oh, Charlotte!"

"You don't know what a plague he's been to me since he decided I was the best match he was likely to m . . . m . . . m . . ." It was significant that Charlotte should be stopped by one of her increasingly rare bouts of stammering.

"He never told you that?"

"He didn't need to. But I see he told you. Wanted you to help bring me round his thumb, I suppose. I hope you sent him away with a flea in his ear."

"I did my best." Not much use denying that she and Trenche had had some conversation about this, but the less said about it the better. She changed the subject. "I wonder how Father is."

"And where," said Charlotte, who knew that Helen had not heard a word from Captain Telfair since they parted. They knew from the newspapers that arrived, weeks old from England, that the *Trojan* was still attached to the Mediterranean Fleet, but that was all they knew. "I'm sure no news is good news," Charlotte hurried to say.

"Yes, I think so too." Helen laughed. "I promise you, I won't worry about him. Really, what hard work this childbearing is, and how tedious."

Sir William and Lord Merritt surprised them with a visit, a few days later, on their way to join the royal hunting party, and to Helen's delight Sir William produced a whole packet of newspapers recently arrived from London with which he insisted he was finished. "We mustn't let you find life too tedious out here," he said kindly in his nearest reference to their exile. "I'm glad to see that you both look the better for the country air already."

"Not missing much in Naples either," said Lord Merritt, unusually civil in Sir William's company. "Everyone looking over their shoulders and saying nothing. No pleasure. Glad to get away myself."

"Has anything happened?" Helen asked Sir William.

"A few more arrests." He did not pretend not to understand her, and she was grateful to him. "And no one released. Nor any chance of it for some time, I am afraid.

But rely on me to do my very best, when I can, Lady Merritt."

"Thank you." It was as much or more than she could have hoped for.

"Lady Hamilton spoke to me," he went on. "She has the softest heart in the world, and, I sometimes think, the best understanding. She told me to give you her kindest love, and tell you she too would do what she could, when she could."

"Oh, thank you." Helen was dangerously near to tears. "Tell her—oh, give her my best love, and thanks."

"Interesting about that volcano." Sir William tactfully changed the subject. "Wouldn't you say there was more smoke than usual, Merritt?"

"Can't say I've noticed it much," said Lord Merritt. "Always look the other way myself."

"I've thought so ever since we arrived," said Helen. "Sir William, you don't think there's going to be an eruption, do you?"

"Oh no, nothing of the kind." He was quick to reassure her. "Just a little extra activity; maybe something to do with the spring equinox. There's no accounting for the habits of volcanoes, though I find it one of my greatest pleasures to try to do so."

Helen, who knew that he had written several learned papers on the subject for the Royal Society, of which he was a Fellow, was only partly reassured. "But you do think there is more smoke?" She pressed him.

"A little more than usual, perhaps, but nothing like what there was before the eruptions in sixty-nine and seventy-nine," said Sir William. "I shall make you my assistant, Lady Merritt, and ask you to keep notes of any activity you see. If the plume of smoke were to double itself, or if there were any great expulsion of stones, then I would suggest that you pack up and come back to Naples. But best of all, send for me, and I will come and advise you. There will be no need, I am sure; but I would really be grateful if you would keep daily notes for me. They would be a blessing for my next paper, and you are ideally situated out here."

"I hope 'ideally' turns out to be the word," said Helen

dryly, but Sir William contrived to leave them both very much reassured. After all, he should know what he was talking about. Luckily for their peace of mind, they did not hear him when he turned to Lord Merritt in the carriage as it drove away. "We must watch that volcano," he said. "Frankly, I don't altogether like the look of it. At the first alarm you must be sure and get Lady Merritt back to Naples. I have always thought Torre del Greco a dangerous site, and am only sorry I did not have the chance to advise you before you took that house. Though it's charming, of course," said the old diplomat, "quite charming."

"Country air. Just the thing. But could move them back, if you think so."

"Oh, no need for that," said Sir William, the diplomat again prevailing. "I really think the ladies are better out of Naples for a while. And if Lady Merritt sends me out weekly bulletins I asked for, I shall have plenty of warning if there should be trouble."

"Good." Lord Merritt was delighted to put the whole vexatious business out of his mind. He did not admit, even to himself, what a relief he found it to be back once more in his comfortable bachelor existence, with Price as an admirable substitute for Trenche. He would certainly do nothing unnecessary to hurry the two girls' return, though naturally he would not dream of leaving them exposed to danger.

In fact, Helen was soon able to convince herself that there was no cause for anxiety. Had she and Sir William imagined that extra large plume of smoke? Keeping a meticulous daily journal for him, she found herself noting, every day, the same occasional clouds shaped like little trees. The weather was calm and dry, and she felt wonderfully placid. Since the moment when she had felt the burden she carried stir to life inside her, everything had been changed. Now she knew that she had been right in what she had done. Whatever happened to her, the child must come first. She was sitting on the terrace overlooking the inlet one fine June morning when Charlotte joined her with a hurriedly opened note in her hand. "What's the matter?" Helen asked. "Not bad news from Naples?"

"Not exactly." But Charlotte was obviously in a state of suppressed emotion. "It's—oh, Helen, could you possibly manage without me for a couple of days?"

"Without you? What in the world do you mean? What's happened? Who's that from?"

Charlotte, who had been white, flushed crimson. "It's —it's Captain Forbes." She said it as if it explained everything.

"Captain?" asked Helen. And then, her amazement mounting, "You correspond with him?"

"Never before. Believe me, Helen. But"—her colour was higher than ever—"he did say something, just before we left the *Trojan*. If ever his prospects improved, he said . . . Helen, forgive me for not telling you, but it seemed so uncertain . . . "

"And now he's a captain?"

"Yes, he was made after the evacuation of Toulon. You must have missed it in the *Gazette*. He went home with dispatches . . . Not good news, of course, but his part in it was gallant. He's got his own command now, the smallest ship in the fleet, he says, and—he's in Naples for two days."

"He should come here." But Helen knew it for impossible.

"He can't leave his command. He writes that Lady Hamilton invites me to stay. He begs me to come. Helen, you'd have Rose?"

"And no carriage," said Helen.

"Oh." Charlotte had not thought of this. "But I'll send it back directly. Lady Hamilton will send me home in one of hers when . . . when he's gone."

Her tone more than her words told Helen how important this was to her. She looked up at the sky. "Plenty of time for you to drive in today," she said. "And if you send the carriage back first thing in the morning . . . "

Charlotte bent swiftly to kiss her. "Bless you . . . I'll never forget . . . He's ordered to the Channel Station. Anything may happen. We might never meet again. But at least I'll have had this."

"Yes." Helen was beginning to think that the "something" Captain Forbes had said must have been something indeed. "You're sure?" she felt she must ask it. "I mean—going in like this—it's as good as a declaration."

"That's what I want," said Charlotte simply. "And," she looked down at the note in her hand and flushed again, "so does he."

"Then I'm so happy for you." Helen stood up to return the kiss warmly. "I always liked Mr. Forbes. But, Charlotte, you won't do anything rash, will you?"

"You mean m . . . m . . . m . . ." It was the first time Charlotte had stammered in the whole conversation. Then, surprisingly, she laughed. "You're a fine one to talk, Helen, but no, I promise I won't marry him on the spot." Her face clouded. "He's got nothing but his profession. If peace should come, my mother's influence might be all important. We can't afford to alienate her. His family's as good as ours." Proudly. "As if I cared."

"But your mother will."

"Yes. I thought I'd give him a letter for her. In case he gets sent home . . . And write myself, of course. And, Helen, will you?"

"Yes, dear, of course I will. When you get back, we'll think it out together." Odd to realise that as Lady Merritt she had, inevitably, an influence with Mrs. Standish that she could never have dreamed of as Helen Telfair. If Mrs. Standish had forgiven her for being Lady Merritt. There had been no mail from England since the news of her marriage, so she had still no idea of how it had been received. But the air was getting cooler. "You'd best pack, love, and be off. I expect he's waiting for you at Lady Hamilton's."

"That's what he says. Oh, Helen, I'm so happy."

"And I'm so happy for you." But alone on the terrace, after Charlotte had gone glowing and sparkling off in the carriage, it was hard to be happy for herself.

It was very strange to be alone at Torre del Greco. What had been peace and quietness in Charlotte's company was now plain, bleak loneliness, and she actually found herself regretting that in the end she had insisted on Charlotte's taking Rose with her. It had seemed essential at the time. Mrs. Standish would be angry enough over the engagement to Forbes. It must at least be entered into

9

with the fullest possibly ceremony. Besides, she herself would not altogether have liked the idea of Charlotte's driving into Naples with only Italian servants.

But she found she did not much like being alone at Torre del Greco with them either. Was she imagining things, or was there a feeling of tension in the house tonight? Certainly her light supper was served with unusual promptness, and she had hardly risen from the table when she heard the group of servants from the village saying good night to the couple who slept in. All imagination, of course. Very likely there was some local celebration in the village, one of those saint's days she had never heard of, and they were eager to be off to it. But their voices, dying away through the trees, sounded subdued.

Maria, the cook, came in to ask if there were any further orders, and Helen found herself on the verge of some foolish question, but bit it back. "I shall go to bed early," she said instead. "Light the lamp upstairs, Maria, and then that will be all."

Bed was what she had wanted. It had been a long day and it was no use pretending that she did not get extra tired these days. Her mind kept harking back to Charlotte and Mr. Forbes—Captain Forbes now, she reminded herself. Strange to think that there had been times in Naples when she had thought Scroope showed signs of caring for Charlotte, had actually suffered, and been ashamed of, pangs of jealousy on that account. Horrible. She blew out the lamp and made herself lie quiet in bed, courting sleep, trying to forget everything but the child she carried. Suddenly, she was sitting up, sweating with fright. The whole bed had moved under her. Not imagination, but earthquake, which, she knew, was often the herald of an eruption. And now a red glow lit up the ceiling. She fumbled her way out of bed and to the window. Yes, it was indeed Vesuvius, its plume of smoke turned to fire, and the whole landscape strangely illuminated. As she watched, a fountain of fire and one vast fireball shot out of the central cone. The noise was as horrifying as the flames and brought with it shivering memories of the *Trojan*'s gunfire that disastrous day in December. But this was no time for wretched memory: she must decide what to do.

What could she do? She had no carriage, not even a horse, nor was there any to be had in the village. She had been mad to let Charlotte go, but there it was. Nothing for it but to say a childish prayer, get the best night's sleep she could, and wait for rescue in the morning. Would the servants come back, she wondered. No doubt they had read the signs early in the day; hence their hurry to get home. But the village was nearer the volcano than the villa. And, besides, it was to the villa that rescue would come. She fought down the temptation to go and make sure that Maria and her husband were safe in their quarters at the back of the house. To do so would only add to their terror, and very likely precipitate a flight that might be avoided.

There was absolutely nothing she could do. She got back into bed, thought, or imagined, that the light had dwindled, and at last, fitfully, slept. Waking, her first anxious thought was for the volcano. Hurrying to the window, she was relieved to see no flame. The whole top of Vesuvius was hidden by thick mist, and she told herself that she must write a note to Sir William about this. It was a strange morning. The sun had a curious dark reddish look, doubtless due to the mist, and there was an unusual chill in the air.

She wrapped herself in the swansdown negligee her husband had bought her, and called down for Maria, and breakfast.

No reassurance here. Maria appeared with stale rolls, watery coffee, and the news that none of the other servants had returned from the village. "The wells have dried up," she broke out with it at last, "and the great fountain hardly flows. They will stay home today and look after their own. When the carriage comes back, the signora had best make haste to Naples."

But the carriage did not come back. All that day, the fifteenth of June, Helen watched and waited and tried to make herself stay calm for her child's sake. Inevitably, as time passed, anxiety for Charlotte was added to that for herself. Had some disaster struck her on the way into Naples? It was all too easy to imagine an attack by panic-stricken peasants; the invaluable horses carried off; and Charlotte . . . what might not have happened to Charlotte?

From time to time, the house shook with a fresh earthquake, and Helen tried to remember what Sir William had told her about these. Were they an alternative to an eruption, or its precursors? Maria, bringing a plate of cold spaghetti for her lunch, reported that an immense stone had fallen through the roof of one of the stables, and followed up this news with an ultimatum. "Angelo says we must go, signora. His mother is alone in the village. The church bells have been ringing all day. He says when you have eaten, we go. Will you come, or wait for the carriage here? Our house is on the other side of the village, away from the carriage road."

"How far?"

"Half an hour. Maybe more for the signora. The path from the village is steep and not easy."

Helen remembered the rough road from village to villa and her heart sank. If the path was worse than that . . . Besides, she was surely safest here, where her husband would look for her.

And if Charlotte had not reached Naples, for whatever reason, she must be here so that no time would be lost in sending out search parties for her. "I shall stay here, Maria," she said. "Is there food in the house?"

"*Si, si,*" Maria launched into a long catalogue, growing more unintelligible by the moment as her dialect broadened with fright and hurry.

Impossible to eat the unappetising spaghetti, with the old woman standing over her, jabbering. Helen pushed away the plate. "Go now, you and your husband," she said. "I will eat this later. Just now I feel sick." It was true enough; the nausea that had passed with the third month had returned with a vengeance.

"*Si,*" Maria nodded her head vehemently. "For the bambino's sake it is best the signora stay here . . . Who knows, a stumble on the rough path to my mother's house . . . " She gasped with fright as a new tremor shook the house. Helen, looking beyond her to the window, saw the darkening sky rent with what looked like lightning.

"You'd best go at once," she said. "Tell the head man in your village, as you go through, that I am here."

"*Si, si.*" But Helen thought that in her eagerness to get away the woman would have promised anything. She made a point of going out to the servants' quarters to say good-bye to Angelo and reiterate her request to him, but got the same eager, unconvincing reply.

As they hurried away up the rough road to the village, Helen wondered if she had added one more to her chapter of mistakes. But what else could she have done? Watching the ruthless pace that Angelo set, with Maria stumbling after him, she knew that in her condition she could not possibly have kept up with them, and knew, too, that they would not have waited for her. Better, surely, to be here, in her own house, than out there, left behind, alone in the rapidly gathering darkness. The lightning had stopped for the moment, and the whole sky was dominated by the huge, mushroom-shaped cloud that hung over Vesuvius.

Shadows crept out from the corner of the room. Soon it would be dark indeed. She made herself go out to the servants' quarters and found, as she had expected, that nothing had been done about replacing the working candles she and Charlotte used. For a horrible moment, she thought the supply had been exhausted, then remembered that Rose, exclaiming over the predatory habits of Italian servants, had locked up an invaluable pound of the best candles in a cupboard. And, looking for it, she now realised that something Angelo had kept hidden under his ragged cloak must have been the windproof candle-lantern that Sir William had given her, but at least an old-fashioned substitute hung from a hook on the wall. If she needed to move around in the dark, this would have to do. But much better not. It was getting darker all the time. No more hope of rescue today. And now, at last, she was hungry. She would eat something, take a book, tinderbox, and a branch of candles to bed with her, and hope for the best. Wryly she remembered all those times on the *Trojan* when she had thought she would give anything to be alone; thought too, suddenly, of something else.

It was something Maria had said. The risk to the "bambino" of the rough walk to her mother-in-law's house. Here, if she only survived, was her reason, ready-made, for what she must call a premature birth. It was June now, and only she and her husband knew that the child was due to be born in September. And if she did not survive, nothing would matter at all. It was curiously steadying to think like this, and she turned with a will to the question of food. More than anything, she longed for some of Maria's good hot soup. Surely that was one of the words she had understood in that excited catalogue of what was available? But in the kitchen, cold disappointment awaited her. She should have realised what that dreary spaghetti meant. Maria had let the kitchen fire go out.

It was completely the last straw. Helen found herself, a while later, sitting on a stool, her head in her hands, at the dirty kitchen table. It was very nearly dark now, or would have been if a fresh fireball from the volcano had not cast its sudden light through the room. It lit up the earthenware bread bin in the corner, and she made herself stand up and feel her way over there in the renewed darkness. The bread felt hard, but did not smell bad; she wondered about cheese, and cursed herself hungrily for those uncounted moments of despair in which she had let full darkness creep up on her. She could light the lantern and take it out into the cold larder. There might even be butter. Something rustled against her skirts. A rat? For a horrible moment she was back in the stinking cable tier of the *Trojan*. Then, reason reasserting itself, she realised that it was too small for a rat. Only a cockroach. She leaned forward, reaching for the tinderbox, and lit one of the branch of candlesticks that she had luckily put down on the kitchen table as she collapsed. It was to see the flagged floor alive with scurrying roaches.

She would not faint. She would not be sick. She made herself sit for a moment, her hands flat and firm on the table top, her feet gathered close under her, away from that horrible army of beetles. Then, slowly and carefully, she picked up the tinderbox and put it in the unfashionably useful pocket of her dress. The bread went under her arm. Her hand shook as she picked up the heavy candlestick. Did it shake too much? Could she safely carry her one, precious lighted candle upstairs? Suppose she were to trip over her own skirts? She moved the candlestick to her left hand, tucked the bread more firmly under that arm, lifted her skirts with the other hand, took a deep breath, and rose.

The light had caused a wave of movement in the surrounding army of beetles; her rising caused another. Just for a moment the path to the kitchen door was clear, and she walked across it, candle in hand, the rustle of the cockroaches louder in her ears even than the rumble of the volcano.

Safe (if safe was the word) at last in her bedroom, she lit all the other candles, realised that she had left *Evelina* downstairs, and knew that there was no question of going back for it . . . A new fireball lit up the room; the candles sickly pale in contrast. The bread lay, grey-brown and unappetising, on the table by the bed. She should have brought up a glass of wine to help it down. But how could she have? And nothing would take her downstairs again to that sea of cockroaches. Besides, she could not eat; not now. Exhaustion overwhelmed her. If she was to die, why not die in her sleep?

And if she was to live, so too must the child she carried. She stood up shakily, like an old woman, and made herself undress, take off the tight corsets that combined with her fashionable high-waisted gown to conceal her advanced stage of pregnancy, and put on the floating befrilled nightgown that Lord Merritt had bought for her in the first flush of their marriage. And at last, creeping gratefully into the chill of her bed, she thought how strange to find her first consideration always the child. Trenche's child.

Chapter 12

ALL night, Vesuvius thundered, but Helen slept the sleep of exhaustion. When she woke at last, it was to a new sound, a crackling. Fire?

Getting fast but shakily out of bed, she had to steady herself by a table against wave after wave of dizziness. The light was strangely dim this morning; the crackling seemed louder than ever. She tottered over to the window and looked out along the ridge of promontory towards the village and the volcano. Nothing but a pall of smoke, and, horribly, the smell of burning. The air was hot, and she did not stop to put on a negligée before hurrying across the hall to look out of the window of Charlotte's room, which faced up the little valley that ended in their inlet of the sea.

Now she was going to faint. The valley held a stream of molten lava that moved slowly but relentlessly down towards the water. As she watched, horror-struck, a giant hiss and a cloud of steam told her that the two had met. Above the level of the lava, trees, ignited by its heat, burned fiercely. She thought with horror of the village, higher up the hillside. Had its inhabitants seen their danger in time?

And what of her own? Moving, stiff with fear, to the window on the north side of the house, she saw that here too the lava was almost down to sea level. She was isolated by the burning flood. And all the time, a fusillade of molten rocks from the volcano splashed and sizzled into the water, where it was not yet heated by the influx of lava. If there had been a chance still of escape by land, she did not think she would have dared take it. Nothing for it but to stay where she was, and thank God that the Villa Rosa was built of marble with a tiled roof.

But the outhouses where the servants kept hens, goats, and, she suspected, a forbidden pig, were wooden. They lay beyond the servants' quarters. She could not let the unfortunate animals burn to death in their sheds. She would go first and make sure that all was well there, then make herself eat something, and take stock of her position. Surely, now that the lava had reached the sea, its level would not rise much more? But might not she, like the animals, burn to death in her marble oven?

She would not think about it, nor let herself admit that the air was hotter than ever. She went down through the kitchen, where not a cockroach stirred this morning, and out down the marble-roofed arcade that divided the servants' quarters from the garden. A stone, landing with a crash on the roof, gave her the speed of terror. The outbuildings were not alight yet, but screams from the animals showed that they knew their danger. She opened the rude latch of the henhouse, watched its occupants flutter and screech their way into the surrounding bushes, and wondered as they went whether she had not saved them from one death merely to condemn them to another, more lingering one.

The goats were in the next shed, baa-ing with fright, and when she opened their door they headed straight down towards the tip of the promontory. Would they perhaps plunge into the sea if all else failed? She had hoped against hope that she had merely imagined the illicit pig, but there was no mistaking its anguished squeals. She had never liked pigs, since she had been knocked down by a bad-tempered sow as a child, but she could not leave this one to its fate. Standing well back, she pushed clear the stick that held the door closed, and watched the immense beast force its way through, and head, like the goats, straight down the spine of the promontory. Should she follow them? Were they perhaps wiser than she? But a flaming stone falling on the henhouse settled the question for her. If it had hit her, she would be dead now. She got herself quickly back into the shelter of the marble arcade and so to the house.

Had she really meant to eat something? What did one do when facing death? It would be sensible, she thought, to get dressed, just in case of some miraculous rescue, but even as she thought this, she found that she had collapsed, shaking with reaction, on the chaise longue in the salon. What she could do, she had done. Now there was nothing for it but to wait, and for the moment she knew that she simply had not the strength to get herself upstairs to her room. Besides, reason came to fortify exhaustion: she was obviously safer down here on the ground floor.

Time ebbed and flowed around her. Sometimes the fusillade of rocks seemed to slacken, but there was no question but that the air got steadily hotter. It began to feel breathless in the house, and she longed more than anything for a drink of cold water. Would the well be boiling too? She found she had not even the strength to go and find out.

She ought to eat something, for the child's sake if not for her own, but was it really worth the effort if they were both going to be dead so soon? She half rose, then thought better of it and sank back on the chaise longue. Idly, she wondered about her husband, about Charlotte. What could have happened? But it was hard now even to worry about Charlotte. Was death really so selfish? It was almost pleasant to feel herself drifting off into a kind of half-consciousness, part exhaustion, part faintness . . . Nothing more she could do . . . And all those plans of hers had come to this. Strange to remember a bright morning, one autumn at Up Harting, when the sun sparkled on the dew and she had turned impulsively to Miss Tillingdon: "I am going to do something—to be something before I die," she had said. And Miss Tillingdon, suffering, she remembered, from one of the chills that plagued her, had wrapped herself more closely in her faded pelisse and breathed a warning. "Oh, Helen, don't be so certain . . . Helen . . ."

"Helen!" But it was another voice now, a real one. "Helen!" Nearer now. "Are you there?"

Charles Scroope. She had known it on the first syllable. Slowly, shakily, she got to her feet, the loose folds of her nightgown billowing around her. "Yes," she called. "Charles! Here!"

His face was black with smoke, and white dust lay like powder on his hair. Entering the room, he brought a smell of singeing with him, but neither of them noticed it. "Thank God," he said.

"You came." She hesitated towards him, and would never be sure whether she fell into his arms, or they came out to find her. Either way, it felt like home, like safety. For a moment she thought she felt his lips, lightly on her hair, then he had picked her up and deposited her firmly on the chaise longue.

"Of course I came." He was on the floor beside her, her hand in his. "As soon as I got Charlotte's message."

"Charlotte? She's safe? Thank God."

"Delayed." He explained. "In the panic. By the time she reached Naples, Lord Merritt had gone with Sir William to Posilipo. Sir William thought it was safer there." Scorn burned in his voice. "It seems to have occurred to no one that you might not be entirely safe out here. Well," with an attempt at fairness, "Sir William thought the main threat to Naples itself. And so did the Neapolitans. You should have seen the panic in the city—and out of it. Most families slept in the fields last night, and the night before, come to that. They must be blessing St. Januarius this morning that the disaster has struck here."

"How bad is it?" She made herself ask it.

"As bad as possible. The village has gone. There's no way through by road." And then, quick to sense her reaction, "It could be much worse. Most of them escaped in time."

"I hope Angelo got his mother out," she said.

"Angelo?"

"The cook's husband. They left last night."

"Yes, they're safe. They told me you were here. Alone." Furiously. "But at least Angelo persuaded his cousin to bring me round by boat."

"By boat?" So far, she had simply accepted his presence as the miracle it was. Now she began to understand.

"Yes. They're waiting down by the point. The water's too hot in the inlet. I'm afraid it might melt the pitch between the planks. Besides, they're under the shelter of a rock. They didn't much fancy running the gauntlet to get here."

She had by now identified the smell of singeing. It came from the left sleeve of his uniform, and she saw that he held that arm awkwardly. "You're hurt?"

"A trifle. But I think we'd best wait a while before we try to get down to the boat. If you think you can manage it. It's rough going, I'm afraid."

"I shall have to manage." Extraordinary to find herself reading his thoughts. Unspoken between them was his inevitable awareness of her condition. She had seen his one quick glance, had wondered whether this was more than she could bear, and tried and failed to think of something light and easy to say. She should have dressed, she thought lazily, and then, what did it matter? What did anything?

"When did you last eat?" His abrupt question brought her out of the dizzy fit.

"I'm not sure . . . Maria brought me some spaghetti . . . But that was yesterday. They'd let the stove go out." She was ashamed now of her own uselessness.

"I thought so. Wait here while I forage." He disappeared, to return almost at once with a glass of madeira. "Drink it slowly," he advised. "It will give you the strength to eat. Your kitchen's a scandal." He was being determinedly matter-of-fact. "If I had your cook on board, he'd be cleaning the heads."

"There are cockroaches." She could speak of it now. "That's why I gave up last night. Oceans of them."

"Bound to be." His voice came from farther off. "Food in a minute." He returned in a surprisingly short time with a wickerwork tray, which he carried awkwardly, taking as much of the weight as possible with his right hand. "Riches," he said before she could comment on this. "The servants' hoard. I don't wonder you couldn't find it in the dark. But what a blessing they forgot it."

"They took my lantern," she said, as he poured chianti from a flask.

"Better eat something first." There was heavily smoked ham, almost fresh bread, and goat's milk cheese, and she thought it the best food she had ever tasted. "That's better." He too had eaten hungrily, and she wondered if his last meal had been any more recent than hers. He got up and moved over to the window. "The dust's thicker than ever; and the stones fall as fast. I wish I knew more about volcanoes." He had come to a decision just the same. "We'll give it half an hour. Then we must go, whatever happens. How long will it take you to dress?"

Thank God those rigorous corsets laced up the front. "Ten minutes." She looked down, surprised now at her own lack of embarrassment, at the grimy frills of her nightgown. "I had to let the animals out," she said, as if that explained everything.

"Yes." He poured her a careful half glass more wine. "Drink that, rest a little, then change into your heaviest clothes and we'll go."

"Heaviest?" It was now almost intolerably hot in the room.

"Muslin might catch fire," he said impatiently, and then, on the same wave of anger, "Helen, I have to know. I've torn myself to pieces wondering. Why did you do it?" And then, quickly. "Oh, God, I know I've no right to ask, except the right of one who has always loved you. I told you, remember, that day at Wimbledon, that I was always yours. It was true, Helen. Do you remember?" And then, bitterly, "Did you remember, when you accepted that idiot? Helen, how could you do it?"

She looked down at herself, then across, very straight, at him. "Do you not see that I had no choice?"

"Dear God." If it only confirmed what he had suspected, it still struck him white. "Helen, you of all people. I can't believe it."

"No?" Suddenly all the bitter loneliness of it rose like bile in her throat. "Nor could I for a long time. But you must see that the child had to come first."

"Whose child?" There it was, the inevitable first question, and more to follow.

She rose unsteadily to her feet. "That I am not going to tell you," she said. "Nor anything else. Believe what you will of me but, Charles, for the child's sake, for mine, for the old days, keep my secret."

"You insult me." But the rage had gone out of him. "Of course I'll keep it. But Helen—when? Surely that you can answer?"

"September, God help me."

"And your marriage in February. Helen, I still can't believe it. Lord Merritt! Did he get you drunk? Force you?"

A great wave of bitter relief flooded through her. So that was what he believed. Well, let him. Best so, however intolerable. "I told you I would say no more." She moved shakily away from him towards the door, "I must dress, and we must go, and neither of us will ever speak of this again. Please, Charles?" When had she started using his first name?

"Never." It came out with the force of an explosion. "And for your sake, Helen, I'll never trust another woman."

"Thank you." It was almost a relief to meet anger with anger. But upstairs there was a moment when she was tempted just to fall on the unmade bed and let herself die there. She did not do it. Both Charles and the child would die with her . . . and there were the unknown boatmen down at the point. Once again, she felt the responsibility of life thrust upon her.

Mercifully, she was used to dressing herself, since she had not dared trust Rose with her secret. It hardly took her the ten minutes she had promised, and she was doing up the top button of a heavy serge riding habit when she heard Charles's voice at the bottom of the stairs. "Helen! I think the stones are fewer. Are you nearly ready?" Was there a hint of apology in his voice?

No time to think like this. She picked up a tricorne riding hat and leather gloves and went steadily down to join him. "Yes, I'm ready. Shall we go?" There was to be, her tone said, no more talk between them.

"Yes." He accepted it. "I really think we have a chance now. And"—he had given her one of his quick comprehensive glances—"I'm glad you're dressed for it."

"And you've no gloves." She reached into a drawer where Lord Merritt kept the heavy hand-knit string ones he used for fishing. "Here."

"Thank you." It was intolerable that after what had passed between them his touch should still send that shiver of fire through her. But they would have fire enough shortly. Might it not, after all, be best to die now, here, together? "Let's go," she said.

The dark sky was lit from time to time by livid flashes of lightning. Stones still fell, but they were smaller now and possibly less hot. The sheds behind the house were blazing merrily and so were trees here and there down the promontory where a particularly hot stone had fallen. And, from the inlets on either side, steam was beginning to rise. "No time to linger." Charles took her arm to guide her down the rough path.

"It's too narrow. I'll be better on my own." She dared not let herself submit to that firm yet gentle guidance. If she did, if she let the current run free between them, she would sob out her whole story before they got to the boat.

"As you will." His tone was cold as he dropped back to walk behind her.

After that, nothing mattered. If a crevasse had opened at her feet, she thought she would have fallen into it gladly. If one of the rocks that fell around them had hit her, she would have been thankful, so long as it had done her business at once. But all the time she was thinking this, her feet, more hopeful than she, were finding their careful way along the path that got progressively more difficult as it neared the point. She and Charlotte had never come this far, and she did in fact have to accept a helping hand from Charles, who went ahead as the path plunged steeply downwards from rock to rock towards the little sheltered cove where the boat was waiting. But by now she was beyond feeling even anguish at his touch. She simply moved behind him like an automaton, putting her feet where he told her to, sitting down from time to time on warm rock to ease her way down from one level to the next.

And now, suddenly, there were shouts from below. The boatmen had seen them coming and were hailing her determined progress with cries of admiration. No wife or daughter of theirs would ever have dealt with the precipitous descent. More important, they were hurrying to push their boat out into water that here, mercifully, did not steam. She was shaking in every limb when they reached the tiny, pebbled beach. "Thank you." She turned to Charles.

And, "Well done," said he, helping her into the boat. Did the boatmen speak English? There was so much that she would have liked to say, and nothing that she dared, or could. Charles had settled beside her on a rough plank below which water showed. "It's nothing," he said. "She sprang a little, coming." He was bailing already with an earthenware mug as he spoke.

"I'll help." The men were pulling strongly at the oars, glad to get away from the burning shore.

"You'll rest. Besides," he smiled momentarily, the old smile, "there's only one mug."

The boat ride, if uncomfortable, was mercifully short, merely taking them a little way up the coast to the next harbour. Here, they found one of Scroope's lieutenants standing, pistols in hand, beside a hired carriage. "Lucky you left me, sir." He saluted. "It's been hard work to hold them—and repel boarders."

"Yes. Thank you." Scroope looked doubtfully at Helen's wet skirts. "I wish you could change."

"But I can't."

"There's a rug in the carriage," said the lieutenant. He was still holding the pistols on the little crowd of wretched refugees from Torre del Greco. "Best waste no time, sir."

"No." Scroope helped Helen into the surprisingly roomy carriage.

She paused for a moment on the step. "It's so large. Could we not take someone?" And then, "Angelo!"

He was pushing his way towards them through the crowd. "It's not for me," he said. "We'll manage, Maria and I, but my mother. She's worn out." She was beside him; a little wrinkled walnut of a woman in shabby black.

"The carriage holds four," said Helen. "Please—" she had nearly called him Charles in front of his officer.

"Yes." She recognised the decisiveness that must have carried him through many a crisis at sea. "It would be wicked not to use the place." And then in Italian to Angelo:

144

"In with her then, quick, and help my man keep the others back, or we'll none of us get away. But where do we take her?"

"She is in the hands of God," said Angelo.

"I'll look after her." Helen too spoke in Italian as they helped the old woman into the carriage. Charles and the lieutenant followed quickly; the door was shut, the relieved postillions cracked their whips, and the crowd, impressed by the show of good feeling, parted before them.

It was a strange enough ride. The old lady, who had probably never ridden in a carriage before, sat shaking with exhaustion and fright, telling her beads over and over. The lieutenant, obviously very much in awe of his captain, sat beside her, holding her up when she began to slide downwards on the seat. And Helen, who had thought this would be a chance to make things at least a little easier with Charles, recognised the impossibility of saying anything, propped herself in her corner, and inevitably slept. Waking at last to a sense of immense peace and well-being, she found herself safely propped in Charles's good arm. Across the carriage, the young lieutenant was doing the same kind office for the old lady, an expression of comic embarrassment on his face. Helen, who had only half opened her eyes, decided to close them again.

But she was awake when the sound of church bells, ringing now in thanksgiving, told her that they were nearing Naples. She made a pretence of coming to herself, moved quietly away from that blessed, encircling arm, and spoke. "Thank you." What more, what less could she say?

"You feel better, I hope." Charles's voice was formal, reminding her of the young officer across the way, who was still uncomfortably supporting his charge.

"Much. I can manage now." She intended to tell him a great deal in this simple sentence, and was almost sure that he understood.

"But what do we do with the old lady?" asked Charles.

"Bring her home with me," she said, and then hated that use of the word, to him. "I said I'd look after her," she went on determinedly, "and I will."

10

So when they drove up to the house Lord Merritt insisted on calling a "palazza," it was the lieutenant who got out first, with the semiconscious old lady in his arms. Helen had passionately hoped that her husband would still be at Posilipo, and she would have time to rest and recover herself a little before she faced him with the knowledge between them of how he had failed her. But there he was, coming out onto the tiny carriage sweep, stopping to gaze with something like disgust at the lieutenant's burden. Helen and Charles exchanged one long, speaking look that seemed to her to say everything and nothing, then he too had jumped lightly down and was holding up his hand to her.

She had not realised what she looked like until she saw her husband's expression. But after all, if Charles's face was black with smoke, and his clothes and hair white with dust, so too were hers. Lord Merritt's horrified expression made everything suddenly much easier. "Don't touch me, dear." With a great effort she let go of Charles's hand and stood unaided. "I'm filthy beyond words, and tired beyond anything. A hot bath, and I will exchange my adventures for yours. I am delighted to see you safe," she added.

"And I you." His tone was strange. "But what in the world is this?" His gesture indicated the old woman, practically a bundle of rags in the lieutenant's arms.

"Angelo's mother. You remember Angelo? You hired him yourself for the Villa Rosa. He begged me to bring her. The servants will look after her, I am sure."

"Begged you to bring her?" Querulously. "This old bag of bones?"

"Because the village of Torre del Greco does not exist any more." She tried to keep the impatience out of her voice. "And because if we had not taken up a fourth in the carriage, we might have been mobbed."

"Can't understand a word!" His tone was more irritable than ever. "Servants enough already, eating us out of house and home."

"This is not a servant," she said. "This is the man who fell by the wayside." And then, aware that once again he

146

had totally failed to understand her, she did the only possible thing. She swayed on her feet, and it was all too easy to do it. The disconcerting thing (yet how pleasant) was that it was Charles, not her husband, who caught her. And then, blessedly, she heard Charlotte's voice, raised in quick question.

"Not hurt." Charles Scroope's arms were gently around her. "Just exhausted. If I could take her straight to her room?"

"Of course." Charlotte was in control. "This way."

But there was one more thing she must do. She opened reluctant eyes. "Dear Charlotte . . . The old lady . . . She's Angelo's mother."

"Lot of nonsense," said Lord Merritt, and Helen let consciousness go.

She lay, somewhere between sleeping and waking, for several days, submitting to the ministrations of Charlotte and Rose, and someone else she could not in her half-conscious state identify. At last, waking with a clearer head and aware that the tide of fatigue had ebbed a little, she smelled coffee, opened her eyes, and recognised Angelo's mother sitting by the bed, cup in hand.

"Va bene," said the old lady. "The signora is better. I said it would be so. And no need for doctors either." She dipped a roll in the coffee and fed Helen expertly as she might have a child.

"No doctor?" Helen was puzzled for a moment.

"No," said the old lady in her quick, peasant Italian. "I told the other signora it was best not. Am I not, I, Angelina, doctor and nurse in my own village—and midwife too." Here was the heart of the matter. "I thought from what Maria told me that all was not quite right. You are best without a doctor. You saved me, signora; I will save your good name, if I can." And then, deftly inserting another morsel of delicious bread and coffee. "That's right. Cry quietly; it will do you good; then sleep and wake better. There is plenty of time to think what we will do."

"Who else knows?"

"The old woman shrugged. "I think, no one. English young ladies know nothing of these matters. And my lord has been away since the day after you returned."

"Oh." Helen digested this for a moment. Then, "He knows," she told this surprising new ally.

"That is good. Then we shall do well enough. And here, in good hour, comes the signora." She rose to her feet, courteously but not at all like a servant, and handed the half-empty bowl to Charlotte. "I told you all it needed was time and my herbs. See; she is herself again."

"Oh, thank God." Charlotte looked drawn and anxious. "I've been so worried about you, Helen." She took the bowl and continued to feed her, and Helen realised that this must have been going on when she was half-conscious. "But all the doctors are worked to death since the eruption, and Angelina seemed sure she knew what she was doing. That's an extraordinary woman." Angelina had quietly vanished. "She was quite fierce when I said yesterday that I thought we really should get a doctor. We agreed in the end that we would give it one more day, and, thank God, here you are."

"How long?" asked Helen.

"Five days. It's felt like an eternity. If you'd not recovered I'd never have forgiven myself."

"Not your fault," said Helen. "How were you to know that the volcano was going to erupt?" And then, as it all came back to her, "But, Charlotte, Captain Forbes . . . Did you see him?"

Hot colour flooded Charlotte's face, and she held out her left hand to show a slim, old-fashioned ring on her engagement finger. "His mother's. I got here just in time," she said. "He was under orders to sail, but awaiting dispatches from Sir William to Admiral Hood. Helen, I'm so happy. That's just why I've felt so terrible about you. To have sacrificed you to my own happiness . . . I don't know what I'd have done."

"Well," said Helen bracingly, "isn't it lucky the question doesn't arise. But, seriously, Charlotte, I'm delighted for you. I always liked Captain Forbes."

"Thank you." She smiled a little tremulously. "So did I."

"And what are your plans? Selfishly, I hope I'm not going to lose you."

"No plans for the moment," said Charlotte. "Captain

Forbes does not approve of women on board ship, and after our experiences I confess I am inclined to think he is right."

"In wartime certainly," said Helen. "When peace comes, it might be another matter. But that seems far enough off, I'm afraid. Tell me," she made it casual, "talking of husbands, where precisely is Lord Merritt?"

Charlotte coloured again, but this time less happily.

"He's at Caserta with the Court," she said. "He left the day after you came back. He said there was no use his dangling about here while you were ill. Helen, I'm afraid he did not much fancy your being rescued like that."

"He would have preferred me to burn to death?" asked Helen dryly. And then, "Well, it's understandable enough. One has to see that he did not cut a very gallant figure."

"No," said Charlotte. "To tell you the truth, Helen, I was relieved when Captain Scroope was ordered away. That first day, with everyone calling to congratulate Lord Merritt on your miraculous rescue and talking about gallant sailors and I don't know what, I was a little afraid of what he might do. You can understand that he didn't much like it. And after all," fairly, "everyone did think that the threat was to Naples."

"Yes. I'm tired, Charlotte dear. I think I'll sleep a little more." And, alone at last, she lay with her face in the pillow and silent tears trickling down her cheeks. Charles Scroope had sailed away, and she would never be able to thank him.

Lord Merritt came back a week later, with Price, as always, in attendance. Helen, watching them ride up to the house side by side, recognised the change in their relationship that she had feared. They were talking like friends, not master and man. But when she went into the hall to greet her husband, she found Price so completely back in his unobtrusive role of servant that she thought she must have been imagining things. It was easy to do, in her present state.

"There you are." Lord Merritt did not ask how she was. "Came for some clothes. Got a villa. Caserta. Handy for the hunting."

"How very pleasant," said Helen. "When do we leave?"

"Not we." Lord Merritt pouted. "Don't understand. Women! Never do. Sir William's ill."

"I beg your pardon?" For once, Helen did find it impossible to understand her husband's inarticulate speech.

Price took a respectful step forward. "If you'll excuse me, my lady, I think my lord would say that it is the merest hunting box he has taken. Not at all suitable . . ." He paused for a significant moment and she felt, for the first time, that he disliked her as much as she did him.

"That's it." Lord Merritt took up the tale. "Hamilton's ill. Someone's got to keep the King company. Mere shooting box. Room for Price and me."

"I see." Helen saw more than she liked. Price must have coached her husband in what he was to say. It implied a degree of ascendancy that Trenche had never attained. Price had used her absence in Torre del Greco to some purpose. And there was nothing she could do about it. "I'm so sorry about Sir William," she said now.

"Nothing serious," said Lord Merritt. "Old man. Lady Hamilton most devoted. Queen sends every day. Lot of fuss."

The two men did not even stay for a meal, and Helen, watching them ride away, side by side again, could not help contrasting Lady Hamilton's situation with her own. If only she had managed her marriage so well . . .

Old Angelina, finding her sitting at her window in tears, gave her a brisk scolding. "You have been ill long enough. It is time to show yourself, to receive visitors, and above all to go out in God's good air. You are not ill now, and you know it. Pray if you like, but do not cry; it is bad both for you and the child."

"Thank you." She knew the advice was good, but had to make a strenuous effort to obey it. It was high summer now, and Naples was empty of people since everyone who could had left for the comparative cool of the country. No wonder. Naples, in this hot weather, stank. Lady Hamilton, paying an unexpected call when she had come into town on business of Sir William's, exclaimed at finding Helen and Charlotte there at all. "I hardly believed it, when they told me up at the palazzo," she said. "But of course, your villa was destroyed, was it not—and Lord Merritt's place at Caserta is hardly the thing . . . I have it—" she rose with her rather heavy grace—"I will speak to Sir William tonight. You must have our other villa. You cannot possibly stay in town through August and September."

"It's wonderfully kind of you." Helen found herself near to tears. "But, my husband—"

"Has not thought about it one way or another, I expect. Don't worry, child. I'll take care of Lord Merritt."

"Thank you." The tears that came too easily these days lurked in the corners of Helen's eyes. "You're so kind . . ." It was a blessed relief to find that Lady Hamilton had apparently forgotten that unlucky scene about Trenche.

And yet, poor Trenche . . . When they were alone she asked Charlotte if there had been any news of the prisoners in the Castle dell'Ovo and Charlotte shook her head. "None," she said. "Nobody dares ask. Nobody speaks of them. Helen, do you not think Lord Merritt might do something? With the King?"

"He might, but he won't," said Helen bitterly. Price would never allow it. Why should he? He was very well off as things were.

It was blessed relief to be safe at the Villa Emma, away from the prying eyes of Naples, and yet not so far from town but that they could get back if necessary. "But it will not be necessary," said Angelina. "I, Angelina, will do everything that is needful, and the signora will find herself much better than if she let some man attend her. Besides, it has to be a surprise, has it not?"

"Yes." Helen blessed the day when she had taken up the old lady in her carriage. After her experience with the doctors who had attended her mother, she was much more inclined to trust to the experienced ministrations of Angelina. If she had been doubtful at first, it had been because Angelo's mother seemed such a very old lady, but then, she had not known at the time that Angelina had spent the last twenty-four hours tending the wounded of Torre del Greco. Now, rested and refreshed, she was looking younger every day, and Helen and Charlotte agreed that she was very likely not much more than forty.

If Lord Merritt was anxious about how his wife would manage in her hour of crisis, he gave no sign of it. A brief note, so coherent that she was sure Price had dictated it, had informed Helen that he approved of her move to the Villa Emma, and announced that he was accompanying King Ferdinand to the island of Procida for the September pheasant shooting. Putting the letter away with a sigh, Helen recognised that her husband would always fail her in a crisis. If only her vital twenty-first birthday was sooner than November. But she sat down, just the same, and wrote a note to Mr. Furnival, the lawyer, to give him her new address and announce that she expected her first child in November. "Perhaps we shall share a birthday." She did not like lying to Mr. Furnival, whose letter of congratulation on her marriage had been couched in heart-warmingly friendly terms, but it had to be done. She was only relieved that he was so far away, and it could be done in writing.

Charlotte, it seemed, felt very much the same. "Thank God we're not in England." She looked up from the letter she was writing to her mother.

"You've not heard yet?"

"About my engagement? No. But I have no hope. I never told you," she coloured crimson, "what she said when she heard of your marriage."

"Dear Charlotte! I can imagine." Unspoken between them was their knowledge of Charlotte's happier position. She might be marrying a poor man, but he was the one she loved. It made Helen wonder, as she had many times, whether Charlotte suspected the state of affairs between herself and Charles Scroope, and whether that accounted for a particular, gentle sympathy in her manner these days. But then, there was her condition, too, to account for that. She was very large now, and grateful that life in the country made it possible to wear the loosest of coolly flowing high-waisted gowns. Angelina continued encouraging. She had somehow slipped into the way of helping Helen to dress and undress, and it was she who decreed that there must be some relaxation in the tight lacing of those essential corsets. "We must not harm the little lord," she said, and once again, Helen agreeing with her, thought how strange it was to be going through all this trouble for Trenche's child.

It was the very next day that they had news of the escape from the Castle dell'Ovo. One of the men had ridden into Naples to do the household's errands and came back full of it. "Only think, signora, the Giordano brothers have escaped from dell'Ovo! They made a rope of their sheets and climbed down into the sea. Michele and another man got clean away, but Annibale hurt himself falling, and was caught."

"What other man?" Helen felt cold as stone.

"It is not known, signora. There is much talk in Naples, but all of it quiet . . . quiet . . ."

"Then we had best not talk of it here," said Helen. She was sitting alone on a terrace overlooking the garden and wished, after the man had left her, that she had asked him to send Angelina to her with a shawl and (she shivered in the warm air) some comfort. Why was she so sure that the nameless third who had escaped must be Trenche? Gradually, she worked it out. Impossible that the escape had not been connived at. How could three prisoners get away from that impregnable sea-bound fortress without help either from outside or in? And everyone knew, though nobody mentioned, that de Medici, the chief of police, was the Giordano brothers' patron. Had he found their imprisonment, and Trenche's, equally embarrassing, and arranged this means to get rid of all three?

Please God he had not stopped at letting them out, but had got them out of the country too. Only now, when she was afraid that he had escaped, did she realise just how much, in peace of mind, Trenche's imprisonment had meant to her.

It was getting dark, and she was shivering more than ever. Time to go in and face the inevitable discussion of this extraordinary escape. She rose, slowly, as she did everything now, and was preparing to move across the shadowed terrace to the lighted doorway of the salon, when a rustling below the balustrade stopped her where she stood. Someone was climbing up the great vine that grew

153

all over that side of the villa. She ought to do something. Scream. Go for help. She stood there, paralysed, immobile, waiting for the disaster she now knew she had expected.

"Helen!" Trenche's voice, very low, from among the vines almost level with the balustrade. "Thank God I've found you alone. You must help me! Food; money; clothes . . . I've nothing. Help me now, and I promise you will never hear from me again."

"Stay where you are." She moved closer to that rustling patch of vine. "If anyone else knows you are here, I can do nothing but give you up. But if I can, I'll help you. God knows I've tried, all this time!"

"Tried!" His voice cracked with bitterness. "Trying wasn't much use to me, Helen Merritt. If the Giordanos had not had friends, I'd still be rotting there in prison. No doubt you hoped I'd be there forever, or better still, secretly killed. Well, you were unlucky! I'm here, and if I'm caught, I'll talk. And you, dear Helen, will provide the corroborative evidence. You look, my lady, rather large for someone who was married only in February."

God, how she hated him. If she could have said the word, there and then, and had him dead at her feet, she thought she would have done it. But she was helpless and knew it. "Hush," she said. "There's no time for talk; no time to convince you that I did try. Wait at the bottom of the vine. I must think what to do for the best."

"Don't take too long about it." It was a threat.

"I won't. Believe me, I want you safe away from here as badly as you could wish." Her tone must have carried conviction, because she heard him begin to work his way carefully back down the vine.

"I'll give you ten minutes." His voice came up to her, muffled through the leaves.

Ten minutes. But how would he measure time, out in the dark there? She was standing, wringing her hands. She must not panic. She moved into the empty salon, grateful that Charlotte must still be upstairs, and rang the bell. Her mind had made itself up, it seemed. "Send me Angelina at once," she told the man who came.

"Yes, signora?" Mercifully, Angelina could not have been far off.

"Angelina, once again I need your help. There is a man waiting at the bottom of the great vine. It is death to help him, but I must. He can ruin me. He wants everything . . . food, money, clothes, shelter. The money I can provide, but how can I hide him here?"

"You cannot, of course. I had been thinking it was time I visited Angelo and Maria. They are rebuilding their house. They will be glad of another pair of hands, and no one will think of looking for him at Torre del Greco. I will bring you food and wine at once—you are always hungry these days, naturally. Give it to him, and what money you think he needs, and tell him to stay quiet in the shelter of the vine until I come for him. He speaks Italian?"

"Yes." How dangerously much Angelina must know or suspect, and what a redoubtable ally she was proving.

The ten minutes must have been more than over when Helen returned to the balcony, but all was quiet. "Are you there?" She leaned down to whisper it.

"Yes. Where else? Cold and hungry. Can I come up now?"

"Only to get the food. I will not have Miss Standish involved in this. And, besides, I cannot trust the servants. I have money for you, food and wine—" She heard the vine rustle as he began impatiently to climb. "Here!" She reached down to give him her purse. "It's all I have, but I will be able to send you more if you need it. An old lady —her name is Angelina—will come for you as soon as she can, to the foot of the vine. Her son and daughter-in-law are at Torre del Greco, rebuilding their house. She says they will hide you."

"And you hope there will be another eruption?" His voice was savage.

"It's the best I can do. Take it or leave it." She made her voice indifferent as she handed down the food and opened wine bottle.

"Oh, I'll take it. For the time being. But for your own sake you will have to arrange to get me away. Best on an

English ship—one of those tame captains of yours surely will take me for the sake of your *beaux yeux.*"

"Why do you hate me so?" she asked, and then wished she had not as his voice came up to her, venomous through the darkness, spitting out the pent-up venom of his months of imprisonment. In that dark solitude, he had convinced himself that she had known of the impending arrests and arranged for him to be included. Impossible to convince him otherwise, and dangerous to stay here trying. "Hush! I hear Miss Standish. As you value your own life, be quiet, and wait."

She had not, in fact, heard anything, but returned to the salon just as Charlotte entered from the stairs. "Do you know where Angelina is?" she asked. "I've been looking all over for her. She promised me some salve for my burn." Charlotte had spent the afternoon in the sun, and was regretting it at leisure.

"Oh, I am sorry. She must have clean forgotten. She came to me for permission to visit Angelo and Maria. . . . They are rebuilding their house at Torre del Greco. . . ." The sentences came out breathless, and to her ears unconvincing.

"At this time of night?" Charlotte's tone was indeed surprised. "What a redoubtable old lady she is. But I hope she's not had bad news?"

"Do you know, I did not think to ask." Absurd not to have arranged some story with Angelina. But at this very moment, the old lady herself appeared, wrapped in her fusty black shawl, the salve in her hand.

"Here, signorina." She handed it to Charlotte. "In my hurry I almost forgot. Maria needs me," she explained now to them both. "But it can be nothing urgent. I will be back in two days, perhaps three."

"Take the mule, Angelina," said Helen. "And travel swiftly. We will miss you."

"For three days you will do very well without me." It was meant to reassure Helen and very nearly succeeded, but with her time so near it was impossible not to fret herself almost to fever point at the absence of her one ally.

Chapter 13

TWO days dragged by, and still there was no sign of Angelina. Increasingly anxious as her time grew near, Helen was exhausted with the effort of pretending to Charlotte that there was nothing the matter. But at least there was one excuse for admitted anxiety. The man who had gone shopping in Naples that morning had returned with the news that the third escaper had indeed been Trenche. The hunt was up, both for Trenche and Michele Giordano. His unlucky brother, Annibale, was back in prison awaiting his long-delayed trial, his prospects infinitely worsened by his attempted escape, but the other two had apparently got clean away.

Charlotte and Helen were sitting down to their frugal supper that evening when they heard what sounded like a considerable body of men riding up to the main entrance on the other side of the house. "What in the world?" Helen broke off at the sound of violent knocking at the door.

"I don't know." Charlotte looked as frightened as Helen felt. Visions of brigands, banditti, or armed refugees from Torre del Greco hovered in both their minds. For the first time, Helen found herself actually wishing for her husband's presence.

"Signora." Carlos, the man who had been to Naples, appeared at the door. "It's the military police!" He too was visibly frightened. "They want to search the house. For those two men."

"Oh!" Helen rose ungracefully to her feet. After all, now she thought about it, it was logical enough—all too logical, in fact, that they should look for Trenche here.

What a mercy that she had not for a moment considered trying to hide him in the villa. "Very well," she said. "Send in the officer in charge. We will naturally do everything we can to help him."

The officer seemed courteous enough, and was apologetic when he saw Helen's condition. "You will understand, signora, that we are searching everywhere that those two might be."

"Of course. The house is small. It is impossible that they should be hiding here without our knowledge, but search for yourselves. We will feel safer so. They must be desperate men!" It was all too easy to sound frightened.

The search was prolonged, alarmingly thorough, and ended in the kitchen, where, Helen suspected, the servants were plying their unwelcome guests with placatory wine. She did not like the idea of this, and was wondering whether it would be cowardly, or wise, to retire upstairs with Charlotte and put a chair against the bedroom door, when the officer returned, less civil than before, and all too evidently the worse for drink. "One of your servants is missing," he said, without preamble or much pretence at politeness. "Why?"

"Not a servant," said Helen. "A guest. An old lady I brought with me from Torre del Greco. She helped nurse me in my illness after the eruption. Now she has gone back to visit her son and daughter-in-law, who are rebuilding their house there. Her daughter-in-law needed her." Too late she saw the danger of this.

"Who brought the message?" His voice was thick with wine. "That's what your servants are wondering."

"A man." His slow speech had given her time to concoct her story. "He did not know the house, and came to me on the terrace here. I sent for her at once. The servant —Carlos—will remember that. It was late in the evening, and Maria took the mule and went at once."

"And the man with her." It was not a question. "I wonder, signora, just who that man was." He leaned towards her, his breath heavy with wine and garlic. "You will describe him for me?"

"I didn't see him." This, at least, was true. "He spoke to me from the foot of the vine out there." She led him out onto the terrace, hoping that the cool evening air might sober him a little.

"He did not climb up the vine to speak to you?" The man moved closer than she liked, took her arm in a rough grasp, and urged her over to the vine. "It looks strong enough to climb. In the morning, we will see."

"You cannot stay here all night." This was Charlotte, sounding extraordinarily like her mother, the dominating British aristocrat.

"You think not, signorina? I believe you will find yourself wrong." But her authoritative tone had made him drop Helen's arm. "We will be no trouble to you ladies." He had remembered who they were. "Your servants will arrange sleeping quarters for us. No need to trouble you further. At least, not until morning." The threat in his voice was hardly veiled. "For tonight," he turned at the sound of a scream from the servants' quarters, "I had best see that my men behave themselves."

"You had indeed," said Helen. "My husband is your king's friend. If any harm befalls a single member of my household, I warn you, King Ferdinand will know of it."

"Old Nosy," said the man affectionately. "But will he do anything about it, signora?" He sketched a faintly mocking bow, and left them.

Alone, the two girls looked at each other in horrified silence for a few moments. Then, "That scream was Lucia," said Charlotte.

Lucia was the youngest of the serving maids, probably not more than fourteen. "I know," said Helen. "Will he stop it, Charlotte, and, if not, dare we intervene?"

"I don't know." They waited, silent, listening.

Another scream, again unmistakably that of the child who helped in the kitchen. Helen looked down at herself. "You go and lock yourself in your room, Charlotte," she said. "I must do something. And they won't hurt me."

"No," said Charlotte. "I'll come too. You can't stop me, Helen. And, besides, with two of us. . . ."

Witnesses. She might be right. Another scream settled it. Helen led the way down the narrow hall that led to the servants' quarters. Pausing in the open doorway, she saw with a breath of relief that the orgy was only beginning.

The soldiers were sitting very much at their ease around the kitchen table, bottles of wine and the remains of an immense dish of spaghetti testifying to the warmth, whether real or feigned, of the servants' welcome. The two older maids were comfortably established in the laps of a soldier each; only Lucia was fighting like a cat, while Carlos, whose fiancée she was, stood in the background, fury and fear fighting each other in his face.

"Stop it!" Helen spoke as one of the two soldiers who were amicably fighting each other for possession of Lucia pulled the shawl away from her brown shoulders. "You!" She turned to the officer who was watching with an amused grin. "Stop them."

"Why?" He yawned and picked his teeth. And then, smiling blandly, "If we find tomorrow what I expect to find, you are all as good as dead anyway."

"And if you do not," said Helen, "my husband will tell your king how his officers abuse women."

"Let him." The man was too drunk to care. "Old Nosy won't mind. He's had enough women himself, in his time. Well, can you blame him with that Austrian bitch for a wife?"

There was a sudden silence. He had gone too far and knew it. Looking around, "I did not say that," he said.

"No?" said Helen. "Let your men go on abusing that child and I will report you to de Medici." She regretted the words the moment they were spoken.

"Will you?" He was dangerous now, a man afraid. "In that case . . ." He had been sitting at the head of the table, but now rose and began to weave his way towards where she and Charlotte stood in the doorway. "In that case . . ." His men were watching him with lazy interest. "What an unfortunate thing that you refused to let us search your villa. Naturally, in a case like that, there may be a little violence." He smiled a vulpine smile. "Nobody sorrier than we shall be tomorrow morning, but the enemies of the King must be tracked down. Anyone who opposes his officers is his enemy. So!"

The men had taken their cue and were rising to their feet, drunkenly and slowly. Lucia screamed again. Helen and Charlotte stood silent, paralysed. Then, "Run for it,"

Helen whispered to Charlotte as the crowd advanced on them. "I'll hold them for a moment." And then, louder: "Are you men? Will you kill my child?" She felt Charlotte move away from behind her, and recognised a moment of surprise. She had wanted her to go, but had still not expected to be left to her fate. She raised her voice. "You have wives," she said. "Some of them perhaps in my condition. What would they say if they saw you now?"

It made them momentarily hesitate, but the officer had too much to lose. "They'd say, 'Rot the British!'" His Italian verb was stronger, and Helen realised that fear had combined with drink to deprive him of what reason he had. "And so do I!" he went on. "I lost my son at Toulon. They left him behind, the scum. And now is the time for the reckoning. Your child shall pay for mine, signora!" The courtesy title mocked her as he moved swiftly forward to seize her arm and pull her into the room. "Mine first!" His tone warned back his followers, who were crowding round him as he pulled her forward to the table. "We've all night," he went on. "Plenty for all, before she snuffs it. *And* the little English lordling." He pushed her roughly back against the table, put his hand to the neck of her flowing muslin dress, and tore it off her with a sound that caused a sudden, startled silence in the room.

And into it, "Don't move, any of you, or you're dead!"

Pulling the rags of her dress around her, Helen swayed dizzily to her feet and gazed at Charles Scroope who stood in the doorway, a pistol in each hand with, incredibly, Charlotte beside him, also armed. "Here to me," he said. "Quick!" And then, unerringly picking out Carlos from among the menservants, "You, go the rounds, disarm them and bring their weapons to me. The rest of you, keep still if you want to live."

Carlos mercifully had stayed sober. He wove his way carefully among the soldiers, who were only slowly realising what had happened, giving them no chance to move behind his back. The pile of weapons at Charles's feet grew. "Charlotte," he said, "give Helen the pistol and tell my men to come in."

"Yes."

Helen sensed something odd in Charlotte's reaction but was too grateful for the shawl one of the maids had silently passed up to her to think much of it. She wound it round her shoulders and tied it behind her, leaving her hands free to take the pistols. "I can use them," she said in Italian. "My father taught me." It was more, she knew, than Charlotte could, and she found herself wondering why Charles had not brought his men.

He was speaking to her now, under his breath, in English. "Does this door lock on the outside?"

"No." She thought for a moment. "But the wine cellar does."

"Where?" His gaze at the disarmed men was unwavering.

"Across the hall. Just behind us."

"Good." And then, in Italian, "You," to Carlos. "Take whichever of their pistols you prefer and help me get them into line."

"I'll help." It was the old major domo, who had been incapably drunk but seemed to have recovered himself in the course of the crisis.

"Good," said Charles.

"And so will I," said one of the younger soldiers. "I wanted no part of this."

"Is it true?" Charles asked Helen without taking his eyes off the officer, who was swearing steadily and horrifyingly under his breath.

"I think so," said Helen. "He was just sitting, quiet, in a corner. I thought he must be very drunk."

"No," said the young soldier.

"It's true," Lucia spoke up. "He tried to make them leave me alone."

"Very well. You three then, get them in line, with their officer at the head. I don't want to lose sight of him." By now, the scene in the kitchen had sorted itself out surprisingly. The women had withdrawn to the corner beside the stove, where they huddled together, sobbing and whispering. The other two menservants were standing in front as if belatedly to protect them. The soldiers were struggling to their feet, fighting the drink that had incapacitated them, still not quite sure what had happened.

Except the officer, who had the most at stake. He was himself again, a terrified self, white and sweating. Helen looked at him coldly. She could see his desperation and was afraid of what might be its results. "What you have done cannot be forgotten," she told him across the room. "But I have no recollection of what you said."

It settled something for him. She could see the desperation drain away. The scene in the kitchen might be explained as a misunderstanding, those fatal words about the Queen never could. His own men would not betray him, the servants would not be believed, only Charlotte and Helen could ruin him. "And the other signora?" he asked now.

"Will do as I say." Helen was beginning to think that Charles's men were a long time in coming, and, in fact, to suspect that they did not exist. She moved across the hall and unbolted the heavy cellar door. "This way," she said. And then, to Charles, "There's wine down there, of course."

"Of course," he said, as the file of men began slowly and cautiously to edge past him and down the cellar steps, shepherded by Carlos, the major domo, and the one sober member of their group. Ex-member, Helen thought, watching the bitter looks that were cast at him as he stood there, pistol cocked, their enemy. The last three men to move had had time to sober up a little and one of them aimed a quick, surreptitious kick at him. For a moment, the whole situation was explosive. Then Carlos lifted his pistol and brought it down with all his strength on the attacker's head. He fell like a log.

"Pick him up, you two," said Charles calmly, "and take him along with you. We don't want him here." And then to Carlos: "Thanks. That was quick thinking." He followed the last two and their unconscious burden into the hall, swung the great, iron-studded cellar door to behind them, shot the bolt, and fastened the large metal hasp. "Have you a padlock for this?" he asked Helen.

"Yes, signor," the major domo answered as he moved across the kitchen to fetch the huge lock, which had been thrown down on a bench. "They made me open up," he said.

"Yes. There's no other way out? No opening for barrels?"

"Thanks be to God, no. But the signora's wine . . ."

"They're going to have a hard time getting it open in the dark. By morning, I hope we will have help."

"Help?" The old man was puzzled. "But the signor's men?"

Charles laughed. "You are all my men," he said. And then, raising his voice. "Charlotte, you can come back now. They're all safely stowed."

"Thank God for that." Charlotte appeared from the salon. "I was just beginning to wonder how on earth to make a noise like an advance guard of sailors."

"You mean you're alone?" Helen had not believed it could be as bad as that.

"Sole alone." And, in Italian, to the soldier who had changed sides, "I think you had best stay on duty at the door. And, I wonder, had you considered going to sea?"

The man's face lit up. "With you, signor? A thousand times yes. I've made too many enemies tonight. . . . "

"That's what I thought. So you're the best man to guard them. Give us a call if you hear anything out of the way, but frankly I think they'll fall asleep pretty soon. What were your servants thinking of to let them at the wine, Helen?"

"I suppose they did it for the best." Her voice shook. Now that the crisis was over, there was time to recognise the pains that were racking her. She pulled the borrowed black shawl more closely around her. No time for that now.

But Charles was giving her a quick look. "Come and sit down. Charlotte, take her other arm."

"I ought to change." She would not think, except practically, about the moment when her dress had been torn off her, about the spectacle she must have presented.

"You ought to go to bed," said Charles, "but, first, if you have the strength, we must talk for a moment." What was the matter with his voice?

"Of course." She would always have the strength, for **him.**

"Good." He and Charlotte were guiding her down the hall to the chaise longue in the salon. "Charlotte . . ." When had they got onto first-name terms? "Could you find Helen some brandy, do you think?" He laughed. "Without going down to the cellar for choice. And a warmer shawl?"

"Yes, of course."

They were alone. He held up a hand. "Hush! I must speak before she comes back. Helen, Trenche came to Naples yesterday."

"What?"

"Yes. I met him in a tavern. He was drunk as an owl and talking—in English, thank God—as if he'd never stop. Helen, how could you?"

"How could I?"

"All of it. Any of it. It makes me sick. But there's no time for that. What I came to tell you is that you are safe. I had him pressed. He's on his way to the Channel Fleet at this moment." He was speaking throughout as if every word hurt him. "He won't do much talking there. Or won't be believed. But, Helen," he said again, "how could you? Trenche!"

She ought to ask him what Trenche had said, what lies he had told, but the pains were coming thick and fast now. "I'm sorry," she said. "Charles—" It ended in a gasp that was almost a scream as the pain ripped through her, blacking everything out for a moment. When the world cleared again, Charlotte was beside her, wineglass in hand, looking if possible even more white and drawn than she had before. Charles had disappeared, and as another pain sobbed through her, Helen was glad of it.

But there he was, returning with the old cook, who looked even more frightened than Charlotte. "We must get her upstairs," said Charles.

"No!" Once again it was almost a scream. "Just go away," Helen begged. "All of you. And leave me alone. Please." The pains were coming faster now. There was no time to think of Charles, or Trenche. . . . No time to do anything but feel the sweat pour down her face, and grasp, when the pains were strongest, at the edge of the chaise longue. "Charlotte. Make them go away."

"Yes, dear. In a moment." Was it possible that Charlotte had still not realised what was happening? Charles knew, of course, but then he knew so much . . . and so much of it so intolerably wrong. She remembered how, just a few nights before, she had found herself wishing Trenche were dead at her feet. Now, she almost wished she had killed him. The pain engulfed her again; the room was emptier now, only Charlotte beside her, and Charles, hesitant, at the door.

He was pushed aside. "This is no place for a man." Old Angelina bustled into the room, summed up Helen's condition with one expert, comprehensive glance, and turned back to Charles. "Get the women heating water," she said. "And you," to Charlotte, "fetch the bundle the signora and I prepared. And the cradle. God knows how soon we will need it." She was bending over Helen as she spoke, timing the pains that racked her. And then, as the other two mercifully disappeared on their errands, "Thank God I wasted no more time. He fooled us properly, that Englishman of yours, signora. But what's been going on here?" Bending to examine Helen, she had become aware of the torn dress, the awkwardly tied shawl.

"Soldiers," Helen gasped. "Looking for him."

"Where are they now?" Angelina was deftly unknotting the shawl, and Helen felt an instantaneous relief. "That's better. Now, the corsets, and you won't have to waste these pains of yours. The sooner it's over, the better. But, these soldiers?"

"Locked in the cellar." It was easier to talk now. "Signor Scroope arrived just in time. But, Angelina, don't let him . . ."

"He can guard the soldiers," said Angelina briskly. "That's man's work. The signorina shall help me. She may as well learn. They did not hurt you, signora? Those ruffians?"

"No. They were just beginning . . ."

"Well," said Angelina briskly as Charlotte appeared laden down with the cradle and the bundle on which she and Helen had worked all summer. "After such an experience, no wonder if the signora is before her time. Is the hot water coming?"

166

"Soon," said Charlotte. "The fire is low."

"It had better be soon." And then, to Helen: "Don't be frightened. It is better with water and rags and cradles, but it is just the same without. I bore my Angelo in a cave in the woods, and neither of us any the worse. At least you're not in a cave, signora, but in your own house." She was searching quickly in the bundle as she spoke. "Here, bite on this." It was a knotted piece of cloth whose use Helen had never understood. "You do not wish the men to hear you scream."

"Just don't let them in."

"I should think not. Now, signora, you may begin to push when you wish to."

After that it was work, and pain, work and pain, with the sweat running down her face in the hot little room, but always the comforting certainty of Angelina's presence, her calm voice, heard in the intervals of comparative ease, directing Charlotte, whom she was keeping at the other end of the room. Once, the door opened, the water was brought, and its bringers sent promptly to the right-about. Once, Helen opened her eyes. "What time is it?" she asked.

"Who knows? Midnight, perhaps. Those ruffians in the cellar are quiet at last, but the signor and that soldier are on guard outside. Carlos has gone for help."

"Not a doctor," whispered Helen.

"Why should we need a doctor? There!" As the pain suddenly exploded through Helen's whole body. "I thought it would not be long now."

Centuries later, or it might have been as little as ten minutes, Helen was lying, weak, expended but content, listening to her child's first squall. "A boy of course." Angelina held the wizened object up proudly. "What else would give its mother so much trouble?"

"Let me have him? Just for a moment?"

"Oh, very well. Here!" The child had been quickly washed and swaddled in one of the shawls Helen had made. Its tiny, wrinkled red face and furiously shut eyes were like nothing and no one Helen had ever seen. Then, it opened clear blue eyes and stared at her with what seemed dislike. "Good God," she said. "My father." How

167

she had dreaded a likeness to Trenche. "Charles," she said. "After him."

"Yes, yes." Angelina retrieved the warm bundle. "After the grandfather and the rescuer; that is good. Now, signora, sleep and sleep and sleep."

But something she had said had rung an alarm bell in Helen's brain. "Ask Lord Merritt," she said, as sleep engulfed her, "what name . . ."

"Yes, naturally. When he gets here." Drifting down and down into sleep, Helen tried and failed to unravel the strands in the old lady's tone.

But waking, what felt like aeons later, she still remembered. . . . Did Angelina suspect Charles Scroope of being the father of her child? Madness to have suggested Charles as its name. But surely there would be time to change it. . . . She slept again and was awakened at last, firmly, by Angelina. "The little Signor Carlos is hungry," she said.

"Not Charles," said Helen.

"Yes, Carlos." Angelina was still holding the tiny, mewing bundle. "We christened him at once; it is always so with children born ahead of their time. Other names may be added later, but Carlos he is. And hungry."

Feeling the angry tug at her nipple, Helen found herself suddenly a different person. She was no longer Helen Telfair, or Helen Merritt, but something quite different, the mother-of-Charles. Or whatever more tactful name she would persuade Lord Merritt to call him. Henry, of course. It had all been worth it, amply worth it. "Charles," she whispered over the tiny, down-covered head, slept again, and did not even notice when Angelina tiptoed in and took the sleeping baby away.

Chapter 14

"CALLED it Charles!" Lord Merritt was in a fury. "As if things weren't bad enough! Thought I was lucky to get you out of Naples; away from the titters. Didn't know the half of it. What kind of a figure do you think I cut now? You and that captain of yours. Talk of the town. And now the child named for him. Passes everything."

He must be angry indeed, thought Helen, to achieve so many complete sentences in a row. But, admit it, he had cause. The fact that it was his own fault he had cut so unheroic a figure would not make him any happier. "Truly, my dear," she said now, pacifically, "I had no thought of Charles Scroope when I suggested the name. It was for my father—and you, of course. He is not to be Charles, but Charles Henry."

"Christened Charles." Lord Merritt was not one to let go of a grievance easily. "Interfering old bag of bones, that Angelina. Sooner she goes back to Torre del Greco, the better."

"It's always done here, with a premature birth."

"Premature!" And then, grudgingly: "True, there's no scandal on that count. Volcanic eruptions; attacks by soldiers; very good cover. Count yourself lucky."

"Lucky!" She could hardly believe her ears. But then, he had not been there that horrible night when she had thought herself and Charlotte doomed to death, and worse. No use discussing it with her husband, who all too evidently wanted to minimise the danger to which he had left her exposed. Well, it was understandable enough. The military police had searched their town house, the Palazzo

Trevi, the day before they visited the Villa Emma. He had been there, cooperated in the search, and then gone off to join King Ferdinand on Procida, without, apparently, a thought for his wife and the danger she might be in, unprotected at the Villa Emma.

"Oh well," he said now, on a slightly more friendly note. "All worked out for the best in the end. Meant to tell you. Letter from Uncle Henry; delighted with our marriage; no more trouble about his will; heir or no heir."

"Oh." Helen put a hand to her brow, taking it in slowly. "When did you hear that?" she asked.

"When?" It took him aback. "Just the other day." Airily. "Last post in . . . can't precisely remember."

She had heard this kind of shuffling lie often enough. He must have known when he left her to her fate at the Villa Emma that he had no more need of her or of the child. Had he perhaps known as long ago as when Vesuvius had erupted? It had puzzled her that there had been no news from the all-important uncle for so long. "Just the same," she said now, "I hope you will write your uncle at once about Charles Henry's birth. It might"—she paused to search for a word—"consolidate the position."

"Con . . . Mighty lot of long words. Married a blue-stocking after all. Laugh of the club when I get back. But, yes, I've written Uncle Henry."

"I hope you said the child was named for him."

"Think I'm a fool, don't you. Course I did. Didn't say anything about the Charles. Sooner it's forgotten the better. Baptised a Catholic too. Don't know what you were thinking of to let it happen."

"I wasn't thinking at all," said Helen. "I knew nothing about it."

"Playing the invalid," said her husband. "Just like a woman. Lots of fuss and nonsense. Soldiers a bit excited . . . fools of servants gave them drink . . . talked it over with the King . . . let off with a warning. Pity about Trenche though. Liked to see him hang, after all the trouble he's caused. What do you think of that fire-eating captain of yours going straight to de Medici? Englishman. English justice. Safe on an English ship. Wouldn't say a word more. Not even to me afterwards. Funny thing," he went on, "almost seemed as if Medici was pleased."

"Very likely he was." Helen did not need to conceal her relief that Charles had dealt so capably with the problem of Trenche. "After all, Naples and Britain are allies; the affair of Trenche might easily have caused trouble. I always thought that escape of theirs must have been connived at from very high up indeed."

"Don't say such things!" He flared up at her. "Idiotish woman. Never learn sense? Hobnobbing with those young revolutionary devils . . . Trenche . . . Eruptions . . . Getting me into trouble every day of your life. Constantly making excuses for you. King Ferdinand calls you—" He thought better of it. "Never mind that. The Queen don't speak of you. Lady Hamilton's given you up. Came to suggest you'd better move out of her villa."

"Where to?" How much more of this was she going to be able to bear?

"Back to Naples, stupid. Autumn now. Cool nights; better start living it all down, soon as you can. But don't fool yourself I'll help. Oh, put in an appearance now and then. Form's sake. Devoted husband; all that; just not over-fond of brats."

"Just the same," Helen had been nerving herself for this, "you had better take a look at Henry while you are here, just in case the servants should think it odd."

"Servants!" he said.

"There's Charlotte too," she reminded him.

"Yes!" He rounded on her. "Another thing. Letter from Mrs. Standish. Seems to think it all my fault that chit engaged herself to another of those captains of yours. Can't think why. Not my idea to have her in my house. Turn her out if I have any more trouble."

"No you won't." Helen had had enough. "Have you considered, Lord Merritt, what might happen if I were to decide to write your uncle the entire truth of what has happened between us? Oh"—she held up a hand to silence him—"I know it would ruin me, but it would most certainly ruin you too. Wills can be changed, remember." If only it was November. If only her own fortune was safe, how gladly she would have ordered him out of her life forever. No; she could not. "My dear," she was persuading herself as well as him, "we must not quarrel, for the child's sake."

"Damn the child." But after allowing himself this explosion, he subsided somewhat. "Child's your affair. All I'm trying to say. So's Miss Standish. Just try to keep out of trouble when you come back to Naples."

After this, it was astonishing to arrive in Naples and find that she and Charlotte were heroines. Everybody called; everybody wanted to know in detail of their adventures; and the more Helen tried to play them down, the more heroic she was considered. She could only assume that Lord Merritt's outburst had been brought on by jealousy, combined with his knowledge, and, inevitably, everyone else's, of the shabby part he had played. Helen soon realised that among the female part of society at least the kind of semi-separation in which she and her husband now lived was considered the most natural thing in the world. Probably the only source of surprise was that she had not got herself a lover, or at least a cicisbeo. The fact that Charles Scroope had rescued her twice was good for an occasional roguish look, but no more. Charles Scroope, after all, was God knew where in the Mediterranean, still believing whatever filthy lies Trenche had told him. It did not bear thinking about, and Helen tried not to.

Lady Hamilton, calling on the occasion of Helen's return to the Palazzo Trevi, settled one question that had irked her. Sir William had known about Uncle Henry's new will as far back as the end of May. "Comfortable for you to have all that settled." The beauty was not given to delving much into the springs of human behaviour. And, besides, she knew nothing of the extraordinary circumstances of Helen's marriage. Why should she be plagued by Helen's horrible suspicions? If she had been killed at Torre del Greco or at the Villa Emma, no one would have mourned more loudly, she thought, or less sincerely, than the husband who had abandoned her both times. And Price? She would rather not think what part he played in all this. It was hard to say which frightened her more, Price's domination of her husband, or the way, in her presence, that he continued to play the perfect servant.

It was no good pretending to anything but relief when Lord Merritt merely escorted her back to Naples, told her to behave herself, and rode away to Caserta, with Price at his side. With them out of the way, it was possible to convince herself that once again she had been letting her imagination run riot. Her husband was weak, not wicked, and Price merely an opportunist. But she was extraordinarily glad they were gone. Naples was very quiet that autumn. The trials of the young men who had been arrested in the spring had begun at last, and though no one discussed them, no one thought of much else. Helen and Charlotte had decided to give up any idea of a box at the opera. The child made an admirable excuse for domesticity. Helen had shocked everyone by insisting on feeding him herself, which happily made most social occasions impossible. And Charlotte was glad to stay at home with her. There was a strange feeling in the air as the trials of the young revolutionaries dragged on, and it was much easier not to meet their silent relatives.

In the end, Annibale Giordano escaped with deportation for life. Most of the other conspirators were either imprisoned or exiled, but three of them were condemned to death, and the riot that followed their hanging caused a new wave of rumours of possible Jacobin uprisings. It was no time for party-giving. The Queen stayed as much as she could at her palace at Caserta, while the King inevitably went on with his bloodthirsty sports.

"But at least they only hanged three." Helen and Charlotte were alone in Helen's boudoir, playing with little Henry.

"Three are too many," Charlotte said.

"Yes," said Helen. "But think of the thousands the French have killed with that unspeakable guillotine."

"I know. And, Helen, there are rumours that they may be going to invade Italy. I do wish we could go home." It was a cry from the heart, and an understandable one since Captain Forbes was now on the Channel Station.

"So do I." Helen, too, was homesick, though she would

have been hard put to it to say exactly what for. But she was buoyed up by a secret hope, which actually came to fruit on her twenty-first birthday, late in November. Lord Merritt had chosen to ignore the celebration, and Helen and Charlotte were sitting quietly together when Carlos announced Sir William and Lady Hamilton.

A visit from both of them was a rare honour, and Helen, glancing quickly round the immaculate salon, felt a pang of gratitude to Charlotte, who never let the servants' standards slip, however quietly they lived. The Hamiltons added to her astonishment by wishing her many happy returns of the day, and Lady Hamilton produced a hand-carved necklace of volcanic jet, which would remind her, she said, of her miraculous escape at Torre del Greco.

Helen, saying everything that was proper, was not entirely sure that she wanted to be reminded of that day, but she was distracted by Sir William. "I have more to congratulate you upon than a mere birthday," he said. "I imagine I may have been looking forward to this day even more than you." And then, aware of their surprised glances (though Helen, in fact, was beginning to guess), "I was approached," he went on, "some time ago by a firm of London lawyers who asked me to have certain—ahem—enquiries made on their behalf. Naturally, I was able to give them a most satisfactory answer, and the result, my dear Lady Merritt, is that you are now a rich woman."

"I beg your pardon?" She had rehearsed this scene in her mind over and over but had never imagined playing it with Sir William. It was evident, however, that he expected her to be amazed, so amazed she was, with Charlotte and Lady Hamilton proving extremely helpful as chorus. Sir William told the story of Helen Glendale Stott both lucidly and kindly, with a wryly apologetic glance from time to time for Charlotte. "I'm afraid your family were a shade tactless," he said, explaining the trouble Mrs. Stott had taken to keep the real terms of her will secret.

"They always are," said Charlotte cheerfully. "Oh, dear Helen, I am so happy for you."

"I am only sorry," Sir William had ended his story,

"that Lord Merritt is not here to share in your rejoicings. He will, of course, take control of your fortune."

"Of course." Helen managed it stoically, but it was a blow just the same. She had been mad to hope that Great-Aunt Helen, who had contrived so much, might even have ensured that she should control her own fortune instead of its passing automatically into her husband's hands. How far away, how long ago seemed the young Helen Telfair, for whom this had been one of the powerful arguments against marriage.

Too late now for this kind of regret, and no time either to wonder just how this would affect her relations with her husband. She must show a happy face of surprise, and entertain the Hamiltons with the wine and fruit that Charlotte had ordered. And Sir William was saying something. "I expect Lord Merritt momently." He leaned towards her. "I sent a messenger as soon as I learned he was from home. There will be, I am afraid, a certain amount of paper work for him, but my secretary will do everything in his power to make all smooth."

"Too kind," said Helen mechanically, at once touched and irritated by the hint of sympathy in his tone. He knew as well as she did that she was infinitely better able to cope with the necessary business than her husband, but there was nothing either of them could do about it.

Lord Merritt returned next day, in a curious mixture of moods. "Dark horse, aren't you?" he greeted her. "Never told me you were an heiress."

"Didn't know it." Lying to him, it seemed natural to fall into his way of speech.

"And what's this about tying it up for the child? Lot of nonsense. Told Sir William so."

"And what did he say?" Sir William's suggestion that she could, in fact, arrange for some of her surprisingly large fortune to be put in trust for her children had somewhat softened the blow of her husband's inevitable control of the rest. And she had been immensely grateful when Sir William had volunteered to propose this to Lord Merritt.

"Said it would look better. Nothing I could say to that.

All very well if it was my child. Serve me right for saddling myself with a bastard."

"Don't speak of him like that!" They were alone, mercifully, but her anger shook him. "You made a bargain. Stick to it."

"Got to." Sulkily. "Letter from my uncle. Lot of fuss in England. You been writing?"

This was the heart of the matter. "Who would I write to?"

"That Miss Whatsername? Clergyman's sister. Tell her about Torre del Greco?"

"Only in the most general terms . . . I said nothing about you, if that's what you mean."

"Certainly is. Some bitch of a gossip's written a pack of lies about it . . . Got back to Uncle Henry in no time. Just as well you've inherited that fortune."

"You don't mean he's changed his will again?"

"Threatens to. Wants us to go home; lead a proper married life; stay with him; under his nose. Damned if I will."

Helen's heart sank still further, but she made one attempt at a recovery. "Perhaps if I were to go home, and take little Henry?"

"No!" Furiously. "Worst thing possible. You'll stay here and behave like my wife."

"Then you had better behave like my husband. *And* pretend a little more interest in the child than you have so far. Oh, don't worry." She had seen his recoil. "I don't want anything but a fake marriage any more than you do, but it takes two, even to create a fake." In her heart she blessed the unknown Uncle Henry who had given her back some kind of small hold over her husband. "Shall we ask your Uncle Henry to act as trustee for the child?" she suggested now.

He looked at it for a moment, sideways. Then, "Not a bad idea," he conceded. "Might do just that. I'll go and consult Sir William. Mind you, Uncle will very likely turn up sweet anyway when he hears your news. Sly old bird that great-aunt of yours, hey?" He laughed his brutally silly laugh. "Like to see old Whatshisname's face—clergyman Tillingdon—that's it—when he finds he's lost the

176

lot. Must have prayed you'd disgrace yourself." And then, "Hey! Lucky for you I took you on. God, wouldn't you have been sick today."

Luckily, the Palazzo Trevi was large enough so that the pretence at married life could be kept up without undue inconvenience, but just the same, Helen breathed a heartfelt sigh of relief one fine spring day of 1795 when she received a letter of her own from the unpredictable Uncle Henry. He had been flattered, delighted, and surprised at being asked to act as trustee for little Henry and accepted with pleasure. "If you would only come home, so that I could see him, it would make my happiness complete," he wrote in his crabbed, old man's hand. "Dear Helen, if I may call you so, do, pray, persuade your husband that it is time to come home. I do not overmuch like the sound of things in Europe, and, besides, I am a selfish old man and long to see my heir."

"Letters?" Sometimes Lord Merritt moved with disconcerting swift silentness.

"Yes." Nothing for it but to hand it to him. "Your uncle has been so good as to write to me."

"To you? That's a new comeout. Losing his mind, like as not. Never was very strong in the attic." He took the letter from her unceremoniously, and began to read slowly, as always, deciphering the difficult hand. At first, all went well. "Capital idea that of yours," he said. "Making the old fool trustee. Pleased him no end, hey?" He turned the page. "What's this? Go back to England? Nonsense." And then, his tanned face suddenly black with rage, "Longs to see his heir? What heir, pray? You been writing behind my back? God!" He broke into a screech of furious laughter. "Going to find myself cut out after all for that bastard?"

"Don't use that word!"

"Darling Henry." His tone was savage, but at least he moved swiftly to the door and made sure there had been nobody outside to overhear. "One thing, Lady Merritt! He ties it up for the child, I'll break the will if I break us all doing it."

"Which you would. But, consider," she was cold with a terror she could not analyse, but kept her voice steady: "I think you are misinterpreting your uncle's words. It is you your uncle longs to see, not little Henry. What does an old man like him care about a six months' baby?"

"Hmm." He read the letter through again, slowly and carefully, a finger tracing the words. "Could be you're right. Hope so, for all our sakes. Going to answer it?"

"I think I should, don't you?"

"Yes. Show me what you say before you send it. And be careful."

She was careful. She knew now what that cold sweat of terror had recognised somewhere below her consciousness. If the child were to stand in his "father's" way, he might well be in horrible danger. She had long since faced the fact that her husband had left her to her fate at Torre del Greco because he thought he had no more need of her. What hope, then, for a six months' infant who stood to deprive him of a fortune? Little Henry was the healthiest of babies, but accidents can happen so easily . . . And particularly in Naples, where the infant mortality rate was so high that it was almost more surprising if a child survived than if it died.

She shuddered as she wrote draft after scratched-out draft. She had been mad—she knew it now—to make that deplorable bargain with Lord Merritt at Toulon. But then she had thought him weak, silly, and guidable. Now she knew him potentially wicked, and as for guidance from her, all hope of that had passed long since. He was guidable indeed, but now it was Price who held the reins. And Price was her enemy. It was he, she was sure, who had encouraged her husband to leave her to her fate before. What might he not do now?

A double accident. That would be the way. That was what she must guard against. And—she must have an ally. Not Charlotte. Fond though she was of her, she knew Charlotte too well to hope for help from her. In some ways, Charlotte was her mother's daughter, with more than a hint of her mother's rigidities. They lived in a world where husbands did not murder their wives, and were incapable of imagining any other. No. Not Charlotte. She rang her bell, and told Carlos to ride out to Torre del Greco and fetch Angelina. "Tell her that now

Maria's child is born, I need her more." It had seemed easier, when she moved back to Naples, to let Angelina go, granted her husband's fury over the Catholic christening and the unlucky name. Now, she must have her back.

The decision taken cleared her mind. She sat down once more to the task of writing to Uncle Henry, and this time produced a draft that satisfied her. She wrote another letter, locked it in her desk, then thought again and enclosed it in a cover to Sir William Hamilton. "Dear Sir William," the words had formed themselves in her mind ready to be written. "I have a great favour to ask of you. Will you, for my sake, and my child's, keep the enclosed, mention it to no one, and open it only in case of my death?" Should she say death by accident or, she shuddered, death by murder? No, that would be an unpardonable slur on Lord Merritt. After all, her fears might be entirely unfounded. And, besides, there was an easier way. She added, "And the child's." God bless Sir William, she thought, signing and sealing the brief enclosure. "I am afraid of my husband," she had written. "I have been ever since the birth of our child. If anything should happen to us, pray enquire closely into the circumstances. I sometimes think a kind of jealousy (totally ungrounded) makes him mad."

It would have to do. She rose wearily and made her way down to Lord Merritt's rooms on the floor below. Price opened the door to her, and she saw that he and his master had been sitting together, playing one of the rather simple card games Lord Merritt enjoyed. Two glasses showed that they had not only been sitting, but drinking together. Not for the first time, she thought that she did not like Price.

Price's manner in face of this unprecedented visit was his usual caricature of courtesy. He ushered her in, dusted a chair for her, as if, she thought crossly, Charlotte did not see to it that these rooms, like all the rest of the house, were always in perfect order, and then, with an apologetic glance at the card table, said smoothly: "I am delighted to see your ladyship. My lord is a trifle out of sorts, and I have been doing my poor best to cheer him. You will undoubtedly succeed far better."

"I hope so." It was depressing to see that her husband was already a little fuddled with drink. "Bring us some coffee, if you please, Price? I have been writing all afternoon and am dying of thirst."

"Glass of wine," said Lord Merritt. And then, sharply, "Writing?"

"Yes." The door closed softly behind Price. "To your uncle. I would be glad if you would look it over for me and tell me if you think it will do." No time to wait for the coffee and, besides, Price's absence was the opportunity she needed.

Lord Merritt was reading, slowly and carefully as always. " 'Dear Uncle Henry—May I call you that?' Soft soap as usual. Works though, don't it? Hope you've done it right this time. Heir . . . child . . . too young . . . hope he'll forgive . . . sure he really meant . . ." He stopped and thought it over. "Not bad; not bad at all. Now. Can't face the voyage back to England. Child not up to it. All right and tight."

"You think so?"

"Yes. Clever woman." It was grudging. "Should do. Can't take it amiss. Either way."

"That's what I thought," she said. And then, quickly: "There's something else. Quite by the way. But I thought you might care to know. Now I'm a rich woman, I have responsibilities—to you, to the child . . . I've written," she paused, "and sent a letter to Sir William, to be opened in case of my death, and the child's." She watched him closely as she said this, and the look of instant understanding on his face told her all and more than she wanted to know.

"Lot of nonsense," he said. "Thank God. Price and coffee. Leave the letter. Add my hand and fist. Hope it brings the old curmudgeon into better tune."

"Let us indeed hope so." She drank her coffee at a lukewarm draught and stood up. "Oh, by the way. I have sent for Angelina. You were saying, the other day, that I spent too much time in the nursery. I have thought about it and believe you to be right. Angelina will free me, and care for the child. I trust I have your approval in this?"

"Not much use asking; already sent for the old bitch,"

said her husband. But returning shakily to her own rooms, she knew that he had taken her point. All her points. What she could do to safeguard herself and the child, she had done. And—she had thought this before— how strange that she would go through fire and water for Trenche's child. The child who had wrecked her life.

Not Trenche's child. Hers. She got up again and went to the nursery.

Chapter 15

HENRY was worth it all, but soon stopped being Henry. Neither Angelina, now in full command in the nursery, nor the other servants, could get their tongues round the name. He became first Henrici, and then, as he began early to feel for words of his own, Ricky. It sometimes seemed to Helen that his nursery was the only sane place in a world where threatening shadows grew always darker and must never be mentioned.

There had been fresh rumours of Jacobin plots, and at last Medici had been disgraced, imprisoned in the fortress at Gaeta, and replaced by a fiercely royalist Council of State. But still the Queen was writing home to Austria that, "I go nowhere without wondering if I shall return alive," and arranging to have her own and her husband's bedrooms constantly changed for fear of assassination. In the end, it was the English minister, Acton, who again took command of the government, and appointed an equally Anglophile Minister of Foreign Affairs, Castelcicala. A new wave of arrests followed, and even the royal bodyguard had to be re-formed, since it was said to be riddled with revolutionary ideas. The French were over the border into northern Italy by now, and disaffected young Neapolitans who could cross the border were making their way north to join them, or to settle at the Court of the Grand Duke of Tuscany, who had actually recognised the French Republic.

There were rumours that King Ferdinand wanted to do likewise, "But the Queen will be too strong for him as usual," said Charlotte, safe in the privacy of Helen's bedroom.

"Yes, for the moment," Helen agreed. "She hates the French too bitterly to compromise with them, and it is doubtless due to her that a detachment of Neapolitan cavalry is actually being sent to help the Austrians against the French in northern Italy."

"And ships to join Admiral Hotham." Something in Charlotte's tone made Helen give her a quick look.

"Would you like to ask for a passage on the *Tancredi?*" she asked. "I'm sure Commodore Caracciolo would take good care of you, and when they join the blockading fleet you could transfer to a British ship and so get home."

"Home!" said Charlotte. "Oh, Helen . . ." And then, "But could you not come too?"

"Lord Merritt would never allow it." This was not something that could be discussed. "And, besides, can you imagine Ricky in a battleship?"

"Easily," Charlotte laughed. "Adored by everyone. You know what the Italians are like."

"Yes, bless them. But I couldn't ask it, and, anyway, Lord Merritt is fixed here, I think, for the duration of the war."

"But must you stay with him?" Helen and Charlotte had tacitly abandoned the pretence that Helen's was a marriage in anything but name.

"Yes."

"Then I will stay too. Don't look so serious, Helen. After all," her face lit up suddenly, "if Neapolitan ships are joining the British fleet, who knows but we may have British ones coming here again."

"Oh, how I wish they would. But things don't seem to go so well with our fleet now Lord Hood's been replaced by Hotham. Only think of having two brushes with the French, and letting them get away each time."

"Shameful." Charlotte, like Helen, was an eager follower of naval news. "But that little captain we met at Toulon—do you remember—Nelson? He distinguished himself both times."

"Yes, Lady Hamilton mentioned him the other day. He seems to have made a great impression on her and Sir William when he was here at the time of Toulon."

"And they on him." Charlotte laughed. "Do you remember how angry he was when someone said something slighting about Lady Hamilton?"

"Yes: he stood up for her gallantly. I remember it well. Poor man. Think of having lost an eye in the service and now having to chafe under Admiral Hotham. Perhaps it's as well Captain Forbes is on the Channel Station. Inactivity would not suit him either." Captain Scroope was on the Channel Station, too, but she did not choose to mention him.

"I wonder how your father bears it."

"Philosophically, I have no doubt." Helen had actually had a letter from her father six months or so after the birth of her child, and knew he was still serving under Hotham in the exhausting, unprofitable attempt to support the Austrian army in northern Italy against the steady pressure of the French. "Who knows," she went on more hopefully, "their need for reinforcements in the Mediterranean may bring Captain Forbes down here."

Charlotte coloured. "I admit I can't help hoping for it. He never writes, of course, about naval affairs, but anything is possible these days. Just think what a fool I'd feel if I took a passage home and then he came here looking for me. And he will come, Helen, when he can. I know that."

"I'm glad." Helen had wondered whether she was right in permitting Charlotte's correspondence with Captain Forbes. It was all too easy to imagine what Mrs. Standish would say if she knew. And here, in fact, was a powerful argument for Charlotte's staying.

She had hit on it herself. "Just think what M . . . m . . ."

She took a deep breath. "You see, Helen, even thinking of her brings back my stammer. No. I won't go home, if you'll keep me, until I can go as Mrs. Forbes."

"Of course I'll keep you, love. I can't imagine how I would manage without you." But Helen wondered if she had been right that summer when the news broke that Spain had signed a peace treaty with France. There had been rumours of this for some time, and Lady Hamilton had gone about, visibly big with important news, but just the same Helen could hardly believe it when she paid a morning call to announce that the alliance was a fact. "And one of which I have taken good care the British government shall have early information," she told Helen. "My darling Queen fought it to the last, and even let me see the letters from Spain, which I copied for our Foreign Office, but it was all no use. That idiot King Charles IV of Spain has given way to his wife and her 'friend' Godoy. Only think, they have created him 'Prince of the Peace.' I only hope it is not a peace that the Neapolitans intend to join."

"Do you think there is a chance?"

"Not while my darling Queen lives, and Sir William and I to give her good counsel. No need to look anxious, Lady Merritt. You and little Ricky are as safe here as you would be in London. You will see; now the French campaign in northern Italy is beginning in good earnest, we shall have all the British tourists coming down upon us, like rats from a sinking ship."

"You think it will sink—the rest of Italy?"

"Sir William is not hopeful. There's a man with a barbarous name—a Corsican, but serving the French. He out-generals everyone. The rumour is that he may be put in command of the army of Italy, and then, Sir William says, heaven help the states that have not made their preparations. Thank God, we are ready here. Sir John Acton has seen to that, with my husband's help, of course. But this is all in the deepest confidence." She rose to take her leave, and Helen wondered in how many other drawing rooms she would impart the same news, "in the deepest confidence."

"But that is unfair, I believe." She had said something

to Charlotte about this. "I truly think that she is careful in her dealings with the Italians."

"I think she really loves her Queen," said Charlotte.

"Yes. And for her, love is everything." It brought back, strangely, a memory long since suppressed, of the angel in that sunlit garden in Hampshire. They had come a long way, both of them, since the angel had come between her and Sir Harry, had said, "Scoot, luv," and little Helen had scooted. "I wonder which she loves best," she said now, thoughtfully, "the Queen or Sir William?"

"Who could help loving Sir William?" It was not quite an answer, and they both knew it, though Helen agreed, wholeheartedly. She would always owe Sir William an imponderable debt of gratitude for the way he had handled the matter of her letter. She had contrived to give it to him in person one day when she was calling on Lady Hamilton, and had asked him quickly, in a private moment, not even to acknowledge it. He had weighed it for a moment in his hand, then looked at her very straight with his wise old eyes. "I will read it when I am alone, Lady Merritt," he had said. "Believe me your servant in anything I can do for you."

She had believed him and had slept more soundly since, though, by her order, Angelina saw to it that little Ricky was never for a moment alone. Angelina had been quick too. "Children's lives are like candles," she had said. "They snuff so easily. But not our Henrici. I, Angelina, have said it. You may trust me, signora."

"I do," Helen had told her.

So Ricky grew from crawling to walking, from odd monosyllables to a stream of childish babble, and learned, among many other things, that when Lord Merritt was at home (which was not often), it was better not to play truant from the nursery. Helen was accidental audience to one of the stages of this discovery. She had come out of her own rooms at the head of the wide marble stairway of the Palazzo Trevi in time to witness a surprise confrontation between Lord Merritt and his "son." Her husband had just arrived unexpectedly, his boots still bloodstained from the hunt, and the slaughterhouse aftermath in which he now joined the King. Ricky, who would not have been loose in the house if Angelina had had any idea of this, had come in from the terraced garden where he must have been busy working in his own patch of ground. His hands and face were black with earth, his dark hair tousled, and his petticoats filthy. He looked every inch a happy little boy.

Lord Merritt stared down at him while Helen caught her breath to speak, then paused despite herself to listen. "Dirty," said Lord Merritt. "Disgusting."

"So are you," said his "son," eyeing those bloodstained boots askance.

One of them was aimed at him viciously. He dodged, was hit, squealed momentarily, then bit his lip. "I don't like you."

"My dear," Helen, leaning over the balustrade, kept her voice even, "how pleasant, and what a surprise to see you." At her voice, the child gave one quick, grateful upward glance and vanished through the servants' door.

"Your child?" asked Lord Merritt.

"Ours," said Helen.

"Filthy."

"A child." She looked, with intent, at his boots.

"Pah. That." But he was disconcerted. "Came in a hurry to warn you. Bad news at Court."

"Oh?" It must be bad, she thought, if it had brought him home.

"That devil Bonaparte's taken Nice and Savoy. Lombardy's next. Talk of throwing the British out of Italy."

"And what does the King say?" or the Queen, she might have added.

"There's to be a service in the Cathedral. Came to tell you. Must go. All of us. Something . . . Acton said . . . United front, that's it."

"Then don't kick our child," she said.

"Your child." She must remember not to provoke him on this.

The lazzaroni turned out in force to cheer the King and Queen on their way to the Cathedral, but many of the nobility's pews were empty. And the news went from bad to worse. Bonaparte had forced the Dukes of Parma and Modena to buy peace for exorbitant sums and had then turned his attention against the Austrian army, which was soon in headlong retreat. Even Queen Maria Carolina had to admit that with the Austrians in flight, Naples could not stand alone. A Neapolitan emissary, Prince Belmonte, was sent to sue for terms from the victorious Bonaparte, but found it difficult to catch up with him in his swift pursuit of the enemy. All that summer, negotiations continued, varying with the fortunes of war. And in the autumn, Helen had another letter from her father. It was dated, "At sea, off Elba," and urged her in no uncertain terms to take any opportunity that might offer to get back to England. "I can say no more," wrote Captain Telfair, "but you and your husband will be fools if you do not take the first chance that presents itself. Show him this letter, with my kind regards."

"Fools!" said Lord Merritt predictably. "Kind of him to say so! Hope I've more sense than to take to the sea at this time of year. Lot of nonsense anyway. Everyone coming here for safety. Prince Augustus . . . those old French princesses . . . Good enough for them; good enough for us. Write your father so."

"He gave me no direction."

"Mediterranean fleet, stupid."

It was not, Helen was to learn, so stupid as all that. With the New Year of 1797 came the crushing news that the British fleet was evacuating the Mediterranean. Corsica, whose conquest had cost Captain Nelson his eye, was evacuated by Nelson himself. And soon Elba, on which he had looked as a last Mediterranean base, had to be abandoned too. In January, Captain Fremantle of the *Inconstant* paid a flying visit to Naples to pick up the ex-viceroy of Corsica, Sir Gilbert Elliott, who had been doing his best to encourage a spirit of resistance both in Naples and at Rome, but without any significant success.

Fremantle had messages for Helen from her father, and offered her and her family a safe voyage home with the retiring fleet. He himself was marrying a girl called Betsy Wynne, whose family he had rescued when Leghorn was overrun by the French, and taking her with him.

"Her family stay behind," said Lord Merritt.

"I believe her father likes the French," Helen said.

"Oh well," her husband shrugged. "Probably not so black as they are painted. Anyway; not coming here. Peace signed. All right and tight. Lot of nonsense that Fremantle talks. Might think it the end of the world the British fleet's leaving the Mediterranean. High time, if you ask me. Just stir up trouble. That Captain Nelson; always taking ships; making people angry; disobeying orders. I don't know what the Hamiltons see in him. Nelson this; Nelson that; a letter from dear Nelson. Pah."

"He writes most interesting letters." Helen had been privileged to hear them read aloud by Lady Hamilton herself.

"Full of blood and battles. Think I'm going to trust myself to one of his young fire-eaters? Lot of nonsense."

At that fatal phrase, Helen gave up. And, in fact, she consoled herself that many other members of the English colony seemed perfectly happy to remain in Naples. Prince Augustus was still exercising his three-octave voice in his apartment at the Hotel Britannia. They French royal ladies, aunts of the dead king, were still infuriating Queen Carolina by insisting on every iota of their vanished dignities. Perhaps this time Lord Merritt was right, and it would be better to stay where they were than to risk the hazards of a winter voyage.

But it was a bleak morning when the *Inconstant's* white sails vanished from the bay, and Helen and Charlotte both had to school themselves to ignore sneering references to the British fleet, "with a fine set of sails for running away." It proved a surprising bond with Lady Hamilton, whose imagination had been caught by that small, plain Captain Nelson who had visited Naples years before and who wrote such vigorous letters.

"He will distinguish himself one of these days," she told them. "You see if he doesn't. Sir William says so. He said it the first time he met him. 'Give him the apartments you had made ready for Prince Augustus,' he said. 'That's a man who will go far.' You just wait and see."

They did not have to wait long. In February, Sir John Jervis, commanding the fleet that had evacuated the Mediterranean, had the luck to encounter the Spanish fleet, now allied to France. Jervis had fifteen sail of the line, against the Spanish twenty-seven. "If there are fifty sail," he said, "I will go through them. England badly needs a victory at present."

Just the same, he would have failed to achieve the complete victory he wanted, if Nelson, in the *Captain*, had not brilliantly disobeyed orders and swung his ship out of the line to risk it and his life against a superior force of Spaniards. His friends, Troubridge and Collingwood followed him with the *Culloden* and the *Excellent*, and the result was an overwhelming British victory, with Nelson capturing not one but two Spanish ships, one of them the *Sanctissima Trinidad,* the largest fighting ship in the world.

"I told you he was a hero." Lady Hamilton had paid a special visit to Helen and Charlotte to read them Nelson's letter on the occasion. "Now what will that nasty French Monsieur Canclaux say, and that naked wife of his." She thought for a moment. "But Sir William says I am not to speak of it. We diplomats have our problems, my dears. And you had best be careful too, with your naval connections. It is not everyone in Naples who is as delighted as we are over this victory of Cape St. Vincent."

"No, I'm afraid not," Helen agreed. "But what a man that Nelson is! And he looks so insignificant too."

"Looks?" said Lady Hamilton eagerly. "You've met him?"

"Yes, once, long ago, at Toulon. He was just back from visiting you here. I've always remembered him. There was something about him . . ."

"Was there not! But I had no idea you had met him. Tell me, what did he say about us here at Naples?"

"Not a great deal." Helen coloured as she remembered.

"But something?" When it concerned herself, Lady Hamilton was disconcertingly quick.

"Yes. I'm trying to remember." Helen felt her face more crimson than ever as she tried to think how to quote Nelson's praise without reference to the slights that had preceded it.

Emma Hamilton laughed that robust laugh of hers. "No need to wrap it up in clean linen for me, love," she said. "We've known each other long enough, choose how." It was the first time she had ever voluntarily referred to that distant encounter at Uppark, and it drew a look of surprise from Charlotte, who knew nothing about it. And, again, Emma Hamilton was quick. "You never told her?" she asked Helen.

"Of course not."

It won her a quick, highly scented hug. "I should have known. Lady Merritt and I met once, years ago," Lady Hamilton explained now to Charlotte. "In circumstances I do not choose to remember."

"And why should you?" said Helen. And then, plunging in, "In a way that's what Captain Nelson said."

"Oh? Explain, love, do. I'm not much good at riddles."

"Well—" Helen plunged in. "There'd been a little talk —men's talk. You know . . ."

"I do indeed," said Lady Hamilton.

"And Captain Nelson suddenly looked about a mile high." Helen was remembering the scene. "I don't know how he does it, because he's not a bit distinguished to look at, but when he speaks, people listen."

"Yes," said Emma Hamilton eagerly. "And what did he say?"

"He said you were the friend of Queen Maria Carolina, and"—she paused, remembering the scene—"a lady who did honour to her station."

"Ah, that's like him. And silenced them, I've no doubt."

"Entirely."

"There's a friend," said Emma Hamilton. "That's the kind of friend we women need."

"Yes indeed," said Helen. Impossible not to think of Charles Scroope, who had believed the worst of her (if only she knew what that worst was) and had still seen to it that Trenche should be immobilised, unable to slander her again.

And, "Yes, indeed," said Charlotte, thinking, they all knew, of Captain Forbes.

"But when will they come back?" Helen voiced the thoughts of all three.

"God knows," said Emma Hamilton.

The next news they heard of Captain Nelson was bad.

In a night attack on the town of Santa Cruz, on Tenerife, he had failed to capture the Spanish treasure ship that might have made his fortune, and had lost his right arm and nearly his life. "He writes that his wife's son, Josiah Nisbet, saved his life," Emma Hamilton told Helen and Charlotte. "If you could but see the pitiful scrawl with his left hand."

"Is it the end of his career?" asked Helen.

"Please God, no. Sir William says we have need of officers like him."

"I am sure Sir William is right," said Helen. It comforted her, in the long, anxious watches of the night, to think of Sir William, caring for that unopened, talismanic letter of hers. It was, she thought, the magic spell that kept Ricky and her alive. Or was she unjust to Lord Merritt? Had she imagined it all? Impossible to be sure, and, being unsure, impossible ever to feel entirely safe.

Rome was in French hands now, and the best of the hoarded treasures of centuries were being sent back to France as tribute, but life in Naples continued merrily, at least on the surface. The lazzaroni, feeling their beloved Church insulted in the person of the aged Pope, who had been summarily packed off to exile in Tuscany, were more devoted than ever to their king, who stood, now, for Church, State, everything. . . .

A new French ambassador, Citizen Garat, who had actually announced the death sentence to Louis XVI, arrived in Naples that May and raised once more the question of the political prisoners who had been languishing in various fortresses for four years now, many of them without pretence of a trial. In the end most of them were set free that summer, including Luigi de Medici, though this made King Ferdinand so angry that he threatened to have the judges who acquitted him arrested in their turn.

"He won't, of course," said Charlotte.

"No, but if I were the released prisoners, I would retire to the country and keep quiet."

A good many of them did more than that. With the French over the border in Rome, it was easy for a convinced Jacobin to slip across and join them. One tended not to ask their families about the whereabouts of the young men who had been released, any more than one asked about their experiences in those four lost years. To Helen's relief, the Giordano brothers seemed to have disappeared. Perhaps they were with Medici, who had wisely retired to his country estate at Ottaiano. Wherever they were, they were silent. One of her nightmares had been that Trenche might have talked while in prison, and that the Giordano brothers might be in a position to ruin her. Another, of course, was that Trenche might not stay forever in the hell of the between-decks. If only she and Charles Scroope had not parted on such bad terms, she would have asked him what ship Trenche was on, and what hope there was of his being kept silent. But then there were so many "if onlys" about that last, wretched interview with Scroope. Sometimes she thought she would never forgive him for believing Trenche's lies about her; sometimes she found herself thinking that it would be only too easy to forgive him anything.

But of one thing at least she could be certain. Trenche, given the chance, could ruin her good name and her child's, but nothing he said could affect her fortune. Helping her husband deal with them, she had read every word of the papers connected with her Great-Aunt Helen's will and knew herself safe, at least on this count. As for the rest, she sometimes thought she hardly cared. Exposure would free her from the misery of life with Lord Merritt, a misery that she sometimes thought only Charlotte's presence and his frequent absence made tolerable. How would she bear it if Captain Forbes sailed into the bay one day and took Charlotte away?

Public anxiety combined with private fear that spring. The French were making massive naval and military preparations at Toulon. Worst of all, the thirty-five thousand men who were said to be ready for embarkation were under the command of the formidable Bonaparte. All this was common and terrifying knowledge. What no one knew, and no one could find out, was where the three hundred transports that lay ready in the harbour were to take them.

Jacobins sang the "Marseillaise" under their breath.

The Court trembled. Where more likely than against Naples?

"They think nothing of peace treaties," said Emma Hamilton, paying a morning call on Helen and Charlotte. "They'll tear it up the moment it suits them."

"I suppose so." Helen thought the Neapolitan Court would do just the same.

"But no need to look so alarmed," went on Lady Hamilton. "You know that privateer that slipped out of harbour so quietly last week? It bore a message from our Court to the Earl of St. Vincent—Jervis that was—asking his help. Any day now, I expect to see British sails once more, out there in the bay, and then we can snap our fingers at the French."

"I do hope so," said Helen.

"Of course we can. Did you not hear what Lord St. Vincent said when there was talk of a French invasion of Britain across the Channel?"

"No. What was that?"

Emma laughed. " 'I do not say that the French cannot come,' he said. 'I only say that they cannot come by sea.' I'll tell you something else," she went on. "Something that's worth everything else. Captain Nelson is back at sea."

"He's really better?" Helen was amazed at the courage of a man who had lost an eye and his right arm in the service of his country, had suffered, by all reports, hideously from the results of the hurried amputation at sea, and was now prepared to risk his life again.

"Yes. That good woman Mrs. Nelson has nursed him back to health. He writes of her in the highest terms. Only think of his insisting on sitting beside her at Lady Spencer's . . . the First Lord's wife," she explained unnecessarily. "Only a man like him could get away with such a gesture, but Sir William thinks him capable of anything. If only we were to see him here, how safe, how happy we would be."

"How is Sir William?" Helen had thought him looking much older the last time she had seen him.

"Fagged to death as usual. They all take advantage of

him. No one can decide anything without reference to him. Truly, if we do not get our leave of absence soon, I shall be anxious about him."

"I am so sorry." Helen privately thought Emma should be anxious already. She was selfishly, and ashamed of it, anxious herself. What would happen to that precious letter of hers if Sir William were to die?

But this was starting at shadows. Presumably it would be returned to her unopened, and, in the meanwhile, she comforted herself with the thought that her husband seemed to have settled down, as she had, to their unhappy situation. He spent most of his time away from home, but when he did come back, treated her with an offhand courtesy that she found perfectly tolerable. From time to time, when convention demanded it, they made a public appearance together, either at Court or at the opera, or, very rarely, at a party.

As for Ricky, Angelina had learned to keep him out of the way when his "father" was at home, and it was merely bad luck that brought Lord Merritt back unexpectedly one warm morning of early summer when Helen had taken Ricky driving with her.

"Good God!" Encountering them in the hall, Lord Merritt put up the glass he had taken to using, to gaze down at the elegant little figure in dark blue silk and lace ruffles. "Can't be the brat?"

"Make your bow to your father, Ricky," said Helen, hoping that the child at least would have forgotten that previous encounter.

"Graceful too," said Lord Merritt. "Does you credit." He thought it over. "Does us credit."

Helen's heart leapt. But there was more to come. "Time he learned to ride," said Lord Merritt thoughtfully. "We'll see to that, Price and I. Father's job; teach his son to ride." He turned carelessly over his shoulder to Price, who was a step behind him as usual. "Remind me, Price. Pony for the boy."

"Yes, my lord." Price's voice had changed a little, and so had his appearance. In private, Helen was sure, they behaved, now, entirely as equals. She preferred not to think about just how they behaved, and the fact that Price was clever enough to keep up the pretence at servility even in front of her frightened her more than anything. The idea of her child in their company gave her the horrors, but what could she do? In the world's eyes, he was Lord Merritt's child too.

Chapter 16

LUCKILY, an invitation to hunt with the King drove all thoughts of Ricky out of Lord Merritt's mind, at least for the time being. Helen saw him and Price ride away with a sigh of relief, but knew that this was merely a reprieve. It was strange that there was only one person she could consult about this new problem, but, she told herself, she was lucky to have even one. She found a moment alone with Angelina, and told her the story of the encounter, baldly, as it had happened.

"So," said Angelina. "He fancies the little one. And the man? Price?"

"I don't know."

"He hates you," said Angelina. "If he can harm the child, he will. You do not think, signora, that you should go home to England?"

"How can I?"

"You did not know? The British fleet is back in the Mediterranean. Take your chance, signora, when it offers, and go. You are not safe here; neither you nor the child. In the meantime, I, Angelina, will see that not a hair of his head is touched . . . And I mean touched, signora." They exchanged long looks. "A child is like a peach," Angelina went on. "Touch it, and it bruises. We will not have our Ricky bruised."

"Please God," said Helen. She did not ask how

Angelina knew that the British fleet was back, but had learned that she was always right about this kind of thing. It had been a lucky day when she took that apparently dying old woman into her coach. "I'm selfish, Angelina," she said now. "I don't know what I'd do without you, but I sometimes think I am keeping you from your own family. From Maria and her children?"

"Pah!" said Angelina. "That Maria! She's afraid of me, signora, and turns the little ones against me. Your Ricky is more my grandchild than her cretins." She used an untranslatable dialect word. "Besides, signora, you need me; she does not. She has Angelo."

"You're right," said Helen. "I do need you, Angelina. I thank God for you."

She was not at all surprised to go to the opera next day and find the whole house buzzing with the news of the British return to the Mediterranean. "I told you so." Lady Hamilton was in the fullest glow of beauty tonight, those remarkable eyes and the fair skin set off by one of the flowing white dresses Sir William liked her to wear. Helen thought him wise. Lady Hamilton loved to eat and drink, as she loved to laugh, and both had left their mark on face and figure. Helen liked her for the laughter lines in her face, but there was no pretending that Romney's sylph had not broadened considerably during the years of good living. The exquisite line of chin and throat he had loved to paint were a thing of the past. It was no wonder that she wrote home to her friend and one-time lover, Charles Greville, demanding the straw hats that could be so becomingly tied under the chin.

But her enthusiasm was as infectious as ever. "It's the best of news," she told Helen. "Lord St. Vincent is in over-all command, and our friend Captain Nelson has an independent squadron under him. No one knows where he is bound, of course, but one could, perhaps, hazard a guess."

"Naturally one will not," said Sir William. He was looking exhausted, Helen thought. It was good to know that he had applied for leave of absence. She only hoped that it would be granted to him in time. Impossible not to wonder what Lady Hamilton thought of their projected return to England, where, Helen suspected, she might not find her path so rose-bestrewn as it was in Naples. The English colony was small and gossip-ridden enough so that it was impossible not to hear the unkind things that were said behind her back by ladies who were glad of the Ambassadress's countenance at Court here in Naples but might all too easily turn her a cold shoulder in London. Here, Goethe might praise her attitudes, Angelica Kauffmann paint her picture, and the Duchess of Devonshire call on her. But, back in England, what chance had she of presentation at the Court of prim Queen Charlotte, and without that, what chance in society? But perhaps, Helen thought, her very real services to her country might outweigh her past history. Certainly they ought to. She had acted devotedly as secretary to Sir William when he was ill, and had almost certainly prolonged his life by her nursing. Was not this more important than a far-off, unlucky past?

A cold prickle of fear touched Helen's spine. Suppose Trenche was on one of the British ships that had returned at last to the Mediterranean? If he had hated her before, now he must be almost mad with it. She tried in vain to persuade her husband that if Sir William and Lady Hamilton did get their leave of absence and return to England it would be an admirable opportunity for them to go too. Lord Merritt was very happy where he was, and might, she was afraid, be happier still if freed from Sir William's restraining presence. He had always been a little in awe of the elegant, elderly ambassador, and this had conditioned his behaviour in Naples.

She knew well enough from servants' talk, repeated by Angelina, that when he and Price were off at the hunting box at Caserta, they behaved more like equals than like master and man. "In fact," Angelina summed up a fear of Helen's, "they say that sometimes Price is more like the master. What will you do, signora, if milord insists on taking the little one hunting with him?"

"I shall refuse to let him go." Helen hoped she sounded more certain than she felt. "It's ridiculous; he's only a baby. He won't be four till September. He'd be a great trouble to them."

"Yes. We must convince milord of that."

It seemed good advice, so when Lord Merritt, entertaining a few of his hunting friends at the Palazzo Trevi, sent for the child to come down and join them, Helen decided to allow it. After all, it was a kind of public acknowledgement of the child, and surely there was safety in numbers.

She herself kept away on these occasions, by tacit agreement with her husband, but this time she found it difficult to keep very far away. She could hear the laughter and talk from the upper terrace where she was sitting, and could occasionally make out Ricky's shrill voice among the deeper ones of the men. They were singing one of the hunting songs she had learned to know so well. Not much harm in that. Most of the words and their implications would go straight over Ricky's head. But she did not like the sound of his treble voice, joining in, stumbling over the strange words and raising a shout of laughter. Now they were trying to make him sing it alone. She got to her feet and took a restless turn along the terrace. She must intervene, but how? To go herself would precipitate the kind of scene she particularly wished to avoid. Lord Merritt hated Angelina. Impossible to send her. The child's voice, quavering to a halt amid a shout of laughter, decided her. She rang her bell and sent for Price.

"Yes, my lady?" Price did not let himself show any surprise at his unprecedented summons. Not for the first time, she found herself wondering how he felt about these occasions when Lord Merritt entertained his social equals, and Price had to behave like the servant he was.

"Oh, Price." She made it casual. "I think Ricky has been in the dining room long enough. I am afraid he will be a trouble to his father and his guests. Perhaps you would be so good as to fetch him for me?"

He looked at her for a moment thoughtfully, and she knew, as plainly as if he had told her, that he was aware of the full facts of her case. She made herself meet his small, mean eyes squarely while he thought it over. After all, he would probably be glad of an excuse to join the party, even if only for a few moments. In the silence, the singing voices rose to a crescendo, then broke into a cascade of laughter, Ricky's voice unnaturally loud among the rest.

"You can hear—" she said.

"Yes, my lady. I'll fetch him."

After a few moments devoted to silent relief, she followed Price out to the top of the stairway, arriving in time to see him emerge from the room below, with Ricky over his shoulder. The child's face was flushed, and he was defiantly singing the extremely improper chorus of the hunting song, kicking Price in the ribs as he did so. Seeing his mother, he struggled harder than ever. "I'm a man. I'll stay at the party." His voice sounded strange, and there were wine stains on the lace at his throat.

"He's been drinking! How could they?" For a moment she had forgotten who Price was. "A baby!"

"A vicious one." A harder kick had got Price where it hurt, and he dropped the child roughly. "Next time, you can do your own errands, my lady."

She held the now sobbing child and looked at Price coldly. "There will not be a next time."

Brave enough words, but when she had got Ricky to bed and persuaded him to drink a mildly sedative draught concocted by Angelina, she found herself furiously pacing the terrace, listening to the noise from below, and wondering how in the world she could make them good. Somehow, she must. She had not staked, and lost, her own happiness for the child's sake, to let him be corrupted now by the "father" she had given him. But what in the world could she do?

Angelina, as so often, provided the answer. Ricky was ailing and fretful the next day, suffering all too obviously from a four-year-old's version of a hangover. "The child is ill," said Angelina. "There is fever. You should have the doctor, my lady."

Helen, whose hand was feeling Ricky's steady pulse, was about to protest that there was nothing wrong that twenty-four hours in bed would not cure, when she caught Angelina's significant eye, which was bent on the maid who had been tidying the room, but had stopped and broken into an anxious wail at the idea that the child was really ill. Ricky, who understood Italian rather better than English, followed suit. "I hurt," he said.

"Poverino." Angelina put a gentle hand on the flushed face. "If I were the doctor, I would recommend country air, I think."

It was a cue, and Helen took it gratefully. No need to tell the doctor about yesterday's party. She was merely the anxious mother of an ailing child, and contrived to slip in the suggestion about country air so naturally that he was sure he had thought of it himself. "The very thing. Send him to the country, my lady, or the sea . . . One of the islands, perhaps. Naples is no place for a child in the summer. In the meantime, a cooling draught, quiet . . . He should be well enough to travel in a week or so."

"I shall take him," said Helen. "I should be glad of some country air myself." Thanks to the lawyers, she had control of a sufficient annual sum so that the hiring of a house of her own was no longer an impossibility.

But when she chose a tactful moment to put the proposal to Lord Merritt, he surprised her with a flat negative. "No," he said. "No, you don't. Send the brat, if the doctor says so. Awkward little cuss. Gave poor Price a nasty kick the other day. Tell you what. Those nuns Lady Hamilton's always on about. They might knock some sense into him. Some manners, at least. As for you. You stay here. My wife. British fleet turning up any day. Parties . . . That Nelson . . . Your father. You're to be here."

"If you say so." Helen's meekness hid a great surge of relief. Price had lost interest in the child; was perhaps even a little jealous of him. Maybe it was not even necessary to send him away, but better safe than sorry. She would miss Ricky horribly, but since Angelina would go with him, she would know he was well cared for, and away from the unformulated threats that hung over the Palazzo Trevi. At least, she thought wryly, if her husband insisted that she be there to put in an appearance at his side when the fleet sailed into harbour, he could hardly be planning her murder.

Or could he? Was this to be positively her last appearance? And the child already out of sight and therefore easily out of mind? It was a thought to chill the blood, and made the parting with Angelina even worse than she had feared. But Angelina was bracing. "Never fear, signora. The child and I can be back with you in a few hours if you want us." She shrugged. "All this talk of the French coming. I suppose they might, and if they do, you will want Ricky at home."

"I shall indeed." Among her other anxieties, Helen had actually forgotten this one. But then, with Captain Nelson in the Mediterranean, it seemed to her most unlikely that the French fleet would even manage to stir out of Toulon.

She was to be proved wrong. A few days after Angelina and Ricky left, the weather changed. All one Sunday night, the Bay of Naples was lashed to a fury by a northwesterly gale, and Helen, lying in bed and listening to the howling of the wind and the roaring of the waves in that usually crystal bay, found herself whispering the prayer for all those in danger at sea. Where were Nelson and his captains tonight? At sea somewhere, in a Mediterranean ringed with their enemies?

Charlotte, heavy-eyed over breakfast, admitted to the same fears. "And the wind still blows. Please God they are safe." She had had no letter from Captain Forbes for some time, but rumour said he was with Nelson's squadron.

Rumour was very active that May and early June. Sir William looked hag-ridden with fatigue, and the Jacobins, as always in moments of crisis, appeared in public and made a point of visiting the French minister, Garat.

And the first news that came was so bad that Helen thought for a while that she would try to keep it from Charlotte. Useless, of course. Everyone in town was talking of it. Nelson's flagship, the *Vanguard,* had been dismasted in the storm, and his squadron scattered. And as if this was not bad enough, the French had sailed from Toulon the night before the storm, and no one knew where they were.

"They've got that Bonaparte, with thirteen ships of the

line; four hundred transports." Lord Merritt was frightened into lucidity. "Coming here, most like. Might have known that Nelson of yours was all smoke and no fire."

Naples flamed with rumour. There had been mutinies that spring in the British fleet at home, and the gloomiest voices were those that said it had infected the Mediterranean Fleet. Others merely insisted that even if Nelson's flagship was still afloat his squadron was scattered and he was bound to sail back to Lisbon to refit. Even optimists had to admit that under the terms of the treaty with France, Naples was officially neutral and therefore could admit only three or four belligerent ships to any port at the same time.

"Much good three ships would do against Bonaparte's armada," said Charlotte gloomily. "Prince Augustus has gone, and most of the other British tourists. Helen, do you not think you could persuade Lord Merritt . . ."

"I'm afraid not." Helen had tried. She had wanted to send for Ricky and take passage on the first neutral ship that offered, but Lord Merritt had been adamant, and, oddly, she found herself respecting him for it.

"Rats," he had said. "Running like rats. I'm a dog. I don't run. And nor will you." He anticipated her next remark. "Send for the brat if you wish. No harm in that. Safe here as anywhere."

Or as unsafe. If the French came, there would be panic, riots, fighting in the streets. An ideal opportunity for the quiet murder of a woman and child. "I think Ricky is best where he is," said Helen quietly. "At least for the time being."

"Your affair." He shrugged it off.

A few days later came good news for a change. Captain Bowen brought the sloop *Transfer* into the bay to report that by quite extraordinary efforts Nelson and Captain Ball of the *Alexander* had saved the *Vanguard*. Despite the hostility on shore, the *Vanguard* had been rerigged at the island of St. Pietro south of Corsica, and Nelson's squadron was now reassembling off Toulon, ready to pursue the French and come to the rescue of Naples if this should prove necessary.

"But still no one knows where the French are headed,"

said Charlotte. She had had a letter at last, brought by Captain Bowen, and knew that Forbes and his *Cormorant* were indeed with Nelson. "Captain Forbes says something about frigates that I do not entirely understand." She sounded anxious.

"Very likely he does not intend you to. I would not speak of it, if I were you. Do you notice how careful Sir William is?"

"Yes. And how tired he looks."

The remark about frigates was explained soon enough. Not everyone had been as discreet as Captain Forbes, and all Naples soon knew that Nelson's frigates, separated from him by the storm, had missed him at the rendezvous he had appointed, and, fatally, sailed back to Gibraltar, thus depriving him of his vital reconnaissance force. "So he must rely on us for information." Lady Hamilton was in her element, hurrying to and fro between Sir William and the Queen. Everyone knew that the Viceroy of Sardinia had refused to allow the dismasted *Vanguard* the least assistance. Everyone wondered what Naples would do in a similar situation. Each ship that entered the harbour might bring news, either of the French position or of the British. Waking, every morning, Helen hurried to her window, wondering if she would see the sails of a fleet on the horizon, and, if so, which it would be.

She sent for Ricky. Impossible to leave him several hours' journey away when affairs might come to a crisis at any moment. He arrived looking well and fat and behaving as badly as possible. The good nuns had spoiled him beyond permission, according to Angelina, who had found it impossible to counteract this by any discipline of her own. "Frankly, signora, I was glad when your message came. He could be ruined just as easily by the doting of those good ladies as by anything else."

Helen wondered if she was right. Her husband had greeted the news of the child's return with a casualness that struck her as somehow false. "Your affair. Brat seems worse behaved than ever. Keep him out of the way."

What were they planning, he and Price? Or, rather, what was Price planning? Lord Merritt was hardly capable of contriving a scheme that would hold together. Left to himself, she was sure, he would let things go on very much as they did. It was not in his nature to do anything but grumble and let things slide. But Price was another matter. She was increasingly aware of something quiet and ruthless in him, behind the mask of the perfect servant that he wore so easily. And what a hold he would have over his master if he could contrive to implicate him in the deaths of his wife and child.

Extraordinary to be sitting in her charming drawing room, embroidering a chair seat, chatting casually and thinking thoughts like those. She looked across at Charlotte. Should she tell her? No. Impossible, and dangerous. Charlotte was as good as gold, but would be incapable of keeping a secret of this magnitude. Besides, she might so easily not believe her. After all, sometimes she thought herself that she was letting her imagination run away with her.

At least Charlotte's presence was a kind of protection. Impossible to imagine a convincing "accident" that would involve all three of them, and Charlotte had the weight of the Standishes behind her, and something of her mother's obstinacy. Price must realise, if Lord Merritt did not, that if Charlotte were to suspect anything out of the way, she would not let go until she had been satisfied.

But that would not be much consolation, Helen thought wryly, choosing a scarlet silk, if she and Ricky were dead. Odd to think that their safety depended to such an extent on Sir William, Charlotte, and Angelina. . . . "I wish poor Sir William didn't look so fagged," she said now.

"Do you wonder? He's with General Acton every day, and still there has been no pronouncement as to how the British fleet would be received, if it were to appear."

"Well, that's not surprising," said Helen. "You must know the Neapolitans well enough by now to realise that they will hedge their bets till the last possible moment. If the French sail into the bay first, I think we will see the most dishonourable of capitulations."

"And what will happen to us?"

"Oh, I expect as civilians we will merely be sent home

on a neutral ship. The French are not quite barbarians. They do not make war on women and children." She hoped she was right, and did not mention her private dread that the lazzaroni, who loathed the French as much as they loved their king, might rise in revolt against such a dishonourable peace. In the chaos that ensued, anything might happen.

The following Sunday, there was to be a service of intercession at the Cathedral, and Lord Merritt surprised Helen by insisting that she and Ricky accompany him. "And Miss Standish, if she likes."

Was this another step in Price's plan, or was she starting at shadows? She was never to find out, for that Sunday morning brought news at last of Nelson. Helen woke to the sight of English colours on the *Mutine* in the bay, and the news that Captain Troubridge was already closeted with Sir William and General Acton. He had left Nelson and his squadron just out of sight, off the island of Ischia, and come, on Nelson's orders, to find out just what the Neapolitans meant to do.

"He'll be lucky," said Helen.

"Yes." Charlotte was deep in a letter that had been sent up by hand from the *Mutine*. She looked up, colour flooding her face. "Helen! He wants me to go back with Troubridge and marry him."

"Oh, my God." She could not help it. Then, with a great effort, she changed her tone. "And you, dear, what do you think?"

"It's not what I think," said Charlotte. "It's what I feel. And, Helen, he thinks it would be safer for me. Oh, could you not come too? You and Ricky?"

"Hardly." Helen's tone was dryer than she liked. It was all too evident that Charlotte's mind had made itself up on the instant. "I doubt if Captain Forbes would exactly welcome us, and my father, you know, is still with St. Vincent and the main fleet."

"Oh, dear." Charlotte's face fell. "I do so hate the idea of leaving you in danger, when you have been so good to me."

"Never mind." Now Helen was glad that she had given Charlotte no hint of the other, private danger that frightened her so much more than the public one. "If Captain Nelson finds the French, you will be in danger yourself. There is plenty for all of us, I rather think. But Charlotte, dear, if you really mean to go back with Captain Troubridge, there is not a moment to be lost. We must start getting your things together."

"Yes." Charlotte was on her feet at once. "John says Troubridge won't wait for me for a second. Oh, Helen . . ."

Helen kissed her warmly. "No time for second thoughts, love. You know you made up your mind the instant you read the letter. Do you go and start Rose packing, and I will write a quick note to Lady Hamilton, explaining the circumstances."

"Oh, thank you. Yes, that would be best. She will help . . ."

"Of course she will. You remember how good she was to that Miss Wynne. She might even delay Captain Troubridge an instant or so for you, at a pinch."

"Oh, I couldn't have that." Charlotte looked frightened.

"No, it would never do, would it, as a beginning. Off with you, love, and get started." She pulled paper and inkstand towards her, then paused at a new thought. "I expect the fleet will be in faster touch with England than we are," she said. "Would you like me to write any other letters for you?"

"To my mother?" said Charlotte. "Thank you, Helen, but you're forgetting. I'll *be* with the fleet. I'll write her when I'm married." And then, hand to mouth: "Did you hear me?"

"Yes, not a stammer to it. Your husband will be proud of you, love. If you ever get to him." It sent Charlotte away, laughing and excited, and left Helen the task of writing her quick note to Lady Hamilton.

It brought as quick a response. The messenger brought back a scrawl in Emma Hamilton's semiliterate hand. She congratulated Miss Standish with all her heart . . . Captain Troubridge was still in conference, and she would send a messenger as soon as it showed signs of breaking up. "I think he is safe here for some time longer. I am afraid, *entre nous,* that it may mean things are not going entirely as we would wish." And then, a touching post-script. "Say nothing of this. But I know you will not. Now you are losing Miss Standish, you and I must be better friends than ever."

For the first time that day, Helen felt tears standing in her eyes. She had refused to let herself face just how much she was going to miss Charlotte, and even Rose, but Emma Hamilton, with her sure gift for other people's feelings, had thought of this. Another postscript had, one of her practical suggestions. "If Miss Standish is ready before you hear from me, bring her and her things here to me. It will save Captain Troubridge some valuable time." And then, "Forgive this scrawl. I must write a note to our dear, dear Nelson."

An hour later, Charlotte was ready. She and Helen reached the Palazzo Sessa just in time to find the long conference broken up. Captain Troubridge greeted Charlotte kindly, if abstractedly. Helen, looking from his face to those of Sir William and Lady Hamilton, thought that it could not be good news that he was taking back to Nelson. But whatever it was, he was impatient to be off with it. Lady Hamilton had been seated at her writing desk when Helen and Charlotte arrived, scribbling a note. Now she sealed it, with an enclosure, and handed it to Troubridge. "For Captain Nelson," she said, "if you will be so good."

"Thank you." This was apparently what he had been waiting for. He turned to Charlotte. "You have sent your baggage direct to the harbour? Good. Then let us go."

A quick kiss, and it was over. Charlotte was gone, and Helen thought she had never felt so lonely in her life. Sir William had disappeared too, and Lady Hamilton took her hand. "Sit down, love, and have a glass of something. You look all to pieces."

"I feel it," Helen confessed.

"Better to feel than not," said Emma Hamilton.

Chapter 17

LADY Hamilton kept Helen with her all that long Sunday, and Helen was glad to stay. Ricky was safe with Angelina, and she was in no hurry to face the Palazzo Trevi alone. Sir William had gone back to General Acton's house as soon as Troubridge had left. "To have another try, I have no doubt," said his wife.

"Another try?"

"For a better reception for our fleet." Emma Hamilton had a ravishing, mischievous smile for Helen. "You can keep a secret, love, can you not?"

"Yes, I think so." God knew she had had practice enough.

"We English must hang together, now the rats have fled. And good riddance to them, I say. That Prince Augustus with his morganatic marriage and his terrible voice . . . What an embarrassment for Sir William." She laughed. "Poor Sir William. I wish I had had a chance to tell him."

"To tell him what?" Helen was not sure that she should ask it, but certain that Emma wanted her to, and curious enough on her own account.

"Why, that my dear Queen has done what that coward Acton would not. He's been shilly-shally all morning with Sir William and poor Troubridge, and it's a glum enough message the captain has to take back to our friend Nelson. Nothing would budge Acton, Sir William says. He sticks to the letter of his treaty with France. No aid for the British; no hostility to the French. It would serve him right if the French armada sailed in here tomorrow and sacked the place. At the best of it they are likely to take Malta and Sicily. Only think of General Acton's actually letting the French minister, Garat, send dispatches with details of Nelson's position. It's enough to make you mad."

"I suppose it is according to the letter of the treaty," said Helen doubtfully.

"Yes, no doubt. Which they'd break soon enough if it suited them. But no need to look so downhearted, love. Things are not quite so bad as they seem. Sir William has seen to it that our dear Nelson has full details of everything we know about the movements of the French. Not much, I'm afraid, but something. And the best of all is that letter I was writing when you and Miss Standish came. That's the cream of it. While Sir William and Captain Troubridge were practically on their knees to General Acton, where was I but with my darling Queen? And not wasting my time either. She's a woman in a million, and hates the French as much as any of us. And no wonder . . . So while King Ferdinand hunts, and General Acton shuffles and palters, what does she do but sit down and write a note for the port authorities, here and in Sicily, telling them to give all the aid they can to the British. That's what I was sending Captain Nelson in such a hurry." She looked at the chiming clock on the chimney-piece. "I hope he obeys my orders and sends it back, for I am bound not to give any of her letters."

"You mean you expect to hear again from the fleet today?"

"I am positive of it. Sir William must be answered, and so must I. Captain Bowen is to come back this evening. Very likely he will have word for you from Miss Standish. And I am sure there will be a letter for me from my dear Nelson. You must wait and see the event."

"I should be glad to, if you are sure I'll not be in the way."

"Never, love. Not you. There's not many here in Naples that I trust, and nor should you. But you and I have been friends for longer than I care to think of."

Helen laughed. "Nor I."

Lady Hamilton turned to one of the large gold-framed looking glasses with which the room was so well equipped. "But we've worn well, that's one comfort."

"Yes, indeed." Had the beauty managed to persuade herself that they were more or less the same age? It was not the first time that Helen had noticed her quite extraordinary capacity for self-deception in a good cause. Was she, just possibly, deceiving herself also about the importance of that letter of the Queen's? Could the Queen give such an authorisation in the face of General Acton's stand?

Captain Nelson seemed to think so. His answer was brought up from the harbour when the shadows were beginning to lengthen across the bay. Lady Hamilton tore it open eagerly, tucked the enclosure in a secret compartment of her desk, and turned to read the crabbed, difficult, left-handed script. "I told you so." Her face glowed with enthusiasm. "He has done everything I bade him. He has kissed the Queen's letter and returned it. Soon he hopes to kiss her hand when no fears intervene . . . Fear not the event, he says, for God is with us." She smiled as she refolded the letter. "No time to write poor Sir William. So much for your official dispatches."

"Does he say what he will do next?" Helen wondered whether she should ask it.

"No, but he has no need to. We know his orders. They are to seek out, sink, burn, and destroy the French fleet. That is what he will do, and presently will return to us crowned with laurels. Oh, I can hardly wait to see that day." Emma Hamilton struck an attitude, and Helen decided that it was time to go home. She thought it would be best to be gone before Sir William returned and found that Captain Nelson had time to answer his wife's letters, but not his own.

"Been out long enough." Lord Merritt was awaiting her in her own parlour. "What's this about Miss Standish?"

"She's left us," said Helen. "She's gone with Captain Troubridge to marry Captain Forbes."

"Good God! Crazy woman. Well, no doing of mine. Mind you tell Mrs. Standish when you write her."

"I suppose I must," said Helen doubtfully. "Charlotte said she would herself." It was so surprising to find her husband in her rooms that she found herself slipping back into the freer communication of the early days of their marriage.

"Certainly must," said Lord Merritt. "In your charge, after all. Least you can do to explain. Soften the pill with a bit of news, maybe? What's gone on up at the embassy all day?"

So that was it. He was curious. And yet it was unlike her husband to show more than routine interest in the news of the day. He had finally convinced himself (or been convinced by Price?) that French or English domination of Naples was all one to him, and nothing would shake him in this belief. Why did he feel so safe? A small worm of suspicion began to crawl at the back of Helen's mind. Price. Everything came back to Price. Just suppose that as well as being her enemy, Price was England's—in the pay of the French? He would be able to promise his master immunity if they landed, and he would be eager, unlike his master, for firsthand news.

But Lord Merritt was growing impatient for her reply. "Ships to and fro all day," he said. "Must have been something going on."

"Of course there was." Helen came to a quick decision. "Captain Troubridge came to ask for help for the British fleet, and General Acton would not give it to him. He's sticking to the letter of the treaty with France." No harm in telling him this, even if he was going to take it straight to Price. And, suddenly, through this new danger, she thought she saw her way to a kind of safety. If Price thought her a valuable source of information, it would be in his interest to keep her alive. "I spent a charming afternoon with Lady Hamilton," she went on now. "She was kindness itself and says we must be friends, now Charlotte is gone. You will not mind, if I spend some time at the Palazzo Sessa?"

"Don't see why not, if you like to. Dead bore of a woman, but that's your affair. Those attitudes . . . Oh, well, time to be getting along." Was he returning to Price for fresh instructions?

She was proved right next morning, when he called on her after breakfast to urge the propriety of her accepting Lady Hamilton's open invitation. He spoke so nearly in sentences that she thought Price must have coached him, and congratulated herself that Price must think her negligible as an adversary. There were, after all, some advantages about being a woman. Men tended to dismiss you as a fool.

She found Emma Hamilton pacing up and down her room in splendidly dramatised fury. "The very person," she kissed Helen warmly, "to share my bad news. Only think of its arriving today, one day too late for Captain Nelson. Oh, it's enough to make one mad. *And* to make one wonder if by any chance it was held up on purpose. If we had only known!"

"What is it?" Impossible to tell, granted the beauty's habitual self-dramatisation, whether this was a great or a trivial mishap.

"The French have taken Malta. The Knights of St. John capitulated without so much as a shot fired. Oh, it's a bad day for England. Soon we will have no friends left in the Mediterranean."

"But is it known where the French are now?"

"Nothing but rumours. Some say they will take Sicily next; others that they are bound for Alexandria."

"Alexandria?" Helen was amazed.

"Yes, to take Egypt and so by way of the Red Sea to join Tippoo Sahib in a revolt against the British in India."

"Good God," said Helen. "It sounds fantastic."

"I'm sure it is," agreed Lady Hamilton. "They'll come here, of course. I've felt it in my bones all along. We must just pray that Nelson has had news of the fall of Malta by now, and comes to our rescue."

Driving home, Helen debated with herself what she should tell her husband. Tell him something, she must, but what? It turned out that he had already learned of the fall of Malta, news of which was all over town by now. "Where will they go next?" he asked her. "Lady Hamilton. What does she think?"

Helen had made up her mind. "She would not say in so many words, of course. But I got the impression that she has some fantastic idea of an attack on Egypt. It sounds like madness to me."

"Egypt, eh? Odd come-out, I'd have thought. Why Egypt?"

"As a means to attack India, Lady Hamilton thought. It seems unlikely enough. Even that daredevil Bonaparte would hardly go half round the world to attack us, when he could do it so much more easily at home."

"Can he?" asked Lord Merritt.

She thought about it afterwards and wondered, in increasing anxiety, whether she had not perhaps picked the wrong bit of information to pass on. How frightful if, intending to mislead, she had actually provided a useful clue. Her husband had left her after that one significant question, which made her think that perhaps the business of passing on information might work two ways. Price inevitably would have to explain a little of his own thinking to his master in order to get him to ask the right questions. It sounded to her as if Price might actually believe the chance of an attack on Egypt.

As the days passed by without a sign of either fleet, the Egyptian venture began to seem more and more of a possibility. Calling regularly at the Palazzo Sessa, Helen learned a week or so later that Sir William had finally received an answer to his letter to Nelson.

"Our friend's not at all pleased with the Court here," said Emma Hamilton. "Who could expect him to be?" She laughed. "He complains in good set terms of the lethargy of Naples—no assistance for him, no hostility to the French."

"But the Queen's letter?" asked Helen.

"Ah ha, he does not mention that," said Emma. "And nor must you. But only to think of his still not knowing that Malta has fallen to the French. He writes urging that Naples make a push to take it. Too late, alas . . ."

"But does he say where he is going next? Or where he thinks the French are?"

"Why, no." She sounded surprised. "Now I come to think of it, he does not." She brightened. "Very likely he had not made up his mind."

Helen wondered. Had Troubridge perhaps warned

Captain Nelson of the gossip-ridden state of Naples? Perhaps even warned him against the charming Ambassadress? After all, it was common knowledge that everything she learned went straight to the Queen, and then, no doubt, from the Queen to the Court of Austria. There were all too many possibilities, on the way, of its falling into the wrong hands.

Meanwhile, they were back at the old, anxious waiting. Helen told Lord Merritt about Nelson's letter, and made a point of telling him that Lady Hamilton had commented on Nelson's failure to describe his own plans. "She thinks he had probably not made up his mind."

"Shilly-shally." It was a phrase Lord Merritt liked. "That Charlotte," he went on. "News of her?"

News of Charlotte would be news of the fleet. "Not a word." Helen wished it did not happen to be true. Charlotte had presumably had no chance to send a letter back by Captain Bowen that Sunday when she had left in such haste. Helen had hardly expected it, but as June warmed up into the heavy heat of July she became increasingly anxious for news of Charlotte as well as of the fleet.

The silence was absolute. "Really," said Lady Hamilton, "one might think the sea had opened and swallowed both fleets. You've heard nothing from Miss Standish?"

"Not a word. I do hope she is Mrs. Forbes by now."

"Yes, indeed, or her reputation's gone, poor girl." Extraordinary to have Lady Hamilton speak in this tone about the loss of reputation. She must indeed feel confident that she had recovered her own. Her next words confirmed this. "A pity there's no news of her. I need news beyond anything, now I am got against my will into the diplomatic line for my beloved Queen. You would not believe how she relies on me. I make my friend Greville write me long letters full of politics from England for her sake. She loves everything that is English, just as she hates the French. So be sure and let me know at once if you should hear anything from Miss Standish. You never can tell, she might find some private means of communication safer than the official ones. Did you know that the first letter Sir William sent to our friend Nelson, about the French armament, never reached him?"

"No!"

"Sent on a Maltese boat, love. The moral is, trust no one. Except each other, of course." A warm, sweet-scented kiss. "And now I must be off to my darling Queen who tells me she quite counts the minutes until I come. We sit together, like mother and daughter, all afternoon, and then, when I meet her at the opera at night, I treat her with such deference you'd think I was still a girl on my probation. It was Sir William's idea. I don't know where I would be without Sir William."

"How is he?"

"Tired. And can you wonder, the burden that he bears. I wish his leave of absence would come—and yet I do not. How could we leave my angel Queen at this moment of crisis? No, Sir William must nurse himself, and keep going, as we all do, for the Cause."

Rising to take her leave, Helen was not quite sure what the Cause was, but very certain that Lady Hamilton did not want to leave Naples, whatever signs of strain her husband might be showing. Interesting that it was on his suggestion that his wife treated Queen Maria Carolina with that pretty, formal deference in public, despite the terms of intimacy on which they lived in private. He was a very clever man, Helen thought. She only wished he was a younger and stronger one.

As usual, July brought heat, flies and stench to the streets of Naples, but to Helen's surprise her husband stayed in town. It was, she was afraid, a sign of the completeness of Price's domination. Town was where news could be had. In town they would stay. It had become a matter of custom, now, for Lord Merritt to call on her, casually, in her rooms after her daily visit to the Palazzo Sessa, and ask, even more casually, if there was any news.

And, daily, she could reply, with a clear conscience, if a heavy heart, that there was none. Anything could have happened. Suppose that mast of Captain Nelson's that had been so quickly re-rigged off St. Pietro had failed to stand up to one of the quick Mediterranean storms that could blow up out of a clear sky? Without him, she was sure, the British squadron would head for safety, leaving the Mediterranean clear for the French. Lady Hamilton agreed with her. "Without him," she said, "they are nothing. I pray for him nightly." She raised her eyes in her Madonna pose.

It irritated Helen into contradiction. "I'm not so sure. That Captain Troubridge seemed like a man of action. And think of Captain Ball risking his own ship to save Nelson's!"

"I should hope so too," said Emma Hamilton. Quick to recognise Helen's moment of revolt, she sent her home early on the pretext that she must get ready to visit the Queen.

At the end of July news came at last from Nelson's squadron. Sir William and Lady Hamilton, and Helen, all had letters, the Hamiltons' from Nelson and Helen's from Charlotte. Lady Hamilton sent this down to the Palazzo Trevi, enclosed in a note urging Helen to come up at once and share the news.

Helen took the precaution of reading Charlotte's letter first, and was glad she had done so when she came to one passage in it. Charlotte was indeed Mrs. Forbes now, and wrote in glowing terms of her happiness. In fact, she spent so much time describing her marriage, her wonderfully convenient little apartments on board ship, and all the comforts her husband had arranged for her, that she had to end by referring Helen to Lady Hamilton for news of their wanderings. A postscript, scrawled down the margin, hit Helen hard. "I met an old friend on my wedding day," Charlotte wrote in her large, free hand. "Charles Scroope has joined the squadron, but, Helen, what have you done to make him so out of temper with you? He positively scowled when I spoke of you, and turned the subject as fast as he could. I thought you two were friends."

"Friends." Helen stared at the letter, her eyes blurring with tears, and wondered, as she had so often in the lonely watches of the night, just what horrible lies Trenche had told Charles Scroope about her. She would never know, and, equally, would never be able to justify herself to Charles Scroope. It was terrible to mind so much.

"Letters, hey?" News travelled fast in the Palazzo

Trevi, and Lord Merritt had come to pay his morning call. "From Miss Standish?"

"Mrs. Forbes. She's married."

"Good thing. Where does she write from?"

Helen picked up the letter. "I did not think to look. Oh —merely, 'At sea.' "

"Fool of a girl. Something about where they've been?"

"Well, not much." Helen was glad to be able to say it. "She seems more concerned with her own happiness. Oh, there's something here about 'such a chase as we have had' but that's all."

"No word of the French?"

"Not one. If they had been in action, I am sure she would have mentioned it."

"Idiotic. Visiting Lady Hamilton?"

"Yes. She asks me to take her Charlotte's letter. They have heard from Nelson."

"Then what's keeping you?" said her husband. "Ambassadress sends for you and you sit around gossiping. Just like you."

It was a relief to get away from his clumsy questioning, but she wished she had more time in which to decide whether to show Lady Hamilton Charlotte's letter or merely quote from it to her. Helen and Miss Tillingdon had always disliked the showing of letters, and in this case Helen was particularly reluctant. She found it hard to face the thought of Emma Hamilton's possible questions about Charles Scroope. Thinking about him was bad enough. Could she possibly speak of him without breaking down?

As so often, she had fretted herself unnecessarily. Lady Hamilton was too full of their own news to be much interested in Helen's. "Writes all about herself, does she?" She laughed indulgently. "Understandable enough. I was like that once, thinking only of dress and parties. Now it's quite other with me. Now I am a politician despite myself." She fell unconsciously into her pose as Pallas Athene, goddess of wisdom.

"Charlotte—Mrs. Forbes—refers me to you for news of Captain Nelson." Helen brought the conversation back to the matter in hand.

"She sends you to the right person." She was the Ambassadress now. "Sir William and I both had letters this time. But it's bad news, I'm afraid. Not a sign of the French. The Devil's children have the Devil's own luck, says our poor Nelson. Only think of his having been all the way to Egypt and back, and still not a sign of them. It's driving him frantic with worry, and no wonder."

"Where is he?" asked Helen.

"Off Sicily. He dates from Syracuse and speaks of taking a look in at Cyprus. If only his supplies hold out . . ."

Two days later, a furious letter from Nelson to Sir William proved that Emma knew what she was talking about. The Governor of Syracuse had had the temerity to refuse the British ships the supplies they needed, claiming that General Acton had sent no orders. "I have come straight from my beloved Queen," said Emma. "We'll soon see whose orders carry weight in this country. But," finger on lip, "not a word to a soul, as you love me."

By now, everyone knew that the British fleet was off Sicily, and Helen felt safe enough in telling her husband this, and also about the fleet's difficulty over provisions and water.

"Both sides against the middle," said Lord Merritt. "Neapolitan game, if you ask me. Best start practising your French."

"Do you think so?" If only she could find out what Price knew, but she dared not rouse his suspicions by cross-questioning her husband.

A few days later came the news that the British squadron had sailed from Syracuse, where, Nelson now wrote to Sir William, their wants had been most amply supplied and every attention had been paid to them. "You see." Lady Hamilton was triumphant. "We all know whose doing that is! But mum's the word."

"Yes, indeed. Though I suppose it will be public knowledge that they have been supplied."

Lady Hamilton laughed. "Bound to be. And the Court will probably give the Governor of Syracuse a public rebuke and a private reward. Only see how cleverly our friend Nelson has worded his letter. See where he writes that he has 'been tormented by no private orders being given to the Governor.' That's put in to save everyone's face, do you see? He's no fool, our friend Nelson."

"No, indeed." Helen knew now what she would say at home. But Lady Hamilton had one more quotation from Nelson. "Be assured," he wrote, "I shall return either crowned with laurel or covered with cypress."

Chapter 18

THE long wait began again. Nelson had sailed from Syracuse on July twenty-fourth, but it was not until September third that Naples learned how fully he had carried out his orders to "burn, sink, or destroy" the enemy. All August, eyes and glasses had been fixed on the bay, where any day a sail might appear with news of a battle that would settle the balance of power in the Mediterranean. Citizen Garat had left Naples in disgust by now, discovering at last that "the infamous behaviour of the Court was not due to barbarity but to ingrained hostility." His secretary, Lacheze, was left in charge of the embassy, but Lacheze had little to do but complain.

September third gave him something to complain about. The sloop *Mutine* sailed into the bay, and Captain Hoste and Captain Capel hurried ashore with dispatches for Sir William and for England. But before they so much as landed, the triumphant pantomime of the sailors who rowed them had told its tale. Miss Cornelia Knight and her mother, who had been watching through a telescope, hurried to tell the news to their next-door neighbour, General di Pietra, and soon champagne glasses were being smashed in honour of British victory.

At the Palazzo Trevi, Helen actually heard the news from her husband, who had been dining with General di

Pietra, but hurried home to tell her (and Price?) the news, and to urge that she go up to the Palazzo Sessa without delay.

For once, there was no need to edit what she learned there. This was victory, unqualified and glorious, and the more Price knew about it, the better. Captain Nelson would indeed return crowned with laurel, and, if he did not, Lady Hamilton was all ready to crown him. She was in a dramatic seventh heaven, weeping, exclaiming, threatening to faint (which she already had), and describing over and over again how the news had been received at the palace. The Queen, too, had "fainted, cried, kissed her husband, her children, walked frantic with pleasure about the room" and then "cried, kissed and embraced every person near her exclaiming, 'Oh brave Nelson, oh God bless and protect our brave deliverer.'" As for the French, "Not a French dog dare show his face," said Emma Hamilton.

The Battle of the Nile had been dramatic enough to satisfy even her. Nelson had found Admiral de Brueys anchored, in the safety (as he thought) of Aboukir Bay, and had sailed in at dusk to fight a bloody night-long action, from which only two French ships escaped. Bonaparte and his army were marooned in Egypt, and the English all powerful in the Mediterranean. But the victory had been bought high. When the two surviving French ships slipped their cables in the morning and ran for it, there was not a British one in a state to give chase. And Nelson had been wounded, at first, he thought, fatally, and though the wound in fact proved superficial he was suffering from the strain of the long chase. He and his battered ships were on their way to Naples to refit and recuperate. Emma was preparing apartments for him in the Palazzo Sessa, and though he began by saying he would rather stay in a hotel, he was soon overruled by the enthusiastic Ambassadress, who was, she wrote him, dressed all over à la Nelson.

She looked, in Helen's view, sufficiently ridiculous, with her blue shawl covered in gold anchors, and more gold anchors for earrings, and her reports of Queen Maria Carolina's rejoicings also began, at fourth or fifth

220

repetition, to have a faintly absurd flavour. Had the daughter of Austria really fainted and cried hip hip hurrah? Helen had to suspect that she very likely had. The Queen and Emma tended to encourage each other in this kind of extravagance. But then, extravagance was the order of the day. There was no talk of neutrality now. All Naples was illuminated for three nights in celebration. "There were three thousand lamps," said Emma, "and there should have been three millions if we had time."

"It was magnificent." Helen said it mechanically. She was finding her role of confidante to the ecstatic beauty increasingly trying, and was grateful to Miss Cornelia Knight for sharing it with her.

"Magnificent indeed!" Emma Hamilton had a sharp look for Helen. She had not lost her disconcerting gift for reading one's thoughts. "You're anxious, love, about Miss Standish—Mrs. Forbes. But you'll see, she'll be all right. Naturally, the private news takes longer. And we know the *Cormorant* was only hit a few times between wind and water."

"Only" seemed hardly the word to Helen, but Lady Hamilton's quick sympathy shamed her out of her critical mood. The trouble was that she had another cause of anxiety, one she could discuss with no one. The *Gannet* was on her way to Naples under tow, and Captain Scroope was reported seriously wounded. It was little comfort to Helen that he was also said to have behaved with the utmost gallantry, joining Foley of the *Goliath* in boldly turning the enemy's line. She wanted to know what his wounds were, and, in the hot discomfort of a crippled ship, what his chances.

Nothing for it, as always, but to wait. A letter from Charlotte painted a gloomy picture. The *Cormorant,* too, was on her slow way to Naples, with a terrible list of dead and wounded. Charlotte mentioned this almost in passing. Her main concern was that her husband was unhurt and that she had had the fright of her life. "Never again!" she wrote in that large, schoolgirl hand. "My dear John says he will not allow me to be so frightened again, and, besides, I begin to think there are reasons why I would be better on shore. So, dear Helen, may I come back to you?

It will break my heart to part with John, but he too thinks it for the best. His anxiety for me, he says, was the worst part of the action to him." And then, one of her sideways postscripts. "Only think of poor Captain Scroope's being so bad! John says he and Foley took a terrible chance. We must just hope the poor man survives." Characteristically, she did not mention what Scroope's injuries were.

On the eighteenth, Troubridge and Ball brought the *Culloden* and the *Alexander* into the Bay of Naples, to a heroes' welcome. Hurrying up to the Palazzo Sessa, Helen found Ball sitting with Lady Hamilton and delighting her by calling her "the patroness of the navy."

"We can expect our dear friend Nelson any day now," Emma told Helen. "But just think, he has lost his foremast, and the *Vanguard* will come in under tow of the *Thalia.*"

"What other ships are in tow?" Helen seized the chance to ask Ball this.

"Oh, several. It was a bloody business, Lady Merritt, make no mistake about that. The French defended themselves like tigers, to give them their due. Think of Admiral De Brueys, his legs shot away, having himself tied in a chair and staying on the deck of his flagship until he was killed by a cannon shot. *L'Orient* blew up later, but we heard the story from a survivor. No, it was a bad night, Lady Merritt."

"But a glorious one," said Emma Hamilton.

"I am so glad to hear that my friend Mrs. Forbes is none the worse," Helen tried again. "She writes me that poor Captain Scroope is hurt. We knew him, she and I, a little. He brought us here, in the *Gannet.*"

"She's under tow," said Captain Ball, and won Helen a quick look from Lady Hamilton. "She should get here about the same time as Nelson. I only hope with her captain still alive. He sustained a wound in the right leg and refused to have it amputated. Well, you can understand that. It would end his career. But, in this climate . . . It's a terrible chance to take."

"Madness," said Lady Hamilton. "It would take the nursing of an angel to save him, and where will he get

222

that? Thank God, our gallant and victorious friend had more sense when his arm was hurt. Oh, how I long for the day when I crown him with the laurel he has earned."

Ball laughed. "Do you know what he said the night before the battle? 'A peerage or Westminster Abbey.'"

"And it will be a peerage," cried Emma Hamilton. "Oh, how well it sounds, Earl Nelson of the Nile. Was not that what they gave Jervis?"

"Yes." Helen thought Ball looked uncomfortable. "But of course he was in over-all command, where Admiral Nelson was not."

"Fudge," said Emma Hamilton. "What difference does that make?"

Word soon got around that Nelson would arrive on September twenty-second, the anniversary of King Ferdinand's coronation. "Tactful, ain't it," said Emma Hamilton with one of the rather touching grammatical lapses that happened only when she spoke English. "Sir William's idea, of course. Would you like to come out in our barge to greet him?"

"No, thank you very much. My husband has arranged to hire a barge for the occasion." No need to say how much the decision had surprised her. Had Price decided to change sides, or was this merely another of his tricks? He had certainly worked doggedly to make sure that the Palazzo Trevi was as well illuminated even as the Palazzo Sessa.

On the morning of the twenty-second, the crowds began to gather early. The mole and quays were thick with people, and the great bay crowded with boats of every kind. The only trouble, Helen was to find, about having their own barge was that inevitably they had to keep back among the gaily bedecked craft of the Neapolitan nobles and gentry. Since there were some five hundred of these, including whole boatloads of musicians, Helen had only a distant and limited view of the Hamiltons' barge, with Emma in white muslin for its figurehead, as it pulled alongside the *Vanguard*. A tiny figure on the quarter-deck must be Admiral Nelson, but they were on the wrong side to see the buxom Ambassadress swayed up in the bosun's chair. The Ambassador's barge was closely followed by the royal one, with King Ferdinand on board. Music played, "Rule Britannia" from one side and "See the Conquering Hero" from another—the ships fired a twenty-one-gun salute in honour of the King, and the barges of the nobles began the slow business of getting their passengers on board the *Vanguard*.

"Take us hours at this rate," said Lord Merritt. "Much better go fishing. Lot of nonsense anyway. Bet the King would rather. Put you on shore first?"

"Yes, if you please." Helen did not know whether to be relieved or disappointed. She had hoped that perhaps someone on board the *Vanguard* would be able to give her news of Captain Scroope, but the sight of the crowds who were thronging on board made this seem unlikely. "What are the other ships that came in with the *Vanguard?*" she asked in Italian.

One of the rowers shouted the question across to a friend and obliged with a list of ships, hardly recognisable in his peasant Italian. But Helen caught the *Gannet*'s name and asked where she was. "Over there—" The man pointed. "Her captain's dying, they say. They're taking him to hospital. That will kill him quick enough."

Helen kept a calm face with an effort and made a quick decision. "My dear," she turned to her husband, "since Lady Hamilton invites the Admiral to stay and be nursed, do you think it would be well taken if we were to invite Captain Scroope? After all, we are under considerable obligations to him, as everyone knows."

"Lot of nursing," said Lord Merritt. "Lot of nonsense. Dead bore of a fellow. Always shoving his nose in." And then, after a pause. "Think it over." He looked down at the embroidered satin of his best suit. "Forgot about my clothes. Not quite the thing for fishing. Go home and change first."

"An excellent idea," said Helen. So he was going to consult Price. Impossible to imagine what view the latter would take, but surely there was a chance that he would think two people to spy on better than one.

Apparently he did. Helen had hardly had time to take off her broad-brimmed straw hat and change the muslin gown that had been splashed with the filthy water of the bay, when her husband joined her, still in his satin. "About that fellow, Scroope—"

"Yes?" She made herself go on calmly brushing her hair.

"Not a good account of him. Dying by the sound of it. Lot of trouble. But might look well—hey?"

"That's what I thought."

"But—*your* trouble." He made his position clear.

"Of course. I count on Angelina. If she can't help him, no one can."

"Old hag," said her husband.

"Shall I invite him?" asked Helen. "Or will you?"

"No need to stand on ceremony. Drive to the hospital. See what's going on. Doctors very likely bleeding him to death right now." Lord Merritt rather enjoyed the idea. "I'm going fishing."

That seemed to settle it. Helen gave a few brief instructions to Angelina and ordered out the big, old-fashioned carriage they had bought for taking baggage to and from the country. With a little judicious arrangement, it was possible to lay a mattress across the seats. She would not let herself wonder whether they would find Charles Scroope alive. If she got permission, she must be able to move him at once.

And all the time, as the servants worked willingly under her orders, her grinding anxiety for Charles was compounded by a more mundane fear that before she could get away, Charlotte might arrive to claim her hospitality and her time. But Charlotte was doubtless at the party that still seemed to be raging on board the *Vanguard*. There was no word from her, and Helen got into the carriage with a silent sigh of relief.

At the hospital, all was chaos, and Helen was afraid for a while that her mission might fail simply because it was impossible to get anyone's attention.

But at last she caught a harassed young doctor and put her question to him. "Captain Scroope? Yes, down there," he pointed. "With the officers. Not much hope for him, I'm afraid." And, when she put her proposition, "Can't make much difference, I'd say, one way or the other. But if you want him—one off our hands. Got enough as it is. No objection that I can see." He was longing to get back to work.

She held him with one last question. "So, if Captain Scroope does not object?"

"Object? Captain Scroope? He's been unconscious since they brought him ashore. Just as well, poor man. No, I don't think the drive will make much difference." All too obviously he thought nothing would. "Must lay him out flat, of course."

"I've made arrangements," said Helen coolly, wishing he had used any other phrase.

"Very good then. I'll just come and give the word."

When she saw the officers' room, Helen wondered what hope in the world there could be for the men. This was an inferno of crowd and noise and stench, where the conscious cried vainly for water, and the unconscious were to be envied rather than pitied. She only just recognized Charles Scroope on his pallet at the end of a line of beds. Flies were crawling over his blanched face, and the bandages on his right leg were dirty and black with blood.

No hope for him here. If taking him away killed him, it would merely hasten the inevitable. She had taken the precaution of bringing with her one of the boys who served as scullions and, on occasion, as pages. Now she sent him to the carriage to bring the men back instantly. "You will hold the horses."

"Yes, signora." He was only too glad to escape from that horrible place.

Helen had forgotten him already. She was kneeling by Charles Scroope's inert body, fanning away the flies, feeling anxiously for a thread of pulse.

"He has no fever." This was a ragged-looking, red-faced woman in a bloodstained gown. "Get him away from here, signora, and he might even live."

"You think so? Oh, God bless you." Helen realised that the tears were streaming down her face and brushed them away with one impatient hand while the other went to Charles's forehead to confirm the nurse's diagnosis. It was true; he was not fevered, but cold as death. "He's cold," she said.

"Then keep him warm. You best know how." A bawdy

wink confirmed Helen's guess that this was a woman of the streets, who had dwindled into the profession of nurse. She looked past Helen. "Here come your people, signora. Take your husband away, and good luck to you."

Scarlet in the face, Helen turned to see coachman and footman grinning widely at this mistake. "Good." Her voice was cold with anger. "Pick him up carefully. You've got the coach as near as possible?"

"Right outside." The coachman had never seen her angry, and it shook him. "We'd best lose no time, or they'll make the boy move it."

The only comfort of that nightmare journey was that Charles Scroope remained unconscious. But Helen, watching more and more blood seep through the filthy bandage, had to remind herself that nothing could be more certain than death in that horrible hospital. Anything was better than that. And there was comfort, too, in that sordid nurse's last words. "No fever," she had shouted down the crowded, stinking room. "While there's life, there's hope."

And at the Palazzo Trevi, there was Angelina to report that all was ready in the room Helen had selected as a sickroom. "Hmm," she, too, put a quick hand on that cold brow. "No fever. He must have the strength of an ox, this one. Bring him in, you, and if you so much as touch that leg, I'll have words with your wives."

All the other servants, Helen knew, looked on Angelina as more or less of a witch, and a threat like this from her was worth any number of exhortations from their employers. They carried Charles in as if he was made of Venetian glass and laid him down tenderly on the bed Angelina had prepared. "Right." Angelina had rolled up her sleeves. "Now send one of the maids to help me."

"No," said Helen. "I will help you." She and Miss Tillingdon had acted often enough as emergency nurses at Up Harting, but then she had been the chief nurse. It was an immense relief to yield this responsibility to Angelina. Their own doctor, for whom she had sent the boy running from the hospital, had still not appeared when they gently got the last blood-soaked layer of bandage clear of the wound.

Angelina seemed rather pleased than otherwise that the doctor had not come. "Ah," she said with apparent satisfaction, while Helen turned away to fight a momentary fit of faintness. "It could be worse. A glancing shot from a cannonball, I would say, and with luck not much lodged."

"Not much?" Helen was horrified that anything should be.

"Not the ball." Angelina was working rapidly at a curious compound she had brought with her. "Shreds of clothing. Sure to be, signora. Just be grateful it was a ball, and not splinters of wood. Then we would have trouble. As it is, he may have been right to refuse to have the leg off. Since he's survived so long, there should be a chance." She had been carefully smearing her compound on a clean cloth. It was greenish grey and added a strange smell of its own to the stench Charles Scroope had brought with him from the hospital.

"What are you doing?" Helen could not believe her eyes as Angelina prepared to put this strange dressing on the wound.

"Dressing the wound," said Angelina. "You told me to care for him, signora. This will save him if anything can. I've used it often enough for wounds like this."

"It looks like mould," said Helen faintly.

"It is mould." With a definite gesture Angelina laid the dressing on the gaping wound above Charles's left knee, then let Helen help her bandage it in place. "Now one of my herbal draughts," she said when they had finished, "and I hope we can snap our fingers at the doctor."

"He will want to see the wound," said Helen.

"He can't. That dressing stays on till it dries. Remove it, and you might as well send for the undertaker."

"How long?" asked Helen faintly.

"God knows. He's lost so much blood. And that's another thing. If the doctor wants to bleed him, turn him out of doors."

The doctor, arriving at last to find his patient lying apparently lifeless in a cool dark room through which a slight breeze blew, was horrified at everything he saw. "You'll kill him with all this air. I'll have those windows closed at once. And now," he moved towards the bed, "let's have a look at the wound."

"I'm sorry." Helen moved between him and the bed. "I do apologise, doctor, but we did not dare wait. The wound has been dressed. It's only a flesh wound, though deep enough. . . ." She shuddered, remembering.

"Oh." The doctor had crossed swords with Angelina before, after Ricky was born, and lost. He thought it over for a moment. "In that case," he said, "I'll just bleed him, to be on the safe side, and leave you a cooling draught."

"No," said Helen and Angelina at once. And then Helen, pacificatory: "The draught, if you please, doctor. There is no fever yet, but we may be glad of it by night."

"Madness," said the doctor. "I wash my hands of the whole crazy business."

It made Helen notice his hands, which were filthy. She looked from Angelina's scrubbed brown hands to her own equally clean white ones. "Very well, doctor," she said. "I can only apologise again for troubling you."

"And pay my fee," said the doctor.

"Well, of course." Helen saw him to the head of the stairs with relief, and was turning back to the sickroom when her husband appeared in the doorway of his own apartments.

"Doctor satisfied?" he asked.

"Not altogether. Angelina had dressed the wound already and did not want it opened again." Best not let him know that she herself had helped in the operation.

"Old hag," said Lord Merritt. "Well, your affair." He looked her up and down. "Disgusting." He summed up her appearance. "Clean yourself up. Double quick. Everyone's up at the Hamiltons'. I'll wait ten minutes."

He (or Price) was absolutely right. This was one occasion when they must put in an appearance together. "Thank you." She allowed herself one backward glance to the sickroom, where Angelina caught her eye and nodded encouragement. "I won't keep you."

"I won't wait," said her husband.

For once, Helen would have been glad of help in her quick change. But Angelina was far better occupied

229

where she was. Certainly, her own reflection in the glass told her that her husband's comment, if rude, had been justified. Ripping off her filthy, bloodstained dress, she washed quickly in cold water, pulled another white muslin from the closet, tied it high with a blue sash, ran a comb through her curls, and was ready.

"Plain, aren't you?" Lord Merritt was waiting for her.

"Lady Hamilton will be dressed like this." It was answer enough.

But, "Jewels," he said. "Great occasion. Diamonds."

The diamonds had been a present from his uncle on the occasion of Ricky's birth; a present, she had often thought, that Lord Merritt resented. She had tended not to wear them as a result, and thought them wildly unsuitable to her simple muslin, but this was no time to be quibbling over trifles. "Very well." She returned to her room, donned sparkling necklace and dangling earrings, and joined her husband in the courtyard.

"Better." He held the carriage door for her.

Arriving at the Palazzo Sessa she was surprised to find that he had been quite right. Lady Hamilton, as she had predicted, was in white muslin, but she, too, was wearing the diamonds Sir William had given her, while all the other women were in full court dresses of silk and satin. And very hot they must be, Helen thought. So must Sir Horatio and Sir William, also in full dress and decorations. But she had remembered something. She held Lord Merritt back, for a moment, as he took her arm to lead her formally into the room. "Captain Scroope," she said, "best if you mention him?"

"Yes." He did it, in fact, surprisingly well, choosing a pause in the conversation just after Lady Hamilton had been describing how tenderly she meant to nurse the victorious Admiral back to full health. "Doing a bit of nursing on our own account," he said. "Least we could do. Old friend . . . Captain Scroope. May be dying, but at least, die in comfort."

If Price had coached him, he had done it well. "Admirable," said Lady Hamilton. "Nothing is too good for our heroes." She went on to describe, not, Helen thought for the first time, how she had arrived on board the

Vanguard, been overcome by her emotions, and almost fainted in the Admiral's arms. "Arm, I should say."

"Always at a lady's service," said the Admiral gallantly. He looked exhausted, Helen thought, and no wonder. Apparently he and Lady Hamilton had just returned from a private interview with the Queen, who was indisposed after the death of one of her daughters. But she also had doubtless wept, and exclaimed and called him, as her husband had, *"Nostro liberatore."* Lady Hamilton might talk about nursing and asses' milk, but she was doing little at the moment to protect her illustrious patient, who seemed to be making rather heavy weather of a conversation with Lady Knight and her daughter Cornelia. Joining them, Helen discovered that the subject of the conversation was Lady Nelson, whom Lady Knight was proud to call a friend. "If only she were here, our happiness would be complete."

"It would indeed." Sir Horatio did not look as if the prospect entirely pleased.

"Yes, yes." Lady Hamilton had heard the remark. "It is all we want. Are we not the *Trio juncta in uno,* Sir Horatio, Sir William, and myself? All we need is a fourth to square the circle. But, come, Miss Knight, the musicians are tuning for you. You must sing us your new verse of 'God Save the King.' "

Miss Knight obliged the Ambassadress with proper reluctance and apology, and everyone stood as she sang:

> *Join we great Nelson's name*
> *First on the roll of fame*
> *Him let us sing.*
> *Spread we his praise around*
> *Honour of British ground*
> *Who made Nile's shores resound*
> *God save the King.*

It brought a round of applause, and to Helen's infinite relief, a gradual breaking up of the party. She longed to get back to that cool room, where Angelina sat quietly by the bed, away from this noise and bustle and confusion.

She had seen Lord Merritt slip quietly away when the singing began, and was preparing to take her own leave, when Captain Forbes and Charlotte arrived. Charlotte looked tired and pale, and, Helen thought, cross. She soon learned why. After she and her husband had paid their compliments to the Hamiltons, Charlotte left him with a quick word and hurried across the room.

"At last!" She kissed Helen warmly. "I thought we'd never get here. Really, I sometimes think John is the most obstinate man in the world. Only think of his insisting that he get all the wounded to hospital before he'd even begin to get ready. As if this wasn't more important than anything?"

"Well, I wonder." Helen thought of Charles Scroope, lying so still. "I can see that your husband might feel the responsibility."

"He seems to feel nothing else. It's always the same, 'The good of the ship must come first.' If I've heard it once, I've heard it a thousand times. Imagine him having me carried below, actually in a dead faint, on the night of the battle. I might have been a bit of furniture for all he cared. He thought only of getting the cabin cleared . . ."

"Well, for action," said Helen mildly.

"He might have taken me down himself! Oh, Helen, I've never been so frightened in my life. That cable tier . . . There were rats."

"I know." Memory rose in Helen's throat like bile.

"And Rose worse than useless. Crying and carrying on as if she was the one to be pitied. I could have slapped her." Helen rather suspected that in fact she had. "And now she wants to leave me," Charlotte wailed. "Just when I need her most. She says she can't face another voyage."

"Another voyage? What do you mean? I thought you were coming back to me, dear."

"Oh, I do wish I was. But that's just it! That's what I was trying to tell you. John is so obstinate. He has taken it into his head that it's not safe for me here in Naples. Did you ever hear anything so ridiculous? Now, when Sir Horatio has made the Mediterranean British at last! John doesn't understand!" It was a wail that had all too evidently been bottled up for Helen's benefit. "He says the place for a lady in my—" she coloured and brought it out—"in my delicate condition is with her mamma. If he would only listen! Oh, Helen, I've had such a letter from Mamma. I don't know that she will even welcome me, supposing I get there alive, which I very much doubt. The voyage will kill me, I'm sure. John just won't understand how ill I am. He seems to think I'm making a fuss! I don't care how his sisters managed. Great country-bred horses of young women." She put her handkerchief to her eyes, and Helen looked round nervously to make sure that Captain Forbes was not in earshot.

The room was thinning of people. This was no place for Charlotte to make a scene. "You had best come home with me for the time being," she said. "A cup of Angelina's herb tea will make you feel very much more the thing. Perhaps Captain Forbes would let you stay with us until he is ready to sail?"

"Oh, yes," said Charlotte eagerly. "He urged it. He says a ship refitting is no place for a lady at the best of times. But I don't sail with him." Here was the heart of her grievance. "Oh, no! It makes him too anxious, he says. I must go home by the packet, or any old merchantman that is most likely to fall a prey to the French. I expect my child will be born in a French prison."

"Nonsense," said Helen, and reminded herself of her husband. "You must see," she went on, wondering as she spoke just how frightful a scene Charlotte had made on the night of the great battle, "that any husband would be specially anxious in these circumstances. Just suppose the *Cormorant* was in action again; it would mean the cable tier, and I am sure that would not be good for you."

"No," said Charlotte doubtfully. "I suppose not. But why must I go home at all? I'd much rather stay here with you, Helen, and Rose says she'll stay with me if I do. Why go back to England, and cold, and fog, when I can stay here? And, besides, there's Mamma! You know her, Helen; you must persuade John that she'll make my life wretched."

"But I'm not so sure that she will." Helen had been thinking about this. "Had you considered, dear, that your case is very much altered since she wrote to you? Your

233

John is one of the heroes of the Nile now, and goodness knows what he may not get in the way of prize money. There may even be a general promotion . . . Who knows? Another action like Aboukir Bay and you may find yourself Lady Forbes, and you know how well your mother would like that." She was ashamed of the arguments as she put them forward, and sorry for John Forbes as she recognised that, in her frantic self-pity, Charlotte had not even stopped to think how the victory had affected her husband.

"Oh," she said now, taking it in slowly. "I had not thought of that."

Chapter 19

HELEN'S announcement that she was taking Charlotte back to the Palazzo Trevi won her a look of such heartfelt gratitude from John Forbes that she could not help feeling anxious for the future of his marriage. "I knew I could count on you," he said. "Charlotte will be much the better for a rest on shore before she starts on the voyage home, and my poor *Cormorant* is no place for a lady just now." That settled, he turned to a subject that seemed to interest him a good deal more deeply. "Lady Merritt, while I was at the hospital I learned what you have done for my friend Scroope. I want to thank you, on behalf of us all. It's . . . it's heart-warming." And then, eagerly, "Do you think he has a chance?"

"I don't know," said Helen slowly. "It would not be right to hold out a great deal of hope, but I've an old witch of an Italian woman, with methods of her own, and I think he stands a better chance with her than he would in that hospital."

"I'm sure of that," he said warmly. "It's wonderfully good of you, Lady Merritt."

"It's the least one can do." She was at once ashamed of the half truth and uncomfortably aware of Charlotte, all agog at her elbow.

"What's this about Captain Scroope?" she asked now. "I thought everyone agreed he was scuppered."

Helen and Forbes exchanged quick, shocked glances, then she spoke fast, before he could. "I do hope not," she said. "I've got him at the Palazzo Trevi. Lord Merritt and I thought it the least we could do, with Lady Hamilton caring for the Admiral."

"But that means real nursing!" Charlotte clearly did not mean to be involved. "Not like seeing that Sir Horatio doesn't overdo it. Not that she is," she added spitefully.

"She will be able to if we take our leave," suggested Helen, her heart sinking more and more at the spectacle of what marriage had done to Charlotte. Or had it merely revealed the real Charlotte, her mother's daughter? Horribly sorry for Captain Forbes, she turned to him now. "Will you give us the pleasure of your company? My carriage is here, and I am sure you would be glad to see Mrs. Forbes comfortably settled."

"Thank you." He smiled at her warmly. "And may I take a look at my friend Scroope?"

"Perhaps." She turned to Charlotte, who was looking cross again. "I have Angelina looking after him; you know what a tyrant she is. But a wonderful nurse." This was to Forbes.

"If only she can save him," he said.

"You men," said Charlotte. "All you care about is each other."

Helen was relieved to get their farewells safely made without any further outbreak on Charlotte's part. Lady Hamilton, kissing Helen warmly, urged her to send up daily bulletins about Captain Scroope's health. "Sir Horatio will be longing to hear," she said, "and so shall I!"

And Sir William? Helen wondered. He was looking exhausted again but had a warm handshake for her and a quick remark about her kindness, which made her feel guilty, as Lady Hamilton's more extravagant praise had not. If they only knew how entirely selfish she was being. . . .

"You and Lady Hamilton seem mighty thick these days." Charlotte's tone was spiteful as she settled herself in the carriage.

"Yes, she's been a good friend to me." Helen did not intend to discuss Emma Hamilton with Charlotte, and was glad of Captain Forbes's presence, which she recognised as having a chastening effect on his sharp-tongued wife, who reminded Helen more and more of her mother, Mrs. Standish. She was even, disconcertingly, beginning to look like her.

Charlotte, it appeared, had taken her invitation for granted, and sent Rose direct to the Palazzo Trevi. It was with a sigh of relief that Helen was able to urge that she go up at once and change from her tight-fitting yellow satin into something cooler. Having disposed of her, she turned to Captain Forbes and found him eyeing her with something like respect. "Now." She ushered him into the small ground-floor salon that opened onto the terrace behind the house. "If you will be so good as to wait here, I will see how my patient is, and if my nurse thinks you may see him."

"Thank you." He glanced anxiously at his watch.

"Yes." She smiled at him. "You must have a million things on hand today. I will be back directly."

"Thank you, Lady Merritt. But, one other thing . . . Charlotte—" He stuck there.

"Don't worry about Charlotte, Captain Forbes. I'll take care of her." She would not let him see how reluctantly she said it.

But obviously he knew his Charlotte. "One of the things I mean to do today," he said, "is enquire for a passage for her. The sooner she is safe in England with her mother the better."

"Yes indeed." She felt horribly sorry for him. "I have been telling her how proud Mrs. Standish will be to welcome a hero's wife."

"Thank you." His grateful smile acknowledged all that

was unsaid between them. "And now I must not keep you from your patient."

In the sickroom, Angelina reported no change, and agreed that it could do no harm just to let Captain Forbes look in. "In fact, a good thing," she said shrewdly. "We're taking a risk, you and I, in keeping the doctor from him. Best get his friends on our side. Just tell him: no exclamations, no fuss."

"I don't think I need to." But Helen duly delivered the warning, before she ushered Forbes into the cool, quiet room.

He stood for a few moments, quite silent, looking down at the still figure on the bed, then surprised and touched Helen by taking Angelina's hand and shaking it warmly. That done, he turned, as silent as ever, and followed Helen out of the room. Outside, "God bless you," he said. "After that hospital, it's incredible. It gives him a chance."

"That's what I hope."

"You're a good friend." His smile could be very attractive when it was unforced. "I see you still believe in fresh air in a sickroom."

"Yes," she smiled back at him. "I've never forgotten how good you were to my mother on the *Trojan*."

"What a long time ago." He looked back over it for a moment, she thought, sadly. "What news do you have of your father and the *Trojan?*"

"Not much," she admitted. "He's still on the Channel Station." She had expected Forbes to leave at once when he had seen his friend, but found that they had somehow got back into the little salon.

"Lady Merritt," he said now, abruptly. "I must ask it, for my own peace of mind. Will you forgive me? If I had spoken up, like a man, back on the *Trojan,* would there have been a chance for me?"

"A chance?" For a moment, she could not take it in, then, understanding, said gently, "No, Mr. Forbes." She held out her hand. "And now, if you will forgive me, I must get back to my patient."

"And I to my ship." He surprised her again by taking

both her hands and pressing them warmly. "Thank you, Lady Merritt, for a straight answer to an impertinent question. You have laid a ghost for me. A ghost of happiness that haunted me. But, do, I beg of you, remember that if ever you should need a friend . . ."

"Very pretty and chivalrous." Charlotte's voice was venomous as she entered the room. "Would you pack Lady Merritt off on the first boat for England, if you had the power?"

"I wish I could. Frankly, Lady Merritt, I don't much like the feel of things here in Naples. All this hysteria can come to no good. Do you not think you should persuade your husband to take you home?"

"Impossible. I have tried."

"Ridiculous," said Charlotte pettishly. "The time to cry woe was a year ago, when our ships were out of the Mediterranean. The case is quite altered now. Lady Hamilton thinks we'll soon be turning the French out of the rest of Italy. 'Boldest measures are safest,' she says."

"Quoting the Admiral," said her husband dryly. His eyes met Helen's, and she became aware, as he was, of the door that Charlotte had left ajar. "Perhaps, my dear, it would be better not to quote Lady Hamilton too freely."

"In Helen's house," she bridled at him. "Ridiculous!"

He moved past her to close the door. "I wish it were." And then, to Helen. "Your husband's man—I remember him—Price was outside, listening."

"Yes," she said. "I'm . . . careful."

"And so must you be." He turned to Charlotte. And then, back to Helen. "You cannot persuade your husband to get rid of him?"

"Oh, no," she said.

"I see." She was afraid he did. He rose to take his leave. "In that case, be very careful, Charlotte, for Helen's sake, and your own."

"I don't understand a word you're saying," said Charlotte fretfully. "Do you know," she turned on Helen when her husband had gone, "I sometimes think he married me because he couldn't get you. Flattering, ain't it? He wakes me in the night sometimes, saying, 'Helen?' That's nice hearing for a wife, isn't it?"

"Oh, my dear," said Helen. "I am so sorry. But remember . . ." She thought quickly. "He *married* you. He never asked me." It was true, or had been, until today.

"He didn't? Truly? You're not lying to me." And then, seeing Helen's face, "No, I know you would not." She sighed and shrugged. "Oh, well, in that case, perhaps in the end we'll rub through somehow. It's thinking always that one's second best comes so hard."

"But you're not," Helen insisted. "Charlotte, you've been imagining things. One does, a little, when one's carrying. Dear Charlotte—" Now that she understood, she found her old affection coming back, combined with a great pity. "For the child's sake, for mine if you like, let me see you and your husband better friends before you leave."

"Before he sends me away." But Charlotte's tone was milder, and Helen felt with relief that the conversation had cleared the air between them.

It made Charlotte a tolerable visitor, but no more. And all the time there was a grinding anxiety lest she say something indiscreet in front of Price, or, perhaps worse still, something that would make Price realise he was suspected. Luckily, Helen thought, Charlotte had been too preoccupied with her own troubles to take in the full import of her husband's warning. And, luckily too, the news that the Court of Naples was actually considering an attack on the French in Rome was soon common knowledge. There were other indiscreet tongues in Naples besides Charlotte's.

They celebrated Admiral Nelson's fortieth birthday on September twenty-ninth with all the pomp and circumstance that Lady Hamilton could contrive. She gave a great dinner at the Palazzo Sessa for eighty officers of the British squadron, and the English residents, who dined off specially made plates emblazoned with the motto, *H. N. Glorious 1st August*. Helen, sitting between Captain Ball and the Admiral's stepson, Josiah Nisbet, found it hard to pay attention to what they said.

"How is my friend Scroope?" Ball's question went to the heart of her anxiety.

"Not quite so well." She had not wanted to come, but

her husband had insisted, and she had known he was right. "There's a little fever, for the first time. But I have the greatest confidence in my nurse."

"So I have heard." Captain Ball had the same direct blue eyes as Forbes. "Sent the doctor to the rightabout, didn't you? Might not look just the thing, if poor Scroope don't recover."

"Oh." She met his eyes. "So there is gossip?"

"Bound to be. You should have known the doctor would talk. Mind you, Lady Merritt," he leaned closer, "I'm not saying you haven't done right. Forbes certainly thinks you have. What I am saying, and feel it my duty, is that if poor Scroope should snuff it, you'd best get that nurse of yours out of town pretty quick."

"I . . . see. And for me?"

"Ah well, you're Lady Merritt . . . another matter." He turned, she thought with relief, to his other neighbour, and she followed his example and turned to Nelson's stepson, who had been sitting moodily silent beside her, consuming, she was afraid, a great deal of Lady Hamilton's good wine.

"This must be a proud day for you." She wished she could remember whether Captain Nisbet had either been at the Battle of the Nile or distinguished himself there. It was odd not to know, but there had been rumours that Captain Nisbet was not in the best of favour with the Lords of the Admiralty.

"Proud? For me?" Captain Nisbet had a significant look for the head of the table, where his stepfather was sitting, wreathed rather untidily in laurel, beside his hostess. "You mistake, ma'am. I did not have the good fortune to be at the Nile. I am the mere captain of a frigate, and the frigates, as Admiral Nelson has let the world know, were not so fortunate as to be with him."

"Oh." She digested this for a moment in uncomfortable silence. "Yes, of course. But," brightening, "think how delighted your mother must be."

"Delighted?" Once again he was looking past her to the head of the table where Lady Hamilton was making a parade of cutting up her guest of honour's meat. "You really think so? At home, my mother does that. I wish we were at home." He gulped more wine. "You know what m'stepfather said the other night? Called this 'a country of fiddlers and poets, whores and scoundrels.' Oh, beg your pardon, I'm sure. But now look at him, eating it up. Flattery by the bushel, and that . . ." Something in Helen's face stopped him.

"Our hostess," she reminded him quietly, and was infinitely relieved when Lady Hamilton rose and gave the signal for the ladies to leave the room. The cream of Neapolitan society were coming to a ball in honour of the hero of the Nile, and more than ever everything was à la Nelson. Buttons and ribbons with the initials HN were distributed to the guests, and the ballroom was decorated with a rostral column engraved with the names of the captains of the Battle of the Nile, and the words, *Veni, Vidi, Vici.* Unveiling this with the attitude of a Boadicea, Lady Hamilton took no notice of a scuffle at the far end of the room. Josiah Nisbet had said something unprintable and was being forcibly removed by Troubridge and another officer.

To Helen, the evening, with its troubled cross-currents of feeling, seemed endless. The Queen was too unwell to come, but was represented by her pregnant daughter-in-law, wife of the heir to the throne, and it was impossible to leave before she did. The interminable dancing was followed by a lavish supper for eight hundred people, and Helen, who had been up a good deal of the night before, watching by Charles's bed while Angelina rested, was almost sick with fatigue and anxiety when the Princess Royal finally took her leave.

But now Charlotte did not want to go. "I'm enjoying myself for once," she said. "You can't drag me away now, Helen, when the bigwigs are gone and the fun's beginning. You can see everyone else means to keep it up till dawn."

"But surely, dear, you, in your condition . . ."

"Oh, fiddlesticks! I'm not carrying the heir to a throne. And, besides, you're the one who's always urging me to take exercise. Well, now I will. The dancing's starting again, and what could be better for me?"

"Bed," said her husband, who had come up behind her in the course of her last speech. "Can't you see that Lady

Merritt is worn out? May I call your carriage for you?"
He turned to Helen.

"Oh, yes, please. I'm a little anxious, to tell you the truth, about Captain Scroope." She wished the words unsaid at once.

"Always Captain Scroope," said Charlotte angrily. "Anyone would think he was your husband, the way you carry on about him. Neglecting your child for him; dragging me away from the first party I've enjoyed for months; and as for poor Lord Merritt . . ." She stopped, aware that she had gone too far, quailing under her husband's black look.

" 'Poor Lord Merritt,' " he said, "left before the royal party even arrived, and I told him I would see you ladies safe home, which I am about to do."

He turned on his heel and left them standing in a painful silence. Charlotte's outburst had made Helen angry, but it had also made her think, and she knew in her heart that it was quite true about Ricky. She had been neglecting him, and so, inevitably, had Angelina. What had he been doing while they were occupied with their invalid? She ought to have thought about this, made arrangements for him, and was ashamed to think that she had actually let out of sight be out of mind. She would do something about him tomorrow. In the meantime, the silence had lasted quite long enough. "Come," she said calmly, "let us say good-bye to our hostess."

"If she can spare the time from her hero," said Charlotte.

Home at last, Helen bade Charlotte a quick good night and hurried to the sickroom. Angelina was looking both tired and anxious. "He's very hot," she said. "And his mind's wandering."

"But that means he's awake." Helen had been increasingly anxious about the way Charles just lay there, inert, apparently lifeless . . . "Surely that's good?"

"Not like this," said Angelina. "Signora, have you thought what we will do if he dies?"

So she had heard the gossip too. "I think you should go at once to Angelo and Maria," said Helen. "Out of sight is out of mind, they say. I'll send for you as soon as it is safe to come back." And then, reminded of him by her own words, "Angelina, do you know what Ricky's been doing?"

Angelina raised troubled eyes to her. "He's been with that Price," she said. "I should have made better arrangements for him. I thought he was with the girl from Torre del Greco. I told her to look after him. And when I asked her today, she just burst into tears, and said, what could she do when Price is so powerful with his lordship."

"Oh my God," said Helen. "But don't blame yourself. *I* should have thought of it."

"There's been too much." Angelina was looking old tonight.

Between them, Charles stirred restlessly, throwing aside the light blanket with which Angelina had covered him. "Helen," he said.

"Yes." Helen sat down beside the bed and took the hot hand in hers. "I'm here."

"Helen!" He gripped her hand feverishly. "How could you? Trenche!" His voice blurred, dwindled into incomprehensible mutterings.

Thank God, Angelina did not understand English. But her own name had been clear enough, and quite obviously Angelina had understood that, and with that, everything. Their eyes met. "Best not let Price in here," said Angelina.

"Has he tried to come?"

"Yes, today. Someone must have told him the signor was speaking. I sent him off with a flea in his ear. But it's one more enemy, if the worst happens." Angelina was looking older and older, and Helen recognised the thing that hung in the air between them as fear.

And no wonder. "You get to bed, Angelina." She made her voice bracing. "In the morning, we will think what's best to do. For now, the signor seems to want to talk to me."

"Yes, signora," said Angelina eagerly. "If there has perhaps been trouble between you in the past . . . if it is weighing on his mind . . . it might do him good to have it clear."

If only she could. "I'll try." She made herself smile

243

comfort. "And now, to bed with you. But, first, has he had his draught?"

"No. For the first time, he wouldn't drink it."

This too might surely be a good sign. So far he had done passively whatever they made him, and it had been unlike enough to the Charles she knew to wring Helen's heart. "Pour me a fresh one," she said. "And I'll try."

It was very quiet in the house. Lord Merritt had either gone to bed long since or, as so often, would be out all night. She wondered if Price was with him and passionately hoped he was. She went across the room to make sure that the door was securely fastened. That settled, she returned to the bed, and picked up Angelina's black-looking draught. "Charles," she said.

"Helen!" Had he recognised her voice, or was this merely more delirium? "How could you?" The same words as before, so probably delirium.

"Charles," she said again. "I'm here. Holding your hand. Trenche lied to you. I don't know what he said, but I know he lied."

"Trenche." He thrashed about on the narrow bed. "I wish I'd killed him." And then, suddenly, in an entirely different tone. "Lied?"

"Yes. He's always been my enemy. He'd say anything." Anything but the truth. If only she knew what he *had* said.

"Lies?" Some part of his mind seemed to be working on it. "All lies?"

What should she say? She took a hard breath. "Yes."

"Lies." Now it was a statement. His breathing, which had been rattling in an alarming way, steadied. "Helen," he said.

"Yes." She bit off an endearment, and then wished it spoken.

"Stay with me. I'm . . . not . . . well. In the morning, we'll talk."

"Yes, in the morning. But, now, for my sake, drink this." She put one firm arm behind him and raised him on his pillows so he could swallow.

"Ouch." It was an extraordinarily reassuring, normal

244

sound. "Nasty." But he swallowed the black liquid dutifully.

"That's better." She settled him back on the bed. "Now
sleep."

" 'Sleep that knits up the ravelled sleeve of care,' " he
said, and slept.

So, in the end, awkwardly, still holding his hand, half
sitting, half lying by the bed, did she. Waking suddenly
into complete consciousness, she heard him talking again,
the same half-comprehensible mutterings as before.
Bending near, she heard her own name, and Trenche's,
and then "No! I won't believe it. Trenche. And her
mother dying. 'It killed her mother.' That's what he said.
Waking to find them . . . Oh . . ." It was a long groan.
And then, clearly, " 'Heaven stops the nose at it.' "

Othello. She knew now what Trenche had told him,
and, ice cold with anger, knew it for even worse than she
had expected. Trenche had claimed to have been her
lover on board the *Trojan,* before her mother died.
Charles had not been there. How was he to know how
physically impossible it would have been. Surely, used as
he was to life on board ship, he might have guessed, but
when was jealousy ever rational? And, clearly, Trenche
had embroidered his story with some horrible description
of a scene when her mother had surprised them. Hard to
imagine how he made that convincing, but then she remembered the cot Forbes had had made for her mother
on the after-deck. By some stretching of the circumstances there, it was just, unspeakably, possible.

And what could she do about it? The answer was:
nothing. Charles's mind was poisoned against her and, if
Angelina was right, that very poison was helping to retard
his recovery. And she could not even allow herself the
comfort of blaming him for believing the worst of her.
After the news of what must have seemed her extraordinary marriage, he would have been in a mood to believe
anything.

He was muttering again. "Lies?" It was a question. "All
lies?"

So he had taken in something of what she had said last
night. Was this a chance for her? She leaned forward and

took his hand. "Yes, Charles, all lies. You should have known Trenche would lie to you."

Very faintly, his hand pressed hers. "Should have known," he muttered, his head moving restlessly. "Trenche . . . lies . . . Should have killed him." And with that apparently settled, he turned his head into the pillow and fell into what seemed like a real sleep. He still had her hand, and she sat there, not daring to move, until Angelina came.

"Ah," said the old woman, putting a hand on Charles's brow. "That feels better. And just as well, signora. There's the devil to pay in the house."

"What's the matter?"

"Ricky," said Angelina. "We should have acted sooner. That Price must have put him up to it, of course."

"To what?" She was on her feet, ready to go to her child's defence. "Tell me quick, Angelina."

"He got into Mrs. Forbes's dressing room," said Angelina. "While she was asleep. He's played hob with her things. She's fit to be tied. Poor little thing, he fell asleep there after he'd done. She found him. You'd best go, signora."

"Yes." One last, quick look at Charles, and she was outside, running swiftly up the stairs to the suite of apartments where she had installed Charlotte. Opening the door, she found Charlotte in hysterics and Ricky in floods of tears. Rose, between them, looked as if she could not decide which to imitate. The room was a shambles. Ricky had found the rouge and pearl powder with which Helen had suspected Charlotte of experimenting, had apparently begun by smearing them on his own hands and face, and then tried to clean himself up with the muslin gown that had been left hanging over a chair.

But even worse than this, he seemed to have pulled out all the drawers of the dressing table, spilling their contents on the floor. Now his face was white under the smears of rouge, and a scarlet mark across one cheek must mean that Charlotte or Rose had hit him. At sight of his mother, he drew in a long, sobbing breath. "No sweets," he said, as if it explained everything. "I couldn't find any."

"Little devil." Charlotte's hysterics had also stopped at sight of Helen. "He must be whipped for this."

"No," said Helen. "Charlotte, I can't tell you how sorry I am, but he's only a baby." Impossible to tell Charlotte of her suspicion—her certainty that Price was behind this. Ricky would never have thought of the possibility of sweetmeats in Charlotte's drawers by himself. Price must have put the idea into his head; had probably even brought him to the door of the room and even—it had a very heavy catch—opened it for him. But to say so would be to precipitate the very crisis she most wished to avoid. "Ricky." She made her voice stern. "You must tell the lady how very very sorry you are, and then you must go to your room. You've been a bad, bad boy."

"I won't," he said. "Nasty lady. She smacked me. Won't say I'm sorry." He began to cry again, and Helen longed to take him in her arms and comfort him. After all, this was entirely her fault.

"I told you he was a devil," said Charlotte. "Whipping's too good for him. Just look at all my lovely things."

"I'll get you some more." Helen moved forward to examine the extent of the damage, but Charlotte was before her.

"Leave my things alone!" she said. "Rose, start packing. I know when I'm not wanted. Now I'm glad John insisted on getting me a passage on the *Dido*. I'll stay in the Hotel Britannia until she's ready to sail."

"Oh, Charlotte," pleaded Helen. "Please . . ." But at last she had understood what Price had intended. He wanted Charlotte out of the house, and she did not like to think why.

Luckily, John Forbes, paying a very early call, largely, Helen suspected, for news of Charles Scroope, made short work of Charlotte's plan of moving to a hotel. "No such thing," he said firmly. "It would be an insult to Lady Merritt, for one thing, and, besides," he hit on a clincher, "what would your mother say if she found I had let you stay with only your maid at a common hotel?"

"I wouldn't go to a hotel," said Rose, and settled it.

Chapter 20

HELEN was glad to leave John Forbes soothing his tearful wife and take Ricky up to his room, where she left him in charge of Lucia, the girl from Torre del Greco, with strict instructions that he was to stay there all day. "Unless you'll say you're sorry," she said severely to the sobbing Ricky.

"Not to her," said the child. "I'll tell him." He looked up at his mother. "I *am* sorry."

It rent her heart. "I'm sure you are, my poppet." She bent to hug him. "I'll bring Captain Forbes. It will be easier among men."

"Yes." She felt him relax at last in her arms, and realised with a fresh pang how far she had let him slip from her. Hurrying downstairs, she found John Forbes just emerging from Charlotte's rooms, and explained Ricky's proposition.

"Yes of course," he said briskly. "Man to man, eh? Charlotte," he turned back in the doorway: "Young Ricky apologises to me, and then it's all to be forgotten."

"Oh very well," she said sulkily. "I might have known you'd be against me, too."

Up in Ricky's room, John Forbes held out a hand. "Well, young man, I believe you've something to say to me?"

"Yes, sir." The child looked up at him. "Please . . . I'm sorry."

"That's the boy." Forbes took the small hand and shook it. "Tell me," his voice was conversational, "who put you up to it?"

"No," said Helen, as the child's face crumpled into tears.

"Oh?" He looked at her. Then, "Very well." He swung the child onto his shoulder. "All forgotten," he said. "When you're a man, will you come to sea with me?"

"Yes, please," said the boy. "And we'll have no women."

Forbes and Helen exchanged glances. "So it was Price," he said softly, safe outside the room.

"I'm afraid so."

"And you do nothing?"

"Believe me, I cannot."

He looked around. "I want to talk to you."

"The sickroom," she said. And then, suddenly radiant: "Captain Forbes, he's better."

"I'm very glad to hear it."

In the sickroom, Charles's more natural colour and breathing confirmed her words. Angelina reported that he had actually taken a few spoonfuls of the chicken broth that had been brewed fresh every day on Helen's orders. "It's the turn at last."

"And thank God for that," said John Forbes as she left the room. "You must have wondered, Lady Merritt, why I chose to call so early."

"To tell you the truth," she said, "I was so grateful . . ."

"It all hangs together." As once before, he moved over to make sure that the door was securely shut. "Someone is trying to make trouble for you. Price?"

"I think so. But you mean there's more than Ricky?"

"Much, much more," he said soberly. "I was so late last night, I decided to stay in town. At the Britannia. A good thing I did. I heard the talk there."

"Talk?"

"About you and your witch, and how you're killing a British officer between you. And how you're bad luck for Naples. Don't ask me how they work it out," he anticipated her question impatiently, "because it don't make sense. But they've convinced themselves. Or someone's convinced them. Which is more to the point."

"Price?" Now it was her turn to ask it.

"I don't know. I doubt if he'd appear in it directly. Not down there. From the way they talked, I'd think they were a parcel of Jacobins."

"But—"

"You think it's the French he's spying for?"

"I'm almost sure of it."

"But still he'd not be seen in it. He's very great with your husband, is he not, Lady Merritt?"

"I'm afraid so."

"So of course he'd not be seen in it. And your husband's away?"

"Yes." It had been a relief when she learned Lord Merritt had gone straight from Lady Hamilton's party to his shooting box at Caserta, though she had been puzzled that Price had not gone too.

"Just so. You'd have been on your own here tonight, with Charlotte at the hotel—oh, that was predictable enough, if I'd not taken a hand. And when they came, the servants would have run for it."

"They?"

"The mob of lazzaroni that's been worked up against you. By the time they had finished with you, and Angelina, and the house, no one would ever have known whether you had really been killing or curing my friend here."

"You mean?" She had imagined horrors, but nothing so bad as this.

"I do. Tonight was the night. They wanted Charlotte out, of course, the people behind it—because everyone knows what vengeance would be taken for a captain's wife. If she stays, I think you are that much the safer."

"But you can't risk her."

"I don't intend to. There will be a guard of Cormorants here tonight, and anyone who comes to make trouble will find more than he bargained for. But, in fact, I don't think anyone will come. This kind of mob-stirring can work both ways. I am going back to the Hotel Britannia now, to mention, in public, how well my friend Scroope is doing in your house. Thank God, it's true."

"Thank God."

She spent as much of that endless day as she possibly

could between Ricky's room and the sickroom, thus at least sparing herself Charlotte's continued grumbling. The first thing she had done after Forbes left was to sit down and write a note to Lady Hamilton with the good news of Charles's improvement. It was the best way she knew to get it into public circulation. It brought her an enthusiastic reply, which also, to her relief, absolved her from the duty of calling at the Palazzo Sessa. Lady Hamilton was very busy indeed, she reported, interpreting for the Admiral. "My duty to him and to my adorable Queen must come first."

No doubt the attack on Rome was being discussed, but Helen had more immediate anxieties, and it was with a sigh of heartfelt relief that she heard Captain Forbes announced at last. "All's right and tight," he assured her. "My men are on duty outside, and I've come to spend the night, if I may."

"Oh, *thank* you. I've not told Charlotte." And then, hurriedly, "In her condition . . ."

"Quite so. And unnecessary anyway. I truly believe, Lady Merritt, that the danger has passed. There are a whole set of new rumours in town today, and I think you and our friend Scroope have been forgotten. An extraordinary people, this . . . And dangerous. I wish you did not have to stay here. But how is Scroope?"

"Still mending, I'm delighted to say. But Angelina thinks it will be a slow business."

The night Helen had dreaded passed without event, and, in the morning, thanking John Forbes warmly, she found herself wondering what would really have happened if he had asked her to marry him, back on the *Trojan*. She had spoken part of the truth when she told him that she would have refused him, but later, when her moment of crisis came, she knew well that it was to him that she would have turned, rather than to Lord Merritt. And, she was sure, he would not have failed her.

All past, all over, and best forgotten. But, for his sake, she worked extra hard all day to make things right again with Charlotte, taking her out on an extensive shopping round to replace the things Ricky had spoiled. What a mercy it was to have her own money, even if it was only pin money, compared with her actual inheritance. But these, too, were thoughts best put out of one's mind.

Charlotte sailed for England a few days later, with Rose in somewhat reluctant attendance, and Helen was surprised to find herself missing them. But then, Angelina had ordered her out of the sickroom. "Your presence troubles him now," she said. "I don't understand it, but you'd best stay away. The maids can help me. It's more suitable anyway."

It was perfectly true, but it made Helen miserable just the same. She had not realised what peace there was in sitting beside Charles's bed, until she was banished from it. Public affairs provided an exciting distraction. Her calls at the Palazzo Sessa had kept her up to date in the long discussions between Nelson, the Queen, and her minister, Acton. The Queen and Acton had hoped for outright support from her son-in-law, the Emperor of Austria, but all they got was advice, and an Austrian general called Mack, who arrived with much pomp and circumstance in the middle of October.

Nelson thought highly of him at first, and a march on Rome was soon a settled thing. In action, Nelson insisted, lay Ferdinand's only chance of safety. His choice was simply, "To die with sword in hand, or to remain quiet and be kicked out of his kingdom." A holy crusade was preached from the pulpits, the lazzaroni took fire at the idea of restoring the exiled Pope to his see, but, characteristically, the Neapolitan Court felt that no move could be made before the Princess Royal had had her expected baby. In the meantime, the whole Court moved to San Germano, where the army was encamped, and Queen Maria Carolina put on a blue riding-habit with gold fleurs-de-lis at the neck, and a plumed general's hat, and reviewed her troops. Her husband, enjoying the camp life, nevertheless had one of his surprisingly shrewd comments when it was suggested that his soldiers should change their blue and yellow uniforms for red ones, like those of their allies, the British. "Dress them in red, dress them in yellow," said King Ferdinand. "They'll run away just the same."

And Nelson, returning in a bad temper from blockading Malta, soon revised his original good opinion of Mack. "General Mack," he said, "cannot move without five carriages! I have formed my opinion. I heartily pray I may be mistaken." But events were to prove him right. When Helen accompanied him and the Hamiltons to watch Mack manoeuvring his troops, it was to see the scene degenerate into total confusion, with the "enemy" masters of the field. But everyone shrugged it off. The Princess Royal had a daughter, and the army marched at last, on November the twenty-second, in the pouring rain.

Helen was not there to see them go. A messenger from Angelina had summoned her home to the Palazzo Trevi. Charles Scroope's leg and his general health were mending steadily, if slowly, but his first action on recovering full consciousness and realising where he was had been to demand that he be sent back to the hospital at once.

"I can't stay here." His voice was harsh as he greeted Helen. "It's impossible. Even you must see that."

"You might thank the signora." Angelina had understood tone, if not words. "You'd be dead if you'd stayed in that hospital."

"And you're not strong enough for it now," said Helen. "Please, Captain Scroope, be reasonable. My husband and I owe you a debt beyond repaying. You must let us do what we can. It was Lord Merritt's idea," she added, with more tact than truth.

"Oh." He took this in. "Where is Lord Merritt? I would like to thank him."

"Off shooting," she made it casual. "He saw no need to stay, now you are so much better."

"I see." He was still pitifully weak, and the short conversation had exhausted him. "Well, then, for a few days more." He managed the ghost of a smile. "And my deepest thanks, Lady Merritt."

Tone as well as formal words convinced her, painfully, that though their strange conversation when he was delirious might have helped in his recovery, he remembered none of it. To him, she was still the woman who had forgotten him, carried on that horrible affair with Trenche by her mother's sickbed, and ended by making an outrageous marriage for money.

And there was nothing she could do about it, except keep away so as not to remind him, and urge Forbes, when he visited him, to persuade him to stay.

"I'll do my best," Forbes promised. "You're quite right. The hospital's no place for him, and nor's the *Gannet*. Her refit has taken longer than it should, with no captain to press things on." Taking his leave of her, before he sailed with Nelson to support Mack's army, he had been encouraging about his last interview with Scroope. "I think he recognises, Lady Merritt, that the good of the service must come first, and that means staying with you for a quick recovery."

It might be painful that it had taken this argument to make Charles stay, but it was reassuring just the same, and Helen was relieved to have Angelina report steady progress and an increasing interest in the news from the *Gannet*. And if Helen strong-mindedly kept her visits to the barest minimum that courtesy required, Charles had a faithful companion in Ricky. Angelina had begun by trying to turn the child away, arguing that he would tire her patient, but Charles had sat up in bed, she told Helen, and insisted that he stay. Ricky brought his toys to his new friend's bedside, and Helen, paying her brief evening call, would find the two of them hard at it in a precarious game of spillikins on the sheets or, somehow more touching still, would hear Charles's voice in the steady rumble that meant he was telling Ricky a story. He always stopped short when she appeared, and no persuasion of Ricky's would make him go on.

"Tell Mamma about the king who lost his voice," Ricky begged, one windy evening when Helen had returned from the Palazzo Sessa with the news that the date for the march on Rome had been settled at last.

"Mamma has other things to think of." Charles's dry voice hurt Helen almost beyond bearing. "Now, off with you to bed, Ricky. Scoot."

If anyone else had given the order, Ricky would have protested, but Charles's will was law. The child picked up the bag Helen had embroidered for his spillikins, said good night, and left them.

"I'm more grateful to you than I can say for your

kindness to him," said Helen. "You've done him so much good."

"It's been a pleasure," he said formally. "He needed some attention."

"Yes, I am ashamed to feel that I have neglected him." Helen would rather have died than point out that in fact the neglect had arisen from the fact that she was nursing Charles himself.

"You ought to take him back to England," Charles said. "This is no place for a child to grow up."

"I know."

"Then why don't you go? You're a free woman, and a rich one. There's nothing to stop you."

"My husband won't hear of it."

"Lord Merritt!" His tone was glacial. "You can't expect me to believe that you aren't able to talk him round. If you put your mind on it."

"It's the truth."

"I still find it hard to believe." While giving her what was tantamount to the lie, he maintained a kind of steely courtesy, and Angelina, sitting sewing on the far side of the bed, had a quick glance for his tone. "Lady Merritt," he went on now, with an obvious effort, "surely, you can't be hoping that Trenche will come back?"

"Hoping!" She could hardly believe her ears. "You are insulting me, Mr. Scroope." It was a relief to forget unhappiness in anger. "I do not know—I do not wish to know what lies Trenche told you about me, but surely, if there was ever anything like friendship between us, you should have given me the benefit of the doubt. And now, I will say good night."

"Helen!" She heard it as she closed the door, and made herself ignore it.

She also made herself keep away altogether from the sickroom, where, Angelina reported, Charles was growing increasingly restless. The elderly first lieutenant of the *Gannet* brought gloomy reports of the progress, or lack of it, in her refit, and Charles was doggedly making himself use his leg a little more every day. Helen had found a new doctor, prepared to take over a patient who had received such unorthodox treatment in the first place, and he and

Angelina were now in agreement that fairly soon Charles would have to go back to the *Gannet,* even if he went on a stretcher.

"I think he'll *make* himself better," Helen told Lady Hamilton, who had returned from seeing the Neapolitan army march from San Germano.

"It would be like one of our hero's captains," said Lady Hamilton, and then, returning to a familiar theme: "Only think of the government insulting him with a mere baronship! 'Baron Nelson of Burnham Thorpe' forsooth. I wonder that wife of his, *and* his family, did not protest on the spot."

It had been a bitter disappointment, and, Helen suspected, had combined with Josiah Nisbet's continued bad behaviour to make a subtle change in Lady Hamilton's feelings about Nelson's wife. Helen sometimes even wondered whether it might not also have changed Nelson's own, but had seen little of him since that tremendous birthday party.

"But, look!" Lady Hamilton had something to show her. "Some people appreciate our hero. See the diamond aigrette and plume that the Sultan of Turkey has sent him! And this fur pelisse." She put it on and struck a heroic attitude. "The Sultan knows who is the saviour of Europe."

"Yes," said Helen. "But what is the news from the army?"

"The best of course." She looked, just for a moment, doubtful, then took up her Boadicea stance. "A pity, mind you, that it rained so when those poor soldiers marched, and that they had to ford the river Melfa, which, I understand, was most inconveniently in flood."

"But surely," said Helen, "one must expect rain and floods in November? Why did not General Mack have a bridge built all that time when he was waiting to start?"

"I don't know," admitted Lady Hamilton. "Between you and me, our friend thinks him something of a fair-weather general. I do hope that for once he is proved wrong."

"So do I." Helen knew that for the moment there was only one "friend" in Emma Hamilton's life.

At home, she found her husband, who had decided against accompanying King Ferdinand to Rome, and was on a flying visit between hunting parties. "There you are," he greeted her with his usual lack of ceremony. "Been at Sir William's?"

"Yes."

"And the news?"

"Lady Hamilton had just returned from seeing the army march." She fought a brief battle between her duty to her son and to her country. But she had failed Ricky before. "My dear," she said now. "I am not quite happy about Lady Hamilton's reports of the army." After all, she told herself, Price would be bound to learn of the army's difficulties soon enough.

"Oh?" At least she had caught his attention.

"Lady Hamilton does not seem to think very highly of General Mack." She would not quote Lord Nelson.

"Yes." It did not seem to surprise him. "Captain Scroope said so too. Gone by the way."

"Gone?" She could not believe her ears.

"Yes. Heard some story about the army marching; told Angelina to pack his things; gone to his ship. Quite right too. Oh, regards and thanks. All that."

"Very civil of him." She had not thought it could hurt like this.

Next day, a formal note of thanks from Charles rubbed salt into the wound. He was sorry not to have seen her to thank her in person . . . He owed her his life . . . He was hers to command, Charles Scroope. And then, a scribbled postscript, "Give my love to Ricky." Safe in the privacy of her room, Helen let go at last, and cried as if she would never stop.

Chapter 21

⟋ A WEEK later, Helen and Lady Hamilton stood at the window of the Palazzo Sessa and watched the *Gannet* sail out of the bay. "That young man will go far," said Emma Hamilton. "Sir William tells me he has achieved as much in a week as his first lieutenant did in the three months since the Battle of the Nile was fought."

"If he doesn't kill himself in the process," said Helen.

"He won't. Our hero's captains are made of stronger stuff than that." Lady Hamilton's mind was elsewhere. "I wish we'd hear from the King."

"There's still no news?"

"Not since we heard of that brush with the French. I wish I knew what General Championnet means to do. It seems strange that he should just withdraw before our troops."

"Yes." Helen had not liked the sound of this either.

But the next day all the church bells in Naples rang out in celebration of a triumph all the more splendid, according to Lady Hamilton, in that it had been bloodless. The French general, Championnet, had withdrawn; the Neapolitan troops had entered Rome unopposed, and King Ferdinand had ridden through the city to shouts of *"Ev-viva il Re di Napoli."* All over Rome, trees of liberty had been torn down, and Neapolitan and Papal standards dusted off and raised instead. King Ferdinand, comfortably ensconced in his own Farnese Palace, had entertained the nobility and clergy of Rome, and the Pope had been invited to return.

"It's the beginning of the end for Bonaparte." The news had sent Lady Hamilton into a fever of joy. "And there is good news from our friend Nelson too. He has received the unconditional surrender of Leghorn, and is returning to join us in our celebrations."

But by December the fifth, when Nelson sailed back into the bay, the news had changed. There was something wrong with the Neapolitan army in Rome. That six days' march through the pouring rain had taken as much toll as a major battle, and General Mack had neither the wits to recognise his army's deplorable state, nor the capacity to rectify it. When the news came that Championnet's withdrawal had been merely a ruse, and that he was preparing to march back on Rome, panic struck. King Ferdinand escaped ignominiously from the city two days before the French entered it. The Neapolitan troops, learning of Ferdinand's flight, felt, with some cause, that they had been betrayed. Some of their officers were French sympathisers or even in French pay. Some, like General de Damas, led their troops brilliantly but unavailingly into small rear-guard actions; others were content to put up merely a token resistance.

In Naples, the triumphant carillons were hushed, and the lazzaroni massed in the great square outside the palace, stirred this way and that by every new piece of bad news. Two weeks to the day from starting on his triumphant march to Rome, King Ferdinand was back, boasting of the terrors he had undergone, but quite prepared to forget all about it and start hunting again.

The Queen and Lady Hamilton had fallen from triumph to despair. A French attack on Naples seemed inevitable now, and what hope of defence had they, with only Mack for general? The King signed an appeal to his people to rise in defence of their freedom, and the lazzaroni terrified everyone by their response. The mob in the great palace square was armed now with sticks and stones and cudgels. An unfortunate royal messenger, Ferreri, taken for a spy, was torn to pieces under the palace windows, and held up, like a slaughtered stag, for the King to see.

Only Nelson was calm, but it was the calm of despair. "If Mack is defeated," he said, "this country is lost," and he and the Hamiltons set to work frantically at plans for the evacuation of the Court to their other capital city, Palermo in Sicily. Calling, as usual, daily at the palace, Lady Hamilton came away with her carriage full to bursting with royal treasure and royal possessions. Other chests came to her secretly at night. Back at the Palazzo Sessa, her mother, Mrs. Cadogan, Cornelia Knight, and Helen helped her pack these miscellaneous treasures into containers sent up from the bay by Lord Nelson. Innocently stamped as "Salt pork" or "Biscuit," they were ready to be taken on board ship when the time came.

And in the evening, tired out with handling heavy gold bars, or priceless jewels, they put on their own court clothes and jewellery and made the public appearances that must keep up the pretence that all was well.

"If the lazzaroni learn the King is planning to leave," Emma Hamilton said, "God knows what they might not do. Who knows, we might even share the fate of that wretched messenger, Ferreri. The mob's capable of anything."

"But they love the King." For once, Helen was not sure that the Admiral's plan was wise. "Surely if he were to stay and lead them, the French would not have a chance."

"The love of the mob!" Lady Hamilton was undoubtedly echoing her "beloved Queen." "We know what that is worth, since Varennes and the Temple. And, besides, we are betrayed on all sides. Aquila has been taken, that coward Vanni has killed himself, and Mack writes that all is lost."

Back at the Palazzo Trevi, Helen found her husband waiting for her, shaking with fright. He, too, had heard of Ferreri's murder. "Time to be packing," he said. "French one thing. Mob another. Price says so. Lot of wild beasts out there. Tear us to pieces."

"Nothing of the kind," said Helen with a certainty she was far from feeling. "It will be time for us to pack up when Lady Hamilton does so."

"She hasn't?"

"Not a thing." It was true enough. Emma Hamilton had been far too busy with the Queen's affairs. "But . . ." She had been thinking quickly. "If Price is anxious, he could make a start. It's true enough that Sir William has shipped out the best of his collection." This, she knew, was common knowledge. Let Price make what he would of it. Her one comfort, those desperate days, was the thought that soon the long, silent struggle with Price would be over. Surely he would stay behind to welcome his French masters and claim his reward?

Lord Merritt was still unhappy. "Wish that captain of yours would come back. Fire-eater. Scroope. Owes us a favour. Know where he is?"

"No." If only she did, but on this point at least she had no need to lie. There had been no word from Charles Scroope since he had sailed away. Why should there be? She would probably never see or hear from him again. And, almost worst of all, Ricky kept asking for him. Ricky had felt the general tension in the house, clung either to her or to Angelina, and asked, over and over again, when "his captain" would come back. It was all Helen could do not to lose her temper with him.

Two days later, the Prince Royal returned from the front with news of fresh disaster. "It's only a question now of which day," said Emma Hamilton. "And me with nothing packed. I shall have to flee in my shift." She rather liked the dramatic prospect, and fell unconsciously into the attitude of Niobe, weeping for her children. Then, briskly: "No need to look so anxious, love. Whatever happens, you shall come with us and the royal family on Nelson's *Vanguard*. It's a promise, but tell no one. I can't even take poor Miss Knight, but you and your Angelina will help us, I know, with the royal children, poor suffering babies, and we cannot leave your Ricky to the uncertain chances of a Neapolitan ship."

Thanking her, Helen wondered how Prince Caracciolo, commander of the Neapolitan navy, would feel when he learned that the royal family had sailed on a British ship. She was also horribly sorry for Miss Knight, who had recently lost her mother, but this was no time for such feelings. Ricky must come first. She thanked Lady Hamilton warmly and promised to have all ready so that they could join the royal party at a moment's notice.

It came on December twenty-first, with the news that Mack could no longer hold Capua. Helen, like the other

English residents, received a scribbled note of warning from Lady Hamilton. The royal treasure was all safely embarked; that night the royal family would follow it. But in the meantime the tragicomedy must be played out to the end. Kelim Effendi, the Turkish emissary who had brought the Sultan's gifts for Lord Nelson, was giving a reception. "You and Lord Merritt must meet us there," Lady Hamilton told Helen that afternoon. "Our hero accompanies us. We will dismiss our carriages as usual and then walk straight to the quay."

"Without even going in?"

"Yes." Lady Hamilton laughed for once. "Poor Kelim, how surprised he will be. But, you see, the mob must not know we are gone until the royal party are safe on board."

"And when will that be?" Helen was wondering what possible arrangements she could make for Ricky and Angelina that would not alert Price.

"Not till nine o'clock. When he has seen us safe on board, Lord Nelson returns for my angelic Queen and her family."

"What shall I do about Ricky?"

"Oh." Lady Hamilton had not thought of this problem, nor did she know of the threat Price represented. "Have that old witch of yours bring him down to the Molesiglio at nine. They can come off with the royal attendants."

"But she can't possibly bring Ricky through town alone, tonight of all nights."

"You've servants, haven't you? That man of your husband's can go with them. No doubt he can make himself useful on board. God knows we're going to have such a shipload of royalty we'll need some extra servants." Again, Emma Hamilton was enjoying the adventurous prospect.

Helen was not. "I think I had best stay home with Ricky myself," she said.

"No." It was final. "Lord Nelson's orders are that everything must seem as usual. If you are not with me, it will be bound to cause comment." And then, seeing Helen still look doubtful, she produced a clincher. "I had trouble enough persuading our friend to make room on the

Vanguard for you and your family. If you find you cannot do as I ask, you will just have to fend for yourselves. Poor Miss Knight will have trouble enough getting passage, I'm afraid. Maybe you could join forces with her?"

"No." Helen was beaten and knew it. "Naturally, if you wish it, Lord Merritt and I will meet you at Kelim Effendi's." She was still racking her brain about Ricky and Angelina when Captain Scroope was announced.

"Shall we see him?" Emma Hamilton had a knowing look for Helen. "I clean forgot to tell you. He's just been made post captain. Our friend told me only yesterday. Yes . . ." She had meant to do so all along. "I think we must see him and offer our congratulations."

Helen did not answer. She was having difficulty with her breathing, but managed to achieve some kind of control before Charles Scroope appeared. He looked exhausted, anxious, and, she thought, angry. Because she was there? No—absurd. She was imagining things again.

Receiving Lady Hamilton's congratulations without enthusiasm, Scroope soon proved that his anger had nothing to do with Helen. "Yes. Thank you," he said with automatic courtesy. "But what a moment to have it happen! I am replaced already on the *Gannet* and must be reduced to the part of mere supernumerary in tonight's adventure." A quick glance accompanied his cold bow to Helen. "I take it Lady Merritt knows?"

"Naturally. She and her husband are to be of our party."

"And my friend Ricky?"

"That's just what we were discussing," said Lady Hamilton impatiently. "Lady Merritt seems dissatisfied with the arrangements I have suggested for the child."

"And they are . . . ?"

She told him quickly, obviously anxious to get back to her own affairs. His eyes met Helen's at last when she mentioned Price. "I see," he said. "Perhaps I might venture a suggestion. I am here with the Admiral's orders to put myself at your disposal for tonight, since I have no command of my own. Would it not be the most natural thing in the world for me to return to the Palazzo Trevi, now I have been turned out of my ship? And then, if Lady Merritt will trust me, I will be responsible for getting young Ricky down to the mole."

"Oh, very well." Lady Hamilton was tired of the subject. "That's settled then. And now, if you will excuse me, I have my own packing up to do."

It was more than a hint, and they took it. Outside, Helen turned impulsively to Charles. "I don't know how to thank you."

"It's the least I can do." His tone was quenching. "I take it you have not made Lady Hamilton a party to your suspicions of Price."

"No. I was afraid it would do more harm than good."

"I hope you were right." Again his tone was chilling. "What do you propose to tell him about tonight?"

"Oh, nothing. That's the easiest part of it. I shall say nothing even to Lord Merritt until we reach the reception. Then, after we have dismissed the carriage, it will be easy, I hope, to persuade him to go with Lady Hamilton's party."

"And your baggage?"
my husband it was merely a precaution against an emergency."

"We have been packed and ready for some days. I told
"So you expect me to bring it, along with Ricky?"

She looked up at him with large, reproachful eyes. "Captain Scroope, I expect nothing of you. But, if you are going to be so good as to bring Ricky . . ."

"I'm sorry," he said, unexpectedly. "Of course I'll bring your baggage—and Lord Merritt's. God knows I'm under obligation enough to you both."

"Oh, obligation!" Her voice came out more bitter than she had intended.

But the footmen were holding open the great doors at the ground floor of the Palazzo Sessa. He took her arm with formal politeness. "May I have the honour of seeing you home?" And then, on a warmer note. "It might be a good thing to pay a visit to young Ricky, preparatory to abducting him tonight."

"I suppose it will look like that," she said a little

doubtfully, as his cold hand helped her up into the carriage.

"Very much like it." He settled himself facing her. "But a minor point at a time like this. If you'll just give the word to Angelina, you may leave the rest to me."

"Including Price?"

"Including Price."

"You won't hurt him?"

"Not if I can help it. You care?"

"My husband will."

"So you want him to come too?"

"My God, no. But I hope he won't want to come."

The desperation in her voice silenced him, and they made the rest of the short drive without another word. Only, at last, helping her down from the carriage, he said, "You trust me?"

"Absolutely."

"Thank you." Still formal, it was a shade less cold.

They found Lord Merritt at home, where he usually stayed these days, since he lived in terror of encountering the lazzaroni. His eyes lit up at sight of Charles Scroope. "Ha!" He held out a welcoming hand. "*Gannet* back. Good."

"Well, yes and no," said Helen into Charles's stormy silence. "Poor Captain Scroope has been promoted out of the *Gannet* and has thrown himself on our mercy."

"Oh." Merritt digested it slowly. "No ship?" And then, hopefully, "Get another one?"

"No," said Charles ruefully. "That's the rub. I shall probably have to go back to England to get one. And until then, if I may, once again, trespass on your hospitality, I shall be more than grateful."

"Trespass?" said Lord Merritt doubtfully.

"He wants to come and stay, dear." Helen had never found it so painful to have to explain an unusual word to her husband.

"Oh, I see. Thought trespass was something else. In the Bible. I suppose he can come. Not much use without a ship." And then with a sigh of relief, "Must go and get dressed. That Turk's affair tonight. You coming?" he asked Charles.

"No, alas. Mere captains are not invited. If I may, I will stay quietly here and keep my young friend Ricky company. Ah, here he is." Helen thought it was a relief to him to see Ricky burst into the room. Returning his enthusiastic greeting, he promised that yes, indeed, he would tell him a story at bedtime. "You and I are to stay home together, while your parents go out."

"Good," said Ricky.

"Parents," said Lord Merritt, and Helen could not decide whether it held a question, and, if so, whether Charles had recognised it. No time to wonder, either. She must change, finish her packing, talk to Angelina . . . She bent to kiss Ricky. "You'll do everything Captain Scroope says, my darling."

"Ricky," said Ricky.

In the tension of planning the escape, Helen had not quite grasped the fact that Ricky and Charles would be dangerously on shore long after she and her husband had been rowed to safety on the *Vanguard*. As she made her quick change into full dress, she remembered what Lady Hamilton had said. Lord Nelson would see the Hamiltons on board, then return for the royal party. It was only after they were safe on the *Vanguard* that he would send back for their attendants, and Ricky.

She could not abandon him like that. Not even with Charles Scroope as protector. She was automatically reaching back to unfasten the clasp of the diamonds she had just put on, when a maid brought her a note. It was from Lady Hamilton, who must have realised, with her uncanny perceptiveness, the way Helen's thoughts would turn. "I count on you," it read. "If you fail me, fend for yourself."

Ruthless. Helen tore the note into tiny pieces with hands that trembled, then put the last touches to her appearance. In the nursery, Charles Scroope and Ricky were absorbed in a game of spillikins. Charles looked up and rose. "You're going now?" Had he too realised the danger to which she was leaving her child exposed? Impossible to explain, and no time for it. It was just one more stone on the mountain of misunderstanding between them.

"Yes," she said. She must not do anything to make the occasion seem unusual. She bent and kissed Ricky lightly. "Good night, Ricky. And mind you do everything Captain Scroope says."

"Of course I will," said Ricky impatiently. "Your turn, sir."

And that was that. She might never see either of them again. She walked slowly downstairs, head up, swallowing tears, and found her husband waiting for her in the hall, with Price in attendance. "Price has heard a rumour," he began.

"Oh, rumours." She cut him off impatiently. "The town's full of them. We must go, my dear. I particularly promised Lady Hamilton that we would be in time."

"Serious rumour." He followed her sulkily out to the carriage. "Laugh on the other side of your face if they all go off and leave us."

"Oh, they won't do that." He had handed her in; the door was shut; they were alone. "We're leaving now," she said.

"Now?" He looked down in amazement at his court dress.

"When we reach Kelim Effendi's house. We are meeting the Hamiltons there. And Lord Nelson. Outside. We dismiss our carriages and walk straight to the harbour."

"Good God." As always it took him a few minutes to take it in. Then his voice rose almost to a scream. "And Price?"

"And Ricky," she said dryly. And yet why should she expect him to care about Ricky? "Don't worry, Captain Scroope makes himself responsible for bringing them." She had no idea what, in fact, Charles Scroope would do about Price, but it would be foolish to precipitate a scene with her husband.

"Our baggage?" he asked now, on a calmer note.

"Captain Scroope brings that too."

"So Price was right," he said with satisfaction. "Confiding in Scroope instead of me. Anything happens to Price, never forgive you. Never. Not sure I won't go back and stay with them."

"It's too late," she said coldly. "Here we are. And I

267

warn you, as Lady Hamilton has warned me. If we do anything out of turn, we lose our chance of passage on the *Vanguard*. So, watch yourself."

"Oh." He was still digesting this as the footmen let down the carriage steps and opened the door. "Very well." He alighted and held up his hand to help her.

"Send the carriage home, dear," she said, her cold hand in his. "Captain Scroope might want to use it later, when Ricky is in bed."

"Home? Not to wait?" He was dazzled by the attempt to assimilate so much information, and she turned impatiently to the coachman and gave the necessary orders. Servants with flambeaux stood ready on the steps of the house. A small crowd had gathered to see the Turk's guests arrive. The great door had been flung open as the carriage drew up. But where were the Hamiltons? Could Emma Hamilton possibly have set a false rendezvous and gone off already to safety? She would not believe it. Whatever else she was, Lady Hamilton was a loyal friend. And experience reminded Helen that punctuality had never been one of her virtues.

In the meantime, she must think of a pretext for staying outside those hospitably open doors. "My dear," she laid a hand on her husband's arm and felt it tremble, "I have the most horrible feeling that I have forgotten something."

"Forgotten something? What? Servants waiting. Ought to go in."

Appalling to be saddled with so inept a fellow conspirator. "That's the trouble." At least, to the servants, who could not understand English, it must look like some routine matrimonial misunderstanding. She stood there in the cold December air, pulled her light shawl more closely round bare shoulders, and looked up at him. "That's just it," she drew it out as much as she could. "I can't for the life of me think. I just have this feeling . . . Something to do with the house? No, I don't think so. With Ricky . . ." It hurt her to say his name, to think of the risks he must run before she saw him again.

"Lot of nonsense," said Lord Merritt. "Can't keep the

men waiting with those doors. Cold, too. Best go in."

"If you do," she said, "you stay."

"You won't come?"

"Of course not!" But what in the world would she do, out here by herself, if he really did leave her? Already the little crowd was beginning to take an interest in their delay, and ribald comments were being passed in the broad Neapolitan dialect. "The Hamiltons are bound to be here any minute," she said desperately. "And what more natural than that we should wait for them?"

"Not natural at all." Impatiently. "Lot of nonsense. I'm cold." He turned towards that welcoming doorway, where, in fact, some kind of argument now seemed to be raging. No doubt the indoor servants were feeling the cold and wanted it shut again.

Well so much the better. She stamped her foot for the benefit of the crowd. It must look like a family quarrel. Easy enough: it was one. "I tell you I'm not going in till they come. I told Lady Hamilton I'd wait." She said this in Italian for the benefit of the crowd.

"Trust a couple of women! Make a mull of things!" He turned angrily away from her towards the door, only to have it close in his face. This made him angrier than ever. His voice rose to a furious squeak. "Think I'm standing here freezing all night?"

"Thank God," she said, "here they come." The familiar carriage had swung into sight, at a most undiplomatic speed. "They were just late."

Lady Hamilton, swathed in furs, confirmed this. They had forgotten a vital packet and had had to go back for it. "Something my beloved friend could not do without." Helen never learned what precious trifle it was that had so nearly cost her her safety, if not her life. But now Lord Nelson had joined them; Sir William was sending the carriage away; the great door had swung open again, and Kelim himself had appeared to greet his guest of honour.

"Come," said Lady Hamilton imperiously, and Helen saw the Turk's jaw drop in amazement as his guests turned away from him and walked off down the road. The crowd parted for them, laughing and jeering, but puzzled out of action. How long would it last? Helen looked quickly at Lady Hamilton and Mrs. Cadogan. Like her, they were wearing all their jewels. And, for protection, they had only the slight figure of Lord Nelson, the ageing Sir William, and her own hopeless husband. She thought the crowd was beginning to realise this too. Comments on the women's appearance became more explicit; conjectures as to the little party's destination more lurid. Helen took her husband's reluctant arm and closed up behind Lady Hamilton. She, too, was walking a little faster, clutching Nelson's arm, looming over him, and, inevitably, making him look slightly absurd.

"Ah," said Sir William. Another party was coming towards them, marching with the brisk casualness of the navy ashore.

"Our preservers." Lady Hamilton struck an attitude for a moment, then let Lord Nelson hurry her along, surrounded now by a protective screen of his men.

At the quay, the Admiral's barge awaited them, but the row out to the *Vanguard* seemed endless to Helen. Time was sliding by. It felt like a nightmare, when every action takes impossibly long to perform.

"I'm sorry we were late, love." As often, Lady Hamilton had read her thoughts. "But don't fret yourself. My hero has allowed plenty of time for everything. He fetches my beloved Queen in a boat from the *Alcmene*. It's all planned like a naval action. You need have no fears for your Ricky; he'll be brought away all right and tight."

"Oh, I do hope so." Tears were streaming down Helen's face, and she did nothing about them.

Chapter 22

ON the *Vanguard*, all was a kind of orderly naval chaos. It had been thought too dangerous to give advance warning of the royal party's arrival, so that no preparations had yet been made for them. Now, while Lord Nelson hurried off, with Captain Hope of the *Alcmene,* to fetch his reluctant guests, Lady Hamilton was very much in her element, giving orders for their reception. The Admiral's cabin must be prepared for the royal ladies, and the wardroom for the King and his sons. Cots must be put up for the princes and princesses . . . Here a difficulty presented itself. Carefully packing the royal possessions in anonymous naval boxes, no one had thought to distinguish cabin necessities. As a result, boxes of treasure cluttered up the Admiral's apartments; vital cases of bedding had been stowed in the hold. "But I've sheets of my own," said Lady Hamilton. "Come and help me unpack them, love."

Helen was glad to forget her gnawing anxiety in work. Her husband waylaid her with an anxiety of his own. "Told you," he said, "if Price don't come, I'll not forget it. Or forgive."

Helen actually found herself hoping that Charles Scroope would have decided it was easier to bring Price than to leave him behind. But this was a minor consideration beside her gnawing anxiety about Ricky. At this very moment, his life might be ebbing away in some dark street of Naples. It would be all her fault. And, doubly horrible, it would also be a judgement for the anxiety she could not help feeling for Charles Scroope.

"Don't fret, love," said Lady Hamilton. "Come and help me make up a cot for the Princess Royal. She'll be exhausted, poor thing, with the baby so new and her strength hardly back." There was no doubt about Lady Hamilton's way with the navy. Things that seemed impossible were achieved with a joke and a laugh; officers who might have resented turning out of their quarters for foreign royalty would do it gladly at the smiling request of the "patroness of the navy."

"I should hope so," said Lady Hamilton, when Helen remarked on this. "And the Admiral would have something to say if they did not. I wonder if he has got there yet."

"Is he going to the palace?"

"Yes. There is a secret passage up from the Molesiglio. Count Thurn meets him at the entrance, and, if all is well, will guide him to the palace where the royal party will be waiting for him. Poor things, what a strange scene for them."

It was indeed. They came on board half an hour or so later, cold, wet, and exhausted. The Queen subsided almost speechless in Nelson's own chair; the Princess Royal lay sobbing on his couch, while the wet-nurse suckled her child. The young princes and princesses ran about, amazed at their unusual freedom and at everything they saw, until Lady Hamilton rounded them up and saw them safely into their cots. Up on deck, the King was enjoying himself. "Only think," said Lady Hamilton, "the King told my hero he was looking forward to good sport in the woods round Palermo. Plenty of woodcock, he says."

"Good God." Helen returned to trying to persuade six-year-old Prince Albert that bed was the place for little boys.

"Have you a little boy?" asked Prince Albert, and wondered why the foreign lady burst into tears instead of answering.

Time dragged. Cabins of a sort had been found for Sir John Acton, for the Hamiltons, and the Russian and Austrian ambassadors. The royal children were settling down at last; even the Queen had consented to go to bed, and the Princess Royal had stopped crying to sip the hot milk and dash of navy rum that Mrs. Cadogan had found for her.

And still the *Alcmene*'s boat had not returned. Helen sat listlessly on her cot in the tiny cabin she was to share with two of the royal maids—and Ricky? She could hardly bring herself to look at his small pallet on the floor in the corner. "There you are." Lord Merritt looked in at the door. "Hope you're satisfied. No sign of the boat. Probably all had their throats cut by the lazzaroni. Too much to hope three boatloads would get away."

She had thought of this too, and raised heavy eyes to his. "If they don't come," she said, "I'll never forgive myself."

"Much use that will be."

It was midnight, and cold. Somewhere, the ship's bell struck, and Helen, listening, wondered if it was tolling for Ricky's death. There was nothing more to do now but sit and wait, and hate herself. How could she have abandoned Ricky as she had? But had she not failed him even before that, when she left him in charge of the servants and threw her whole heart into nursing Charles Scroope? If the two of them were dead now, it would be no more than she deserved.

"Here they come, love." Lady Hamilton stood in the doorway, and for the second time in her life Helen thought her an angel.

"You're sure?"

"It's the boat all right. Can't see who's in it, of course, but they've got a full load. You can see how low she lies in the water. Come up on deck? Here—" Emma Hamilton had brought a warm boat cloak and wrapped it round Helen's shoulders. "I knew you'd want to come."

Impossible to make out faces in the boat that looked so small and tossed so restlessly as it came alongside in the dank darkness. The bosun's chair was swinging down. Helen found she was holding Lady Hamilton's hand, tight. The chair came up with the King's major domo, sweating with fright, shaking uncontrollably as he was deposited on the deck.

"Wait here, love. I'll ask." Lady Hamilton loosed Helen's hand gently and went over to speak to the man in her fluent Italian. Returning, "All's well," she said. "Your Ricky's down there having the time of his life. A proper young devil, the man says. But something must have gone wrong. Captain Scroope's wounded."

"Badly?" If so, all her fault.

"He didn't know. Hold on, love. You can't faint here."

"I suppose not." With an effort she pulled herself together. "No time for that anyway. Lady Hamilton, I do thank you . . ."

The beauty laughed. "Am I your angel again, then? And, look, here comes your young devil. Scoot, love."

Ricky, released from the bosun's chair onto the deck, was in a seventh heaven of excitement. "Oh, Mamma!" He was touchingly glad to have her for audience. "I had an adventure." And then, thinking about it, "Captain Scroope and I. A real adventure. Captain Scroope said I was a very brave boy. I held the lantern while he fought Price. Just think: a real fight, and I held the lantern."

"Who won?" Lord Merritt had been close by, invisible in the darkness, waiting too.

"Captain Scroope, of course. The good man always wins. He told me so. And Price was very bad."

"Was?" Helen had not thought her husband's voice could contain such naked feeling. If only she could warn Ricky, but the child's voice was already tumbling on.

"I think Captain Scroope killed him," he said. "He had his sword on. Price said, 'Stop,' and he said, 'Why,' and Price said, 'I'll show you,' and then I took the lantern and they fought. Look," he held his hand proudly to the light. "I'm all over blood from where I gave the lantern back."

"Boasting, Ricky?" said a new voice, Charles Scroope's. "All's well, Lady Merritt. We had a little trouble, but all's well."

"Well?" Lord Merritt's voice grated from the shadow. "Where's my man? Where's Price?"

"Dead, I hope," said Charles Scroope.

"Ooh," said Ricky. "I thought he was dead."

"Young devil!" Lord Merritt emerged from the shadows to strike him a ringing blow on the head. "Say that about my friend!"

"Price?" the question came simultaneously from Charles Scroope and, through surprised sobs, from Ricky.

"Price. My only friend." He turned on Helen. "Warned you. Watch yourself, that's all. Just watch yourself. I'll get even." He turned and vanished into the crowded darkness of the deck.

"I'm sorry." Scroope took Helen's arm to guide her below-decks. "There was no help for it. Price had had a very good idea." He switched from English to his fluent French. "He was going to keep the child as hostage for your cooperation."

"Oh, my God."

"What are you saying?" Ricky let go of his mother's hand and stopped crying to look up impatiently. "I don't understand."

"I'm telling your mother about our adventure and how brave you were."

"But you're wounded." Helen had actually forgotten it in the scene with her husband.

"It's nothing. A scratch on the arm. Price was no swordsman, and I no hero. I'll have it seen to when you are safe below."

"Much better let me bandage it."

"No thank you, Lady Merritt." His tone was cold again. Had he had enough of her nursing?

It blew and rained all night, and in the morning the exhausted passengers of the *Vanguard* found themselves still at harbour in the storm-tossed bay. And Naples woke to find its King gone, and the royal standard flying from the British flagship in the harbour. All day boats plied to and fro with messages, petitions, prayers, but only Cardinal Zurlo, the Archbishop of Naples, was allowed aboard, and he got little satisfaction from the King, who merely told him that he would return when he saw that his subjects did their duty.

Watching from the deck, Helen and Ricky saw the mole and quays thronged with thousands of would-be refugees bargaining frantically for passage on one or other of the merchantmen in the bay. Two Neapolitan warships were also making ready to sail, but half their crews had deserted in order to stay and protect their families, and Lord Nelson had to lend them British sailors. "The only reliable men in the world," said Lady Hamilton.

"Just the same," said Helen doubtfully, "I would have thought it would have been more tactful if the royal family had sailed with Prince Caracciolo in the *Samnite*."

"Impossible," said the patroness of the British navy. "How could they have trusted that wretched lot of deserters?" And then, "What's the matter with Lord Merritt, by the way? He looks sick as a dog. And the way he's treating you . . . !"

"He's angry about his man Price," Helen explained reluctantly.

"No need to take it out on you," said Lady Hamilton. "Shall I have a word with him? Or ask the Admiral to?"

"Good God, no. Thank you very much. It will pass. I hope." Helen had also hoped that everyone would be too busy to notice how her husband behaved to her when she was so unlucky as to meet him, but she might have known that this was just the kind of thing that Lady Hamilton *did* notice. "If only we would sail!" It was a cry echoed by every one of the passengers. Now that the first urgency of the escape was over, they were beginning to feel the full discomfort of their crowded condition.

They did sail at last next day, December the twenty-third, but Helen was puzzled to see that the two Neapolitan ships were not accompanying them. "I wonder why not."

"Cowardice, I expect," said Emma Hamilton.

That night they learned that Prince Caracciolo knew his weather. The wind rose to gale force; the sails split, and sailors stood ready, axe in hand, to cut away the mainmast if it should fall. Below-decks, conditions, bad before, were now as near intolerable as made no difference. Suffering already from fatigue and nervous strain, the royal party were now prostrate with seasickness. Servants were in as bad case as their masters, and only Lady Hamilton, Mrs. Cadogan, Helen and Angelina kept their feet.

Helen had her hands full with Ricky, who was suffering from the inevitable aftermath of his adventures, but as soon as she had got him off into a restless sleep, she joined the other two women in providing what comfort they could for the occupants of the crowded, stinking royal cabins. To get up to the heads was to risk death. It was no wonder if the below-decks smelled.

"How is Sir William?" Helen met Lady Hamilton, basin in hands.

"In his cabin." Emma Hamilton's voice was scornful. "With a pistol in each hand. He says he will shoot himself if we sink. He won't die with the 'guggle—guggle—guggle' of salt water in his throat. Much use he is." She summed it up once and for all. "Oh." A happier thought. "My hero has invited you and Captain Scroope to join us for Christmas dinner. I said your husband was too ill."

"It's true, thank God," said Helen. She had tried to minister to her husband but had been turned out of his cabin with a volley of helpless curses. Of Charles Scroope there had been no sign. Doubtless he was up on deck, helping the Admiral's depleted crew to fight the storm. "I wonder where Prince Caracciolo is," the question rose naturally from her thoughts.

"Lucky if he's not drowned," said Lady Hamilton.

The wind eased a little on the night of the twenty-fourth, and by Christmas day they were merely encountering the rough aftermath of the storm. The royal family were still prostrate with sickness, but Ricky was sleeping more naturally, and Helen felt it safe to leave him and join the Hamiltons at Christmas dinner with the Admiral. It was a strange enough occasion. Sir William had changed from an elderly, upright man to a shuffling, shaking, old one, and his wife seemed to have stopped noticing him. All her attention was for the man she now called "my" rather than "our" hero, and all his for her. Sitting side by side, they might just as well, Helen thought, have been alone in the crowded cabin. Sir William, drowsily drinking port, apparently noticed nothing, but Helen caught Charles Scroope's eye across the table and knew that his anxious thoughts ran parallel to hers. There was something at once touching, and, alas, ridiculous about the two of them as they sat there, aware of nothing but each other. They might have been a boy and girl in the throes of first love, and the world well lost. But they were not. It was an elderly, crippled Admiral who flushed like a boy at the touch of the buxom charmer by his side. They could hardly have made their situation more obvious, Helen thought, if they had written "We Are Lovers" on one of those bits of ribbon Lady Hamilton was so fond of.

Horrible. And Sir William sitting there, sipping away at his port, apparently oblivious. Charles Scroope caught her eye again, and this time she read his message clearly, and obeyed it. "Forgive me." She rose with a flood of apologies and thanks, the gist of the matter her anxiety for Ricky. It effectively broke up the party, and she was more relieved than she cared to admit at the sight of Lord Nelson tearing himself away from his enchantress to go up on deck.

They sighted land at last at three o'clock that Christmas afternoon, but there was no chance of going ashore until next morning. And that night little Prince Albert died of exhaustion in Lady Hamilton's motherly arms.

It was selfish, after watching Maria Carolina mourn the death of her son, to feel such joy at Ricky's recovery. Their two cabin mates were better too, and had tottered out to minister to their unhappy mistress. Helen was alone with Ricky when Lord Merritt appeared, white, exhausted, and shaking. "You." He leant against the open cabin door. "Want to talk to you. Killed my friend Price. Go your own way. Don't want to hang for you. So: go your own way. I've done with you."

"You can't . . ." But he had gone, and she faced the fact that he could. There was nothing to stop him leaving her penniless in the strange city of Palermo. So much, she thought bitterly, for Aunt Helen Stott and the independence of women.

"What's the matter, Mamma?" Ricky was pulling at her skirts. "Why's he so cross?"

"It's nothing, dear." Helen had noticed long before that Ricky never referred to Lord Merritt as "Papa." "We're all tired, that's all," she said. "It will pass." Would it?

"I'd rather live with you," said Ricky. "Oh good." The door had opened again to reveal Charles Scroope. "Now we'll be all right and tight. Mamma is crying," he said, as if it explained everything.

"Helen." Charles looked round the empty cabin, came in and closed the door. "I won't apologise. I was outside. I heard what Lord Merritt said. I'd been wondering what to say; what to do. About you—about us. Now I know. You can't go on like this, if he'd let you. With him. Bullying you; swearing at you; threatening you for what I did. For Price! And not fit to be in the same room . . . Now he's settled it. He's freed you. You're free, Helen. In the eyes of God."

She looked up at him, eyes dull with shock. "I don't believe in God."

"So much the simpler. You must come away with me. You and Ricky. I'll send in my papers. I'll take you"—he stopped for a moment, thinking it over—"to America. I've friends there."

"And they'd welcome your mistress?" She rounded on him, savage with the pain of it. "And her child." She had nearly said bastard. "It's mighty kind of you, Charles Scroope, when you don't even *like* me."

"Like? Who said anything about liking? Helen, you know I've always loved you. I can't help myself. God knows I've tried."

"Thank you. I've noticed. I've seen, too, how ready you are to believe the worst of me." It was a relief to have it out at last. "Everything that wretch Trenche told you. I suppose this flattering offer of yours follows naturally enough. Why should I not be your mistress, since I was Trenche's?"

"So you admit it."

"I do not!" She spat at him, then remembered the child who was standing between them casting puzzled, anxious glances from one to the other. "But this is not the time, still less the place to be talking of such things. Not that there is anything more to say. I thank you a thousand times, Captain Scroope, for your most flattering offer, which I must decline."

"But, Helen, what will you do?"

"Anything but that," she said. "You were there, at dinner. Did not the very sight of them make you sick? As

279

if no one else was in the room with them. Doting . . . and Sir William there . . . and poor Lady Nelson at home in England . . ." She had not quite known until now, when she found herself so unexpectedly speaking of it, how much she had minded that scene. "I thought her an angel," she said now. "She's only the shadow of one."

"Or fallen. Like Lucifer."

"Twice. She had made such a recovery. That's why it's so sad. It is so sad, Charles." How had it happened that she, who a moment before had been so furious, was now appealing to him like this for comfort? And yet, how natural.

And, equally natural, he did his best to give her the comfort she needed. "Nothing's happened," he said, and then spoiled it by adding, "yet."

"But it will."

"I'm afraid so. God knows what will come of it."

" 'Afraid.' Charles, there's your answer. What won't do for them, will do still less for us. But—" she smiled up at him through a dazzle of tears—"thank you, Charles. Oh . . ."

He, too, had heard voices outside and had turned quickly to tell a puzzled Ricky that he could not take him up on deck just now. If Helen's two cabinmates thought it odd to find her entertaining a naval gentleman with no better chaperon than Ricky, they kept their thoughts to themselves, and soon forgot them in the excitement of preparing to go ashore. Nobody slept much that night, since everyone knew that in the course of it, the *Vanguard* would make her battered way into Palermo harbour. Helen had finally fallen into a light doze when Ricky woke her. "Mamma, I think we're there!"

Listening to the familiar sounds above-decks, she knew at once that he was right. There was the anchor cable roaring out. The horrible voyage was over. And a bustle outside the cabin told her that her fellow passengers knew it too. Now a knock on the door was followed by a low-voiced summons to the Queen's two maids. "Her Majesty goes ashore at once," said the anonymous voice.

"It's the middle of the night!" Ricky was amazed and

delighted. "Mamma, do let's go and watch them! Or are we going too?"

"I don't think so." What should she do? There had been no chance to discuss her plight with Lady Hamilton, and even if there had been, she did not think she would have done so. She would never forget that scene over dinner the day before, the overblown beauty and the shrivelled little Admiral sitting there and languishing at each other. And now, inevitably, she remembered other scenes. She had not been present when Lady Hamilton had fainted into Lord Nelson's arms on his own quarter-deck, but she had heard about it often enough. And then there had been that extravagant, vulgar birthday party, when Lady Hamilton had been in such an exalted state, and Nelson's stepson had made a scene. At the time, Helen had blamed Josiah Nisbet; now she felt only sympathy for him. He had been right, and she wrong. The gallant friendship she had admired had carried the seeds of disaster, and now they were ripe for the sowing.

She wanted no part of it. Lord Nelson, she knew, intended to share a house with the Hamiltons in Palermo. If she went to Lady Hamilton with the news that her husband was abandoning her, she would undoubtedly be invited to join them. She could not bear it. But why? What had happened to her? She was Helen Telfair, who had so often shocked Miss Tillingdon by preaching the liberation of women and the equality of the sexes. And here she was, behaving, or planning to behave, exactly as Miss Tillingdon would. Dearly though she loved him, she would not live, unmarried, with Charles Scroope, and neither would she expose Ricky (or herself) to the kind of affair that was so evidently coming into rank blossom between the Admiral and the lady. She was just a prude, after all.

Time was slipping away, and she had decided nothing. "Very well," she made her first decision, thinking it a small one. "Let us go up on deck and see what is happening." Was she, admit it, hoping to meet Charles Scroope? She would never be his mistress, but she thought she would have to let him help her. For Ricky's sake? Or for the sake of the friendship that had somehow, through yesterday's scenes, made itself felt between them? That was it. She would never be his mistress, but at least she could be his dear friend. If they had not been interrupted she would have told him so. Now, suddenly, it seemed of the first urgency to do so, before they went ashore. She knew the navy well enough to know how easily they might be swept apart, with only the memory of her angry words between them.

Unbearable. She hurried Ricky into his warmest clothes, and out into the bustle of the companionway. The door of Lord Nelson's cabin was ajar, and she could see that preparations for departure were going on apace among the royal ladies. But pausing outside the wardroom door she found all quiet, and the sentry on duty there told her that the King had given orders that he was not to be disturbed until morning.

"Come on, Mamma." Ricky tugged at her hand. "Let's go up and see."

"But there will be nothing *to* see." She had just heard the ship's bell and realised that it was much earlier than she had thought. "It will still be dark up there, Ricky. We'll be horribly in the way." She had been mad to hope to find Charles Scroope in the confusion of a landing.

"But you said we'd go." It was a wail. Did he feel that she was failing him once more, as she had done so often?

And her head ached from the heat and smell of the cabin. "Very well, just for a moment. But hold tight to my hand. I don't want to lose you up there."

"Don't worry, Mamma. I'll look after you."

The deck was alive with men, their ordered activities uncertainly lit by here a lantern, there a flickering torch. Only on a British ship, Helen thought, could a disembarkation by night, and a royal one at that, be so capably managed. She was taking deep breaths of refreshing, salt-flavoured air when Ricky squeezed her hand. "Look," he said.

Lord Merritt was at the rail, staring out into darkness. And, fatally, he heard Ricky's voice. He turned and moved towards them, his ravaged face bent on Ricky. "Well," he said. "Here's luck." Suddenly, while Helen

282

stood aghast, he dived forward and grabbed Ricky. "My sweet son," he spaced the words out slowly. "Feed the fishes."

"No!" Helen screamed as he carried the struggling child towards the rail. "No!"

"No," said another voice. A sailor who had been working nearby had witnessed the scene, and Helen gave a thankful gasp as he moved forward to intercept Lord Merritt. Then she screamed again. "Vengeance is mine," said Philip Trenche. He took the struggling child from Lord Merritt and put him down on the deck. "Run along, you." There was a note Helen had never heard before in his voice. "This is no place for boys."

"I want to stay with Mamma." Ricky ran over to grab her hand.

"Too bad." Trenche had Lord Merritt by the collar. "Now," he said. "I don't know which of you did it to me, but you will both pay, even if my son goes too. God! How I've prayed for this day, down there, below-decks, in hell. And God heard me. Now! This is the first install-ment." What had he in his hand? It came down with a thud on Lord Merritt's head, then he lifted him, swung him as if he were weightless, up and over the rail, to fall with one stifled scream into the darkness.

"Dear God." Helen clung to Ricky's hand and watched as this gaunt, white-haired, unmistakable Trenche ad-vanced on her. She looked around wildly for help. Surely someone must have noticed? Why had there been no cry of "Man overboard"? Then, hopelessly, she understood. Above her, in a glow of torchlight, Queen Maria Carolina was taking her leave of Lord Nelson. All eyes were fixed on the royal party.

And Trenche was upon her. "Let go the child's hand," he said. "If you want him to survive you." He smiled at her, horribly, in the dim light. "If only there was time to rape you again." He lunged at her.

"Ricky!" She pushed him away. "Run!"

"No." Ricky clung to her, and then, as the mad face loomed close, the air reverberated and the deck shook as a broadside saluted the Queen's departure. And, surely, nearer, one single shot? Trenche's face, close to Helen's, changed, became calm, became almost peaceful, then fell away, as she fell, too, into blackness.

"I couldn't do anything." Charles's voice. She seemed to be lying on the deck, her head in his lap. "Not while you were between him and me. But I saw and heard it all." The emphasis on the word "heard" spoke volumes. "Ricky pulled you out of the way just in time, God bless him. They're looking for Lord Merritt. But, Helen, there's no hope. That was a wicked blow. And I had to think of you first. Trenche was mad; raving. It *was* Trenche?"

"Oh, yes," said Helen. "It was Trenche. And, in a way, it's our fault, Charles, yours and mine."

"Then we'll share it," he said.

"Am I a hero?" Ricky was dancing about on the deck, tired of being overlooked.

"Indeed you are. And your mother's a heroine."

"Not an angel?" The world was still swooping and dipping around her.

"Angel enough for me."

"I was looking for you." How pleasant it was to lie like this, her head in his lap, leaving everything to him.

"Well." He pulled her firmly to her feet. "You found me." And then, his strong arm still holding her, "Oh, God, look!"

On the quarter-deck, Lady Hamilton had appeared beside Lord Nelson to watch the Queen's departure. Now, as the loaded boats moved away towards the shore, a lantern, swaying with the ship's movement, revealed the quick gesture with which, in what she thought was darkness, she took and kissed his hand. Then, suddenly aware of the light, she moved away to the rail and struck a familiar attitude. "The Goddess of Victory," said Charles.

And, "God help them both," said Helen.

ABOUT THE AUTHOR

JANE AIKEN HODGE was born in Boston, Massachusetts, and educated at Oxford and Harvard. She is the daughter of Conrad Aiken, the distinguished poet and critic. Her novels include *Watch the Wall, My Darling; The Winding Stair; Greek Wedding; Marry in Haste; Savannah Purchase; Strangers in Company,* and *Shadow of a Lady.* In 1972 she published a biography of Jane Austen, *Only a Novel,* to enthusiastic response on both sides of the Atlantic. Mrs. Hodge is currently at work on a new novel.

JANE AIKEN HODGE

HERE COMES A CANDLE

A fine novel of romance, betrayal and mystery.

When the Americans sacked the English capital of
Canada at the outbreak of the war of 1812, Kate Croston,
newly widowed and seemingly lost, was only too glad to
flee her shadowed past and accept the offer of help given
by an American civilian, Jonathan Penrose.

But as soon as she took charge of Jonathan's daughter,
little Sarah, Kate found herself caught in a web of intrigue
and suspicion. Was Jonathan wise to defy his arrogant
wife, Arabella, and place Sarah in Kate's care? And
what was the role of the handsome Englishman, Captain
Manningham, in this whole mysterious affair?

'Highly entertaining and diverting . . . anyone who enjoys
full-blooded historical novels will certainly enjoy this
one.'

The Scotsman

CORONET BOOKS

JANE AIKEN HODGE

GREEK WEDDING

A young girl's romantic adventures in the bloodstained muddle of the Greek War of Independence.

The adventure-seeking Brett Renshaw despised the Greeks almost as much as he did women and his relationship with his reluctant protégée, Phyllida Vannick, was a stormy one, since both her brother and her Greek wooer were fighting the Turks. Yet, bankrupt as he was, how could he refuse to let her charter his yacht, which bore the name of Helena, his lost lover?

'All the lightness of Georgette Heyer and with added substance besides.'

New Statesman

CORONET BOOKS

HISTORICAL ROMANCE FROM CORONET

JANE AIKEN HODGE

- ☐ 10734 0   Here Comes A Candle   80p
- ☐ 16228 7   Greek Wedding   80p
- ☐ 18806 5   Strangers In Company   70p
- ☐ 17412 9   Savannah Purchase   70p
- ☐ 02892 0   Watch The Wall My Darling   75p
- ☐ 16465 4   Maulever Hall   75p
- ☐ 15029 7   Marry In Haste   60p
- ☐ 19862 1   Runaway Bride   75p

DOROTHY EDEN

- ☐ 20001 4   The Millionaire's Daughter   80p
- ☐ 10884 3   Siege In The Sun   70p
- ☐ 02927 7   Never Call It Loving   80p
- ☐ 12800 3   The Vines Of Yarrabee   85p

FRANCES MURRAY

- ☐ 20759 0   The Heroine's Sister   60p
- ☐ 19891 5   The Burning Lamp   40p
- ☐ 18293 8   The Dear Colleague   35p

All these books are available at your local bookshop or newsagent, or can be ordered direct from the publisher. Just tick the titles you want and fill in the form below.

Prices and availability subject to change without notice.

CORONET BOOKS, P.O. Box 11, Falmouth, Cornwall.

Please send cheque or postal order, and allow the following for postage and packing:

U.K. – One book 19p plus 9p per copy for each additional book ordered, up to a maximum of 73p

B.F.P.O. and EIRE – 19p for the first book plus 9p per copy for the next 6 books, thereafter 3p per book.

OTHER OVERSEAS CUSTOMERS – 20p for the first book and 10p per copy for each additional book.

Name ....

Address ....

....